Taking Stephan Home

Taking Steaphan Home

VIVIENNE KING

THE CLOISTER HOUSE PRESS

First published in the United Kingdom in 2020 by
The Cloister House Press

ISBN 978-1-913460-19-8

Contents

Foreword		vii
Preamble		ix
Chapter One	**Bombshell**	1
Chapter Two	**Place of Safety**	22
Chapter Three	**A Deep Breath**	40
Chapter Four	**News at Last**	49
Chapter Five	**A Rustic Spell** – in more ways than one!	57
Chapter Six	**Making Memories**	74
Chapter Seven	**Tragedy, Defeat and even Dismay**	101
Chapter Eight	**Prowlers, or Predators?**	121
Chapter Nine	**A Gruelling Move**	138
Chapter Ten	**An Unwelcome Surprise**	164
Chapter Eleven	**"Derring-Do"**	176
Chapter Twelve	**Frank and The Fugitive**	185
Chapter Thirteen	**The Proposal**	209
Chapter Fourteen	**Completing the Journey**	223

Foreword
by Lucas Gates

In 1937, at the age of fourteen, my Grandmother started work in an engineering factory where she was soon polishing glass lenses for Spitfire gun cameras. Her wartime stories as a young woman were often sad although many were hilarious especially after she wangled her way onto a farm working alongside Italian POW's.

One story was particularly poignant. Her father, my Great Grandfather, was a member of the London Fire Service when the Blitz began. Sent to quell the fires raging in the docks, he witnessed mass destruction of warehouses and factories including the sugar refinery and a few days later, attended the remains of a school.

Exhausted physically and emotionally, Granny said he returned home the following week with a distinct smell of burnt sugar.

Preamble

Initially, there was great excitement amongst some people when the uncertainty of whether, or not we would go to war was at last decided and the nation had accepted the need to fight fascism. Others saw it in a different light and '*Here we go again*', were the words on many older and wiser lips.

For the most part though, we all felt very patriotic and invincible. Dad searched the attic space for his dusty Union Jack flag, which hadn't had an airing since 1918 and Philip Atkinson from next door hoped the war would go on long enough for him to become a daring fighter ace, or heroic submarine captain picturing himself in a dashing uniform of some kind when he turned eighteen; only four years to wait then. We all laughed at that for different reasons. A lot of people compared these days to the Great War, saying that it wouldn't go on for such a long time and we were all sure that Hitler was a madman who couldn't run a tap let alone a war.

Classroom gas mask drills with the few children who hadn't already been evacuated were made into a game although most of them couldn't begin to understand what it was all about. Then the so-called, 'Phoney War' saw the return of bigger classes when it was believed that we weren't in danger and little ones came home in droves; a disastrous decision in some cases but how could we know what was to come?

In the very beginning, I admit we were all lulled into a false sense of security because nothing much happened although almost immediately it was announced that petrol was to be rationed and we noticed a big change in what the shops had to sell – or rather *didn't* have. Most people bought a daily newspaper or avidly listened to the wireless for any sort of news or information and neighbours we'd been used to seeing in work clothes or their Sunday best were suddenly in all sorts of uniforms, dashing or otherwise.

It was several months later that everything began to change. Of course, little did we know then that it was the start of something monstrous. Something so dreadful that it would go down in the annals of history leaving a painful legacy to haunt countless people for the rest of their lives. And we certainly didn't know that it would push some of us to the very edge, while at the same time it was to bring out the best and worst in people.

Years before, when Mum was alive and Germany was just another country with good beer, there were happy, as well as sad times. Normal life was – *well,* the same for everyone, I suppose. Somehow, I managed to go to Grammar School. Dad said I had mum's brains and mum said I had dad's brains but wherever they came from soon after I finished my normal education, my brains were good enough for me to start training to teach young children. I couldn't have gone off to college unless Grandad had died though. He'd been coughing for months and just didn't wake-up one morning. Nan turned-up on our doorstep in a right old state and it was all incredibly sad, especially when she gave his pigeons to the club he'd belonged to. How he loved those birds. Fortunately for Nan, his stamp collection turned out to be worth a lot of money and she sold it straight away, which amongst other things paid for my lodgings at college.

I struggled a lot, maybe with the worry of Mum being ill, but managed to gain my certificate, and had at least seen a bit of the outside world living in the college hostel. I'd even been kissed a few times although I struggled with that too since the kisser smelt of a substance to repel moths, had hair dripping with '*Brylcreem*' and insisted on buying me the new energy balls called 'Maltesers'; I had so many, I could have opened a sweet shop.

It was soon obvious that Mum was desperately ill and wouldn't recover. Adamant that she wanted to die at home,

Nan moved in with us to help look after her and never left. With Mum gone, it was just the three of us living in one of the terraced houses snaking all the way up to the new viaduct on the main road at Canning Town. Dad and I used the cosy sitting room for our meals and to listen to the wireless around the fireplace, with or without a fire and Nan took over the front parlour, which she filled with very old furniture, including a bed and her beloved piano. There was just enough room for her companion, 'Miss Bluebell' a so-called budgie who bounced around her cage singing importantly and wasn't blue at all. In fact, she was a yellow Canary, but Nan was often '*au contraire*', as they say in France.

Upstairs were two bedrooms. Mine overlooked the back of our house and Dad's the front. He spent a lot of time in there saying he was reading. Of course, Nan and I knew the real reason because we often heard his grief as he sat on the big double bed where Mum had died. We also had a box room where we kept all manner of things including the commode she had used. We tried to pretend it wasn't there although it really should have gone back to the Red Cross, but when I caught Dad stroking it one day, knew it was much too soon for that.

At the very top of the house was the attic space. It wasn't visited enough to warrant a runner on the three stairs leading up to it, but when someone did, the sound of footsteps on wood was unmistakable. I was always curious as to the reason for the visit and couldn't resist running up the first flight to see what was being added or taken out making sure I used the three extra stairs as a safety barrier. It was a dark and mysterious place. The small oval window threw only a little light on the junk and old photos waiting there for a new purpose and the cobwebs hanging from the ceiling were an indication that it was a haven for spiders. As a child, I tried to avoid it until I was big enough to reach the light switch and even then, paying a call to the room triggered a sudden urge to rush to the toilet.

Talking of the that I should add that there'd been a lot of new houses built in the area with a bathroom and toilet inside, but Mum was adamant that she'd never move from the house I was born in, so there we stayed; outside lavvy and all. We cooked on the gas stove in the tiny scullery, where in the same big sink with one cold water tap, we washed the dishes as well as ourselves, scrubbed the veg and flowerpots, cleaned shoes and rinsed out our smalls.

On washday Monday, Nan would have the copper on to boil, which caused no end of trouble. Every window streamed with water and in winter she insisted on drying everything indoors; that was after squeezing it all through the mangle three times. She had the biggest bloomers you had ever seen and what with them dangling like huge white flags and her questionable culinary skills - *well*, have you ever smelt Tripe and Onions boiling?

Apart from this, Nan's contribution to our lives was something magical. The house was always full of music because her piano-playing was marvellous. She was able to read most pieces but was miraculously able to play a tune as soon as she heard it as well. When they weren't covered by sleeves, the tops of her fat arms swung in time to the music, which always made me smile. She was a wise old lady and knew exactly why I smiled.

Dad had been a Fireman for as long as I could remember. Obviously when war was declared, it was thought his experience would come in especially useful and this was when he was promoted to Leading Fireman. Nan and I were immensely proud to see him in his special helmet, although we had no idea then that his job would turn out to be so dangerous. In the beginning putting it simply, some of us were young and very naïve but by 1945 we had grown into razor-sharp souls ready to take on anything that was thrown at us.

Anyway, 1945 was a date far from my mind when I gained my qualification, but it wasn't long after, that what we all expected finally happened and war broke out with Germany. A lot of young men, including my 'mothball marauder' and several teachers were amongst the local lads who went straight off to a training camp and this did me a favour. It made sense for me to take the place of someone who had joined-up and living so close to a Primary School, I was snapped-up for what I hoped would be a long-lasting job with regular pay. Women were of course, paid less than their male colleagues and becoming a wife while teaching was frowned-upon, but at least we were now more readily accepted as teachers. Nan was happy to have me at home, but Dad was overjoyed, especially since he knew I really wanted to join the Navy and become a Wren. I didn't exactly know what a Wren did and was worried that like Auntie Win, I might suffer from seasickness, but I just loved the uniform.

Our house had a postage stamp-sized garden. The toilet was out there too beside the coal hole in what Nan called the 'area' and it was here that Dad and the men from the families either side of us had spent hours digging deep holes in each garden to erect an air raid shelter. Named after Sir John Anderson who was responsible for such precautions, they were made of corrugated iron sheets strong enough, we were told, to protect us from a falling bomb. Once erected, the shiny surface was covered in mud and grass and Mr. Atkinson even grew vegetables on his. Nan insisted that Dad use the shears to keep our surface short, unlike Mr. Craig on our right who let his grow with Dandelions and Daisies. I thought it looked quite pretty, but Nan was appalled at such laxity.

We hoped never to use the Anderson but with the many false alarms of air raids and the threat of gas attacks we were in there quite often and 'Miss Bluebell' came too. Maybe Dad had dug a bit too deep because there was usually two inches of water above the wooden floorboards, it smelt horrible and was always teeming with Worms, Centipedes, and Woodlice. Our blankets were damp and musty, the matches to light the lamp never ever produced a flame, the tea mugs had gone rusty and something had eaten the contents of the First Aid kit. Retreating to this place of safety as little as possible, a whole year had passed, but in the months since, I learnt my first German word - *'Blitzkrieg'*.

CHAPTER ONE

Bombshell

Trapped.

Trapped in a vast, eternal whirlpool comforted only by silence and the gentle embrace of vivid rain clouds, I hummed a tune without a care in the world. On and on I drifted in blissful contentment until without warning the spinning ceased and an unwelcome commotion began. Violently tossed upwards and sucked into a dark tunnel, the sound of whistles and clanging like the pealing of bells, high-pitched whining and the gushing of air replaced the silence. I wished it would all go away and leave me in peace.

At the very end of the tunnel, a pinpoint circle of light quickly grew. It was mesmerising and unable to look away, I felt myself sliding towards it at great speed until Dad's voice echoed softly, *"Lelly. Lelly. Lelly."*

It caused my heart to skip a beat.

With lids as heavy as lead, I struggled to focus on the two similar-looking girls standing beside me until I saw the girls become one. It must have been this revelation combined with a strong smell of antiseptic that caused my stomach to spew its contents and the young girl become my saviour.

"Sorry, Lesley", I heard, *"I just had to shine the light in your eyes one last time, and you've been sick again, but we'll soon have you cleaned-up."*

The taste of something very bitter in my dry mouth was disgusting. It burnt my throat as I looked from left to right in panic - my head spinning like a top, but all I saw was 'Skinny Steven' lying in a bed. Deciding now that I was either in the middle of a nightmare, or had gone mad, I quickly sat up. And promptly fell back down again.

"You take it easy now, luv," came a kindly female voice from beside me. *"You and your littlun took a nasty bang you did. Come off better than most though. Dreadful in it?"* She tutted.

Without a clear view of the speaker, all I could do, was smile because I hadn't the foggiest idea where I was, who the lady was, or what on earth she was talking about. I turned to look at Steven, which confused me even more and in doing so, noticed bits of gravel had fallen out of my hair and onto the white starched pillowcase. I was fully dressed, apart from my shoes, in someone else's bed and my fingernails had dirt underneath them, which was most unusual. My nose was running and sneezing several times, I reached for my hankie only to discover that it was wasn't in its usual place. I was terribly thirsty and noticing a glass of water on the surface beside me, grabbed it, greedily swallowing the contents.

I felt water dribbling down either side of my mouth and wiped it away with the back of my hand making one much cleaner than the other. My head hurt, I felt dizzy and how did I get so dirty? Propping myself up on an elbow, I tried to take in my surroundings. I was in a hospital. But why?

Dear, skinny little Steven, who never stopped talking or asking questions. He was there too. That lady thought he was my son. My son? I'm married? I quickly looked down at my left hand. No, of course I'm not married and of course, he's not my son. He's in my class at school and I'm his teacher! I scolded myself for this ridiculous thought and would have shaken my head too, had it not felt so heavy, but the relief at remembering something concrete at last was wonderful. I took a deep breath but that just made me feel queasy enough to vomit again. My mouth was so dry with a dreadful sour taste that Nan would have said was like the bottom of a birdcage after one too many Dubonnet's and I really needed my hankie.

Panic returned when I realised that Steven was hurt. No blood. At least I couldn't see any, but his thick, ginger hair was covered in a bandage and he looked so pale. He always looked pale though, probably because he was always hungry. The mixture of baby teeth and big ones, which seemed to have sprung up in all the wrong places did nothing to benefit his appearance and the Impetigo around his mouth didn't help much either. My mind continued to wander. I wanted to sleep and closed my eyes. I pictured his mother, Coral – a pretty, delicate-looking young woman who did her best but without a husband really struggled to give Steven and his sister a decent life. Funny thing though, she was very well-spoken with a bit of a 'twang' of some kind and kept herself-to-herself. Some people even avoided her saying she was stuck-up. I'd never heard young Beth speak but Steven's accent was the dead opposite of Coral's; he spent far too much time with the other boys rampaging around the streets and fitted-in with them well.

My dreamlike state followed in the same vein, and now I had an image of Steven. I knew I was smiling again and tried to stop, but my thoughts were pleasant and comforting so I blissfully let them go on. Gorgeous eyes. The only thing in Steven's favour as far as looks went, were his gorgeous eyes. A piercing blue, with the longest, thickest lashes most women would have given their eyeteeth for. I had only taught him for a few terms but loved his never-ending chatter and cheerfulness despite his dire living conditions. He was a real trooper and I never heard him complain once.

I was startled when I heard him speak. Opening my eyes as wide as I could, I turned my head wildly in the direction of his voice and almost toppled out of the bed.

"Cor, Miss", he chirped, *"Fought you'd never wake up."*

I gulped a mouthful of air and what little saliva I could muster and said in a croaky voice, *"Well I'm awake now. Does your head hurt? Shall I find a nurse for you?"* My speech was slurred, but I was sure I wasn't drunk.

The 'helpful' lady in the next bed answered the question.

"Oh, e's alright. This isn't the proper 'ospital. We're just 'ere for

a while. Nowt wrong wit 'im, sept the blast. Ee asked for a bandij and they let 'im 'ave one".

Smiling again, I thanked her politely, hoping she wasn't going to carry on listening-in.

Steven was anxious to talk and said excitedly, *"Was it 'cos the sugar factory got 'it Miss? Or was it that rubber place wot got burned dan?"*

With no idea what he meant, I answered him with nothing but a frown. *"Yeah. The soap works is gone too, Miss".* He added.

The teacher in me replied, *"Steven, what are you talking about? Is this another one of your stories?"* Chuckling in an awkward sort of way, I felt sick again and made another desperate search for my hankie. *"Ooh no!",* came 'Helpful Lady'. *"They've all got bombed."* And leaning towards me, she added in a whisper, *"School's gone too, but the littlun don't know about that yet."*

I watched as a nurse wheeled a screen towards the lady's bed removing her from my view. This was ridiculous. I was sure she was mistaken. Sirens had been wailing for days and there had been a few air raids in the suburbs in August and then I'd seen bombs dropped on the docks, but surely they wouldn't want to bomb a school; what purpose would that serve? Anyway, if the school had been damaged there would have been more casualties like us, and all the other beds were empty. Steven had dozed off and I was glad because I needed to be quiet, retrace my steps and try to make some sort of sense out of all this. I laid flat, looking up at the lightshade suspended from a long cord on the ceiling recollecting the past.

Almost twenty-three, I had led a quiet life apart from Teachers' Training College mainly because mum was ill on-and-off for two years and the last few months of her life I helped nan nurse her when I was home. It had been hard, although in a funny-sort-of-way, I was able to accept her death more readily. But as if that wasn't bad enough for our family, in May - when all the blossom was on the trees and the birds

4

were singing – *you know*, that lovely 'fresh' time of the year, we heard that dad's brother had been killed.

Uncle David had lived in Whitstable with Auntie Win and my cousins, Hattie, and Geoffrey. He owned a Cockle boat and did quite well out of it collecting Cockles, Whelks, Crabs, Oysters, and Winkles depending on the season. Geoffrey had been helping since he was tiny, and Uncle David hoped he would take over one day; I think Geoff had other ideas though. Hattie was never allowed out on the boat, which was probably sensible what with her daydreaming, fancy ideas, and suffering from her nerves, which Nan said came from Auntie Win - *the one I said gets seasick*. She was always a bit delicate.

The highlight of our year for as long as I could remember had been a family get-together at the annual Oyster Festival when for several summer nights the female members of the family would cram into their two bedroomed house while the four 'boys' topped-and-tailed inside Uncle David's old tent in the garden. Hattie always shared her room with Nan and I, and on the first night we would humour Nan by saying that we'd never heard the story of how she met Grandad on a Kent Hop Farm when she was twelve and how she knew even then that they would marry. The story grew romantically the older we became, but we loved it just as much every time she told it while wiping away her tears.

We hadn't been able to go to the festival for the last five years and I missed our much-loved jamboree terribly. Grandad had died, Mum was ill and then the war started so time passed without seeing them in Whitstable, although they attended both funerals and Hattie and Geoff had stayed with us in 1937 when King George and Queen Elizabeth were crowned. That was a disaster though. The weather was awful, and we didn't even get a glimpse of them or any of the procession because we couldn't find the right place to stand. Hattie cried the whole time frightened by the crowds and we had lost Geoffrey for most of the afternoon so all in all, it was a dreadful day.

And then in a heartbeat, disaster struck. Events just seemed to overtake our hopes for more happy times at the seaside when there was an unusual and desperate call from the Navy. We knew the British Army was in France as a direct response to Hitler's invasion and things had not gone well for them. Our men had been overwhelmed by the strength of the German forces and had no alternative but to retreat. There were grave concerns when they were trapped at Dunkirk on the French coast because unless they could be brought back to England, we would have no army to continue the fight.

Transport ships had been sent to collect them, but with such large numbers of soldiers it was taking time. Time was not on their side though. Some of the ships had been sunk blocking the harbour and the decision was made to pluck the men from the beach. This had its own problems. The water was very shallow, and the big ships were unable to come close enough to get them, which meant the soldiers wading out and standing in water up to their necks for hours just waiting to be rescued.

I don't know whose brainwave it was, but someone realised that the only way to get the men off the beaches safely was to ferry them in boats small enough to navigate the shallow water. Boats just like Uncle David's. It sounded an impossible task, but he didn't hesitate to offer his boat. The 'Merry Mollusc' had a mind of its own though and the high-ups thought it would be better if he took it over himself with his mate Bobby and a Naval Rating. With petrol supplied by the Navy, they chugged down to Margate and then continued to Ramsgate where a huge flotilla of little boats had assembled – safety in numbers, maybe, then courageously crossing the Channel together, each either delivered men to the destroyers, or returned to England with a boatful of them. It was simply miraculous and saved the country from impending doom.

A sketchy account of a second journey however proved to be true and neither Uncle David, Bobby or the Rating survived to rescue more. The only saving grace was that Auntie Win had forbidden Geoffrey from going too. We never knew what had happened exactly, but Uncle David would always be my hero. Dad didn't say much about it, which I thought was bad for him and Nan cried constantly for a whole week. I did wonder whether this coming so soon after Mum's death and Grandad leaving us without saying goodbye magnified the third blow, but even worse for Nan was the decision not to hold a service of any kind since poor auntie and my cousins had nothing to bury. It was cruel.

Long before it happened, the government knew that war with Germany was inevitable and with the certainty of bombing said that children must leave some towns and cities. Consequently, thousands of children had been evacuated to the safety of the countryside. Alas, as the months went on it seemed that there was no danger after all and some Mums – *Coral being one of them*, fetched them back. Now we lived in uncertain and potentially dangerous times. The threat of invasion was real, and we should protect ourselves.

An announcement from the Home Secretary, Herbert Morrison told us that deep shelters would be dug, but ours' had yet to be built. Meanwhile, other arrangements would be made for those without their own shelter. So, each time the sirens started their terrifying wail, anyone without a garden to build their own Anderson either shut themselves in the cupboard under the stairs with the meters for company or went to the huge basement beneath our school. There they would wait for buses to take them to a public shelter a few streets away.

That Saturday, I had volunteered to go to school for a few hours. Some of my class, including Steven had fallen behind their peers due to the disruption that initial evacuation, 'Operation Pied Piper' had caused, and it was hoped that with a bit of extra coaching they would catch-up. Halfway through our lessons, the sirens moaned. Steven cheered. The others followed suit. Books disappeared beneath the lid of their desks and each of them stood to attention with their gas mask boxes over a shoulder. We were well-rehearsed.

Everyone was frightened when bombs were dropped over Harrow the week before last and hearing that many of our airfields had also been attacked, it wasn't long before their families and other locals began flooding-in to the basement to wait for one of the deep shelter buses. Once the children had been collected by a parent, I too went down into the area beneath the school. It had been organised with wooden benches and bunks and was well-lit, although it wasn't designed to be used for long; it was simply a waiting area really. The atmosphere was quite jolly to begin with and although it was a bit of a squeeze with so many of us down there most of us waited patiently. But time went on and on and with no buses arriving, some people left the safety of the basement taking their chances with the threat of bombing. Maybe they hoped to get to a relative, or friend and I could understand the difficulty trying to keep several children happy in such unpleasant and restrictive surroundings.

Sirens warned of imminent danger one minute and confused us with an 'all clear' the next. There were cheers, big sighs and rapturous applause when we thought we could leave, but as soon as we began to gather-up children and our belongings, another 'red warning' began and the cheers turned into groans as we all sat down again. Places vacated were soon filled with new people and the basement was now crammed full. I wondered what Dad was doing. He was probably wondering what I was doing, and Nan would have been wondering about the two of us.

The afternoon dragged-on. Where were the buses? Nothing had happened, apart from a few loud bangs and I was in two minds whether, or not to dash home and sit with Nan in the Anderson. But before I could make my decision, the loud bangs grew into deafening explosions. People screamed and children cried. Gas masks went on. We cowered together in terror as the noise of aircraft above us intensified.

Bigger explosions rumbled like thunder. Anti-aircraft guns fired. Bells rang furiously and at one point, I was sure the floor

8

had moved. We were under attack in a way none of us thought possible. That night was a new experience for us all. We thought it would never end, but morning came with the 'all clear' although it was far from clear about what had happened. The Warden tried to stop us leaving the basement, saying it was too dangerous to walk around with fires burning and buildings falling, but an elderly couple insisted they'd rather die in their own beds and left anyway.

Somehow, a WVS van parked outside and the ladies came down with tea and biscuits. Exhausted and anxious, uncomfortable, and needing some fresh air, I left my place and headed to the toilets, only to find that they had stopped flushing. I had to use one though and at least there was a trickle of water from the cold tap. I swallowed a mouthful from a cupped hand and splashed water over my face. An acrid smell of burning wafted through the air and standing on tiptoe to look out of the window, saw only smoke and flames. Men were shouting, bells continued to ring, and the sound of water gushing reminded me that Dad would be fighting the fires. This was an awful experience, but surely it would stop soon. Promising myself that I'd be back home before long, I returned to the basement.

The rest of the day saw more people arrive. Some were in nightclothes and little else. Graphic accounts of their experiences and the description of the carnage outside horrified all who would listen. The canteen van was replaced by another, this time with bread and dripping ferried down to us in batches. It was glorious and gratefully accepted. The Warden said he was 'making enquiries' about the buses, but some roads were blocked, and it might be a while longer before we were moved. I just wanted to go home.

Why I was surprised when the sirens went again, I don't know. I didn't expect another air raid, but that was what we had a second night. It was as bad as the night before and went on and on. Surely, there couldn't be much left to bomb. We still had electric light, which was a miracle, although it flashed on and off as each 'crump' of bombs hit the ground. I longed to take a deep breath, but the air was stale and smelly. Children were inconsolable and so were some adults when they ran out of cigarettes. Old Mrs. Crabb from number 29 reluctantly shared her bottle of Milk Stout, the toilets overflowed and the lady sitting opposite held her baby wearing what by now must have been a very dirty nappy.

Nan would have expected me to be safely in the big shelter and I knew she'd be in the Anderson with 'Miss Bluebell' and whatever she was 'knitting for victory' this week; that is, apart from taking constant trips to the lavvy. I'm sure the needles clicked faster and faster with every siren. At least the weather was good, which meant the shelter wouldn't be ankle-deep in water. I shuddered at the thought of the creepy crawlies that must be joining her, although right then, I would have joined her in a flash.

Terrifying noises outside and choking smoke drifting inside made it difficult to sleep. Embarrassed at first, mothers feeding babies were now a sight we ignored; at least they were kept nourished and quiet. My head ached. None of us had eaten or drunk enough for two days and the conditions worsened when the Warden produced fire buckets to use instead of the toilets. One bomb landed so close we felt the building above us tremble.

There was a lot of crying, screaming and prayers asking for salvation. And so, it continued until the early hours of Monday morning when the 'all clear' droned on. It was such a relief although the mood amongst us was mixed with most not knowing what to do next. We seemed to have been in the basement forever with conditions deteriorating rapidly and the promised buses still hadn't arrived. I stood and dusted myself off and as I did, had a sudden urge to leave. My pulse racing, I felt a sense of daring I'd never known before as I decided to run home as fast as I could.

The Warden looked dreadful. He couldn't have had any sleep at all by the look of him but was still feisty. "*No love,*" he said with authority, "*You can't walk around up there. The buses will come soon.*" Totally deflated, a wave of tearful exhaustion replaced my earlier sense of daring. I wanted to believe him but was rapidly losing faith. The men behind me weren't having any of it though. Pushing past him, they headed up the stairs, only to return seconds later looking shocked. "*Unbelievable.*" Said one. The other said nothing and sat down again.

My seat had been taken by a sleeping child, so I leaned against the wall instead. Steven stood in front of his mum and little Beth, who had been clutching the same slice of bread and dripping since the day before. My mouth turned up at the edges when I heard Steven say, "*If you ain't 'ad that by the time I count to an 'undred, I'm 'avin' it.*"

The fact that Steven couldn't count to one hundred didn't matter, because Beth began nibbling round the edges and Steven folded his arms in a huff. For some reason, he always had one sock up and one down, which made him appear even more lovable. I smiled. He smiled back revealing the assortment of teeth. He was still smiling as he squeezed his way towards me with his gas mask box over one shoulder unaware that it was bouncing off several people. Sliding down the wall we sat on the floor together.

Turning to me, he said, "*Ot in 'ere, in it, Miss? Are ya scared?*" I couldn't admit that I was petrified, so just smiled.

Another warning. Sirens came and went incessantly and in between we slept any way we could. A woman and three children in grubby nightclothes and with ashen faces left their corner quietly with only the blankets they'd been given by the Warden. With no other belongings, it was obvious they'd been bombed-out. How would you explain all this to a child? I will never forget the look of fear and confusion on their faces. Where were they going? Would they be okay? But then with no further thought for their well-being, I took advantage of their decamping and curled up on the space they'd left, although I knew I was lying in a puddle of something rather unpleasant.

The next siren woke me. I was stiff and cold from being on the floor and longing for a cup of tea, wished the WVS van was still outside. My clothes were damp, and I smelled awful. What day was it? Why hadn't we been moved? Crying and coughing, sneezing, and moaning, we were a sad and miserable bunch of people. Where was Dad? Was he alright? If only I could go up to the playground and see what was going on, perhaps there'd be a fireman I could ask.

Our third night in the basement was no different. It was almost second nature to prepare for another onslaught as the siren wailed urgently warning us that the loud whine of aircraft engines meant they were directly overhead. This alarmed us all and some people put on their gas mask again. Beth protested while her mum fitted the horrible thing around her face - the remains of the bread and dripping squelching in her hand. Steven loved wearing his though and had it on in a flash blowing into it with gusto. Most of the boys and even some of the girls did this to make a very rude noise and I had to bite my lips to retain some decorum during classroom gas mask practice. Mask in place, the usual sock at half-mast and his school cap backwards on his head the way he liked to wear it, he stood stiffly with arms beside him. He looked quite a sight.

With bombs dropping and our own guns firing, even hands over our ears couldn't block-out the noise. I tried to sleep, but every time I closed my bleary eyes and began to doze off, there was another '*BOOM*', or bang. It was 3.35am. Boys and girls should have been safely tucked-up in bed. Rubbing my eyes fiercely, I decided. That's it. I've had enough. I'm going to see if I can find out about Dad. The Warden can stick it in his pipe and smoke it. Goodness knows what I thought I could do, but I felt useless doing nothing; I had no intention of putting that foul rubber contraption on my face though and slung it over my shoulder. Lengthening the strap around my handbag so I could wear it across my body, I tiptoed carefully through the dozens of people sleeping on the floor. Trying to be careful where I stepped, saying, "*Sorry. Sorry*", there was still a groan from someone whose fingers I trod on. Eventually reaching the stairs, the Warden was thankfully not on guard. Using this opportunity, I took the steps two at a time, sped through the corridor, and gingerly stepped into the playground realising with horror that the school was surrounded by an inferno.

As light as day and as hot as hell, the building next door was now a pile of burning rubble. The sound of gunfire turned my attention upwards where bullets rose in an arched stream of white dots, while searchlight beams swayed in the dark hoping to catch an aircraft in the sky like torchlight attracting moths. It was a shocking sight and almost beyond belief. A stomach-churning smell made me retch and I thought my ears would burst. I couldn't catch my breath and when I did, the smoke-filled air made me dizzy and my eyes sting. Why had I left the basement?

When I realised that Steven had followed me, I thought I would faint. Standing quite still his attention was drawn to something behind me. Turning sharply my eyes narrowed at what I saw. Steven walked towards it. Sensing danger, I shouted at him to stop going any further. He didn't hear me. I hurried over to him and we stood looking at the long, sparkly, fizzing object lying on the part of the playground that had been marked with white lines for games. The lines had been painted over to make them less visible from the air, but the pure white brightness of the fizzy thing showed them up again. I had never seen anything like this pretty object before. Its brightness grew. It seemed to be melting.

Catching Steven's hand, we moved backwards, our attention drawn to the clear sky and the planes flying in it. I was astonished at the amount of aircraft the Germans had. This was nothing like Nan's description of the Zeppelins flying silently over London in 1915. Resembling giant insects, the planes flew along the river - quite high at first although they seemed to be circling in a perfectly orchestrated way. Shells exploded all around them, but the pilots held their course.

More of the fizzy long things tinkled down from the sky and had we not been in danger, I'm sure we would have stayed looking upwards. This spectacle was hard enough for me to take in, so it was difficult to know what Steven was thinking. I knew it was really happening, but it was like some sort of unearthly dream. It was ludicrous to think that the German men flying above – *maybe tall, handsome blondes* hated us this much, but my romantic notions ceased when one of the fizzy things suddenly burst into flames.

Despite the compulsion to stand and watch, my heart was beating nineteen-to-the-dozen and I knew we should go back to the safety of the basement but before I did maybe I could just stand on the wall on the far other side of the playground to get a bigger and better view of what was going on, or at least see if there was any sign of the buses. There was no point in trying to speak to Steven through the noise and there seemed to be no end to the planes, which just kept flying over us.

Steven gazed into the sky with a hand over his school cap. His small frame top-heavy with the apparatus on his face and a reflection of the aircraft flickering on the transparent part like a cinema screen. He was spellbound. Sensing even more danger, we had to move. Planes kept coming, their outline coloured by the fires below. In the distance, we saw them turning back towards us releasing their bombs as they flew, the resulting explosions causing great clouds of dense smoke and flames shooting high into the sky. Steven ran over to me and flung his arms around my waist. We needed to shelter, but where?

The playground wall was much nearer than the school building. I grabbed Steven's hand and we ran. My legs felt heavy and although I wanted to run faster, I seemed to be stuck in mud. Finally reaching the lowest part of the wall enclosing the school playground, we squeezed behind the little brick house with the bins inside and rather than have him fall off the wall and hurt himself, I managed to lift Steven over it where he sat propped-up still gazing at the sky. Clambering on top of the wall onto my knees, I was just about to stand up when I think there was an almighty bang and a big rush of wind. These were my last recollections before finding myself in the hospital bed.

A young, pretty nurse walked towards our end of the ward. I followed her without moving my aching head and it was then I noticed how lovely her uniform was. The calf-length dress in thin white and Lilac striped material with a starched apron enveloping it, had long billowy sleeves with white cuffs. Lilac was my favourite colour and I pictured myself wearing it. I think I preferred this to the uniform of the Wrens. Her hair was long, although I was unable to see how long, because most of it was underneath a round linen cap with a sort of bow at the back. Stupid how my mind was blithering. I should be concentrating on getting up and brushing my teeth, not thinking about fashion.

Looking at my watch, I brought it closer to my eyes because I couldn't make out the time. The glass was shattered and listening for the tick, realised it had stopped. There was a clock above the doors of the ward though; it was almost one o'clock but what day? I must get home. Nan and Dad would be agitated by now. Steven's mum might not be able to get to the hospital easily, so perhaps I could take him back with me.

I stopped the nurse who was removing the screens from the lady beside me and pointing to Steven, said, "*Excuse me Nurse, I think Steven and I were knocked over by a blast of some kind, but we've not been hurt, so I could take him back with me. I suppose his mum knows he's here. We've been in the same clothes for ages*", I added with a skittish laugh.

Her reaction was a surprise. She said nothing and literally turned tail towards the swing doors. I stared at the helpful lady, who pursed her lips and stared back at me. Maybe I should speak to someone in authority. I desperately needed to spend a penny anyway and hoped my feet would hold me up if I placed them on the floor although before attempting that I had to find my shoes. Each bed had a wooden locker beside it.

15

Recognising Steven's school cap and gas mask sitting on his and assuming the one on the right with the water I had drunk belonged to my bed, I opened the door. My handbag, shoes and my own dreaded gas mask box were all there covered in a thick film of dust.

I swung down into the locker and retrieved my shoes. After that, I felt giddy again and sat still for a moment before slipping them on. Noticing several ladders in my stockings corresponding to some cuts on my legs I cursed under my breath, knowing that I had only one decent pair left in the drawer at home. I felt sure my bag would be safe enough to leave and I'd conveniently forget about the gas mask, but took out my comb and then leaning on the bed to hold myself upright, worked my way down to the end.

"*Miss, Miss*", Steven called, "*Where ya goin'? Don't leave me ere*".

"*No, I won't leave you, Steven. I'm just going to talk to someone about us going home. They might even take us in an ambulance!*" I tempted.

Aiming for the swing doors, the space in between looked a long way off. I wasn't sure I would make it without help. Just then the young nurse I had spoken to earlier swept through the same doors pushing a wheelchair and the next thing I knew I'd been pressed into it. Ignoring the squeals from Steven she steered me out of the ward. "*Would you take me to the toilet, please?*" I begged.

Stopping abruptly, the nurse turned the chair in the opposite direction and at top speed, wheeled me to the WC where she helped me out of the chair and into the cubicle without saying a word. When I'd finished, she did the reverse, speaking only when I asked to wash my hands and face and comb my hair, saying, "*Yes, but be quick, we have to go to Sister's Office they're waiting for you*".

I didn't know who was waiting for me, but I wanted a bit of a wash and brush up. Sitting so low down in the wheelchair, I could see only half of my face in the mirror above the basin.

The reflection horrified me because what I could see looked dreadful. My eyes were bright red and there was dry blood around my nose and ears. Soaping my hands and rubbing my face, my mind was still in a whirl. Using my comb, I managed to dislodge even more of the stuff in my hair but before I could examine it the nurse grabbed the chair and hurtled back in the direction of the ward. Stopping at a door with 'SISTER' written thickly on the mottled glass panel, the nurse tapped on it gently.

A lady in a dark blue dress and ornate white cap opened the door. Nodding to the nurse and taking the wheelchair she placed me in front of a big desk where an elderly gentleman with gold-framed glasses sat. At one end, I noticed that buff-coloured folders piled into a wire basket were in danger of slipping onto the floor. I wondered if I should mention it. A jug of lovely flowers brightened the room. Crossing her arms as she sat on a chair in the corner, the lady looked rather unfriendly. Trying to sit up straight, I was glad I'd managed a bit of a tidy-up even if I hadn't brushed my teeth. Turning towards me, the man smiled faintly and said, *"Hello, Miss Cooper, how are you feeling?"*

"Oh, you know my name." I replied. Nodding slowly, he produced a pipe from his pocket. Filling it with tobacco from a pouch, he continued to speak. *"My name is Doctor McKeon. Now you have suffered Concussion caused by a bomb that exploded quite close to you. Do you have any memory of that?"* I didn't react, so he went on. *"Yes, you and Steven were discovered unconscious during a bad air raid. One of the ARP Wardens found your identity card in your handbag and Steven has told us all about you too."* He lit a match and held it to the pipe. *"Well, yes, err … what exactly is Concussion?"* I asked. There was no explanation. Instead, he gave the lady a quick look and took my hand. *"Miss Cooper, what I have to tell you will cause you some upset."* I lowered my eyes and took a deep breath. Was it about Dad?

Sucking on his pipe, which wasn't actually alight, he said

slowly, "*You were both in the school basement and then for some reason left the building. This obviously saved your lives because it was then that a bomb was dropped knocking you off your feet ... but I'm afraid the bomb hit the school*". Staring at him, I didn't move. "*Do you understand what I'm saying, Lesley? The school took a direct hit.*"

"*Yes, I understand*". I replied, "*The school was bombed, but then what happened? We were all in the basement. Did the buses come?*" I was confused and shook my head. This time, it was fine, sand-like gravel that landed on my lap. The Doctor looked away for a few seconds before turning back. "*Lesley, there have been many casualties in the last few days. The docks, the factories and some of the streets in between have been demolished and most of the people in the school basement were killed. I'm afraid that Steven's mother and sister are on the list of those confirmed dead.*"

The lady stood up and moved towards me. Now she looked almost sympathetic. Staring at the Doctor for what seemed like ages, I began to ramble. Wringing my hands, which had suddenly become cold and clammy, I burbled, "*Yes, well if we can go now in the ambulance ... Nan will be so worried. So ...*"

I continued to talk nonsense while he wheeled me into another room with the gentle assurance that Concussion often made you do and say funny things and I wasn't to worry about it; I would be better soon. The room was empty of people although full of armchairs and he left me in a gap beside the fireplace. From the chair, I closely examined every silky petal of the orange Roses in a vase on the hearth. My head hurt too much to bend down to take in their aroma, although I doubted their scent was as good as Mum's. After a while, I looked up at the mantlepiece where there was one of those tear-off calendars showing what was obviously today's date. To my horror, I realised I hadn't seen Dad or Nan for four days.

Repeating the doctor's words to myself, it was too shocking to believe that the people in the basement – *Mrs. Crabb ... the lady and the baby ... pretty Coral and dear little Beth* – might all be dead. No, they can't be dead. What would happen to Steven?

A lady wearing a green overall came into the room carrying a big cup and saucer also in green. Strange how you recognise things even at bad times. *"There's sugar in the spoon if you like it"*, the lady said. I managed to nod and took it from her, slowly pouring the spoon of sugar into the tea. Sugar. Even the sugar factory was bombed. This nightmare was slowly beginning to sink into my mixed-up mind when yet another lady, about the same age as my Mum but without a uniform this time knocked on the open door. Peering round it, she said kindly, *"Hello, Lesley, I'm Mrs. Johnson, the hospital Almoner. I'm also helping the local Council at the present time and we'll soon have you sorted-out".*

"I don't need to be sorted-out". I said abruptly and close to tears, *"I just want to go home."*

"Yes, but first we need to have some details". It's all official stuff these days". She told me softly.

Mrs. Johnson explained what was known so far about the school, the docks, the factories and the streets around them and the horror of those details could only have been worse if she had told me that Dad was dead. She didn't know anything about him, or Nan, or even if our house was still standing, but said that gas mains were burning and even buildings that hadn't been hit were so badly damaged that the area had been evacuated. Then she asked me if I was strong enough to do something awfully hard.

By the time Mrs. Johnson had finished talking, the sirens went once again and she wheeled me to another part of the hospital, where to my delight and his joy, Steven and I were reunited; his head bandage removed. *"Cor Miss, you left me wiv that old bag".* He said with a laugh. I doubted I would ever laugh again.

We were not a religious family, but when Mum was suffering as she did, I prayed most nights. I had no idea if it was the right, or wrong way to contact God, or even if He was listening but it secretly gave me some comfort to share my feelings instead of keeping the stiff upper lip Mum had thought so important.

Sitting in a corridor without windows did little to muffle the sound of the dreaded air raid siren and the incessant clanging of ambulance and fire engine bells outside. A bomb must have landed not far from the hospital. The floor shook, plaster fell from the ceiling like talcum powder and the light went on and off as if someone flicked the switch. One explosion seemed so close and made such a loud bang, that Steven left the bench to sit on my lap in the wheelchair. I put my arm round him and held his hot little hand and we trembled together in silence amongst the dozens of other frightened people sheltering there.

Some were crying, some whimpered pathetically. Many had an arm in a sling, an eye bandaged, an ankle in Plaster of Paris, some with nasty cuts and bruises – some with plasters covering them, some not. Others didn't seem to be hurt at all, including a Jewish family who gently rocked their heads while praying quietly. I decided that this was as good a time as ever to do the same and prepared myself as best I could by closing my eyes and taking a deep breath.

The prayer almost amused me though because I wasn't asking God to keep us safe. No, it wasn't that. I asked for much more because I knew I would need all the help I could get to fulfil the task I'd been given. Screwing-up my eyes tightly I practised by saying to myself,

'*Dear God,*
Please help me tell Steven in the nicest possible way that his
mum and sister are dead. Thank you very much, Lesley
Cooper.

20

OR should I say,

'Dear God,
Give me the strength to tell Steven that his family has passed
away. With thanks, Lesley Cooper'.

Both prayers were as bad as each other and I was disappointed I couldn't do better than that with the education I'd had. I wasn't even sure if this might be the sort of thing you could ask. However, I felt that the first version would do, since even though he was only nine, Steven would know what 'dead' meant. We had a dead cat in school when the Caretaker had laid poison for the rats and most of the children had seen it. But what would God make of this? Why had He allowed Coral and Beth to be killed leaving Steven alone? Why was my street in ruins? Where were Nan and Dad?

Remembering vividly what Mrs. Johnson had said, I went over it again. As far as she knew at this time, Steven had no known Father and until perhaps a copy of his Birth Certificate could be obtained and investigations on Coral and Beth made, maybe no other living relative. That technically, would make him an orphan. A lot of houses in the street where Coral lodged had been flattened and although we didn't know if hers was one of them, it might mean Steven had no belongings either. Mind you, he was rarely seen in different clothes, so I was sure his 'belongings' were few.

It would appear, that I was now the only person Steven had an attachment to. Under the circumstances, rather than take him to a Council-run children's home where a stranger would tell him about his mother and sister, arrangements were to be made for us to go to a Reception Centre together. We could have a bath, be given a change of clothes and stay there until other plans were made. Meantime, it was my job to give Steven the awful news, which would need to be done soon.

CHAPTER TWO

Place of Safety

___

Thankfully, the last air raid hadn't magnified, and the Jewish family left together in a dutiful line behind the older man as soon as the 'all clear' sounded. I wondered where they were going, or why they had been there in the first place. Two male Orderlies arrived and ferried others away and I was asked by another if I felt well enough to vacate the wheelchair, which I did with pleasure. Steven and I sat on an empty bench until boredom overcame him and he slid up and down the corridor on the dust that had settled on the floor. I hoped someone knew we were there.

I was thirsty again and knew we should both go to the toilet although I was concerned that if we did, we might miss whatever it was we were waiting for. Steven had slid to the end of the corridor and I asked him to peer around each corner to see if there was a WC.

Looking in each direction, he called, "*Dunno, Miss*".

Dizzy, thirsty and hungry and still not quite back to normal, I stood slowly. Something fell onto the floor and looking down, saw it was my comb. Then I remembered that my gas mask and handbag were still in the casualty ward locker. I caught my breath. All my money and paperwork were inside. I had to retrieve it somehow.

But first things first. Inhaling deeply and gingerly taking a step, I too almost skated across the floor towards Steven. Relieved to reach him without tumbling, I placed a hand on his shoulder to steady myself and guided him into the next corridor where the first thing I saw, was a long piece of metal protruding above a door saying, 'LADIES'.

"*What does that say?*" I asked Steven, pointing to the sign. "*It don't say, WC, does it Miss?*" He replied cleverly. I pulled him towards the door where he stopped dead in his tracks squawking, "*I aint no lady. Aint goin' in there, Miss.*"

"*Yes, you are, Steven*" I told him, "*It's alright.*"

With the door closed behind us, it was a quiet haven of peace and normality. You wouldn't have believed there was a war going on outside. It was clean as a whistle with four flushing toilet cubicles and a row of basins, which we both used. There was nothing to say we couldn't drink the water, so we both slurped from a cold tap. I splashed water on my face, combed my hair and told Steven to freshen-up a bit. This he did, by wiping his nose on his sleeve and standing up straight. The expression on my face told him he needed to do better than that and pulling-up the one sock that was always at half-mast, he rubbed the front of his shoes on the backs of both socks. Believing this to be a vast improvement, he held the door open for me in readiness.

"*Thank you, kind Sir*". I said.

His smile said it all and we went back to the empty corridor and sat on our bench.

Feeling worried about so many things as I was, I didn't know what to worry about first. However, retrieving my handbag was the priority now and as soon as a nurse passed-by, I asked for her help. After I had explained my predicament and the fact that we didn't know what was supposed to happen to us next, she looked at the upside-down fob watch pinned to her beautiful uniform saying she was just going on her break but would see what she could do. She would also find someone to sweep the floor before Matron saw it.

All we seemed to do was wait and I was still agitated for some time after she went until one of the tea ladies wearing green turned-up with Steven's gas mask, my bag and my own dreaded gas mask box. Unfortunately, she had no information to give us but promised to speak to 'Staff Nurse', who could speak to 'Sister'. Thinking there was obviously a stringent pecking order here, it also sounded as if Matron was a real tyrant too.

Steven was asleep with his head on my lap. Trying not to disturb him, I opened my bag and peered in to examine the contents. Nothing seemed to be missing but I was unable to go through it properly, so just stuffed my comb inside. I dozed fitfully with flashing lights appearing before my eyes every now and then, until we were gently roused by the same lady in green holding a tray with a glass of milk, a cup of tea and two Corned Beef sandwiches. I was so grateful for such wonderful refreshments, I had tears in my eyes when I took the tray from her. We devoured every scrap in the few seconds it took for her to tell us that we were waiting for the others. When I asked who the 'others' were, she told us that 'Sister' had told 'Staff Nurse' that we and the others would be leaving soon. I was intrigued. However, this had given me something else to think about and Steven and I made a bit of a game out of it by trying to decide who these people might be. "*Soldiers, Miss*", Steven supposed. "*I ope it's soldiers! Wiv guns!!*" "*I think it will be people like us, Steven,*" *I doubt there will be guns.*" At least I hoped not.

By the time we had exhausted our long list of 'others', we heard the air raid warning go again. My heart sank. Not another one. Hadn't they done enough damage by now? Let's hope they run out of bombs. This was nothing like the Great War Dad told me about and the Zeppelins that dropped their bombs; nothing remotely like what was coming down now. Exhaustion coupled with our uncertain destination made us both feel uneasy and the bench seemed to be growing harder to sit on by the minute. Steven's lovely eyes were turned to the floor with those thick lashes sweeping up and down with each blink and I wondered if he was thinking about his mother and sister. He hadn't mentioned them once and I didn't know if this was good, or bad.

Almost as soon as it had begun, the siren stopped. The

24

threat had passed. No bombs. What a relief. Steven cheered but his whoops were interrupted when as if my magic, a lady in a very frilly cap and an almost black blue dress appeared. Holding what looked like a Bible, before speaking, she took a long look at the floor, pursing her lips as she did. Steven shuffled the dust around a bit with a shoe, but it did nothing to hide his antics. Turning to me, she looked terribly tired and sad. The lady smiled and in a softly spoken voice at last told us our fate.

The idea was to get as many fit people as possible out of the hospital while there were no aircraft above us. We would be driven to the Reception Centre Mrs Johnson had mentioned and were not to be alarmed because it was a place of safety. We would be well-taken-care-of, for a short time before moving on. I was asked if I felt well enough to undertake the journey and prepared to accept responsibility for Steven and as she said this, we both turned to look at him. He had a finger up his nose, which stayed there while his eyes widened revealing even more of their colour. The finger stayed there until he saw me shake my head slowly and grinning like the cat that got the cream, indiscreetly rubbed it on his shirt.

I repeated my name and address and my position at the school where I taught, at which point the lady frowned and said, "*Yes, a terrible thing.*" These details she wrote in the book, which wasn't a Bible at all, and I signed my name beneath. Then we were told to "*Come along,*" so I grabbed Steven's hand, threw my bag over a shoulder, gathered up the gas masks and quickly followed her down several flights of stairs outside into the ambulance bay.

Outside. We were outside at last, where the smell of burning and the colour of the sky was a bit of a shock. I felt Steven's grip on my hand tighten. I couldn't make out where we were because there were no recognisable buildings and it might sound odd, but they were all hollow, like a skull with smouldering sparks for hair. Bells rang in the distance and I was sure the gushing noise was water from a hose. Could it be

Dad? Men in uniform were doing their best to sweep the ambulance bay free of debris with long brooms. The sound of shattered glass and falling masonry muffled their voices although believe it, or not, one of them was whistling.

It was getting dark and my bloodshot eyes were still adjusting, but I could just make out several other walking wounded pressed onto the benches in the back of an ambulance. A man I assumed to be the driver held the door open and cheerfully said to them, "*Budge up. One-and-a-half more,*" Then he turned to the lady and I heard him whisper, "*Don't worry Matron, I'll look after them, they'll be fine.*" He closed the doors with us inside and we set off with the light from a blue bulb giving us all a peculiar complexion.

There were no windows, apart from two that had been blacked-out at the back, so it was impossible to see where we were going, or even what direction we were taking. I thought I was going to be sick again and began the deep breathing recommended by the doctor. Steven looked very apprehensive although we were still tightly holding hands. He was a sweet little boy and I wanted to cuddle him. What was he thinking? Would I be able to look after him when I had trouble looking after myself? If only the buses had come.

It was obvious the driver was having a difficult time picking his way through the damaged roads. We were thrown around a lot to begin with, which caused a lot of groaning from some of the passengers and the driver often shouted, "*Sorry!!*" until we were far enough away from the bombed areas for a better surface. Two ladies in a tight embrace had wept softly since we left the hospital and between 'tutting', an elderly gentleman constantly mumbled something about 'The White Hart'. Sleep had overcome Steven who was laying with his head on my lap now and the other five simply stared at the floor. Soon the air was stifling, made worse when the old gentleman's trousers started dripping with what I assumed was urine. I hoped our journey would end soon.

I hadn't felt this anxious since Mum's last few days, but my feelings were mixed with emotion of a different kind this time. I had no idea where we were going, but it was obviously far away from home and neither my father, nor my grandmother knew where I was. I shouldn't have left the hospital. I should have tried to contact Dad. Why did I get in the ambulance? I was in a panic and knew I must calm down. It seemed that Steven and I were lucky to be alive, but the twist of fate that meant we were together when the bomb dropped on the school had given me the biggest responsibility of my life so far. How I'd tell Steven about his family, I didn't know. He still hadn't mentioned them. Maybe I should start hinting a bit. So much was tearing through my mind. I felt ill and closed my eyes.

By the time we reached the Reception Centre, wherever it was, we were all asleep until the ambulance came to an abrupt stop jolting us all awake with a frightened start. The driver jumped out and opened the rear doors expecting us to do the same but quickly realising that we weren't in the best of shape stood there for a while until at long last he said, "*Sorry folks, but I need to get the lights of my vehicle switched-off. Quick as you can now*". With the doors open, we could see stars twinkling above us rather than enemy aircraft and the rush of fresh air was wonderful. Steven lifted his head off my lap and said, "*Are we 'avin' our tea 'ere, Miss?*"

I told him we would be having a lovely tea because a growing boy needed all the food he could get. At least I hoped we were as I felt quite weak with hunger myself. Being nearest the door, we stepped out of the ambulance and although my legs were still very shaky, I managed to help the driver get the other poor souls out. It was dark, but I could see Steven pinching his nose when the elderly gentleman finally made it onto the gravel. It was so good to see the stars and breathe air mixed with the sort of aroma, which only comes from trees. The bliss was short lived, however as the rumble of guns and explosions behind us turned our attention to the orange glow on the horizon. No one spoke, which wasn't peculiar, since we all knew we weren't looking at a beautiful sunset. One of the two ladies, who were still cuddling began to whimper and the elderly gentleman started moaning again about 'The White Hart' and the fact that 'Flo' had bought it. Poor old thing, I thought. This is his second, or even third war.

Dim light from the building silhouetted the outline of a tall lady in the doorway. *"Come along now, think of the blackout"*, she snapped. Her scolding startled us all and we dutifully trotted with greater speed along the path towards her and our 'safe place'. The ambulance driver started his engine. I was sorry if he was having to drive all the way back. Fortunately for him though, I saw that he was turning the ambulance round to park.

In stark contrast to the freshness of outside, the atmosphere in what I assumed was a large village hall was quite different. The door was banged shut, a heavy curtain drawn across and with all the windows blacked-out, it felt as though we were in a stuffy prison. How I wished to go outside again. Artfully arranged tables and chairs were empty of people so I assumed we were the only group there. Several buckets of sand hung from the walls and the smell of sawdust mixed with the faint odour of carbolic did nothing to help my nausea, which had returned with a vengeance. Steven held my hand tightly and looked even more anxious. We needed to eat and were both extremely weary.

Our travelling companions were strangers, but we congregated in the security of a huddle. The tall lady who did not give us the courtesy of introducing herself looked very posh, or 'well-to-do', as Nan would have said. Holding a clipboard in a very official way, she told us to wait until she had ticked-off all our names to make sure we should be there; had she told us to go elsewhere I think there would have been a mutiny.

Once 'ticked-off', she waved in one direction telling us that we were to use the toilets and then have a cup of tea and a sandwich, although as soon as she came to the elderly gentleman, he was whisked away somewhere before he even had the chance of a cup of tea. The tall lady looked Steven up-and-down with pursed lips. This was the moment I decided I really didn't care for this tall lady very much at all.

Steven and I headed straight for the toilets, two side by side, one with 'men' scribbled on a piece of cardboard and attached to the door with a drawing pin. The two ladies were already using both cubicles next door and two others had formed a queue so increasing their number, I stood behind them. Steven hesitated at the door of the men's toilets. I could see he was worried about going in alone and pulled him towards me. I was glad I had, because the commotion in there would have scared the life out of him. The door swung open revealing the old gentleman kicking and punching the air. With his opponent out of sight, he screamed at the top of his voice, "*Get awf me!*" *I'll tan yer ide for ya, ya little bugga. Git yer own Long Johns.*" Steven gave me a knowing look.

After the satisfaction of using the toilet, we sat at a table with our tea, which was strong and sweet. Sardines sitting between doorstep-sized pieces of bread were gone in a flash and we would both have liked more. My nausea gone, I looked longingly at the remainder on the trolley but just then, a nurse wearing an apron with a big red cross on the front came towards us. With a huge smile exposing the biggest front teeth you'd ever seen, she bobbed down in front of him and said in the kindest of ways, "*Hello, you must be Steven. Come with me and I'll give you a nice bath*".

Steven's reaction was such a surprise, I nearly fell off my chair. He was heading for the front door at great speed. Oh, Steven, bath time at home was obviously not a regular occurrence, was it? I went after him, but he was too quick for me and by the time I got to the door, he'd torn open the curtain and was out into the darkness. I couldn't see a thing when I left the hall but then heard Steven shouting and footsteps crunching on the gravel, which grew louder until I recognised the driver of our ambulance wearing a wide grin and Steven over his shoulder.

Reaching for his hand, I tried to calm him down as the driver marched with him and the nurse towards the bathroom. *"I hear this happens a lot with children from that area"*, the tall, posh-looking lady said to the driver as we swept past her. I gave her a backward stare long enough to make her feel awkward but really wanted to poke my tongue out at her; it made me grip Steven's hand even tighter. She looked embarrassed and said pathetically, *"Well, we can't have the door open, can we? Think of the blackout."*

Almost an hour later, I was relieved to see him tucked-up in bed. The nurse and I had coaxed him into the bath where he had allowed us to stay if we promised to turn our backs. I think he secretly enjoyed pouring the jug of water over his head and was rinsed, if not properly washed because the towel he used after was streaked with dirt. The pyjamas he was given were too big and smelt of carbolic soap, but he was soon fast asleep in the bed assigned to him with a postcard above it stuck on the wall with adhesive tape saying, 'STEVEN'.

The lovely nurse explained that the Reception Centre had been set-up for adults and consequently, there were no fresh clothes small enough for him, so she gave his shirt and socks a bit of a wash. He hadn't been wearing a vest or anything under his short trousers and she left them thinking they would take too long to dry for him to wear in the morning. This was fortunate since she discovered his Identity Card in the back pocket. While she did this, she pointed me in the direction of a room housing the boiler and mops and buckets where I would find nightgowns stacked on a shelf and a selection of other clothes to replace my own. I was to leave my skirt and blouse in the bucket marked 'dirty', in exchange. Shuffling through the clothes, I found a dress that Mum would have loved and tried it on. It fitted me perfectly and, although it wasn't really the type I would normally wear, found it comforting to think that Mum would have chosen it. Standing still for a moment I stroked the material. I wanted to cry and had to take a few deep breaths and swallow several times to stop myself from howling like a banshee. That wouldn't do at all.

Pulling a pair of men's pyjamas from another stack even though they would gape at the front, I took the clothes with me to the bathroom. I was the last of our little lot to use the bath and although the Red Cross Nurse had assured me that she had cleaned it adequately between people, I had the elderly gentleman in mind and sloshed a jug of water around anyway before turning on the taps. I would have loved hot water up to my neck, but the tepid trickle rose just a few inches before I sat in it forgetting I was still wearing my watch.

Nan had bought it for my 21st Birthday using some of Grandad's stamp album money and apart from being the only piece of proper jewellery I had, it was precious to me for obvious reasons. I removed it from my wrist and in vain, held it to my ear to see if I could hear even a slight 'tick'. Nothing. Not a sound. Gently placing it onto the chair as if it were a sleeping kitten, I fought back my emotions while I washed.

Vigorously using the medicated soap on my cuts and grazes and this time, sloshing a jug of water over my own head, I hauled my aching body out of the bath. I was exhausted but my mind wouldn't rest. I still had no news of Dad, or Nan and in the morning, I had to talk to Steven. I sat on the chair beside the bath and rubbed my hair. More bits of grit and gravel fell out when I pulled my comb through it and I was glad that it was cut short in a 'bob'; had it still been waist-length, it would have taken ages to dry. I rinsed my stockings and thought twice about doing the same with my corselet but plunged it into the warm water anyway. Wringing it out and shaking it as hard as I could, I left it hanging in the boiler room and went to the dormitory.

Whoever had set-up the village hall as a Reception Centre knew what they were doing. The nurse had told me that it was an unusually large building, having had a room added-on to house a large Scout Troup, an even larger

Women's Institute and the new Home Guard as they were now called. The recent air raids had scuppered those plans though, which turned out to be fortunate for people finding themselves displaced and in need of immediate respite. Not so fortunate for the Scouts, WI, and Home Guard who despite the reasoning behind the decision now had to use the much smaller Baptist Church Hall. They were not amused with this arrangement apparently.

Beds with less than six inches between them lined the walls along two sides of the biggest of the rooms and some even had a screen giving a little privacy. It was all done in a very military fashion. Having had our lives turned upside-down, we all needed to feel that someone else was in charge and with my current responsibility, I for one, had no problem with that. I had begun to feel very protective towards Steven and had asked to stay as near to him as possible; after all, I had signed Matron's book! The circumstances were not just unusual, they were quite bizarre and I thought back to the few days before all this happened when all I had to worry about was whether I was doing a good job in class and trying not look like an idiot in front of the other more experienced teachers; I could do with a few of those 'energy balls' from my mothball marauder right now too.

This was only the second time in my life that I'd been properly away from home and I felt very apprehensive. Creeping past rows of sleeping strangers in the dimly lit hall, holding the front of my pyjamas for the sake of decency, I tiptoed towards Steven's bed in the corner and mine beside him with a screen. Perfect. The bed was far from perfect though. It was rock hard and so was the pillow. I suddenly felt another wave of sadness, which really made me want to cry, something I hadn't done throughout the insanity of the past few days.

Maybe this wasn't the right time though. I needed to remain in control at least until Steven knew what happened and he was suitably settled elsewhere, or even better with family. He hadn't been hurt. Thank goodness he was the other side of the wall when the bomb was dropped protecting him from the blast. I was also grateful that I hadn't been standing on the wall, which had been my intention. Had I done so, maybe I wouldn't have been so lucky. I planned the morning beginning with the hope of finding my corselet where I'd left it. Then I'd make every effort to locate Dad and Nan. It was a good plan until a big sigh reminded me to add Steven's bad tidings to the list.

I woke several times in the night and each time wondered where I was. I could see in the half-light that Steven hadn't moved an inch though – maybe because of the tight way the nurse had tucked him in, or maybe just through sheer exhaustion but when I opened my eyes the last time, I saw that he was awake with the Lark standing on his bed jumping up-and-down trying to peer through a torn piece of blackout on the window. It was a good job his pyjama bottoms had been wrapped around his waist and fastened with a safety pin.

He smiled at me saying, "*Ungry, Miss? I am.*" And looking around the room waving his arms added, "*They've all gone, we'd better 'urry*".

At the bottom of our beds were our freshened-up clothes and Steven's shorts with his Identity Card sitting on top. His shoes had been cleaned and left underneath – *probably by the Red Cross Nurse* and I was relieved to see that my dry corselet and stockings lay on top of the dress I'd chosen. My shoes had also been cleaned and placed in a similar fashion. What a kind and thoughtful lady she was.

After such a fitful night I didn't feel rested, although I hadn't seen the nurse at all, so must have had some sleep. Reality hit me like a ton of bricks, and I was instantly anxious and irritable. I shouted at Steven telling him to stop bouncing and then felt dreadful when he did as he was told and sat with his arms folded. My thoughts jumped from one thing to another. I didn't want this responsibility and felt scared and lonely but knew I had to be stout-hearted for his sake at least.

33

My head hurt again and so did my tummy. Oh, no. Not that as well. It was bad enough that I hadn't brushed my teeth for days. Why couldn't I have been a man? So much seemed to be going on and all in all, I was quite miserable; I just wanted to go home.

Forcing myself to stop being selfish and think of Steven whose priority was relieving his hunger pains, I gave him my best smile under the circumstances and told him to get dressed. He beamed at me with the grin that got me every time and that sideways glance of those icy blue eyes, which would melt someone's heart one day. Quickly throwing-off the huge pyjamas and dressing himself in the clothes he hadn't noticed were mostly clean, he proudly tied his shoelaces looking up at me a few times to make sure I was witnessing the spectacle. I directed my gaze towards his pyjamas. It took a couple of seconds for him to realise that he should fold them neatly and place them under his pillow and having done so, looked at me for further instructions. I replied by asking him if he was ready to face the world to which he frowned and scratched his chin like a wise old man.

Steven stood on the other side of the screen while I dressed. To my dismay I felt the ladders in both stockings grow in length as I pulled them on. Now in tatters, they were beyond reasonable wear. Without them, the suspenders on my corselet would dangle annoyingly but there was no alternative. Pure white ankles with brown shoes would hardly look attractive, but it couldn't be helped. The dress was a bit of a success though once I'd struggled with the zip.

I took Steven's hand as we walked between the row of beds, which had miraculously been straightened in that military way. There was a dustbin outside the toilet and lifting the lid, I reluctantly dropped my stockings inside. Steven complained when I suggested he wash his face and behind his ears, saying that the bath the night before would '*last a long time*'. I had to smile. Returning to the big hall where we ate the night before, I was pleased to see that the tall, posh-looking lady had been

34

replaced by a short, fat one in a green WVS dress. Meeting us at the door with a beaming smile, she was the exact opposite of the tall lady. I was relieved.

"Aah", she sighed, *"We let you sleep – you were late going to bed. Now, come and have some tea and toast; there's SPAM as well,"* she said, enticingly. I had never really liked SPAM but ate it because I was so hungry. Steven swallowed it so fast, I doubted he even tasted it. The toast was alright although it was spread with margarine and we could have as much as that as we wanted. It would have been nice to have Nan's jam on top, or even honey from the bees Mr. Lomax kept at number 42, but these thoughts led me back to the reason we were at the Centre and I declined a third slice.

I would stick to the plan. Locate Dad and Nan then find a way to talk to Steven. I was prioritising, not putting anything off. The WVS lady enthusiastically spread margarine on more toast as I interrupted her task. *"Excuse, me"*, I begged politely, *"I'm Lesley. I'm sorry, I don't know your name, but I need to get some information".* She turned towards me with that lovely smile revealing some very yellow teeth, *"Yes, dear, what can I do for you? I'm Mrs. Stokes and I help to run the Reception Centre with the Women's Voluntary Service."*

Giving her a potted version of the last few days with the fact that I wanted to contact Dad's Fire Station and the ARP Office in my town, I asked if there was a telephone I could use. *"Well, there's a telephone I can use for you, but we need to find the numbers first"*, she said. I called to Steven to tell him to stay where he was and that I would be gone a few minutes. He nodded with a massive mouthful of toast and margarine dripping down his chin onto his clean shirt. Mrs. Stokes stuck the knife in the margarine and taking my arm led me into a miniature 'office' – I think it had once been a cupboard, but now had a chair and a small table with a telephone on top. Sitting on the chair, she picked up the handset and tapped the button furiously to call the operator until a muffled voice could be heard the other end. Mrs. Stokes replied by saying,

"Hello. Hello. Doris? Yes, it's Ethel Stokes here. Yes, fine, fine. Yes, a lot of people. Look, is there any chance of getting through to the Fire Station at the docks, or the ARP Control Centre there?" She paused, listening to Doris's reply, and continued, *"Okay then, yes, I see, well thanks anyway".*

Apparently, telephone poles were down everywhere and at the present time, the only means of contact in that area was by messenger. However, she said they hoped to have something sorted out later that day unless there was more bombing. That was more than likely because there had been raids every day for some time now. All this did, was increase my anxiety and take me closer to the next thing on the list which I was dreading. I thanked Mrs. Stokes for trying and asked if we could leave the building for a while. This was permitted so long as I signed a book with the time we left and reminded me that I had the added responsibility of Steven. That, I didn't need reminding about.

There was a local map on a board and easel near the front door and she suggested I get my bearings. However, Mrs. Stokes told me that all the road names had been crossed-out in case we were invaded! Should we lose our way, we were to head for the church, as the hall was right beside it. Studying the map showing nothing much except a load of lines, was the word 'forest' and I suddenly realised I had been in this town before; we had picnicked here before Mum became ill. I couldn't remember where exactly but vaguely remembered Mum taking me to a row of nice shops and a small department store after our tramp through the forest. I was elated with these memories and almost felt happy for once.

Steven was on his fourth piece of toast and second cup of milky, sweet tea and Mrs. Stokes had given him an apple, so he was more than enjoying his breakfast. I told him I was going to find my handbag, which I'd placed under my bed and emptying out the contents on the counterpane, found my lipstick intact although the compact mirror was in pieces. Using the biggest shard to see what I was doing, I filled-in my pale lips until they were oily-red and powdered my nose a bit, finishing only when I decided I looked much better than I had in the hospital mirror.

Fortunately, my Identity Card and Ration Book were undamaged and so too, was my Post Office Savings Book. Flicking through the pages to the last entry, I congratulated myself on the total. Putting a little away each week – just a shilling, or two had added up to a nice sum, enough now to buy some new stockings and see if there was a shop selling children's clothes. We both needed a toothbrush and paste and as I had no idea how long it would take to resolve Steven's plight, would spend a little of my money on him; he certainly deserved it. I picked up my little change purse next and was pleased to see it contained the grand sum of £1,11/6d. This led me to wonder about my last pay packet, which I hadn't received.

At the outbreak of war, everyone was advised to keep anything 'official' with them. This was easy for me since I didn't own anything, although I did have some important documents. I kept my Birth Certificate in the zipped compartment of my handbag and unfolding this, was reminded that my twenty-third Birthday was not far off. When I saw Mum's name on it, I had to scour the counterpane for my errant handkerchief. It wasn't there and ridiculous as it sounds, my disappointment was unbearable. Grabbing my handbag, I frantically looked inside. There it was. My handkerchief. The relief I felt was excessive and totally out of proportion, but these were emotional times.

The Certificate I was presented with following my Teacher Training was in the same place. Dad had framed it behind some glass and hung it on the landing wall when I first received it as he was so proud of my achievement and no one else in the family had been 'Lettered', as Nan called it. If our house had been damaged, I was glad it was safely with me at least for the time being. The thought of our nice little home being damaged produced a huge sigh as I looked to see what else had survived. Coming across the dogeared photo of Mum and Dad together at Southend produced another huge sigh and tears that had to be dabbed with my hankie. I couldn't believe all this has happened in such a short space of time. One minute, I was teaching a little boy to read and the next, I was giving him terrible news. One minute, I had a regular salary and the next, nothing coming in at all. How on earth would I manage? This was selfish of me though. We were the lucky ones.

I was still going through my treasures placing them back in my bag, one-by-one, when someone bounced onto the bed beside me making me jump. I put my hand to my heart and turned to scowl at them but when I realised it was Steven, my eyes softened.

"You alright, Miss?" He asked.

"Yes, I'm fine, Steven", I said, *"Shall we go to the shops now?"*

Steven still hadn't mentioned his mother, or his sister and this troubled me. Where did he think they were? He looked rather dishevelled to be seen out, with his Impetigo covered in grease from the margarine and his cheeky grin revealing an apple pip stuck between his front teeth. I combed his hair and did-up his shirt buttons in the right order, then took him to the toilet where he washed his face with a soapy hand, which dislodged the pip. Suggesting he stand up straight like a soldier, a second look showed a great improvement.

The book I had to sign dangled from a piece of string on the easel and just as Mrs. Stokes had said, there was a column to add the time of departure to our names. Dutifully attempting to do so, I glanced at my broken watch remembering that it couldn't give me the information I needed. Noticing this, Mrs. Stokes shouted, *"Twenty to Eleven, dear."* And despite no call for a Ration Book, added, *"There'll be some lunch if you want it."*

Steven smiled. I nodded.

Deciding that there was just enough time to buy the things

we needed, I looked at Steven and said, *"Ready, soldier?"* With one sock up and the other down again, he saluted perfectly even though it was the wrong hand and we marched through the door out into the sunshine together.

CHAPTER THREE

A Deep Breath

The sun poked through white fluffy clouds in a light-hearted way and the sound of birdsong made it hard to believe that we were at war with people who might also be enjoying a pleasant day. The smell of burning in the air was unmistakable though and the view of smoke on the distant horizon towards the far south confirmed that we were indeed, involved in deadly conflict.

Trying to look cheerful to prepare Steven for the awful news I was to give him, my own worries rose to the surface once again. I only hoped that when we returned to the village hall, I would be given some positive and reassuring personal news rather than something devastating that would need coping with; I wasn't sure if I could handle anything else.

We walked past St. Edmund's church – a solid building with a tall tower and a fine testament to the Victorians. Gravestones lay either side of the path winding to the great oak door, which had a sign on it saying, "Come in and pray" and this gave me an idea. This is where I would talk to Steven.

It was a lengthy High Street from what I could see, with shops on one side, dense forest on the other and a narrow road in between. Apart from what was going on at the village hall, the war didn't seem to have touched this town, although there were several shoppers in a uniform of some kind. I reckoned the docks were about eighteen miles away and maybe the fact that the area was heavily forested, the enemy decided that it wasn't worth bombing.

A man leading an enormous Shire Horse clopping slowly-by delighted Steven no end, especially when the horse stopped to drink from the water trough. Watching the horse take just as enormous slurps fascinated Steven and he asked the man why the horse was wearing "*Them fings on is eyes*". Even with the explanation, Steven was worried that the horse couldn't see where he was going and asked the man to take them off.

He was a lovely boy, Steven. I had more than a soft spot for him and the thought of him ending up in a children's home and what might happen to him when he left there years later was upsetting. Surely these places were unable to offer the same care and direction as a loving family would. Steven was a good kid and didn't deserve a difficult life. It would be hard enough as it was for him without his mother and sister.

I couldn't buy much without first visiting the Post Office to withdraw some money but was in a quandary about just how much to take out. Having never bought children's clothes before it was difficult to estimate how much I'd need, but it would be better to have too much and avoid the embarrassment of not having enough, so I decided on £4, which was an enormous sum of money added together with the change in my purse.

Tearing him away from the horse, Steven walked backwards beside me waving to the man until man and horse carried on their way. We came to a shop with a sign above it written in gold letters saying, 'J.H. Jenkin Jeweller', which I thought was a bit of a mouthful. In the window was an advert for watch repairs and I wondered how much it would cost to have mine mended, so we went in to ask.

The bell above the door jingled sweetly, just as the sound of the air raid siren went and I stopped dead in my tracks. "*They're a long way off, it'll be a green alert again,*" the gentleman behind the counter told us, "*Do come in, we'll soon be told if we need to shelter*". Smiling warily, I went to the counter with Steven following and pulled-up my sleeve to reveal the damaged watch. "*Would it be very expensive to mend this?*" I asked.

Taking a monocle from his breast pocket and placing it in his right eye, which widened it to twice the size, he said, *"Well, I can have a look at it for you."* Steven was fascinated by this procedure and in a whisper said, *"Does it 'urt Mister? Can I 'ave a go?"*

Although Mr. Jenkin would not allow Steven to wear his monocle, he couldn't help but be charmed by his innocence – *Steven had this effect on people* - and allowed him to peer at my watch through the enormous magnifying glass he kept on the counter. An inspection revealed a better outcome than I'd hoped. The little hand had dropped off but was still there and if it went back on easily, it would just need new glass.

"I'll clean it up and reconnect the hand. I have this size window and can fit it easily. How does two shillings and sixpence sound?", Mr. Jenkin asked eagerly. *"Very reasonable"*, I replied. We would return to collect it and pay the money after doing our shopping and left Mr. Jenkin and his monocle, with the 'all clear' sounding. Beside the jewellers was a large 'Boots the Chemists'. The dull ache I was now feeling in my tummy reminded me of the fact that there was something else to purchase. That was all I needed on top of everything else. The chemist would be the last stop on our way back, well, before we visited the church, of course.

I wondered how far down the street the Post Office and the department store might be and stopped a lady on a bicycle to ask if she knew. Wearing the uniform of the Land Army and looking very dapper in her jodhpurs and hat, she told me that they were both about a minute further on and 'Percival's' was much bigger than it looked from the outside. Thanking her for the information, I looked round for Steven only to see him standing in the middle of the road bent double, one sock up, one down as usual, staring at something in deep concentration.

Shouting at him to move immediately, he stood up, took one step back and continued his investigation. The road was empty, apart from one parked car but I feared something

42

might suddenly appear and shouted to him again. This prompted another step back, but he was still in the road and I had no alternative but to walk quickly over to him. "*What are you . . .*" I began, until I could see he had stopped to examine a pile of horse dung.

Deeply engrossed in the contents his gaze was interrupted when a woman with a large shovel appeared from a door between 'Boots' and the jewellers. Expertly scooping up the dung in one fell swoop, she turned to Steven and said, "*Roses*", vanishing with it as fast as she had appeared. "*Din look like roses to me*", Steven said, with a huge grin.

Finally, we reached the Post Office and went in. Three people stood waiting to be served, but it wasn't long before we reached the counter and I gave my Savings Book and Identification Card to the Post Mistress sitting behind a wire grill. I hesitated when she asked me how much I wanted to withdraw knowing that the amount left in the account would be small. No, I would stick to my original decision and take out £4. "*Are you sure, dear?*" she asked. "*It's a lot of money to be walking around with.*" This remark rather ruffled my feathers and with an indignant look simply said, "*If it could be made up with three £1 notes and two Ten Shilling notes, I would be much obliged.*" Raising her eyebrows, she scribbled the date, banged an ink stamp in my book and handed over the money with my documents.

Carefully adding the notes to the money in my purse and placing that in my handbag, I gave my thanks and we left the Post Office. I felt quite worried. Was I doing the right thing? I had no job. How would I survive when I'd spent this money? At that moment, Steven touched my arm and said reassuringly, "*Don't you worry, Miss. I won't let no robbers take ya money*" and instantly, I knew I was doing the right thing.

The department store, oh, the department store. It was so wonderful. A real Aladdin's Cave just like the one we saw in 'Ali Baba and His Forty Thieves' at the Picture Palace. Steven's eyes widened and I'm sure mine did too, as we looked around at the wonderful things for sale in the big mahogany display cases. *"Can I help you, Madam?"* asked an unfortunate lady with a bad Permanent Wave. Desperately trying to ignore Steven's reaction to the corkscrews dangling from her head, I asked if there was a Children's Department. *"First Floor, Madam,"* she said, gesturing to the stairs making the corkscrews expand and retract. Open-mouthed, Steven lifted a finger towards a corkscrew, but before he could touch it, I dragged him away. Tact perhaps, was not one of Steven's strong points.

Clothes in the children's department were mainly school uniforms for those in the area. I was glad we weren't buying any of them, since they were very expensive and obviously for children being privately educated, however after a brief explanation of our needs to a helpful, quite normal-looking lady this time, we were pointed in the right direction.

One grey flannel shirt, one cardigan, two undershirts with briefs, two pairs of socks, one pair of pyjamas and one nightshirt – as there was only one pair of pyjamas in his size. It came with a nightcap complete with bobble at the end of the long piece of material and Steven asked if he could wear it now. I knew he would look a bit odd walking along the High Street in a nightcap, but he'd been such a good boy I didn't want to deny him this tomfoolery. Seeing my nod of consent, he grabbed it from the counter gleefully pulling it on over his hair and wobbling his head to make the bobble bounce.

Picking up a pencil, the saleslady licked the lead end a few times while she wrote down the prices in the sales book, silently adding together the long line of numbers. She smiled when she had finished her arithmetic and announcing the total, rang-up the sum on the till. My mouth was very dry as the final amount popped-up, but I handed over two £1 notes, seventeen shillings and a sixpence as if this was a regular occurrence. Secretly though, I was frantic with worry. I tipped the small amount of change into my purse while she skilfully placed the clothes in the middle of a large piece of brown paper, folded it into a parcel and tied it with string. Steven took the parcel and despite its bulk, held it proudly in front of him as if it were Gold, Frankincense, or Myrrh.

"What do you say to the lady? I asked him. "*Eh? Oh, yeah, ta very much*".

The things I'd bought, together with what he was standing in would have to do. New shoes were out of the question. The ones he was wearing looked quite reasonable and there hadn't been any complaints of 'pinching' so that was Steven done.

Or so I thought, because now he looked longingly in the direction of the toy department. Reluctantly, I allowed him to lead me there and as if I had suddenly been a winner on one of those Football Pools Dad loved so much, purchased a jigsaw with a picture of a train and a small brown tipper truck. That really had to be it now although the look of delight on Steven's face made me feel that if was worth spending so much of my money.

Back on the ground floor, I hunted high and low for my usual brand of fully-fashioned nylon stockings. There was nothing in my size or even in the colour I preferred. The saleslady on this counter told me that production of nylons had stopped, "*The factories are making other things now.*" She told me, "*We've even heard that there will be rationing of all clothes if the war carries on for much longer*", she added. This I found hard to believe. Surely, we couldn't have this too. Food rationing was bad enough.

Shaking my head in unison with the lady, I carried on looking for something to attach to my suspenders. All I could find were those awful-looking Lisle stockings, which Nan wore. Well, I thought, autumn would be here before we knew it so it might be sensible to have a warm pair and I did have an unopened pair of nylons in my drawer at home; I would have to be very careful with those though if they were hard to come by for a while. Mentally adding-up the expense so far and remembering that I still had to go to the chemists and pay for my watch repair, I was beginning to wish I had emptied my Savings Account. I paid for the Lisle stockings and noticing the assistants watch realised how time had flown. It was twenty past twelve. Better get a move-on.

Steven, still wearing the nightcap and ceremoniously holding the parcel with the jigsaw and truck balanced on top said he was feeling very hungry and I had to admit I was too. He clutched the jigsaw and truck to his chest as I took the parcel from him and leaving the store, we made a dash for 'Boots' where the personal things I needed were swiftly placed in a brown bag, together with new toothbrushes and paste. We were loaded to the gunnels, what with my handbag and our gas masks and it was a bit of a struggle to walk with everything.

Back in Mr. Jenkin's shop, he greeted us like old friends and with great pomp produced my watch. It looked brand new and was ticking! I thanked him profusely and handed him a half-crown and in return he gave me a receipt. Thanking him once more, Steven said, "*And a good afternoon to you, Sir.*" Mr. Jenkin smiled and reached into the till again pulling out a sixpenny piece. Handing it to Steven he said, "*This is in payment for your help, my boy.*"

Steven was astonished.

When the church came into view, my stomach started doing somersaults at the thought of what was to come next. I tried to convince myself that I wasn't qualified for this sort of thing and should pass the responsibility on to someone else but knew deep down that this simply wouldn't do. Steven should be told that his family had been killed by a person who cared about him.

"*We just have time to go in here a minute,*" I told him as I turned onto the path. "*But I'm hungry.*" He moaned back.

I walked on. Steven, ever curious, had to stop at every gravestone to try and decipher the words on them and tell me what they said. Anxious to get this over with, I told him to take off the nightcap, stop dawdling and hurry up. The church was empty. It felt cold and damp and despite the lovely arrangement of Lilies either side of the altar had that musty smell that all churches seem to have. Placing our parcels beside us, we sat quietly in one of the heavily polished pews and remembering the words of my first prayer I closed my eyes repeating it silently several times hoping that hearing my plea, God would help me get it right.

When I felt I'd practised enough, I looked up just as a beam of sunlight shone through the huge stained, glass window at the far end. The brilliant shaft of light radiated straight through the panes flooding the altar with colour turning the lilies a delicate shade of blue, while the scene on the window depicting a heartbroken Mary cradling a dead Jesus in her arms grew in intensity. It was quite beautiful in the saddest of ways and made tears sting the back of my eyes.

Steven sat beside me feeding the bobble of his nightcap through his fingers, until he became unusually still, silently staring at the same window. This was it. I had to speak. Taking a deep breath and turning to look at him, I said, "*Steven ...*" But before I could go on, he interrupted me.

"*They're dead, aint they Miss?*"

I froze, hardly believing what he'd just said and then in one sudden move pulled him onto my lap. Closing my arms around him tightly, I felt his little body inhale deeply. It stopped momentarily until he was engulfed in the type of grief that no little boy should ever have to endure when he let go in one long piteous howl.

Holding him as he sank lower in my arms, his skinny white legs dangling on the floor, I gazed at the window reflecting a similar image and knew that my prayer had been answered. It had been answered in the strangest of ways, yet I was grateful and silently sent my thanks up to heaven.

We wept together and I cuddled Steven until my arms ached and his breathing had returned to normal. He looked up at me, the tears welling in his eyes trickling down his cheeks. I knew I should have armed myself with my hankie before sitting down and wasn't sure what to do next but then through my own tears, saw a hand offering me a large, folded handkerchief. I took it gladly, wiping my own face to begin with and then mopping Steven's dear little face looked round to find the owner. It was difficult to focus but I soon recognised the tell-tale collar around the man's neck.

"I saw you come in and wondered if I could help in any way." He said, softly. I thanked him for the handkerchief that was now soaking wet and handed it back to him. Smiling at us both, he replied, *"Shall I just sit with you for a while?* I nodded and with a croaky voice said, *"It's all been a bit much these last few days,"* which made me cry even more.

The vicar sat between us with eyes tightly shut. He held our hands, but we didn't speak. Steven's face was deathly white, and I must have looked frightful too. I swept my hair back with my free hand and sniffed to control my runny nose, thinking that I had at last managed to perform the duty I had dreaded and had also been able to release some of my own emotion. I glanced at Steven, who was resting his head on the vicar's shoulder. It was a tender moment proving that this little boy had a great deal of love to give. All he needed was a family to return that love. The lump in my throat returned and once again, my tears flowed.

Sitting in the peace and calm for a few more minutes allowed me to find the strength to recover my self-control and able to leave this beautiful peaceful place. Squeezing the vicar's hand, he opened his eyes and Steven sat up with a huge sigh. He tried to smile at us both, but his dry lips were still trembling, and he didn't quite make it. As we left, the vicar placed a hand on each of our heads and mumbled some words. I didn't know why but I found it very comforting.

CHAPTER FOUR

News at Last

———

Through blurry eyes, we struggled back to the village hall to find that while we'd been out, chaos had emerged. Five, or six vehicles were parked on the gravel outside and there were people everywhere. By the look of them, they were more walking wounded needing initial respite before going elsewhere.

A WVS canteen had also arrived dishing-out tea and sandwiches from the side of the van with their usual efficiency and we headed for this. Steven still looked very pale. I told him to sit on an upturned box and piled everything on his lap so that I could collect our much-needed refreshments.

He hadn't said a word since the awful scene in the church and I hoped some sort of permanent damage hadn't been done to him. We would have to deal with anything like that later, but first things first. I returned with a feast. Mugs of tea, two Beetroot sandwiches and two biscuits all balanced on a cake tin lid, to find our parcels, and Steven's jigsaw on the box, but no Steven and no toy truck.

I thought I was going to faint and almost dropped our feast on the floor but composed myself enough to ask those close by if they knew where he'd gone. No one had seen him, and I began to panic. Where had he gone? Why had he gone? Was he in some sort of shock? What do I do now?

Oh, there he is. Thank goodness. He was walking towards me, one sock up, one down, swinging the nightcap in one hand and the truck in the other as he walked. He looked much better. Trying not to sound cross, I asked him where he'd been. "*Lavvy, Miss.*" As simple as that. I was beginning to behave like a parent, not his teacher and I blamed my maternal instincts on the female curse that would soon be upon me.

The tea and biscuits went down a treat, the Beetroot sandwiches not as well, but they would stave off the hunger for a while. We returned the cake tin lid and mugs, collected our things, and went into the hall where there must have been forty people milling around. Everyone was dusty, or dirty and dishevelled and a strange sweet smell wafted around; it seemed to me to be a repeat of the night Steven and I arrived but in a much bigger way.

Signing 'returned' beside our names in the book dangling on the easel, I was disappointed to see that the tall, posh lady rather than Mrs. Stokes was in charge. It looked as though I would have to ask her for the latest news, but before I was able to do that, she approached me.

"*Oh, Miss Cooper*", she said, with a sickly grin, "*Why didn't you tell me you had such an important father?*"

"*A what?*" I asked.

"*Yes, he's been waiting in the office for some ... time now ...*"

Her words tailed-off as I bolted for the office like a Jack Rabbit before she had time to finish the sentence. I held my breath as I went into that stupid little room and there he was. My Dad. I burst into tears as we hugged each other. He hadn't shaved and looked as if he hadn't slept for days. His hair was dirty and with eyes so bloodshot it was difficult to see any of the usual steely grey. Then I recognised the smell. Sugar. Everyone, including him smelt of burnt sugar, but he was alive. I couldn't believe it.

I hugged him and kissed his sugary face and hadn't noticed that Steven had squeezed under the table with his jigsaw and truck until Dad said, "*And there's young Steven. You look a bit better than you did when I saw you last*". Steven gave him one of his left-handed salutes and Dad laughed.

Questions. I had so many questions. What had been going on all this time?

"*Dad, is Nan alive?*" I asked uneasily.

"Yes, she is and she's fine" He said, *"But let's start from the beginning"* and gesturing in Steven's direction whispered, *"What does the littlun know?"*. He sighed when I just gave him a sad look although I didn't know that his account of what had taken place would make me even more miserable.

Perching on the desk and rubbing his sore eyes every now and then, he quietly told me that the situation down at the docks was serious. Factories and warehouses had been destroyed, with rats pouring out into the streets. Molten grain and boiling sugar stuck to boots like treacle making it difficult to walk and whole streets of houses were gone, with hundreds of casualties. Then in a whisper, he went on. The buses meant to evacuate the people sheltering at the school had been sent to the wrong place and before this was realised, the bomb landed in the centre of the building causing it to collapse into the basement. Very few of the hundreds down there survived. This, of course I knew.

Steven and I had been caught in the blast and were saved only because we were far enough away from the actual explosion. The dustbin store in the playground had taken the brunt of the shock wave and we were discovered soon after by firemen fighting the blaze where one of them recognised me. Steven was found first under the rubble of the wall where I left him, bewildered although virtually unscathed and still wearing his gas mask and school cap, but I was unconscious. Dad had managed to see me and held my hand before I was taken away in the ambulance, which is how he knew where I was now.

"I heard you call my name, Dad". I whispered. *"Honestly, I did"*. I'd heard him call me by the name he always used. The one I'd learnt as a child before I was able to pronounce an 's'.

He went on. When the siren sounded, aircraft were soon overhead. Nan had gone to the Anderson with the budgie in its cage and as usual, had made several trips to the lav. It was during one of these visits that the Anderson was flattened by a huge piece of machinery hurled into the air from one the factories. "Miss Bluebell's" cage was damaged badly at one end and sadly, there was no sign of her dead or alive. The house was not in danger at present but the whole area had been evacuated.

Cousin Geoffrey had managed to beg some petrol from somewhere and had collected Nan in the van driving her back to Whitstable where she would stay indefinitely but before she went, there had been time to pack a few clothes between raids. They'd even managed to get Nan's piano in the van. Thoughtfully, Nan had stuffed as many of my things she could into my carpet bag and Dad had brought it with him in the coach outside.

"Well done, Nan!" I said. And then felt terribly selfish again.

"There's more". Dad said, directing his gaze towards Steven who was still under the table. *"Let's go and find your bag and then I must get going. You hang-on here, Steven-me-lad, in case the telephone rings!"*

Dad had been given a lift in a passenger coach, which had to get back to what was left of the city and he and his crew were moving to another Fire Station for a rest. The 'stand down' would last only another six hours as he had already used up two, but it would be long enough to get a bit of sleep, which by the look of him was very much needed. I walked outside with him and he hauled out the bulging carpet bag from the luggage rack.

Before we said our goodbyes, he handed me a large envelope, saying it was from Mrs. Johnson, the lady at the hospital and contained information about Steven, which would explain a lot. The driver started the engine and hooted for Dad to climb aboard. As he did, I told him that if he didn't take care of himself, he would have me and Nan to answer to and he smiled in the way he did when Mum was cross with him and I cried again.

I waved him off in the coach and watched until it was out of sight. Struggling with the carpet bag, I was desperate to have a look at my things; it was a connection to home and my real life. I was excited, which seemed a bit daft, but it felt like all my Christmases had come at once. I would tip everything out on my bed and make an inventory. Squeezing past tables and chairs loaded with noisy, dirty, sad, and desperate people, I reached the dormitory. The only thing was, I didn't have a bed anymore! Neither did Steven. Two strangers were asleep in them. I turned tail and rushed out to look for the tall lady, but instead, bumped into the lovely Red Cross nurse.

"Our beds are gone", I said in panic. *"I mean ..."* I went to say, realising this sounded ridiculous.

"It's alright, you and Steven are going elsewhere, it's all been arranged. Mrs. Dobson-Smythe will give you all the details." She told me.

"Mrs ..." Oh, the tall lady", I said. This was the first time I had heard her name.

The nurse nodded but was obviously so caught-up with the new intake that she was suddenly gone. Wrestling with my carpet bag and dodging several pale and dusty people, I looked for Mrs. Dobson-Smythe. I found her eventually in the small office trying to remove Steven from beneath the desk. He wouldn't budge saying that the soldier had told him to answer the telephone, while she insisted that there were no soldiers and that he certainly must not pick-up the telephone!

"Not a soldier, Steven. That man was my dad and he's a Leading Fireman." I said in a loud voice. *"Aah, Miss Cooper."* Mrs. D-S cooed – her attitude changing immediately, *"We've made some lovely new arrangements for you and ... the little boy."*

She went on to say that investigations continued into Steven's background and some progress had been made. However, there were many loose ends and as no family had yet been uncovered - and with my own circumstances being as they were, I was asked to continue his care for a little while longer. It didn't take long for me to decide. I felt I should carry on and see it through – whatever the outcome and told Mrs D-S this. I didn't have anywhere to go apart from maybe

Whitstable but the house there was tiny and although Geoffrey might be called-up any day it would be a squeeze with us all there. With this settled, the good news was that Steven and I would leave the Reception Centre together. It was a relief to hear because it would be wrong for him to stay with strangers, especially now that what he'd suspected for days was in fact true. With such terrible news, he needed time to adjust; somewhere lovely that he could be quiet and take it all in.

Mrs D-S said that my decision was anticipated but when she told us where we were going, I was so astonished, I might as well have been told we were going to tea at Buckingham Palace with the King and Queen. We were going to stay on a farm! I couldn't believe what I heard. What could be better? I could have kissed Mrs. D-S and the surprise on her face at my elation was rather comical.

"*A farm, Steven!*" I exclaimed. "*They might have some animals! Won't that be marvellous*"

Steven shot out from under the table banging his head but didn't seem to mind.

"*When we goin', Miss?*" He asked, rubbing the top of his head with his truck.

"*Well, now actually.*" Mrs D-S said. "*It won't be for long, so don't get too comfortable there, it's only because they're waiting for two new Land Army girls that the beds have become available,*" she added snottily.

Our carriage awaited. An enormous tractor with a trailer attached, which would transport us to Middlewych Farm, where there was a room available because two Land Army girls had gone home after harvesting. Two new girls were expected next month to work on the farm in the village, with one remaining to carry on working with the animals and poultry at Myddlewych. It was she who would be driving us there. I was terribly excited, but Steven was consumed with the adventure of it all.

The vehicles in the gravelled area outside had all gone apart from the tea van and the tractor, which was huge and extremely ancient. Rust had replaced most of the green paint once covering it and the enormous tyres were caked in dry mud, but it looked marvellous to us. The driver jumped out of the cab wearing the same uniform as the girl on the bicycle – another member of the Land Army. *"Hello. I'm Linda. And is this your husband?"* She joked pointing to Steven.

Steven frowned, sucking-in his lips and slowly shaking his head, making her laugh. Linda was tall and slim with short, dark brown hair. Her brown eyes were almost black with eyelashes and brows to match and a straight nose seemed to complement her high cheek bones. She was quite striking in a masculine sort of way.

It wasn't a special trip to collect us Linda told me. In a very potted and speedy history, she told me that eggs were delivered to the Reception Centre twice a week, so at least I didn't feel as though we had used up precious fuel. The tractor was owned by a big farm in a village where they kept chickens as well, although they concentrated on their beef herd. I nodded enthusiastically and tried to take it all in. We would be staying on an agricultural farm outside that village. They also kept chickens and while they still had too many to count, they could sell as many eggs as they had, although with poultry becoming scarce, she could see this coming to an end. There were a few animals as well, but the farmer concentrated on crops.

With so much information in such a short space of time, I felt I should have taken notes! Linda went on to tell me that the journey would take a while, as the farm was nine miles out of town, and it would be a bit bumpy in the trailer. Had I been told to run behind it, I would have. Anything to stay on a farm. For how long exactly, would of course depend on the investigation into Steven's family – if one existed and if the new girls arrived on time.

I hadn't been in many cars. Plenty of buses, the Underground, and a few steam trains but never a tractor and wasn't quite sure how to get into a trailer so high off the ground. Realising this, Linda said she would move the tractor near the wooden bench to use as a leg-up and started the engine. This startled me – I didn't expect it to be so loud and it shook and rattled as it was manoeuvred next to the bench. Steven clambered in wearing his nightcap. It was an odd sight, and only then did I remembered he was missing his school cap, which must have been left at the hospital. He was more than attached to his truck already though and wearing a grin that was surely mixed with glee and trepidation, he sat cross-legged in the big steel tray with the truck held tightly in his hand.

Making sure that nothing was left behind, I threw my carpet bag and our parcels into the trailer and was just about to join him when I thought of something important. Mouthing to both Linda and Steven that I wouldn't be a minute, I hoped they thought I needed the toilet. The real reason was that I had to ask Mrs D-S one last thing and went back inside to find her.

She was talking to a group of people and left them when she saw me standing at the door. *"Is there anything wrong, Miss Cooper?"* She asked. *"Nothing wrong,"* I replied, *"I need to ask you something though."* Mrs D-S looked at me curiously as I hesitated with my question. *"Erm … Do you know what happened to Steven's mother and sister? I mean … them actually – after the … Bomb?"* Her face coloured as she whispered. *"It has been taken care-of. They've all been taken care-of there. All done in the nicest possible way, with flowers and mourners in the municipal cemetery so we were told."*

I didn't need to hear any more.

CHAPTER FIVE

A Rustic Spell -
in more ways than one

———

Fortunately, it was another lovely day. I hoped it would stay that way because if it rained while we were in the trailer, we would get very wet. I wasn't so worried about us personally although we didn't want to arrive looking like two drowned rats, but it wouldn't do to have our few belongings soaked through. Scrambling in beside Steven, it was obvious it would be too noisy to talk. It hardly felt safe in the back, so I hung on for dear life as we trundled off.

I can only describe the next hour, or so by saying that bouncing around in the back of the trailer did us the world of good. It might sound silly but being thrown around along a winding country lane beside open fields with trees and birds galore was simply wonderful and was nothing like the journey in the ambulance. This one really swept the cobwebs away.

Steven began to stand up to see more but I'm sure he would have bounced right onto the road, so I shouted the word 'dangerous' and shook my head. He sat down like the good boy he was, content to sit with me pointing to the myriad of lovely things we saw and laughed when we had to scramble for his parcel, or my bag each time they slid away from us. It was wonderful and Steven had some colour in his cheeks for a change.

It was a while later – I'm not sure exactly how long, because I had forgotten that my watch was working and hadn't noticed the time, that the engine noise changed to a whine and we slowed down. Steven and I had been seeing where we'd been, rather than seeing where we were going, if you see what I mean and it wasn't until we turned onto cobblestones that I saw an old wooden sign saying, '*Middl ch arm*'. Some of the letters had been erased over time, but we had obviously arrived. With a beaming smile, I turned to look at the farmhouse. My smile dwindled almost immediately however, as I took in the view of a dilapidated thatched building; the chocolate box image conjured up in my mind disappearing in an instant.

The first thing I noticed was a dreadful smell. Nan would have described it as a '*stink*' and hunted for something dead. Quite long - or maybe I mean wide, the place looked derelict. Constructed in red brick mostly cracked or crumbled, lengths of rusty iron girders leaned against it. Were they holding it up? Green slime covered most of the thatched roof apart from several bare patches surely letting in the rain and thatch drooped sadly across two of the upper windows crossed with scrim tape - perhaps to hold the glass in place, rather than an air raid precaution. Sparks flew amongst thick black smoke puffing from the precarious-looking chimney and the porch was covered in such a thick vine, I wondered if we would pass through it. I hoped my disappointment was not apparent – at least to Steven.

Linda brought the tractor to a halt and switched off the engine, allowing birdsong to reach our ears until this sweet sound was broken by distant and urgent barking. I had never been sure of dogs and had no idea if Steven was used to them so before we left the trailer, I asked Linda if the dog we could hear belonged to the farmer and more importantly, if it was friendly. "*Oh, we have two dogs.*" She told us. "*Bonnie will growl at you to begin with, but it won't take long for her to like you. She's our ratter. And Bella is just an old softie.*"

One of the dogs appeared and bounced towards us. Steven gasped and crept backwards in the trailer. I held my breath and stayed put too. Linda shouted at the black Labrador. "*Sit Bella.*

Good girl. Stay." If this was the 'old softie', what was the other one like? At that moment, we heard more barking and the tiniest little brown and white creature raced up to us from behind the house. The moment she saw us, she stood perfectly still growling fiercely showing tiny pointed teeth.

"*Oh, shut up Bonnie,*" Linda said, scooping her up from the cobblestones. "*They're alright.*" However, Bonnie continued to growl and was dribbling all over Linda's arm. As small as she was, this dog worried me and the thought of her being a ratter worried me even more. Steven and I quickly escaped from the trailer with our bags and parcels and I wondered what would come next. My heart was sinking rapidly and there was no sign of any proper farm animals, although the smell might mean otherwise.

A voice called the dogs. Bella sped off and Bonnie wriggled out of Linda's arms to the porch where camouflaged by the vine, stood a very fat, bespectacled lady holding a carving knife. Her floral dress was covered by an apron streaked in something bright red but despite her threatening appearance, she looked quite jolly. The dogs sat at her feet beside a scraper covered in dry mud and a pair of big boots swathed in an equal amount of mud.

"*Come in, come in,*" she shouted, "*You must be hungry.*" Little did she know then that we were always hungry, but did we want to eat here? Clutching our belongings as best we could, we passed through the vine without mishap and into the kitchen, a huge room with peeling paint and plaster revealing thin strips of wood here and there. There was a musty smell with a hint of paraffin and what might have been the pungent odour of wet dog. Shutters replaced curtains adding to the stark surroundings. The low ceiling had cracks big enough to stick my fingers in and on the floor were what I assumed had once been orange tiles. Some were missing but most of them were mottled and so ingrained with dirt, it was only those intact at the edges showing their original colour.

Dominating the kitchen, loomed a long rectangular

wooden table with benches either side. It was laden with a motley collection of glass jars and two big lamps, which I supposed meant no electricity. Around them lay piles of carrots, beetroot and onions and several bottles. Then my attention was drawn to a huge green dresser. One of the shelves seemed to be crammed full of assorted china, old books, and mud-caked newspapers. On the other an empty cigarette box sat beside an overflowing ashtray, a chewed dog lead, bits of string and more china. A mouse trap primed with a mouldy piece of cheese on a bread board complete with loaf was on the dresser top and amongst it all, I was surprised to see a sleeping one-eared ginger cat. It was then I noticed a similar-looking cat with two ears in an open drawer who stretched and flicked its tail before opening one eye. Later, I was to learn that this was quite normal because she did only have one, but never discovered the reason for the other cat's missing ear.

The bulky concrete sink standing on a metal frame was without a tap, which I thought was rather peculiar and on a wooden table beside this, a rusty upturned bowl and china pitcher, a bar of soap and two washboards of similar size. The dogs had settled down in front of a huge cooking range. Bonnie showed me her teeth whenever I looked at her and I noticed that Steven was trying not to look at either of them. Above the range on a laundry rack a pair of wet, moth-eaten dungarees dangled. Water dripping from them landed on Bella's head, which looked comical because she was oblivious to this and blinked each time a droplet landed on her nose.

I'm not sure if it was my sharp powers of observation, or that I was so dismayed with our new surroundings I'd been able to absorb all this in the time it took to place our things on the floor, dust ourselves off and for Linda to walk in minus her boots. I was beginning to think that perhaps this wouldn't be the idyllic setting for Steven to recuperate after all; maybe we should have stayed at the Reception Centre. Well, it probably couldn't get any worse.

"I'm Gladys." The lady said, placing the knife on the table and wiping her hands on her apron. *"Gladys Albright. Mr. Albright's wife. Now he isn't here right now. He's in the top field having a look at things there, but he'll be home in time for supper."*

Introducing myself, I looked at Steven hoping he would do the same but he just stared at the floor without saying a word, so I spoke for him adding that we'd had a bit of a rough time and were very grateful to be staying there for a while away from the Reception Centre. Gladys asked for our Ration Books and when I explained that Steven had to be issued with a new one, she said we weren't to worry because the dogs always left a few scraps.

This alarmed Steven enough for him to look up at me and say, *"But Miss …"*

We three ladies chuckled and when the penny dropped, Steven showed his cheeky grin. We would be fine here. The surroundings were strange to us, but Gladys was nice. Linda was nice. The dogs were – *probably* nice. We just had to meet Mr. Albright now and hope he was nice too.

Just as these thoughts were going through my mind, heavy footsteps grew louder as whoever they belonged to, stomped into the kitchen. Bonnie left her position at the range and padded towards the person who I supposed was Mr. Albright home early but when he came closer, I realised that he was much too young to be the farmer. He was the biggest man I had ever seen, and it took Steven a few seconds to look him up and down, his wide eyes telling me that he was a little scared of this giant. The giant stared first at me and then Steven and then back again, finally resting on Linda's face.

"Hello, Alec," Linda said quickly, *"What are you up to today? These are some friends who will be staying with us for a while, like the other girls have, but they won't be wearing Jodhpurs."*

"Yes, this is my son Alec." Gladys told us. *"He's very good around the farm, aren't you Alec?"*

Alec didn't answer and left through the front door into the

cobbled yard as swiftly as he had appeared; the dogs following quickly behind.

"*Well now.*" Gladys said, ignoring Alec's disagreeable manner and untimely exit, "*Linda will show you upstairs. You can drop your things there and then it'll be time for supper. We have it early so we can get to bed. We're up at dawn, see.*"

My heart sank further.

Linda beckoned for us to follow her and we quickly stuffed our parcels under our arms and processed up the stairs behind her. We climbed two flights, and on the way, passed three closed doors, which I assumed were bedrooms for Alec, Linda and the Albrights and then came to a small flight of six stairs with another door. I stopped at the bottom, while Linda and Steven climbed them to reach the door. Jiggling the knob, Linda kicked the bottom of the door twice before it creaked open.

"*Door sticks,*" she said. "*Best not to close it completely. Should have been left open for a bit of an airing.*"

It was the attic space, just like the one at home.

I was suddenly unable to take a deep breath and couldn't move. How would I go in there? Saliva filled my mouth and I felt the muscles in my underneath tightening. What will I do?

"*You okay?*" Linda shouted. "*Coming up?*"

"*I, I . . .*" I croaked, "*Yes, erm . . .*"

The next thing I knew, Steven was standing beside me and taking my hand said in an assuring way "*It's alright Miss, it's a nice room. Come on, I'll show you*"

I managed to swallow the mouthful of saliva, although my underneath was still to recover and slowly took the stairs. Standing at the door, I peered in. It wasn't nice. At least I didn't think so. It was not unlike the one we had at home where the eaves of the roof protruded into the room. It wasn't filled with junk, although there were a few cobwebs and it was just as dark. With the door wide open, an odour wafted under our noses and Steven screwed-up his, saying, "*Cor, wot a pong!*" Apologising, as she opened the small window, Linda said,

"You'll need to take your potties out every day. The girls who had this room found that difficult to do for some reason."

The floorboards were bare. There was a small fireplace although newspaper dangled from the chimney hole, so I supposed it wasn't in use. The one small window was grimy with scruffy curtains threaded onto a piece of string and beneath it, a thin piece of wood lay propped-up against the wall, which I assumed was for the blackout. Either side of this were two single cast iron beds covered in bedspreads made from cotton ticking and just as I thought my heart was unable to sink any lower, I noticed a chamber pot poking out from beneath each of them.

An odd-shaped brown and white rug dividing the space between the beds looked familiar. I couldn't think what it reminded me of at the time. At the far end sat a tall chest of drawers with big white knobs. On top of this was a bowl and a chipped pitcher with a hunting scene on the side and two small, frayed towels. Beneath the far bed I could see a pile of ripped newspapers, an empty candleholder, and a box of matches. A rather unusual combination, the purpose of which I assumed would become clear later.

Several deep breaths helped me calm down. I was being stupid. It was just a room and I would share it with Steven. There was nothing sinister in it and there were six stairs up to it, not three. I felt as though I'd managed to challenge a deep fear. Fear of what, I had no idea because all I'd done over the years was assume that the attic at home had something very creepy in it. Anyway, for all I knew, maybe the attic wasn't even there now.

I thanked Linda saying that it all looked '*fine*'. The expression on her face was one of surprise at my comment as though she was expecting me to balk at the austere accommodation offered, so I added, "*Beggars can't be choosers.*" And she nodded. I asked where the toilet was. She told us that it was outside the back door. It didn't flush with water because the farm used a well. All the water was pumped-up manually and nothing else but paper and that which came out of your body must go down it. Then, directing the next explanation to me personally added that absolutely everything else had to be burnt in the kitchen range. Of course, I understood what she meant.

"Anything I've forgotten?" Linda said to herself. *"Where's the animals?"* Steven asked. *"Gotta Tiger?"*

"No Tiger", Linda replied, *"But we do have Roger."*

Steven frowned and looked at the floor. I could hear his mind working overtime wondering what a 'Roger' was and although I knew it would be rude to mention, casually asked, *"Is Alec, erm, rather quiet?"* Linda told me that he worked like a Trojan around the farm and was extraordinarily strong but could only do this if he was told exactly what to do. Linda added that he rarely spoke but was gentle and loved animals and that he would like us after a while – *just like the dogs.*

Steven chose his bed. I had no idea what he'd been used to at home with Coral and Beth, but he seemed quite content and although we didn't have the security of the Reception Centre, we had each other. We'd been through so much together in such a short space of time that we were no longer teacher and pupil, so I decided that this was as good a time as any for him to stop calling me '*Miss*'.

I suggested he call me 'Lelly', which he thought was a strange name for a lady until I told him how it had come about and then he thought it was funny. He agreed to use this if I would call him 'Stevie', which is what Coral and Beth used to call him and we shook hands, which he also thought was funny. He did have one of his quiet moments after this though and I wished I knew how to deal with those.

Stevie grabbed his truck and we went back downstairs into the kitchen. I told Gladys that our room was more than adequate and that we would be quite comfortable there, but we had better see where the toilet was. Linda wiggled a finger in the air, which was a signal to follow her again and we moved from the kitchen into a small hall where there were two, or three cupboards with wire fronts and a door leading to the back garden that could be opened in two halves for some reason. Above the door, a heavy-looking shotgun sat on two big spikes, which Stevie noticed with a *"Cor!"*

The garden was mainly set out to grow vegetables. In the first plot amongst a network of canes tied together with string, spindly broad bean pods dangled here and there and in the next sat a row of cabbages in various sizes. It would appear from several empty areas that this is where the produce on the kitchen table had come from. I recognised carrot tops and huge rhubarb leaves floating above dark pink stalks and could see lots of berries amongst potato leaves, which hopefully meant a large crop.

A thin, wooden shed housed the toilet. Linda suggested that if we *really* wanted to use it, we should knock loudly before entering as there was no lock. Alternatively, she pointed to a small hole in the door, saying that we could peek through to see if there was an occupant. Taking a deep breath and sticking a finger in the hole to open the door, she revealed a wooden toilet seat on top of a rusty oil drum. The smell drifting from the drum was dreadful and Stevie pinched his nose as I peered into the drum just long enough to see a deep hole. This made me wonder if the vegetable patch had conveniently been dug there to receive nutrients from the toilet waste and with horror pictured the vegetables on the kitchen table being readied for eating. Unlike the scratchy paper on a roll we used at home, a length of wire with roughly torn squares of newspaper skewered along it was nailed to the door. I would later suggest to Stevie that we used our potties and decant the contents into the toilet rather than make the journey down to the shed. I was sure that this was what Linda did. Either that or suffer from constipation!

After the tour of the toilet, Linda walked us round the outside of the house, stopping at the water pump to demonstrate its use. Stevie operated it with great gusto producing a huge gush of water, which seemed adequate, but when I asked if there was a public bath house like our own near the docks, Linda laughed.

"Well, what we girls did in the summer, was walk down to the stream." She said. *"It's a few feet deep in places and wasn't too cold then but in winter ... well, maybe not,"* *"The Albright's don't seem to bother."* She added with a wry look.

It was dusk by this time and Gladys called us in for supper. Linda said the animals were all shut in now, but she would show us them and more of the farm tomorrow. Back in the house, the kitchen had been transformed. The dresser remained the same, although both cats had gone. The window shutters were closed, the table had been laid with plates and cutlery and the paraffin lamps had been lit giving the room a warm glow.

The fire in the range had been stoked giving off radiant heat and Linda moved the dogs away, so they didn't absorb all the warmth. I was glad of this as there was a definite chill in the air. I shivered as I asked Gladys where Stevie and I should sit because there were seven places laid.

Just at that moment, we heard the back door open and slam shut. Someone said, *"Hey-Hey"*, to which Gladys shouted, *"Yoo-Hoo"* and in walked Alec and an older man I assumed to be Mr. Albright, another giant. Before speaking to any of us, he walked over to Gladys and kissed the top of her head; she looked embarrassed. Then, clapping his hands and making Stevie jump, he said, *"Well, who do we have here then? Foreigners?"*

Stevie mouthed the word, *'foreigners'* as if he'd never heard it before and I stood up to introduce myself explaining that presently, we were in 'limbo'. Stevie also mouthed the word, *'limbo'*, in an exaggerated way while he drove his truck round and round the plate in front of him. Mr. Albright nodded and said he understood and that we could stay until the new girls arrived, which of course we already knew. He sat at one end of the table and Alec took a chair next to Linda. Stevie and I sat on the other side and Gladys next to me, which meant that there was one place spare at the head of the other end. Surely, this was simply a mistake as it seemed that no one else would be joining us.

Despite the Spartan surroundings, our supper was marvellous. Stevie's eyes were the size of saucers when he saw what was offered. Great hunks of bread and real butter, jam, Goat cheese, boiled eggs and some sort of meat mixture set in a long tin, which Gladys cut into slices with a dangerous-looking knife after turning it upside down to empty it out. We drank tea sweetened with runny honey and finished with stewed fruit and more honey. It was sumptuous and I told Gladys so as she took the simmering kettle off the range. I stood up to help clear the table, but before I could collect the plates, Linda used the leftover bread to wipe them clean. "*The chickens will have it*", she said as she placed the messy slices back on the board.

Gladys poured the contents of the kettle into the tin bowl at the sink, dropped the soap into the steaming water and taking a whisk hanging on the wall, began making a few bubbles, although by the time the crockery went into the water, the bubbles had all burst. Gladys sloshed everything around a bit with the tips of her fingers, rubbed the plates over with some sort of old rag, stirred the water with the cutlery and then piled everything up beside the bowl. The cooking utensils remained unwashed on the range. I asked for the tea towel to dry-up, but Gladys insisted that this wasn't what she did. Mum would have been horrified to witness this washing-up 'lick and a promise' and I wondered if we would all die from some terrible disease.

Stevie looked exhausted and I thought that by the time we had our things sorted out and undressed for bed, our tummies would have dealt with all the food. Secretly, I wasn't feeling very well, but the reason for this was something that I couldn't discuss and anyway, nothing could be done about it. All I wanted to do, was tuck-up in bed and get a good nights' sleep knowing I would feel better tomorrow.

Mum would have filled a hot water bottle for me, but I doubted there was one in the house and didn't dare ask for one; I couldn't possibly have explained my reasons to a stranger. I thanked Gladys and Mr. Albright, who told me to call him Joe and instead of doing the same, Stevie held up his truck for everyone to see, which seemed to be quite acceptable as a '*thank you*' to them all. It was so sweet. Gladys took a candle out of a drawer in the dresser. She lit it and handing it to me, said "*Night, night, love. It's not quite dark yet but put the wood in the window and bring the candle down with you in the morning.*" Linda smiled and gave us a little wave, and Joe told Stevie that he "*had a fine truck there.*" Alec said nothing.

Stevie and I walked slowly up the stairs to our room by the light of the candle. I would love to say that I didn't hesitate at the bottom of the six stairs, but I did. Only briefly, but I did. Stevie opened the door and went in. It was alright. Nothing terrible happened. I followed him in and stuck the candle in the holder then picked up the wood to use as a blackout but before fixing it in place, peered out at the dusky evening sky. I guessed the front of the house faced north, because I'd become accustomed to that awful glow on the southern horizon and couldn't see it. My thoughts turned to Dad and I mumbled, "*Please stay safe, Daddy.*" I knew the air raid last night was bad and if there was another tonight ... Oh, I couldn't bear to think about it. Surely it would all stop soon, and everything would be alright again. I pushed the wood against the window, probably a little too hard, because I heard a '*crack*'. I would have to own up to that tomorrow.

Although I was desperate to get to bed, I really wanted to go through my carpet bag to see what Nan had managed to put in, although Stevie had to be settled first. I found the 'Boots' bag and our new toothbrushes and paste and told him to spit into the potty after he had furiously brushed his teeth. He rinsed his hands and face in the cold water I poured into the bowl and while he undressed, looked for the nightcap and shirt, which would be warmer than wearing pyjamas. In the candlelight, he looked like a figure from a Charles Dickens novel, especially when he jumped onto the creaky old bed and slipped beneath the thin quilt.

I was amazed how good he'd been in such difficult circumstances. Given terrible, life-changing news, torn from his home, and dragged from pillar to post but despite this, had managed to show an amazing and resilient temperament. He was a real character and everyone he met - *except Mrs. D-S of course*, seemed to like him. I shouldn't have, but I couldn't help kissing his cheek and in return, he showed me his truck for all of one second before it disappeared safely back under the quilt.

Emptying my wares onto the bed as quietly as possible, I moved the candle closer being careful not to drip wax on anything. Nan had done me proud. At least two changes of clothes and underwear, my washbag – *now I had two toothbrushes and paste,* my slippers, a nightie and a pair of pyjamas, the mackintosh that folded-up to hardly anything, my canvass shoes and the best thing of all, my stockings! Right at the bottom of the bag I saw a small cardboard box. Inside, I found a letter from Nan, a photograph of us all in the garden when Mum was alive and three, pound notes!

Nan's letter told me all about the air raid that had squashed the Anderson and that she was grateful to be alive and how sad she was to lose 'Miss Bluebell'. She wasn't keen to live with Auntie Win and would look for an alternative as soon as possible – ' *I rather fancy one of those bungalows*' were her exact words and that I was welcome to live with her if that was what I would like. Nan asked all sorts of questions about what happened to me and *'how on earth'* I had managed to find myself living with one of my pupils. She finished by telling me to look after myself, not to trust a soldier and certainly not a sailor, to write soon and said she was sure the war wouldn't go on much longer with that silly little man in charge of the Nazis.

By the time I had finished reading the letter, the top of my dress was soaked with tears. I rummaged around to find my hankie and blew my nose gently without waking Stevie. Live with Nan in a bungalow? Yes. That was a good idea. Did she mean on the coast? That would be lovely, and Stevie would like it too.

What was I thinking? Stevie won't be living with me. As much as I would have liked that, they must find some relatives so that he doesn't have to go into the children's home. I could keep in touch with him and maybe we could even visit from time to time. No, I would have to put thoughts of him staying with me right out of my mind; I wasn't even married, so I would be the last person they'd choose.

It was then that I remembered the large envelope Dad had given me and shuffling through the parcels came across it. Inside was quite a weight of papers held together with a large paper clip and a letter from Mrs. Johnson. In a smaller envelope, was Stevie's school cap and a pretty brooch with a mauve thistle.

The letter from Mrs. Johnson read,

Dear Lesley,

I do hope you are coping well. This is a difficult time for you but even more difficult for Steaphan. We discovered Coral's real name to be Aisla. She was buried with her daughter, Elizabeth in the local cemetery with great respect. Flowers were provided, and the Mayor attended the service. Steaphan will be able to visit the grave later.

It was here that I wondered why Mrs. Johnson had spelt Stevie's name in that way but supposed it was a mistake and read on.

The house where Coral rented a room was still standing when I called there to continue the investigation into Steaphan's family. The Landlady allowed my colleague and I to go through the few belongings they had and what we found was immensely helpful. The boys' clothes really weren't worth getting to you although you will find Steaphan's school cap in the envelope, which had been left at the hospital. A few of Aisla's clothes had been of good quality once upon a time and those, together with a lovely coat, we gave to the clothes appeal people.

The Landlady knew nothing of consequence, as Aisla hardly spoke to anyone. However, she did know that she had been married and that her husband was killed in an accident not long after Elizabeth was born, Aisla had moved with the children from that area to somewhere cheaper and looked for work but without someone to look after Elizabeth, it was impossible and they had to live a very simple life.

Enclosed, several documents and a piece of jewellery that now belong to Steaphan. I trust you will keep them safe until he is relocated into the care of an adult, whoever that may be. You will find Birth Certificates for both Steaphan and Elizabeth, a Death Certificate for Alasdair Stewart, the Marriage Certificate, and a newspaper cutting about the accident he was involved in.

We managed to obtain a new blue child Ration Book for Steaphan but haven't located an empty gas mask box for him. There are several expired Pawn shop receipts and a letter, obviously from Aisla's mother, which offers an insight into the past.

The investigation is now in the hands of the Police, not because there is any hint of wrongdoing, but as this is the only way to discover the family that obviously exists. With the war continuing in this way, it is quite possible that their records no longer exist, and they say it will be some time before they can give this matter the time it requires.

Meantime, I will endeavour to find you both more suitable accommodation and will be in touch again very soon.

Yours Sincerely,
Anabelle Johnson

This was hard to take in. I spread the documents across my bed and held the candle close. The first thing I wanted to see was Stevie's Birth Certificate and sure enough, his name was spelt that way – Steaphan, Douglas Stewart, born in Paddington on October 12th, 1930. He would be ten years old next month. Beth was only six when she was killed and never knew her father, because his Death Certificate showed that he died in 1934 of 'INTERNAL HAEMMORHAGE' sustained through catastrophic injury, but Stevie would have known him.

Sifting through the Pawn Shop receipts, I could see that each one described a piece of jewellery. The brooch was quite big. It glittered in the dim light and looked expensive. A mauve thistle on a stem, surrounded by what might be diamonds for all I knew. The scruffy newspaper cutting was brown with age and difficult to read in candlelight; I would have a better look at that in the morning but the letter from Aisla's Mother was in large, beautiful handwriting and easy to read. I studied this avidly.

Home, August 12th, 1932

My Darling Aisla,

Father and I did not want this to happen. The Police were involved only because of our desperation to find you and the child and it was never our intention to label you a thief. We have made it quite clear that the jewellery you took was bequeathed to you by Granny and was nothing but your own to do with as you pleased, which means that the Police have decided not to press charges realising our mistake. I beg you to bring your little one home, with or without your husband. Father will come to terms with this eventually, but you must understand that his bitterness stems from the fact that unlike Alasdair, your brother did not survive the war in France and to add insult to injury, an employee took our only daughter from us.

Please write to me. Mother.

The Marriage Certificate showed that Aisla, Bonnie, Blair MacClintock and Alasdair Stewart were married in Paddington in June 1930. *Aisla* – not Coral. If that's a Scottish name, does that mean Stevie's family are at the other end of the country in Scotland? What are all the Pawn Shop receipts for? Had Coral run away with Alasdair? Who was he? I was beginning to feel as though I were in an Agatha Christie novel. I needed Hercule Poirot! Still wondering about all this, I carefully placed everything back into the envelope.

There was still a lot to go through, but the candle was just a bit of a stub now and if I carried on, there'd be nothing to take downstairs in the morning. I'd have to wait. How on earth would I sleep tonight? More had happened to me in the last few days than in the whole of my adult life. My mind was in a whirl and if I didn't have such a tummy ache, would have felt exhilarated.

With everything churning in my mind, I poured a little water into the bowl and brushed my teeth. It was good to have my washbag and pulling out my bath size bar of Camay, held it to my nose to smell the perfume. Echoes of home swamped my mind. Visiting a Bath House was obviously out of the question; it was the stream or nothing. That would be a challenge. My sponge was a bit musty as it had been in the bag for a while, but I rinsed it a few times and once it had a bit of Camay on it, it was fine.

Stevie was fast asleep, so it was safe to strip-off and have a good wash-down. I had the usual sluggish feeling associated with what Mum used to call my 'visitor' and wished I'd had an 'Aspro' to swallow at supper. Remembering Linda's words that the contents of our potties would have to be thrown into that foul toilet in the morning without anything else, I wrapped-up the item for burning in the kitchen range in a piece of newspaper and left it beside my potty. My winceyette pyjamas smelt of home, which I found very warm and comforting - what with the Camay fragrance as well, then I blew out the candle and felt my way into bed. I think I was asleep in a flash.

CHAPTER SIX

Making Memories

———

A chink of light woke me. That and the smell of bread baking. I had difficulty remembering where I was and it took me a minute, or two to think straight but then it all came flooding back. Stevie was still sound asleep and didn't stir as I removed the piece of blackout wood from the window although he whimpered a little when I pushed open the pane of glass and let in some fresh air. A thorough examination of the glass thankfully did not reveal a crack, although the frame felt a bit wobbly – hardly surprising with the state the house was in. Yawning loudly, Stevie moved his arms above his head and opened his eyes. He was still holding his truck in one hand. *"Good morning, Stevie"*, I said cheerfully. *"Mornin' Miss"*, he replied, quickly correcting himself with, *"I mean morning, Lelly. Dunno if that sounds right really, Miss."* I assured him it did.

There was just enough water left for us to rinse our faces and slosh some around our important parts and then decant the used water into our chamber pots. It would be difficult to get them downstairs without spilling any of the contents and I wasn't relishing the thought of trying; maybe later I would look for a bucket to use. I rifled through all the clothes and found my dungarees, which would be perfect while we were here and once again thanked Nan for her thoughtfulness. Everything else fitted nicely into the deep drawers in the chest. We combed our hair and pulled the beds straight and remembering the candle at the last minute, stuffed that under one arm and my 'parcel' under the other. I covered each potty with a piece of newspaper, which to my dismay instantly sank, realising too late that it just meant there was more to carry. We picked them up as carefully as we could, opened the door and slowly took the stairs - *all twenty-four of them*, potties full to the brim with goodness-knows-what.

It was such a relief to make it to the back hall but then we had to get to the toilet shed. I could hear Gladys being busy in the kitchen and told Stevie to carry on walking. How we managed to get there without mishap, I don't know, but get there we did. We couldn't help giggling quietly. I took a deep breath, opened the door with my finger in the hole and just as I was about to toss the lot into the oil drum, realised that Alec was sitting there; I had forgotten to knock on the door!

I must have stood looking at him for several seconds before apologising and quickly closing the door. As usual, Alec said nothing. Stevie was laughing so much he was spilling his potty contents and I sternly told him to put it on the ground. *"It's not funny, Stevie, I could have thrown it all over him."* I said. However, I could see the funny side too and had to stifle my own chuckle as I pictured Alec covered in – *well,* you know ...

We waited and waited and finally, Alec came out of the toilet shed looking rather dishevelled, his face impassive. I wondered if he would wash his hands considering we were about to have breakfast and smiled at him sweetly while Stevie sucked-in his lips. When he had gone, we chucked our waste into the oil drum and rubbed our hands on the small area of grass beside the vegetables and then washed them at the pump, where Stevie pumped and I rinsed our chamber pots. Had I bought down my bar of Camay perhaps it would have banished the odour from the shed; something else to remember.

Stevie hurtled upstairs to place the pots back under our beds and I walked into the kitchen. I greeted Gladys with a 'Good Morning' and she asked if we slept well. I told her that we had. I felt a little sheepish asking if I could put my parcel into the flames, but Gladys simply lifted the round lid of the range with a hook and I quickly threw it in. Then I asked if there was anything I could do to help with breakfast, remembering to tell her that I had a new Ration Book for Stevie. The huge table was already laid – *once again with seven places*. Curious, I thought. Curiosity went from my mind instantly though, as I was tasked with cutting the freshly baked bread. It smelt wonderful but was difficult to cut with the heavy knife because the big crusty loaf was so soft in the middle. I did as good a job as possible and enjoyed the lovely smell emanating from it as I cut.

Stevie bounced into the kitchen. Gladys threw her arms around him as if he were one of her own, which rather startled him and surprised me somewhat, then asked if the truck had a name. Hesitating, Stevie replied, *"Trucky"*. *"Well, that's a perfect name."* said Gladys.

He sat down where he had been the night before and I did the same, having placed the sliced bread on the table and asked where everyone else was. *"Well let me see"*, Gladys began while smoothing her apron and peering through the window, *"Linda and Joe were up at 4am. Daisy Mae and Tess, the cows have to be milked early you see, or they'll be all upset and then the chickens come out."*

4am? The middle of the night! Stevie wasn't listening and just stared at the bread.

"Then there's the goat to be milked too, the horses want their breakfast and the eggs to be collected ... lots to do." She added.

Gladys obviously kept everyone fed and made all the bread, butter, and cheese, which was all very time-consuming. She was pickling vegetables for winter now, so her day was also filled from dawn to dusk. Harvesting must be even worse with long hours and ridiculously hard work and it was no wonder the other two Land Army girls had gone home afterwards; but why was Linda still here? I told myself off. I was always asking questions and such things were none of my business. Stevie was my business now, which was a huge responsibility. I had more things to read from Mrs. Johnson and the story unfolding was so surprising that I didn't know what to expect next. With no idea of our length of stay on the farm, we just had to make the most of it even though it wasn't ideal. These were truly kind people to take us in and I shouldn't query everything going on; but I couldn't help it. Mum said I had an 'enquiring mind'. Nan said I was just nosy.

Gladys was cooking bacon! My eyes nearly came out on stalks and Stevie had his nose in the air sniffing as Linda and Joe walked in. They were both very jolly – even though they'd been up before dawn and sat down in their usual places. Gladys banged a huge enamel tea pot on the table and slopped a jug of milk beside it. Then came such an amazing sight, Stevie and I sat wide-eyed. On a white, oval enamel tray with blue edging, a dozen fried eggs wobbled and beside them, enough frizzled bacon for an army of hungry people. I wanted to ask where the bacon had come from, but it might have been awkward, since that amount of bacon was so difficult to come by. Perhaps I would ask when we'd eaten it all.

Gladys buttered the bread throwing it onto a plate as if she were dealing a pack of cards and poured the tea. At this moment, Alec and the dogs appeared. Scraping the chair on the tiled floor, Alec pulled it way from the table and stood while he loaded his plate with four slices of bread, three eggs and at least six rashers of bacon. Gladys told him that he had enough now, to sit down and eat up. Alec thought for a moment, sat down with his plate, and tipped tea from the cup into his saucer, where he proceeded to suck it up noisily until it was all gone. Stevie stared and looked at me. I knew what he wanted to ask and shaking my head mouthed, "*No! Use the cup!*"

The enamel tray was soon empty. We ate in silence, with only the sound of cutlery scratching the plates; it was only for a few minutes because the food was gone in that short space of time. It was delicious and I felt very content despite the toilet shed incident, which hadn't upset Alec at all. He and Joe left the table without saying a word, the dogs following closely behind. Thanking Gladys, I offered to help clear the table, but

Linda was to keep her promise saying she would take us on a proper tour of the farm and Gladys was happy to relieve me of the chore. I was surprised that none of us licked our plate, but that would have been another 'no-no' for Stevie and they were almost clean anyway, with every streak of egg yolk mopped-up with that wonderful bread and nothing left for the chickens.

We would both need boots as everywhere was very muddy and knowing that neither of us possessed them, Linda took us through a green door to a room at the far end of the house. The door allowed enough light to see the cobblestone floor and big double doors at the far end. It had a cold, sweet smell and I thought this might be because for some reason there were no windows. I felt this was not a nice place and it made me shiver.

It was the slaughterhouse. Stevie was naïve enough not to understand the reason for the room and was simply interested in what was hanging from the ceiling, where an array of knives and other tools of all shapes and sizes swung gently on a bar amongst fierce-looking hooks. On the floor in one corner, were three big enamel pails with wooden handles and a hay bale. Beside these a large wooden table with wide legs and draped across it, a long red rubber apron and a scrubbing brush. I shivered again, but not because the room was cold. Pointing to a pile of Wellington boots in various sizes and condition, Linda told us to find a pair that fitted us, but to make sure there were no spiders in the toes. Stevie and I looked at each other in horror. It took a while to find two boots of the same size and since I said that Stevie and I wouldn't know what a spider felt like, Linda was kind enough to shove her hand inside to check for any, although her sideways glance at us meant that she knew the real reason.

Adequately booted, we followed Linda yet again out into the farmyard. The noxious smell was still in the air with no flowers in pots to disguise the smell. There was nothing remotely pretty and it certainly wasn't the chocolate box picture I'd expected. On the left side of the farmhouse was a barn in desperate need of repair. It had lost many of the planks of wood and Nan would have said that it was "*Holier-than-Thou*". We went in through one of these gaps, rather than using the actual door. It was full of hay, or straw – I wasn't sure of the difference and hanging from the eaves we saw a saddle and other horsey-type-of-things. There were four compartments, but no horses, just a cart of some kind.

"*But where are the horses and the Roger?*" Stevie asked, waving his truck in the air. Linda explained that Mildred, the pony which pulled the trap was 'out' and the two Shires, Peggy and Polly were pulling the plough for Joe. We would see them and 'The Roger', later. The sheds and barns seemed to go on and on and I hadn't realised just how big the farm was until Linda told us that Joe's family had owned more than one-hundred-and-sixty acres for as long as anyone could remember. Joe kept dairy cows when Linda first came here and had also grown Flaxseed, which had the prettiest blue flowers in summer, but the 'Ministry' – *the Ministry of Agriculture* – had ordered Joe to grow root vegetables, so the cows had to go and so did the Flax.

Daisy Mae and the younger animal, Tess were kept for milk and had to be attached to the machine powered by a small generator twice a day. Daisy Mae was coming to the end of her milk-producing days, but Tess fortunately had a long time ahead of her. Between milking they stayed out in the yard, or in their shed eating from a trough loaded with silage and Linda said that this was one job that Stevie and I could help with; she would tell us how later. Silage?

We walked on to find a goat, something I'd never actually seen before. It was very smelly and looked a bit stupid, but Stevie was delighted to be so close to a real live animal at last. I was glad she was tied to a post on a long chain although completely ignoring us as we stood looking at her, she didn't seem to mind Stevie patting the top of her head and asking her name. We were surprised to hear that she didn't have one. Her predecessors were never named because they were eaten when they stopped producing milk and replaced by a new one, which would account for the rug in our attic room. Stevie thought it was sad that she didn't have a name and decided to call her 'Billy' although Wilhelmina would have been more appropriate.

Stevie told 'Billy' he would see her later and we carried on. A noise baffled me as we neared a much larger shed. I couldn't imagine what the sound was and didn't like to show my ignorance by asking. Anyway, Linda was jabbering on and on and I wouldn't have interrupted, so with one ear listening to her and the other trying to put a name to the noise, she explained that two more Land Army girls and several farmhands from other areas were needed during harvesting potatoes and turnips and the new tractor promised by the Ministry was still to turn-up. The old tractor they shared with the other farm was no good for ploughing, so the Shires, Peggy and Polly were vital, although they were both quite old and when the new tractor arrived there would be the dilemma of how to warrant keeping animals that had no purpose; feeding them would be a huge problem.

Having reached the furthest point of the dusty farmyard, where fenceposts held back tall grass, Linda stopped outside the largest building. The noise was intense now and realising we were at the chicken shed I was glad I hadn't asked about it. We didn't go in, because Linda said they were very broody and shouldn't be upset but behind the shed was their open area surrounded by a tall wire mesh fence driven deep into the ground to stop anything burrowing underneath it. The dogs kept predators away most of the time, but every now and then something would try their luck. They were very funny to watch, and Stevie laughed, pointing to individual chickens, and giving them names.

Listening to Linda's knowledgeable information intently, we were captivated by it all. It was all so interesting. For example, I had no idea that chickens kept laying eggs so long as they were removed each day, but that none would hatch into chicks if there was no rooster. I must have missed that bit at school and of course, Stevie had only seen a piece of a chicken served up on a plate – and that wasn't often. Linda said things changed almost daily with chickens and egg production. Joe was constantly worried about what instructions might come next from the Ministry with talk about drying eggs into powder form for longer storage and ease of transportation. Farming was always unpredictable, but the war was making the job even harder and meeting the demands of the Ministry were almost impossible with the threat of a hefty fine for any variation always there.

Then came the best visit of all. We went to meet 'The Roger', who was lucky enough to have a home of his own on the other side of the chicken shed; a small rectangular house built with layers of flat stones and a roof of very old thatch. Several holes in both the walls and the roof had been plugged with mud, reminding me of the Anderson shelter next door at Mr. Atkinson's because the mud had dandelions growing in it giving it a 'cottage' look, but without the roses. Roses would have been nice to have helped with the dreadful smell though, which was overpowering.

The corrugated iron door with 'Roger' painted on it in very dribbled letters was propped up beside the entrance. Wooden shutters on the windows were held back by plaited rope looped round huge nails driven into the stones and beneath the windows was a tin bath and string wound into a filthy ball almost the size of a football. The little house was complete with a garden area in front, although without grass and here and there, flies were buzzing around some sort of sloppy mess spilled on the earth. Surrounding The Roger's domain was a fence of intertwined willow branches, which had grown leaves in places, and I thought that if it wasn't a place fit for a King, it was certainly a palace for a Roger, whatever it might be.

Linda said that he must be sleeping because he was usually pleased to have visitors. Stevie looked nervous and quietly asked, *"Does it bite?"* Linda didn't answer because just then, a rustling noise came from inside the house and the next thing we knew, 'Roger' – *all 200lbs* of him, had dashed out of the house towards us. I gasped and put a protective arm across Stevie's chest as the huge animal leaped a foot into the air, landing heavily with two front hooves resting on the willow branches. Snorting uncontrollably with a sort of mucus dripping from his nose, he was indeed pleased to have visitors. Filled with relief that it wasn't anything more sinister, our anxiety turned to laughter. *"It's a pig!"*, Stevie shouted with glee, *"It's a pig!"*

Without being warned that we'd be so close to such a large animal and not knowing how to handle this sort of thing, Stevie and I stood back while Linda fearlessly stroked Roger's ears and patted him on the head. I was sure he was smiling when she spoke to him like an old friend, saying, *"Hello Darling. How are you today?"* Covered in dry mud, we could just make out the pink of his skin where several trails of mucus had made clean tracks. I thought of the bacon on the breakfast plate and was glad it had been frizzled.

Roger grunted and 'oinked' shaking his head from side to side, sending trickles of slimy stuff into the air and onto Linda's jumper making Stevie and I move back even further, then sliding off the fence, he trotted over to his ball of string, which he rolled around using his huge snout for a minute, or two. It was so funny and so good to hear Stevie laughing. Having had enough of the string game, he somehow managed to bounce into the tin bath where he stood looking at us. I wondered if he was *our* entertainment, or were we entertaining him? Linda said he was in the tin bath hinting that it was empty and would need to get him more water. While she did this, we stayed with him enjoying the company of our new friend and neighbour with immense satisfaction.

With Roger busy drinking, we waved him goodbye. Having watched Stevie hold his tummy where it ached with laughter, I could see he was beginning to look more robust each day. I felt such an attachment to him, although I knew I shouldn't. The

Impetigo had cleared-up, his face had filled out and his cheeks had a rosy glow. Best of all, he didn't seem to have been greatly affected by the events of the past week, which pleased me no end. Could it be this easy? I wasn't sure he'd accepted the loss of his mother and sister, or even if it had sunk in properly. Was this some sort of calm before the storm? The future would be challenging for him and I wanted to do everything I could to make the short time we were together as painless as possible; at least I would try.

Linda said she must carry on her work now but after supper, would explain the way we could help make silage. I wasn't even sure what silage was but was willing to have a go and nodding furiously, so was Stevie. I really wanted to go over the papers in the envelope but should ask Gladys if I could help her, so we wandered back to the house. I pulled off my boots at the front door, but Stevie went straight into the kitchen where Gladys was just about to skin a rabbit lying dead on the table. *"This one's for the dogs",* Gladys told him. *"They'll eat the whole thing, buckshot an' all if we let 'em, so we've taught 'em to bring 'em back. Just means I have to do the dirty bit".*

Stevie asked if he could touch the rabbit and Gladys stopped for a moment while he put his truck on the table and rubbed the fingers of both hands through the dense fur. *"Still warm."* He said. *"But it's dead, right?"* He wasn't asking anyone specific and didn't look up. Gladys and I glanced at each other to see who would speak first. *"Yes, it's dead".* Gladys answered. *"Gone up to heaven to be with the angels."*

Gently stroking the soft, grey fur, we watched Stevie examine every part of the loveable rabbit without saying a word. He came to the wound on its side where it had been shot and with a deep sigh, rubbed around it with his fingers causing blood to seep. Suddenly, he began to rub more vigorously until he was rubbing so intensely, he could have been kneading dough. At first, I found this comical, but when he stopped and lifted the rabbit off the table with arms outstretched, I realised he was in some sort of trance. Staring into space, with huge unblinking eyes, his little body began to tremble. Blood collected in his palms and trickled through his fingers as he slowly squeezed the rabbit so hard it altered its shape. Stevie's sickly grin revealed clenched teeth and saliva dripped from his mouth as he uttered a peculiar growling sound.

I went to grab the rabbit from his hands, but Gladys stopped me raising a finger to her lips warning me to say nothing. It was horrifying to see Stevie like this. A moment passed. Blood dripped onto the table in dark treacle-like pools. The rabbit had taken on a different appearance and was now a wretched looking thing. Stevie's lips were tinged with blue and it was then as Gladys gently prised it from Stevie's grasp that he slid onto the floor in a dead faint. Kneeling beside him, I held his blood-stained hands and burst into tears. Once again, I felt useless. Pulling a jumper from the rack above the range Gladys placed it under his head. *"He was ready for that"*. She said softly. *"Needed to come."* Between sobs, I begged, *"What do you mean? What happened to him? What shall we do?"* Gladys answered wisely, *"Nothing to be done . . . Won't be the last time."*

I was so confused. Stevie looked dreadful, just when I had begun to think he was looking well and happy. How wrong I was. Alec walked in at that moment and looked quizzically at Stevie laying on the floor. *"He needs to go to bed, Alec. Will you take him?"* Gladys asked. Without hesitating, Alec carefully lifted him from the floor like a rag doll. As he headed for the stairs Stevie's boots fell off; I knew they were a size too big, but he had insisted they were right for him. With me following closely behind we quickly went upstairs. Alec laid him on his bed and left the room. Stevie was perfectly still and felt cold, so I wrapped the bedcover around him and swept the hair off his forehead. I heard Gladys clomping up the stairs cursing them. She came into the room holding a three-legged stool in one hand, a glass of milk in another and Stevie's truck tucked into her cleavage. *"Bit of honey in the milk."* She told me softly. *"Said anything yet?"* She added, looking at Stevie.

I shook my head, took the stool, and sat on it placing the

milk on the floor and the truck beside Stevie. Glancing over her shoulder as she went back to the kitchen, Gladys said, *"The milk is for you, dear."*

I took a sip but couldn't drink more. I would give it to Stevie when he woke up. So, this was a reaction to everything was it? I really didn't know. Should he see a doctor? What would a doctor do? He stirred. I held his hand, still covered in blood and fur. Smiling down at him, he looked back at me with those lovely eyes and whispered, *"Cor, Miss. Didn't feel quite right for a tick. Where's Trucky?"* Pressing 'Trucky' into his hand gave him some reassurance and sitting up on one elbow, he looked around the room rubbing his head. *"Ow did I get 'ere?"* He asked. I smiled and offered him the milk, which he swallowed in one go, then fell back onto the pillow sleeping more peacefully this time.

After a few minutes, I quietly went to the drawer where I'd hidden the envelope from Mrs. Johnson and emptied everything out on my bed again. It was much easier to read in daylight and I went through it all in greater detail. Holding Stevie's cap in my hand I thought of the last time I'd seen him in it on top of his gas mask. On that dreadful day, he'd come rushing into the classroom wearing it with the peak at the back and I'd told him off for not having it on properly. It seemed important at the time. I held it to my chest as I read the letter to Coral from her Mother; it reminded me of my own mum and my eyes welled with tears. Then I came across the newspaper cutting about Alasdair's accident.

PADDINGTON TRAGEDY

"Alasdair Stewart, thirty-four years of age, a man of this parish who served bravely in France during the Great War, died on Tuesday of injuries received following the heroic and selfless attempt to halt a runaway carriage and pair in a crowded street near to his work at the station. His actions most certainly saving the lives of the occupants and many others, he leaves a wife, young son, and a baby daughter. 'Tragic', said Alderman Hume.

I wiped my blurry eyes. So, Stevie's father was a hero. He was working at the station – there must be records of past employees, surely details can be found to help find his relatives. How dreadful for Coral, I meant Aisla of course although I found it difficult to use that name. Pieces of the puzzle were coming together. Aisla and Alasdair were together somewhere in Scotland and it sounded as if her family were not happy with this arrangement. They were married, lived in Paddington, and had two children. When Alasdair was killed, the three of them left to live in a cheaper area. It all made sense, Aisla must have come from a wealthy family. The coat, the pawn shop receipts, the brooch. If family exists, perhaps Stevie will be well-looked-after. Oh, how I hoped I was right. Mrs. Johnson must have come to the same conclusions and I was sure she would be making all the right inquiries.

Maybe this wasn't the best time to give Stevie his cap though and I put it back in the envelope with everything else for later. When he finally woke, he told me that he needed to change his trousers and this we did without speaking about the wet clothes he took off. Thank goodness we'd bought new things. The water used to rinse his hands took off enough rabbit blood until we could get to the pump and I would take my bar of Camay down with us to do a better job. The pink water smelt horrible when I poured it into the chamber pot and that would have to go downstairs too.

Stevie's Identity Card had been in his back pocket with the sixpence given to him by Mr. Jenkin. The card was rather damp and so was the bed, so I pulled the covers back and left the sixpence and card there for it all to dry together; it wouldn't take long with the window open. I had already started a pile of clothes for washing and added his to these, remembering that before long, I would have to ask Linda what she did about laundry. By the time Stevie was dressed - truck safely in one hand, sixpence in the back pocket and both in our stocking feet, it was gone one o'clock; no wonder I was hungry. I popped the bar of Camay into my cardigan pocket, gathered up the potty and water jug and we went down the first flight of stairs together to the landing, where one of the doors was open a little.

None of the doors on the stairs had been open before and I couldn't resist peeking in. It was a bright room with two windows and similar scrappy pieces of material for curtains as there were in the attic. The wardrobe had a long rusty mirror on the door, which was hanging off its hinges and by the look of the clothes draped over two of the open drawers, was sure it was Gladys and Joe's bedroom. In the middle was a big cast iron bed with an amazing patchwork quilt and on the floor, a huge cow-shaped black and white rug.

Rickety wicker tables sat on either side of the bed with a clock and candle holder on one and a photograph in a frame on the other. From what I could see from a distance, the photograph was of a soldier in uniform. Stevie had carried on down the stairs and I thought I'd better leave the bedroom. It was hard not to slop the potty water and when we reached the bottom of the stairs, I left it there while we put on the shoes we'd left at the front door.

Although it was raining a little, I took Stevie out to the pump to wash his hands with soap until I was satisfied that any reminder of the blood was gone. He said nothing about the rabbit or fainting and being outside freshened us up a bit returning the colour to his face. I for one, was very hungry despite the emotional time we'd had.

It was as if Gladys was a mind reader because there was

another feast on the table. She was her usual cheerful-self and once again, greeted us like long-lost family. I remembered the china at the bottom of the stairs just as I went to sit down and excused myself to deal with it. This time, I was careful to make sure that no one was sitting inside the toilet shed and knocked on the door before opening it releasing several flies before throwing the potty contents into the putrid hole. I filled the water jug from the pump, swilled-out the potty and left them both at the bottom of the stairs to go up later.

We sat at the table alone because everyone else had eaten at noon and we tucked-in to bread with home-churned butter, cheese and pickle and a nice cup of sweet tea. What a morning. It had started so well with the tour of the farm and the fun of seeing all the animals. I still didn't really understand what had happened to Stevie to make him behave in that way and knew I should try not to dwell upon it, but I felt so sorry for him. With each passing day, there came new experiences for us both and for me, the emotional responsibility increased with each encounter.

The rain had stopped by the time we had eaten, and the sun was shining brightly through the kitchen windows. Linda came in and hung-up her damp jacket.

"What-ho", she said. *"Shall I do the village run now, Gladys? We need to register our guests at the shop too."* Already prepared for this question, Gladys handed Linda a massive rectangular wicker basket containing a pile of Ration Books, a shopping list written on a piece of newspaper and a purse. *"Coming with me?"* Linda asked.

"We'd love to", I said, looking at Stevie. *"Just let me get Stevie's new book and some money from upstairs."*

Linda suggested that while I did that, she and Stevie would hitch Mildred to the trap, and we'd meet in the stable. Stevie was almost through the door before he remembered to thank Gladys for his bread and cheese, but waiting for him to go, I turned to Gladys to thank her not only for our food, but also for her handling of the earlier thing. She put her arm round me and kissed the top of my head. I think she had tears in her eyes but couldn't be sure.

In my haste to get to our room, I spilt a little water on the stairs but doubted anyone would be going up before it dried, so left the spots where they were. I delved into my handbag and felt for my purse. With only a little change in it I thanked goodness for Nan's money. At the last minute, I remembered Stevie's new Ration Book and took that from the big envelope. Did we need our gas masks? Linda didn't carry one. Why should we? I knew it was rather foolish to feel this excited about a shopping trip, but once again, it was another new experience. I had never travelled in a pony and trap and doubted Stevie had either and obviously we'd never been to the village.

Leaving the potty and water jug on the floor, I was halfway down the stairs when I realised that I still had the bar of Camay in my pocket and had to return it to our room. The spots of water on the stairs were almost dry with my footsteps skimming them and I had to smile when I saw that they had left clean places on some of the wood. Dashing down again, I passed Gladys who shouted, "*Have a good time,*" and I waved back at her before heading to the stable.

We still hadn't seen the Shire Horses who were out once again with Joe, but Mildred had spent the night in the stable. A sleek, brown horse - *I think the colour has an actual name,* she seemed quite happy to be attached to the trap and once Linda had finished fixing everything in place, she told Stevie to hop-up in the back and that I was to sit with her at the front. I realised I had performed in a rather ungainly fashion when I saw Linda plop into the seat with one big hop, hardly touching the step. She was used to the trap and this was all new to me, but I was still a little envious of her skill. She waited until we were settled and told us to "*Hang on to the handrails at all costs*" and picking up the reins in one hand cracked the whip in the air with the other giving Mildred the cue to move.

The trap was very bouncy, and Stevie immediately began to

laugh as we trundled across the cobblestones turning right onto the narrow lane. Mildred walked slowly beside the hedgerows and trees, the sun shone at us, the birds sang for us and insects swooped down at us. It was wonderful.

After about fifteen minutes of utter calm and beauty, I noticed a peculiar-shaped building in a distant field. It wasn't a house, because the windows were simply tiny slits and there was no proper roof. Turning a bend bought us closer and it was then I noticed the soldier standing next to it. Mildred stopped a few feet away from him and pointing a rifle towards us, he shouted at the top of his voice, "*Halt! Who goes there?*" A bit too old to be a soldier with his white hair and glasses, his appearance was still quite menacing, and Stevie put his hand on my shoulder. I patted it with mine in the reassurance that we weren't about to be shot.

"*Hello, Mr. Tomkins,*" Linda answered.

Replying in a friendly way, he said, "*It's you, is it Linda?*" Then in a more threatening and sarcastic voice, added, "*You have to show me your Identity Cards you know.*"

Linda smiled as she took her card from a jodhpur pocket and I delved into my handbag to find mine. Turning to Stevie to take his, I saw that he was fumbling in the back pockets of his trousers. Of course, they were the new trousers and the Identity Card wasn't there. It was drying on his bed!

Realising we were one card short, Linda explained that Stevie was staying at Middlewych Farm for a few days before moving on and that she would vouch for him. At this, Mr. Tomkins stood to attention with his rifle across his chest and with eyes rigidly fixed on Stevie, called, "*Fred. Fred, you'd better get out here.*"

Fred appeared from behind the strange building holding a tin mug. Placing the mug on the ground and grabbing a rifle leaning against the wall, he marched over to us. Fred looked even older than Mr. Tomkins but wore two stripes on his uniform obviously giving him an amount of authority. "*What we got here then?*" Fred said. "*Oh, hello Linda.*"

Linda gave the explanation again and I told them that I was Stevie's teacher, that I was responsible for him at the present time and as he was only nine years of age, he could hardly be a threat. Fred and Mr. Tomkins whispered together and walked round the trap to look at Stevie, where he sat cross-legged and bemused, but gave them one of his winning smiles.

"*Well,*" Fred began, "*We're here to protect the village you know. This is our post, what they're calling a pillbox' cos of its shape. Indestructible. We'll show them Jerrys!!*"

"Can't go letting in every Tom, Dick and Harry without a card." Mr. Tomkins added.

Pushing her hat above her forehead with a forefinger and with a deep sigh, Linda asked who was guarding the other side of the village. Fred and Mr. Tomkins looked at each other.

"*Well, we'll be marching there when we finish our duty here.*" Fred told her.

"*Look, we won't be very long shopping for Gladys and if we can get back here to your guard post before you leave for the other end of the lane, will that be alright?*" Linda begged.

They whispered together again.

"*That will be in order, but just this once, mind.*" Fred said. "*Can't go wandering around the country . . .*"

We didn't hear the rest, because Linda had told Mildred to 'walk on' and we left them behind us.

"*Home Guard.*" Linda said.

I nodded slowly.

A few minutes later, we were in the village – *what there was of it.* It did have a big church though, which was strange for such as small place. Trotting past the churchyard, I could see it was full of old tombstones and curiosity getting the better of me, asked Linda if she knew anything of the history of the area. She told me that it had once been a thriving community with a manor house and a huge district farmed by hundreds of people until the Black Death arrived.

I wished I hadn't asked.

The narrow lane continued through the village and out the other side. Some of the buildings were old with thatched roofs and the whitewashed Boar's Head Inn was no exception. The ancient and well-used pub dominated the village and to the right of it, was a large courtyard where stables must have once been used by coaches and passing travellers. The front door had a horse trough either side and beneath the lower windows were well-stocked flower beds. This time, it was a perfect chocolate box scene. A row of houses continued the terrace, until it was broken by a brick-built schoolhouse with a slate roof; it looked as though it was still in use, although by the look of the dusty windows, perhaps not recently. The Post Office was next door to the Village Hall and in between the two, a telephone box.

Then there was the shop laying back off the lane with a muddy turning area in front and a square of steps up to a stone memorial to the fallen of the Great War. A small building with a roof thatched on one side and slates to a small extension, there was no name above the door where several ladies crowded under a calico awning. In front of the large windowpane on the shopfront were boxes of potatoes, and propped-up against them, two blackboards showing the prices of their contents written in chalk.

Linda steered Mildred off the lane just outside the shop where the horse stopped automatically. As we sprang from the trap, Mildred walked towards a pail of water conveniently placed on the memorial steps sticking her head in it to suck-up the contents, having perfected this routine over time.

Everyone seemed to know each other. Linda began to talk to another Land Army girl in the queue and the girls carried on a conversation shouting above the chatter of the ladies in between them. It was all rather chaotic in a friendly sort of way, but Stevie was soon bored until he spotted a small plane circling above. Eventually, it flew low over the village and he waved and waved even when it was long gone and then used his truck to mimic what he'd seen. This kept him busy for a while longer and then the queue went down enough for us to stand inside the shop.

The shelves weren't packed solid. There were gaps replaced with signs saying, '*maybe next week*' and '*no more*', but the ladies serving were still busy weighing and calculating, reading shopping lists, slapping pieces of meat in paper, and shaking their head a lot.

Stevie had his eye on the sweet jars. There were four of them. One was almost empty of what must have been Liquorice, but the others had a reasonable amount of Barley Sugar Twists, Black Jacks and Pear Drops. Sweets weren't rationed yet, but because the country was short of sugar, they weren't being produced and supplies were dwindling. I wasn't sure how much we could have and decided to ask, but first we had to get to the counter. Stevie had the same idea and was holding his sixpence in readiness.

At last, Linda made it to the counter and after exchanging niceties with one of the ladies, handed over our Ration Books, saying that there were two to register, even though it was a temporary arrangement just for a few days. This was easily and quickly done, with Linda's validation and no mention of checking Identity Cards, fortunately. Items on the shopping list were crossed-off one by one as they were taken off the shelves or produced from the rear of the shop attached to the farm with the lady expertly referring to the Ration Books when necessary and the basket was soon piled high. Linda asked Stevie to help carry more in a string bag she produced from her jodhpur pocket, which seemed a bottomless pit for all and sundry. He did this without complaining and returned the sixpence to his back pocket, although he kept his gaze in the direction of the sweet jars until he left the shop.

Linda struggled back to the trap with Stevie, leaving me to buy some washing powder, and another bar of soap. I wanted to write to Dad and Nan, so bought a pencil and sharpener and a notepad. Then I noticed a tumbler containing an assortment of crayons and thinking Stevie could do some drawing, or even some writing, bought one each of red, blue, yellow, and green and a pad of plain paper. Then I plucked-up the courage to ask about the sweets. "*For the little boy.*" I said.

By the time I had finished making my purchases, Stevie and Linda were waiting for me in the trap and having drunk all the water in the pail, Mildred pawed at the ground in anticipation of the trek back to the farm. I would love to have hopped-up using the same method as Linda, but holding my bag and the shopping, was even more clumsy than before and landed sideways on one shoulder. Linda smiled and hauled me up with, "*Here ya go.*"

Before we set off, a young girl called to Linda from the pub and jumping down from the trap, she eagerly ran over to her. The girl was small, pretty, and blonde and greeted Linda with a peck on the cheek. Linda held her hand while they chatted, and this gave me a moment to study the names on the memorial dedicated to those who fell in the Great War. There was only time to get down as far as 'D', but there were no Albrights on the list, so it was good to know that the soldier in the photograph beside Gladys's bed hadn't been killed in that war.

I felt Linda jump in the trap beside me and as Mildred turned around, I had a better look at the young girl, who waved with her fingers, rather than in the usual wavy sort of way. Linda touched her hat and nodded to her and as we moved on, she looked back at the girl who wiggled her fingers again.

Stevie had the basket and string bag in the back with him and with no room for anything else, I somehow balanced everything on my lap for the return journey. Of course, Fred and Mr. Tomkins were waiting eagerly at their pillbox to inspect us once again and after several minutes with them, time was getting on, so Linda put Mildred into a trot, making it even harder for me to steady my purchases. We arrived intact though, and Stevie and I took the shopping in to Gladys, who always seemed to be in the kitchen, while Linda dealt with Mildred and the trap, saying that I was to tell Gladys that she'd had the last of the vinegar for a while and that the WI wanted as many apples as possible for canning. Placing it all on the table, it seemed a lot of food, but I suppose there were six of us to feed, or maybe seven if the mysterious extra person ever turned up.

I gave Gladys the message about the vinegar and she sniffed the air and 'tutted'. I asked about the WI wanting apples and she told me that the local Women's Institute had been given a canning machine, which had been sent all the way from America so that absolutely nothing would go to waste, canning anything and everything as often as they could. I thought this was marvellous. Was there no limit to the strings in Gladys's bow?

Noticing my box of washing powder, Gladys told me that if I needed to do some laundry, I might have seen an old brick oven near the water pump, which she used to heat water in a big tin bowl. There was a washtub and board and of course, I must have spotted the mangle. If the weather was okay, she used the line beside the toilet shed, or hung things over the range. I hadn't noticed the mangle and thought the brick oven was another well. It would certainly be different to the usual way of doing laundry and for once longed for Nan's copper.

We were lucky to be living in the country Gladys said, because others in the towns weren't having enough to eat, although if the war carried on, goodness knows what would happen. There was sure to be more rationing, and the Ministry would be telling farmers what to do even more than they were now. It was all very worrying. She sorted through the food and asked me to carry some with her to the pantry. I didn't know what she meant by a pantry but followed her out towards the garden anyway and we came to a door I had assumed was just a cupboard.

Gladys opened the door, which had concealed a dark cavernous room. She struck a match from a box on the side and lit a candle revealing shelves from floor to ceiling on two sides and a stone shelf across another with cupboards above. It was what we called the larder at home, although much, much bigger. With no windows, it was very cold, and the mixture of smells confusing, until I realised there were three dead pheasants and a rabbit hanging on a hook from the ceiling and the large green object on the stone shelf was in fact a big chunk of cheese covered in mould. There were too many glass jars and others made of clay or pottery on the shelves to count. It seemed they were all stuffed full of unidentifiable vegetables, fruit, and other food and to determine this meant lifting the cork lids or removing the cotton covers. It all looked very eerie and somehow reminded me of the Frankenstein book I'd read, which scared me to death.

Back in the kitchen, Stevie was changing into his boots. Linda had told him that she would show us how to make silage and to hurry up because the sun would soon be setting. I didn't want to appear stupid by asking what silage was and nodded with a grin. Before changing into my own boots, I went quickly upstairs and took out the bag of sweets I'd tucked secretly in the front pocket of my dungarees and placed them on Stevie's bed, then rushed back downstairs to find Linda. She was walking towards the cow shed carrying a pitchfork and a rake and we quickly caught up with her.

It was a lovely evening. The earlier rain had made everything sparkle and there was still a little heat left in the sun, which was setting fast as Linda had warned. She led us to a grass bank behind the cow shed where a big three-sided hole had been dug out. I was surprised to see Alec there; we hadn't seen much of him and I had wondered what he did all day, but now he was pulling cut grass from a hayrick and throwing it into the hole. Linda did the same with her pitchfork, while we watched fascinated.

When the hole was half full, Linda told Alec to stop and then picked up one of three large enamel jugs. Walking on top of the grass mound, she began to pour the contents slowly all over the grass until each jug was empty. It was thick brown stuff, which smelt sweet and sour at the same time; what she did was most peculiar but not wanting to appear even more stupid, I didn't ask questions. Stevie was desperate to help and asked Linda what our job was going to be. She said there had to be more grass on top before the fun could start and nodded to Alec who carried on piling the grass onto the brown mess.

With the hayrick empty, Linda told Stevie and I to walk up the bank and jump onto the grass and this we did, standing there for the next instruction. Linda joined us and with a deep breath said, "*Now jump!*" I thought she'd gone a bit mad when she began to jump around the grass as if springs were attached to her boots, but when Stevie did the same, I joined in too. It was hilarious. I couldn't imagine for a moment why we were doing this, but Linda obviously knew best and the three of us laughed and bumped into each other while Alec looked on stony-faced, until we could bounce no more. "*Don't sit down, unless you want your clothes to get all sticky*", Linda said, "*It's Molasses.*"

We were 'pickling' the grass. Jumping about on it would remove a lot of air and help the pickling process, eventually turning the grassy-brown mess into silage – winter food for the horses and cows when the grass ran out, or when it was covered in snow. Joe had been cutting grass for days and had dug several silos, which were dotted around the farm. We bounced until the sun had almost set and Linda said we'd done such a marvellous job we could stop. I think Stevie would have carried on bouncing until he exhausted himself, but it was time for supper. We left Alec and Linda laying a tarpaulin over the grass and went back to the house, where we washed our hands under the pump and changed out of our sticky brown boots. It had been exhilarating fun and had made us laugh; something that was greatly needed.

The table in the kitchen was ready for us and once again, it was laid with seven places. Stevie and I sat in our usual seats and hearing Linda and Alec using the water pump, Gladys began to pour tea into the cups. The back door slammed shut and the dogs rushed in. Bonnie growled at me and then went to sit in front of the range with Bella. Joe followed with a "*Hey-Hey*" and Gladys gave her usual, "*Yoo-Hoo*". Joe was covered in dry grass but sat with us anyway; at least a few of us were reasonably clean. Gladys told Joe that Stevie and I were certainly earning our keep, which of course wasn't the case since they were being paid one whole guinea a week to feed us with the going rate for an evacuee being ten shillings and sixpence. Not that I would have ever been so rude as to mention it when everyone was being so kind.

Linda and Alec sat down, just as Stevie let out such a howl it made me, and the dogs jump a foot into the air. The earlier episode sprang to mind, and I caught my breath.

"What's wrong, Stevie?" I gasped.

"*Trucky! My Trucky! I've lost 'Trucky'.*" He screamed.

In one way I was relieved he didn't seem to be going into another trance but knew the consequences of losing the precious truck wouldn't help Stevie's present state of mind either. Joe slurped his tea, regardless of the grass dropping into the cup and said nothing, while Gladys and I tried to remember where we'd seen him with it last. Linda put her arm round him saying, "*We'll find you another truck, Stevie. I promise.*"

"*I don't want another one, I want that one.*" Stevie howled. "*It was special. Lelly bought it for me.*"

Alec immediately left the table and went outside. Seeing Stevie so distressed had obviously upset him. Stevie wouldn't eat. Tears streamed down his face and pushing his plate forward, he laid his head on his arms. He was in a bad way for the second time that day and I despaired. The dogs were agitated by all the fuss and left their places at the range to sit at the open front door. Maybe they were waiting for Alec. Gladys put the tea on the range to keep warm with the remains of the stew for Alec to have later, but we were unable to coax Stevie to eat a morsel or drink his tea.

Stevie continued to whimper while the rest of us finished eating whatever was in the stew and devoured apples with custard and had more tea. Barking signalled Alec's return. His appearance shocked us all. The smell radiating from him was terrible and he looked as though he'd fallen into a muddy pond. It was soon clear that he was covered in Molasses and grass, but in his hand was Stevie's truck. Stevie's face was a picture. We three ladies clapped, and even Joe looked up and smiled. I couldn't thank Alec enough. It was incredible that he'd managed to find it amongst the silage, or even cared enough to go and look for it. Stevie kissed the sticky truck and held it to his chest, beaming at Alec.

"*Thank you.*" Stevie whispered.

From that moment on, Alec and Stevie were best friends. They ate their stew together and drank so much tea, Stevie needed to use the toilet shed although it was dark by this time and we had to take a lamp with us. The scene in there was even worse at night, with many more species of creepy-crawly enjoying the waste.

When we went upstairs that evening, Stevie discovered the bag of sweets on his bed. I was so glad I'd bought them even though the lady at the shop was reluctant to give me an assortment for some reason and charged a lot more than in peacetime. It was worth it to see the look on his face, but then he did something so touching, I had that stinging in the back of my eyes again; he offered me his sixpence. I told him to keep it for a rainy day and that he could have one of the sweets before he brushed his teeth. He never failed to amaze me. I was beginning to feel a type of love I had never known before and had to remind myself that there would come a day when we would be separated. Stevie would never be separated from his truck again though and once we'd managed to wash it enough to take to bed, he held it with both hands before it slipped safely beneath the covers.

Every day seemed to have a new encounter, catastrophe, or intense emotion attached to it and as I undressed hoped for a more relaxed day tomorrow. I didn't know when the time would be right to give Stevie all the information we had so far and decided to think about that another time, but just as I was about to snuff the candle, Stevie said,

"*Where are they, Lelly?*" I hesitated because I knew where this question had come from, but unable to think of the right answer asked him what he meant.

"*Well ... Mum and Beth ... I think they've gone to 'eavan, but I don't get where that is, or 'ow they got there.*" He explained. This was difficult to answer because I didn't know either but had to say something.

"*Well, we're told heaven is a lovely place Stevie and I don't think anyone comes back so they must like it there. It's a sort of secret. Their spirit has gone there, but their bodies are still here.*" That was the best I could do. I knew it was totally inadequate and now would be worried that I'd said all the wrong things and done even more damage to his mind.

"*What's 'spirit'?*" Stevie asked. Oh, my goodness, how do I explain this one?

"*Well, it's all your memories and nice feelings and the love you have inside you. Your spirit can't be seen – it's another sort of secret.*"

I was making a mess of this and knew I had to stop the subject somehow before I made it even worse, so I blew out the candle and said,

"*Is Trucky asleep yet?*"

"*Don't be daft, Lelly*" Stevie said wisely.

CHAPTER SEVEN

Tragedy, Defeat and even Dismay

Our next day on the farm was a wet one. After breakfast, Gladys was busy pickling anything that didn't move, and I asked if we could help. She was rather reluctant with an answer, so I said that maybe Stevie should do a little bit of schoolwork if we could have the end of the table; it was certainly big enough. She nodded and was obviously relieved that we wouldn't interfere with her routine.

I left Stevie watching the pickling process, with Gladys explaining what she was doing, while I went upstairs to our room. On the way, the same door was open on the first landing and I peeked inside again making a beeline for the photograph beside the bed. There was nothing to say who the young man was, but it was obvious that the uniform he was wearing was from the Great War. Maybe I would ask Linda if she knew anything about it, although of course, I was being terribly nosy again.

The jigsaw, or the paper and crayons? I couldn't decide, so took everything down to the kitchen, where Gladys was in the middle of blinding Stevie with science about the way vinegar 'did a marvellous job' and that if she didn't do all this now, lots of food would go to waste and they'd not have any nice things to eat in the winter.

"*Chip shop.*" Stevie said. "*We'd go dan the chip shop. They 'ave pickled eggs, but I like chips best.*" Gladys chuckled. I asked where I might find a piece of wood to do the jigsaw on rather than dismantle it halfway through and she suggested I wait for

Alec because he knew where the perfect thing would be hiding.

"He might not be able to tell you where to look, but he'll find it for you," she added. Then before I realised what on earth I was saying, I had said it, *"You only have one son, Gladys. And no daughters?"*

My face coloured as she turned to look at me. *"Just Alec."* She replied with a downward glance. I felt as if I had betrayed her. She must have known that I'd been poking around and seen the photograph. It was rude of me to ask about such a thing and intrude upon her personal life; I was furious with myself and apologised.

"I'm sorry for asking Gladys. It's none of my business. My mum always said I had an enquiring mind and I know we've only been here a few days, but you've made us feel like part of the family." Gladys said no more and hacked through a cabbage like a Lumberjack.

Rolling the paper in the opposite direction to flatten it out a bit, Stevie held the crayons in readiness. I thought he could draw for a while and then we'd go through the alphabet and numbers. I asked him what he was going to do, and he told me he would draw a picture of Roger. Carefully positioning 'Trucky' on the table where he could be safely guarded, Stevie took great care with his drawing, but the finished product looked nothing like a pig, especially as he'd used the green crayon.

The outline of Roger's house was at least recognisable though and there was no mistaking the sun in the sky. We all laughed, and Gladys said it was so good, she would prop it up on the dresser. Stevie groaned when I suggested he write out the alphabet in capital letters and I had to promise that he could draw some more after he'd written every letter. To make it a little more interesting, I held the crayons behind my back and told him to point to one of my hands and use the crayon I was holding. It's amazing what fun can be had from such small things and I enjoyed myself too.

I hadn't noticed the rain had stopped, but Stevie had,

probably because he didn't want to write any more of the alphabet and he asked if we could go and see the animals again. Gladys was sure we could, even though Linda was busy, but not to get into any trouble and to be back at noon to eat. Stevie rushed to find his boots and had mine waiting for me at the door when I'd put the paper and crayons together.

It was a bit windy, but the sun was strong. Only a week had passed since we were in hospital and it all seemed like a weird dream, or was it that we were in a dream now? Away from bombs dropping and people being killed, life seemed to have taken on a different complexion and today, I felt optimistic.

Standing on the cobblestones in front of the house we decided what to do first. Probably a visit to the chickens, then there would be just enough time to see the goat before getting back at noon. As we began to walk towards the chicken shed, we heard the tinkle of a bicycle bell and both turned to see the Postman riding towards us. *"Gladys inside?"* He asked. We nodded as he propped-up his bicycle against the porch wall and went into the house.

The chickens were all very funny to watch and ran around as if they needed to be somewhere in a hurry pecking at the food on the ground in between. The goat seemed to spend all its time rubbing against the fence posts; maybe she had an itch she couldn't scratch. Then at long last, we saw the Shire Horses, Peggy, and Polly. Joe was bringing them towards the farm, and I thought they'd had a short day's work until I remembered they would have been out at dawn. They were huge, marvellous-looking creatures. We followed them and Joe into the stables to watch them being relieved of their harnesses and much to Stevie's approval, have their blinkers removed.

Once they were free of their shackles, the girls seemed to know that they had finished for the day and they whinnied and snorted gleefully as Joe slapped them both on their rump. They would spend the afternoon in the top field, which had a good view of the farm and Joe asked if we would like to go with them. Of course, we said we would and when Stevie was offered a ride, he gave me a winsome look for my approval. I smiled back, secretly wishing I could have a ride too.

Joe lifted Stevie onto Peggy's back and told him to hang onto her mane. Then he stood beside Polly and bent down cupping his hands for me to use as a step-up to scale her enormous size. I had a moment of panic when I realised that he was offering me a ride but couldn't possibly refuse such an offer. With a deep breath, I placed a muddy boot into his hands and in a flash was catapulted onto her back.

It was another experience for us both but this time, a wonderful one. The horses didn't seem to mind us being on them, or even having their mane pulled – *and I certainly pulled Polly's with both hands*! The journey took us past fields with deep furrows and the horses proudly walked past them as if to say, "*We did that!*" Several rabbits scurried about the ruts and it was a surprise to see the dogs appear from nowhere chasing the rabbits between them as if they were playing a game of Tag.

It was all so enjoyable that Stevie and I were both reluctant to leave Peggy and Polly's silky backs. It was also a long way down to the ground, but Stevie slipped into Joe's arms and I did the same, landing on the spongey grass. The horses stood quite still, until Joe said softly, "*Get on then, girlies.*" And despite their size, they raced into the field like children. I could have watched them all day.

Joe beckoned for us to follow him to one corner of the field to see the view, which was breath-taking. We were quite high up. The countryside seemed to go on and on for miles and once again, there was no sign of the war. That was, until we heard an engine noise that Joe recognised. It began as a sort of hum and grew louder until it changed into a growl and we saw a small yellow aeroplane above us. "*Tiger Moth.*" Joe told us. "*Trainer from the airfield*", he added, pointing in the opposite direction.

It wasn't something you saw every day and even the dogs sat watching. Assuming it would fly straight over the field, the three of us stood shielding our eyes from the sun gazing into the air as the little yellow machine flew past. We watched as it began to circle, slowly losing height and performing the same action, circled once more until Joe said, *"They're landing."*

Stevie and I looked on with wonder, as the pilot brought the aircraft to the ground where it bounced a few times before coming to a standstill on the grass below us.

"Cor, weren't that good?" Stevie shouted excitedly. And just as it landed, it turned and trundled off again lifting into the air as if by magic. *"Off again".* Joe said, *"Teaching some poor young'un to fly so's he can be shot at by the Hun."* He said under his breath.

"I'm gonna do that one day," Stevie assured us. *"In a bigger one than that though."* He promised.

The Tiger Moth flew off into the distance and Joe reminded us that we had to get back to eat otherwise there'd be hell to pay, but just as we turned away from the view, we heard the familiar humming sound again. Thinking it was the little yellow plane, we stopped to watch, except what we saw flying towards us this time wasn't a little yellow plane; what we saw was incredible.

A dense, black cloud of what could have been a swarm of insects was heading our way. Without knowing who, or what they were, Joe told us to quickly lay on the grass although It wasn't long before he mouthed, *"RAF. They're ours'"* and we stood up. The thunderous roar was the loudest thing I'd ever heard - even louder than on that awful day. We covered our ears but even then, it was deafening. Despite their size, the horses ran around the field in sheer terror, until the swarm began to break up and batches of planes flew off in different directions.

Some were immediately above us. Stevie was jumping up and down shouting, *"Yahoo! Yahoo!"* Joe waved at them furiously and the dogs were in a frenzy chasing their tails and barking madly. My heart was thumping like a sledgehammer as I blew kisses and shouted, *"Come back safely."* It was such a thrilling sight; one I would always remember with a mixture of fear and pride of what would come to be known as 'The Battle of Britain'.

With the noise gone and the sky empty again, the horses settled down and we left them chewing the grass as if nothing had happened. The dogs didn't settle down though and we walked with them running backwards and forwards in an excited state while we chatted in our own excited state about the spectacle we'd seen. Reaching the farmhouse door, we removed our boots and the dogs headed for the range. Joe shouted his usual, *"Hey-Hey. Did you see the planes? Well, of course you did, you couldn't miss them!"* but this time, there was no reply from Gladys.

For once, the kitchen table hadn't been laid and there was no sign of anything bubbling away merrily on the range, or even a hint of the smell of bread. Gladys sat at the table holding a handkerchief with Alec on one side and Linda on the other. Her eyes were red and watery, and her face was very blotchy as if she were all hot and bothered. On the table in front of her was a letter, which she picked-up and held out to Joe. None of us spoke until Joe read it, said, *"Oh"* and sat down. Stevie looked as confused as I felt and we both sat quietly in our chairs hoping for an explanation.

It seemed that the rollercoaster we were travelling on was set to continue. Our lives were lurching from one lovely thing to the next disaster and today was no exception. The letter was from a relative in Birmingham giving Gladys the terrible news that the city had endured heavy bombing and that her younger sister had been killed along with her two children.

Joe took Gladys upstairs to their bedroom. Linda went into the pantry and returned with some cold meat, a dish of butter and what was left of yesterday's bread, while I filled the kettle from the pump and placed it on the range to boil. Stevie and Alec sat still for a while, and once the food was dished-up onto plates they both began to eat. We finished with tea and an apple each and when Linda and I had cleared everything away, Linda took a tray of tea up to Gladys and Joe.

Alec left the table and went to the back door, returning just as quickly holding a rectangular-shaped piece of wood, which he offered to me. I was rather confused, until I remembered that I had asked for a base for the jigsaw. Thanking him very much, he went out through the same door with the dogs.

"*Well*", Linda said, scratching her head, "*Now what? They'll need to go to Birmingham for the funerals, it's just lucky that we've finished drilling.*" I was worried about Stevie. He hadn't said anything. He moved his truck up and down the table, but I knew he was taking-in every word. "*How long will they be gone, do you think?*" I asked Linda. She bit her lips while thinking and then said, "*With all the disruption, a day to get there, a day to get back. Maybe three days there. They'll have to go tomorrow – the letter took four days to get here and the funerals are on Wednesday.*"

"*What's funerals?*" Stevie asked, while he moved his truck slowly around the table with one finger. I took my time to explain in the best way I could. I said a funeral was a way to say goodbye to someone when they had died and that afterwards they were safe in the churchyard, while all their love and feelings went up to heaven, as I had explained before.

"*Is that what them big stones with names are for then?*" Stevie asked. "*They're all under the ground?*" Linda and I nodded. Stevie carried on wheeling his truck.

Joe came downstairs. He looked awful. The dogs stood up, wagging their tails assuming they were going out with him. Joe spoke sharply to them and they sat down again disappointed with his response. He asked Linda if she would be able to handle the farm while he was gone and then added, "*If only ...*" Unable to finish the sentence he went back upstairs.

"*Stevie,*" I said, "*Go and get your jigsaw. You can use this nice piece of wood to put it on.*" While he was gone, I told Linda that I would do anything to help and that we would be fine. "*We'll hold the fort.*" I said. Linda nodded, saying she had better look in the pantry to see what she could rustle-up for supper and I went with her. While we were scanning the shelves for inspiration, I asked about the photograph upstairs.

"I know I shouldn't have", I said apologetically clutching a jar of pickled carrots, "*But I couldn't help noticing the picture of that young soldier beside their bed. Who is he?*"

"*Toby*", Linda replied. "*You've noticed that Gladys always sets an extra place at the table, haven't you? It's for him.*"

"*Toby?*" I asked. "*Alec's twin brother.*" She went on. "*My friend at the pub knows everything going on and before her mum died, she'd been great friends with Gladys. The story goes that Toby had begged his Dad to let him go off to France, but he was needed here on the farm, then he went and joined up in the July of 1918.*"

"*But he wasn't killed in the war though, was he?*" I asked, "*His name isn't on the memorial in the village.*" Shaking her head slowly, she replied, "*Nope. Ironically, just before the Armistice, he was shipped back to England with serious wounds. Trouble was the doctors decided they were self-inflicted, and he was going to be Court Marshalled. If he'd been found guilty, he would either go to prison, or be shot but before that could happen, he died of Spanish Flu.*"

I put the carrots back on the shelf.

She went on. "*No name on the memorial because he was seen to be a coward. He was buried in the village churchyard and some people didn't even want that, let alone have his name on the stone.*" I was visibly shaken enough for Linda to put a hand on my shoulder. "*And Alec,*" I asked gingerly, "*Was he always ….. Was he born, slow?*" Linda shook her head. "*The boys caught Chickenpox when they were thirteen. Toby completely recovered, but somehow Alec had it badly and it affected his brain. Simple as that.*" Linda said, lifting two tins of corned beef off a shelf. So now I knew. I was shocked and terribly upset for Gladys and Joe. How dreadful for them. Two sons. Their lives taking such different and tragic paths.

There were plenty of potatoes, a cabbage, carrots, and the corned beef, so Linda said she'd make a Hash, whatever that was. The pheasants hanging in the pantry smelt bad and one of the heads had fallen off onto the floor. Linda kicked it out into the hall for the dogs to find, which I thought was rather unpleasant. Stevie was back at the table with his truck and the jigsaw. He emptied out the pieces and we rummaged through them to find the straight edges, positioning them on the wood. I was sure we'd be alright – the three of us and Alec. The dogs would be a comfort too, but I still felt uneasy at the thought of Joe and Gladys being away for so long.

Linda made a grand job of the Hash, which she'd put in an enormous enamel dish covering it with a tray until it was time to put it in the oven and by the time she'd finished, we'd found a lot of the sky shown in the picture on the jigsaw box. Alec came in with three dead rabbits and a jar of honey and I asked Linda where they'd come from. *"He didn't kill them with a gun, did he?"* I asked quietly. *"He doesn't have a gun, does he?"* Linda assured me that Alec didn't use a gun, although rumour has it that he was an amazing shot before he caught Chickenpox. Joe kept his shotgun above the back door and Alec knew he wasn't allowed to touch it. These rabbits were trapped by Kenny, the local poacher who while providing customers with rabbits, hares, pheasants, and ducks, also gave them a jar of honey from his own bees. It was 'fair game', Joe would say, which would make Linda laugh.

What a sad story. Alec being brain damaged by something as ordinary as Chickenpox and Toby dying of Influenza, although I suppose it was better than being shot by our own army. Their twin sons virtually wiped out within a few years of each other and now Gladys had lost three of her closest family; children as well. My worries were nothing in comparison. I wondered how Dad was getting on and if Nan had fallen out with Auntie Win yet – *that was inevitable.* I must write to them both tonight.

Before we could have supper there were many chores. The chickens had to be checked for new laid eggs and be put to bed in their shed, Mildred had to have fresh water and oats, Roger and the goat had to be fed and she and the cows had to be milked. Stevie and I followed Linda around, helping wherever we could. Stevie was much more useful than me with his natural ability around animals. I tried not to look at Bonnie who had cornered a rat, or the one-eared cat. It wasn't only his appearance that made me feel queasy, he was chewing a mouse that wasn't quite dead and the crunching sound from each bite was horrible. Obviously, Stevie had to investigate each of these incidents. He was a boy after all.

Linda was marvellous and knew exactly how and when to do everything. I admired her so much but had to admit that I was a little envious at the same time. The cows had been plugged in to the machine attached to the generator and above the noise, I asked Linda where in the country she had come from. She said that her home was in Surrey but had been educated at a boarding school in Sussex. Unable to become the type of person her parents wished for, she had jumped at the chance to get away with the Land Army and live the way she wanted. Her dream of becoming a Jockey would probably not be fulfilled, but at least she could be with animals and feel free. Years later, I discovered that she was in fact, Lady Lucinda Cavendish, the daughter of an Earl.

It was gone six o'clock by the time we finished everything. With her foresight and planning, Linda ran ahead of us to put the Hash in the oven. I was exhausted, although she'd done all the work. Where her energy came from, I wasn't sure, but I grew to like her more and more each day. Stevie said he was 'starving' and I told him off saying he didn't know the meaning of the word. We rinsed our hands under the water pump but then decided we needed to spend a penny, so it was necessary to wash them again after visiting the dreaded toilet shed.

While we waited for the Hash to cook, we helped light the oil lamps and close the shutters on the windows for the blackout. The kitchen was warm and peaceful, the dogs were snoring, and Stevie wheeled 'Trucky' round and round the table again. For the moment, there was no war and I turned my mind to compiling the letters I wanted to write. I would ask Dad how things were in the city and to tell him to look after himself. I would ask Nan what she had been playing on the piano lately, what the weather was like on the coast and let her know that I was still in charge of Stevie and living on a farm; she would be proud of me.

Linda took more tea upstairs for Joe and Gladys, but it wasn't a surprise to hear that neither of them wanted to eat so I laid four sets of knives and forks on the table. Alec seemed to spring from the shadows whenever food was ready, and this evening was no exception. He stared at the table for quite a while before sitting down and I thought he must be studying Stevie's truck, but when he went to the dresser carefully picking up three more knives and forks, I realised my mistake.

"Oh, thank you, Alec," I said in a matter-of-fact sort of way, *"The other knives and forks, of course."*

Taking them from his hands, I quickly laid three more places at the table, with Linda acknowledging my reaction by looking up to heaven. The Hash was good and very filling. The plums and custard afterwards a treat and a cup of tea finished it all off. Linda had done another marvellous job. Stevie was falling asleep at the table and although his tummy was full, I took a candle and led him to our room, where he had a cursory wash and was soon asleep with 'Trucky'.

Needing to use the table to write my letters, I went back downstairs with my notepad. If I could finish them tonight, we could walk to the village to post them although this time, we must remember to take Stevie's Identity Card. Linda sat at the other end of the table reading 'The Land Girl' magazine. She caught me glancing at her every now and then and smiled. There was much more to write about than I thought although I said much the same in each of the letters, but I was sure the fact that I had written at all would be enough to satisfy them. Linda said she was going to bed and rather than stay downstairs alone, we turned down the wicks in the oil lamps, opened the shutters and I did the same. Passing Gladys and Joe's room there was a hardly a sound. I hoped they were asleep.

Realising I had slept quite well, another day dawned and then I remembered the awful news that Gladys had received about her sister. Was the husband away fighting I wondered. Did he even know what had happened to his family? Why, oh why are we at war with Germany anyway? It was all so ridiculous. With Birmingham being bombed so badly would it be safe for Gladys and Joe to be there? What if they were killed and didn't come back? There I went again. Questions, questions.

Stevie had poured a minute amount of water into the bowl and proceeded to dab a wet finger behind his ears as if putting on perfume, but it really didn't matter if he wasn't clean. In the last few days, I had begun to change my mind about a lot of things and cleanliness was now exceptionally low down on my list of importance.

We crept downstairs because the house was unusually quiet. Perhaps Gladys and Joe were still asleep. Dealing with our chamber pots as quietly as we could, I cursed the water pump for making such a creaking noise and went into the kitchen on tiptoe. There was no sign of anyone – not even the dogs but there was a note on the table which read,

"4am: Lesley, Taken Gladys and Joe to the station in the trap, as they have to catch the 8.30 train from London. Have told Alec to let the chickens out and collect the eggs, feed the other animals and muck-out. Hope he understood. If you can make sure he has, I'd be grateful and If you felt able to attach the cows to the machine and milk the goat too, that would be very helpful because they'll be in pain if left too long; you've seen me do it a few times. Back by noon after stopping at the pub. Linda. PS: Don't let the fire in the range go out. Keep it stoked."

Milk the cows? Milk the goat? Fire? I took a sharp intake of breath and sat down with the note to make sure I had read it correctly. Well, yes, I'd seen her operate the machine twice, but to put me in charge of something like that and get milk out of the goat with my bare hands was another thing. Why couldn't I have been told to collect the eggs?

"*We 'avin tea?*" Stevie asked. I was unable to answer immediately and stared at the note hoping I had read it wrongly. "*Erm, yes, of course and some bread and butter and ... anything else we can find in the pantry.*" I replied. He dashed to the pantry and I followed. He was standing there with hands on his hips looking at the jars and potions as if he were surveying his kingdom. I noticed the head of another pheasant had dropped off and kicked it out into the hall as Linda had; maybe I had some 'country bumpkin' in me after all.

"*Shall we 'ave some of that stuff?*" Stevie said, pointing to the remains of the Hash. "*No.*" I replied curtly. Tea, bread and butter and an apple was quite enough for breakfast. While we ate, I thought about the milking machine and remembered that it was first filled with petrol, but for the life of me couldn't think what came next. As for the fire in the range, there was a pile of wood outside under a tarpaulin; I'd deal with that first. "*Well, Stevie.*" I tried to say cheerfully, "*We've got our work cut out for us.*"

I went on to explain Linda's instructions. His face lit-up and before I could finish, he'd gone through the front door like a steam train to collect the wood. While I rinsed our cups and tidied things away, he returned struggling to walk, or even see where he was going with a huge pile of logs in his arms. Unable to hang on to them any longer, he dropped the lot with a thud onto the floor beside the range and disappeared again.

Realising the log basket in the corner of the kitchen was already full and the amount we now had, I was sure we wouldn't need the second load he brought in, but having put so much effort into the task, I didn't have the heart to say that there were now more logs inside the house than under the tarpaulin. I picked up a few smaller sticks and copying my move, Stevie did the same. Lifting the cast iron lid with the long hook, we peered into the hole. It was difficult to know

113

how much wood to drop in, but surely if the fire kept going, it must be okay. Filling it to the top with each piece Stevie enthusiastically handed me, leaving just enough room to replace the lid we'd come back soon to check on it. Even this was an achievement and Stevie and I looked at each other with a great sigh.

"*Now for the cows.*" I said confidently.

Stevie was off again with 'Trucky' in his pocket, skipping in great leaps towards the cowshed where Daisy Mae and Tess looked pleased to see him and I followed slowly deep in thought. By the look of things, Alec had fed and watered the cows, which was something and the stall looked as though it had been swept and washed down. The girls fidgeted making their udders swing, which looked heavy and full and I hoped they didn't sense my apprehension, because my mind was in a whirl as I tried to think what to do next.

Using logic, it was quite simple. We have two cows and a milking machine. The milk is taken out of the cows and ends up in the churns. All I need to do is complete the bit in between. Four shiny milk churns sat beside the machine. Were they the ones we should use? I lifted the top off one and was almost knocked over with the smell that came out. Not that one then. I tried the next churn, which smelt just as bad. Slowly lifting the lid of the next one, I was ready for the same overpowering smell, but this time it smelt of nothing, thank goodness and neither did the one next to it. Two clean churns. Good, we were well on the way to reaching our goal.

Stevie dragged the petrol can out of the alcove and I found the funnel and between us, we managed to remove the cap and pour some fuel into the chamber. Then we stood back looking at the machine hoping it would tell us what to do next. Stevie looked backwards and forwards between the cows and the machine and said,

"*We 'ave to wash our 'ands an put on that white dress.*"

He was quite right. I pictured Linda washing her hands and donning the gown before connecting the tube things to the cows but had no idea where she kept the gown. We went to the pump, washing our hands well and hoped this would suffice on this one occasion and returned to battle with the machine. It didn't seem to have an on-off switch, so I turned my attention to the equipment. The long rubber tubes were hung over a pole and this was attached to ropes on a beam using the same principle as the drying rack over the kitchen range allowing it to be raised up and down. Releasing the rope from its hook, it was a relief to see the tubing on the pole drop to knee height and not crash onto the concrete floor. The pole swung from side to side, the tubing dangled in readiness and for a moment, all was calm.

Now what?

"*The fire!*" Stevie hollered – his shriek making me jump, as he dashed off towards the kitchen. "*Don't let the range fire go out*", Linda said. Must keep it stoked, I mumbled and ran after him. Noticing us leaving, Daisy Mae and Tess began to 'moo' loudly, and I shouted, "*Won't be a minute,*" which of course, they didn't understand at all.

We fed the range fire with more wood and then ran back to the cowshed. This was exhausting work. Time was moving on and the thought of the cows being in pain was awful. Stevie sucked-in his lips and looked up into the beams above us for inspiration and then began to point between the generator and the cows as if he were conducting an orchestra.

Yes, he had the right idea. The tubing had to be stuck onto the udders. I took one of the tubes, which had two black cuplike bits on the end and pulled it over to Daisy, who helpfully lifted a leg. This was easy. Yes, I had the hang of it I thought. But when I tried to attach it to the teats, it promptly fell to the ground. We stared at it on the floor and Daisy put her foot down again; I'm sure she was 'huffing'.

"*It's gotta suck. We 'ave to switch the thing on first.*" Stevie said. "*Oh, and we forgot the washing of them fings,*" he added *pointing to the udders.* I nodded. He was right again. However, taking a good hard look at the pendulous bags, I decided they wouldn't be having a wash today.

Stevie had more common sense than me because he was quite right, we had to switch the generator on, but how? We went over it with a fine toothcomb. There was no switch. I tried to picture Linda operating the machine, while Stevie playfully spun the big wheel on the side. I could almost hear him thinking. Asking me to do this job was above and beyond my capabilities and although loath to admit defeat, thought I'd have to. It was then that Stevie triumphantly picked up the metal handle in the alcove, which fitted the centre of the wheel perfectly. Clever boy! His memory was better than mine. Of course, this started the motor. Now all we had to do was turn it fast enough to get it going.

I began turning as fast as I could until my arm hurt. Then Stevie tried. We were like Laurel and Hardy, egging each other on to turn the wheel faster and faster and getting nowhere. Then I remembered Linda saying there was a 'knack' to this. We were failing though. It just wouldn't work and if we didn't stoke the range soon, we would have failed with that too. Reluctantly, we downed tools and ran off once again to do the only job that we were capable of it seemed. With the fire stoked, I thought we should have a go at milking the goat, which surely had to be easier than using that machine, but to our amazement, we heard the noise of the generator coughing and spluttering between the odd 'bang'. There must have been some sort of delay in it starting up, or maybe we did have the 'knack' after all. We ran back to the shed, where the generator was working at full steam, or whatever the expression was and standing beside it, was Alec and the dogs. Bonnie growled as soon as she saw me. It was obvious we'd never be friends.

Bella came towards us in a friendly way though and laid down when Stevie began to stroke her gently. It was both a relief and a disappointment to see that Alec had started the engine, but I thanked him very much anyway. He watched as I clumsily attached the cow part of the tubing and cup-things to the udders and the vacuum pump began to do its work. I could have sworn that Alec smiled when we realised that I hadn't anchored the other end into the churn, so milk was flowing out onto the ground. Stevie dived onto the straw to catch the end, which saved me from further embarrassment, but it took several attempts to make the connection with the churn and our boots were white with milk.

For a moment, I felt victorious. Stevie and I stood together with hands on hips jubilantly, until I began to think that the churn was filling up faster than it should. How do I stop everything happening and move it to the other cow and the next churn? Disconnect the cow from the machine? Switch it off without a switch? My heart began to race and raced even more when I realised that Alec and the dogs had gone.

I had said before that I was not religious, but I don't think I'm the only person to ask for God's help in an emergency; the incident in the church with Stevie proves my point, I think. Well, I did that again – prayed for assistance, which came in the shape of the strangest of people. Above the noise of the generator, we heard the tinkle of a bicycle and who should pedal into the courtyard, but the Postman. I ran over to him. *"Gladys in?"* He said, asking the same question of us as yesterday. I quickly told him the sad story from the letter he delivered and that I was somehow in charge of things until Linda returned. I also admitted that I was in a bit of a pickle with the milking. *"Pickle, is it?"* He replied. *"Let's see then."*

Leaving the bicycle in the same place, The Postman took off his jacket and cap, rolled-up his sleeves and washed his hands at the pump. My relief was obvious when I realised that he knew exactly what to do. I asked his name and introduced Stevie and I at the same time. How marvellous that a Postman called Donald could turn his hand to this sort of thing and how stupid I was that I was unable to work a milking machine. When he'd finished and had rolled the churns into the darker part of the cowshed, Donald told me to fill the smelly ones with water, so they would be easier for Linda to deal with when she returned, and this Stevie and I did without mishap.

117

Donald's post sack was hanging on his bicycle and after donning his uniform jacket, he rifled inside and bought out a letter handing it to me saying, "*I wondered who Miss L. Carter was, care of Middlewych Farm.*" It was a surprise to receive something and instantly thought it was from Dad. 'Saint' Donald went on his way after the greatest of thanks and Stevie and I went into the kitchen where we stoked the fire yet again. I didn't recognise the writing on the envelope, but it was stamped 'Whitechapel E.C.1' and although I was keen to open it, decided that we should eat something first; all this tension had made us hungry and we still had the goat to milk. 'Trucky' came out of the safe place in Stevie's trouser pocket and had a bit of an airing round and round the table, while I put the kettle on the range, which was so hot the water was boiling in less than a minute. We were good Stokers at least.

I stuffed the letter in my dungarees while we had a cup of tea and took a slice of bread and butter out with us to where the goat was tethered. She looked at us so angrily, I was sure she was frowning. We stood looking at her from a safe distance while we ate our bread, glad that she was tethered. "*We need a clean pail and the three-legged stool,*" I told Stevie. "*Stool's in our room, ain't it?*" He replied, skipping towards the house. I looked at my boots, knowing that I would have spent a long time looking for it, since I'd forgotten it was there and that once again, Stevie's mind was sharper than mine. The goat made the usual strange noise, but this time I thought she was laughing at me. Stevie returned with the stool, which he set beside the goat and seeing it, she hopped-up onto the wooden milking crate while Stevie skipped away again knowing exactly where to find the clean pail. I would have to spur myself on a bit more to survive on the farm; I just wished I had Stevie's insight.

The squeaky pump halted my daydream and I joined Stevie to wash my hands. Of course, he had found the pail and before I finished shaking the water from my hands, it was positioned at the udder end of the goat. It all seemed to come quite naturally to him. Offering me the stool with his open hand as if he were a salesman selling a new product, he grinned in anticipation of what was to come.

Clapping my hands together and taking one of those deep breaths when courage was required, I sat on the stool, and poked the udder. But before I was able to make any progress, Stevie screamed, *"No, no, naughty goat."* He had lunged towards the head end of the goat, where I saw with horror that she was chewing my letter! I couldn't believe it and felt in my pocket, knowing it wouldn't be there, looking in disbelief at the remains in Stevie's hands.

"Oh no." I moaned, *"I don't even know who it's from."*

"Not too bad," Stevie said reassuringly, *"Be a bit like a jigsaw, we're good at them."* Then handing the tattered envelope to me, he sat on the stool and began to milk the goat as if it were the most natural thing in the world. I took what was left of my letter into the kitchen, where I stoked the fire; at least that was alright and using a knife to saw round the tooth marks, carefully pulled three pieces of paper from the envelope opening them out on the table. The letter was from Mrs. Johnson, that much was clear. A few words were missing and some of them were smudged by goat saliva, but I was able to piece together the gist of what she was telling me.

Unfortunately, the Police had made no progress with their investigations into Stevie's family. Her job had become even more difficult and demanding, especially since her own home was without water and electricity and she and her husband had moved into a room at the hospital, which was bursting at the seams. Morale was exceptionally low everywhere and no one was able to get enough sleep because of the constant air raids and working long hours.

It was depressing to read her words and immediately, I thought of Dad; my letter to him must go in the post today. Surely, I would be told if anything bad happened to him. I read on, not expecting much more, so I was surprised when I came to this part, having to decipher the words thanks to the goat.

"*My Dear Lesley.*

Trusting you and your charge are well.

I   relieved to know that you   n a safe part of the country and feel sure that the   air will have done you both good. However, I have news that I hope you will view as making a different   of progress. I have taken the liberty of securing a position for   as a teacher at Witherleigh Hall, a boys' boarding school in Wiltshire, where staff are in short supply.

Consequently, we ask that you remain Steaphan's guardian for the time   . His education can continue there, while you are able to utilise your skills and earn a modest   , with your lodging costs being   of.

Whether or not, you decide to move on once Steaphan is relocated, will be a matter   , but I believe this to be a more suitable   rather than have you alloc   in another remote area.

You will need to   your professional credentials and make the journey on the   . I have enclosed Travel Warrants from Paddin   and assuming it will take time to make your way there,   you aim to catch the train to Lond   , which leaves at half-past two that day. Once there, I am told the school is   ride away.

luck.

Annabelle."

I read the last part three times, filling in the words as best I could and discovered the warrants ticked inside the envolope, thankfully intact.

Just two days away.

We had to leave the farm in two days' time.

CHAPTER EIGHT

Prowlers, or Predators?

My emotions were all mixed up. I couldn't think straight. Did we have to go? Could they make us go? If only I could speak to Dad, or Nan, but there wasn't time for that. How would Stevie feel about going to a boarding school? How did I feel about teaching in a boarding school? No, we won't go. We were happy here on the farm.

We were certainly happy on the farm and in a short space of time, had settled into country life; well at least Stevie had. To leave for a job teaching in a big school with no animals and living there too, was quite out of the question. I had decided to join the Land Army anyway and Stevie could go to the local school; what was wrong with that? This was the selfish Lesley talking. In my heart I knew we couldn't stay. The other Land Army girls were expected and had there been news of Stevie's family, of course, he would be leaving me sooner, or later anyway. He had to have an education and maybe this would be just what he needed. Maybe it was what I needed too. My career hadn't exactly taken off with a great start, had it?

I decided to break the news to Stevie by way of making it a great adventure as soon as I had told Linda what was going on; I needed to ask her a favour anyway, so put the letter in my pocket and went outside. Roger was playing with his ball of string, which was amusing Stevie no end. Each nudge of the filthy mess caused laughter that turned into a croak the more he laughed. He was beginning to look much healthier now. No longer skinny, no pale face covered in Impetigo and even his teeth seemed to be taking their rightful places, although that could have been wishful thinking. Stevie had managed to express half-a-pail of milk from the goat. I told him I was extremely impressed and that it would make wonderful cheese. I had no idea if it would make wonderful cheese, but he seemed terribly proud of himself and that was all that mattered. We carried the pail together into the pantry, where there was a basket full of eggs courtesy of Alec and as the mix of aromas had become even more unusual, quickly closed the door.

It was then that we heard Mildred's hooves clattering on the cobblestones and went outside to greet Linda. Following them to the stable, where Mildred seemed glad to be uncoupled from the trap, Linda told us that Gladys and Joe caught the local train, which was on time although they'd been warned of massive disruption on the main line from the city to Birmingham and would get there, when they got there. Then she asked how things had gone at the farm and I told the truth, singing Stevie's praises. He blushed and drove 'Trucky' around through the air while making engine noises to cover his secret delight of this recognition and Linda patted him on the back, which made him smile.

I asked Linda what if anything, I could prepare for our late midday meal and supper and tried not to look horrified when she asked if I knew how to pluck and skin a pheasant. I told her that I was willing to learn, but neither of us believed Stevie when he said that he'd "*done loads.*" Fortunately, Linda said she would deal with the three hanging in the pantry, with Stevie's help, if I would cook them. At this, I nodded with all the aplomb of an experienced chef, along with that sinking feeling I had with each new encounter.

Pheasant for supper sounded very grand and it was in the back of my mind when I scoured the pantry for something quick to have straight away. What was foremost in mind though, was the impending move and how I would break it to Stevie. With only a crust of bread on the shelf, I decided to cut some of the mouldy-looking cheese and chop the last of the bacon which was going green. The most bruised apples should be used-up and I'd pick some tomatoes and anything else I could find in the vegetable garden and went out there to have a look at what was dangling from the stalks.

I found broad beans, plenty of tomatoes and a cabbage, which I picked making sure I didn't identify the proximity of the toilet shed to the growing area and took it all inside to wash. With the bacon, beans and cabbage cooked on the range, I rolled-up cubes of cheese in the leaves, sliced the apples and tomatoes and mixed the beans with the bacon. When I'd put everything together in a big bowl, I had to congratulate myself, because it all looked rather tasty and colourful. Carefully laying the table with seven places, Alec and the dogs sensed the food and came into the kitchen. Alec looked a little concerned that Gladys wasn't there, but Linda's presence and the table arrangement seemed to do the trick. We ate the lot and I was rather pleased with myself because I had somehow managed to prepare a decent meal.

A little later, Linda was cleaning the smelly milk churns and rather than disturb her, I sat on a bale of hay until she had finished. Watching her work, I realised I'd miss her. She was a wonderful person; not exactly feminine but that made me feel safe somehow, which was an odd thing to feel about a woman. The churns were very heavy and awkward to hold, although Linda was making light work of scrubbing them out and that was another noticeable thing - her strength.

Stevie skipped into the cowshed and I thought this would be a good opportunity to tell them both together about our move, so did exactly that. I made it sound as exciting as I could, but really wasn't ready for the reaction from either of them. I'd come to the part where we would need to catch a bus from Swindon Station when Stevie suddenly ran off. Linda chased after him, leaving me sitting on the hay bale alone. "*That went well*", I mumbled to myself sarcastically.

Walking into the courtyard, they were nowhere in sight. Standing there, I closed my eyes and turned my face to the warm sun. I could hear birdsong and the dogs barking in the distance, which no longer alarmed me. I knew that I would forever recognise the distinct smell of cows and even quite liked it. I had ridden a horse and helped to make silage, which I didn't know existed. I would always be able to picture the funny chickens running around urgently, the mad goat who ate anything and knew I could always conjure up a picture of Roger and his ball of string. With more challenges in these last few weeks than I ever thought possible, it had been the most unnatural time of my life. More importantly, I had cared for a little boy and helped him through dire circumstances and these experiences had surely widened my limited knowledge of the world.

Walking out of the farmyard, I gave Roger a pat, something I could not have done before living on the farm and passing the stream, saw Linda sitting on the bank dangling her feet in the water. I sat beside her, kicked off my boots and did the same; it would be nice to have clean toes for a change although the cold water was almost painful on my skin. I asked if she knew where Stevie was, and she pointed a finger up to the sky. My frown told Linda that I didn't know what she meant and she silently mouthed, "*In the tree.*" The massive branches above us held crinkly-brown brown leaves and amongst dozens of spiky green conker cases I saw a hand holding 'Trucky'.

"Oh, well," I said loudly, "*I'll just have to go to the new place on my own. I don't know how I'll manage though. I shall ask Gladys and Joe if I can come back here for a holiday in the spring, but it won't be the same if I'm alone.*"

Stevie stayed put. I knew he'd heard what I said, and I could feel him watching as we walked barefoot back to the edge of the farm. I had never walked on grass without shoes and felt connected to the ground, a strange feeling which I vowed to repeat. There were many things I wanted to repeat. Another was cooking; maybe even grow my own vegetables. One day perhaps even live on a farm.

Linda went off to finish the chores for the day saying that she would be back soon to deal with the pheasants and hoped that Stevie was down from the tree by then. I went back to the house thinking about supper rather than our move and decided to roast some potatoes, stuff the pheasants with apples, onions and herbs of some kind and mix a few vegetables together. The range would need to be hot, so I stoked the fire; something I was now quite good at and did with ease, then picked some runner beans, and pulled up the last of the carrots.

I'd noticed earlier that the Blackberry bush growing in the hedgerow near the stream was laden with fruit and by the time I eventually coaxed Stevie out of the tree, he had watched me pick a bucketful of berries. The sun was setting fast and it was a little chilly, but I think it was hunger rather than anything else that eventually persuaded him down. Linda was waiting for him outside the front door with the pheasants in a pail and without a word, Stevie sat beside her, his eyes firmly on the birds. Not wishing to witness the gutting and preparation, I made an excuse to go inside and left them to it, hoping that Stevie wouldn't be traumatised at the sight of death all over again.

I laid the table in the correct way, scrubbed the carrots and stringed the beans. As I said, the range would need to be hot to cook the pheasants and roast the potatoes, so I piled as much wood as possible into the top, doing so without burning my fingers; strange how you can quickly get used to doing something completely unfamiliar. Stevie came in carrying the pail containing the innards, claws, and skin. I asked him where the heads were and before I'd finished asking, remembered that the dogs had already had two of those. Linda followed him in, saying that he was a natural feather 'plucker' and that she was surprised at the way he was able to handle the job.

Although secretly pleased with yet another acknow-ledgement, Stevie was still sulking after the news of our impending move, His silence at supper was a combination of having his mouth full most of the time as well as feeling grumpy, but at least he ate everything on his plate. We finished with Blackberries, Rhubarb, and runny honey and even Alec seemed content. The dogs were also very content by the look of their blood-stained mouths and the slimy entrail dangling from Bonnie's chin.

As predicted, Alec left the table the minute he had cleaned his plate and as sure as '*eggs-is- eggs*', the dogs followed. No one seemed to know where they went. His bedroom didn't look as though it was ever used, and it was surprising that he didn't smell bad, considering he was always in the same clothes. As I mentioned earlier though, my priorities had changed so much recently, that cleanliness wasn't so important anymore.

I cleared away the dishes, while Linda prepared the blackout. Stevie was busy pushing 'Trucky' around the table and with just the three of us in the kitchen, I thought it was as good a time as any to continue with my news. *Well, Stevie,*" I said happily, "*What an adventure we're going to have.*" He stopped the truck but didn't look up.

"*Yes,*" Linda chimed in. "*You'll be with lots of other boys and be able to play Rugby*". Linda obviously had inside information on this subject, although I doubted Stevie knew what Rugby was. We struggled to gain his attention and with these words making no impression, packed him off to bed. I joined him soon after and then Linda knocked on our door. She came in ready for bed wearing men's pyjamas, her hair pulled back off her face in a short ponytail accentuating her high cheekbones. I envied her thick eyebrows and with her sharp features and weather-beaten skin, thought she really could have passed for a man. I wondered if she would have preferred that.

We sat on my bed and with Stevie fast asleep, went into greater detail about the job and the school. She thought the whole thing was a good idea and would be perfect us both. I was disappointed because I hoped she'd have told me not to go and that I would make a good Land Army girl, but no. I knew she was right and the chances of me making a good Land Army girl were almost nil. We went on to plan the next few days, working out the time frame to get us to Paddington

Station and the onward journey to Swindon. With plans formulated, Linda whispered 'goodnight' and opened the door to leave, but hesitated, saying, *"Oh, one other thing, I'll be staying at the pub tomorrow night, but I'll be back just after dawn the next morning. My barmaid friend asked me over for supper and what with the blackout, it would be silly to try to get back in the dark. You can manage, can't you?"*

Linda could see I had nodded in approval before I blew out the candle, but any attempt at sleeping was interrupted by thoughts of Stevie and I being alone in the house and what I could find to cook for supper. Perhaps Linda would take us in the trap to the village to buy fresh supplies. With this extra plan conceived, I didn't give the word, 'manage' another thought and was relaxed enough to sleep.

Something disturbed me though. I was suddenly wide awake again and Stevie's bed was squeaking, which meant he was awake too although it was still as black as pitch outside. I knew this, because with the dawn there was usually a chink of light showing through the wood jammed in the window and it wasn't there. *"Woss going on?"* Stevie whispered. *"Woss that noise?"*

"I don't know Stevie," I replied, *"I'll look out of the window."*

Removing the piece of wood from the window, I lifted the latch and pushed the glass to open it but to my complete surprise felt a burst of fresh air as it disappeared onto the cobblestones below violently smashing into smithereens. As if this wasn't enough of a shock, the door suddenly flew open. *"Quickly, quickly, get up!"* Linda shouted before hurtling down the stairs almost without touching them.

Ignoring the latest mishap for the more urgent-sounding matter, I fumbled around in the dark and ignoring the blackout for once, lit the candle. The dim light revealed the raggedy curtains fluttering around in the breeze and a gaping hole where the window had been. Were church bells ringing? Was it the invasion? Stevie had his shoes on already and slipping into my own, I somehow managed to tread on the handle of my potty spilling some of the contents. Frustrated with my clumsiness, I cursed myself for being such an oaf; it would have to wait.

Reaching the kitchen as fast as we could, the noise of something awful carried on outside. I couldn't take a deep breath and was sure I could hear my heart beating. Linda blew out both candles and opened one of the window shutters. I shivered a little as we stood together listening and really needed the toilet. Stevie jumped up onto the bench to get a better view through the window and with the moon giving a little light between the clouds said slowly, *"There's a man."*

I didn't want to see a man. I was scared and wanted to go back to bed but peered out of the window anyway. I didn't see anything. The noise continued. I couldn't think what it was. It sounded like high pitched 'clucking' mixed with piercing screams. Was someone trying to steal the chickens? Without saying a word, Linda went towards the back door. Stevie followed and not wanting to be left alone, I went too. Stevie with his constant insight into everything opened the cupboard with the wire front and pulled at the lid of a box. Linda reached above the door, but what she wanted wasn't there. *"The gun."* She said, *"The gun has gone."* *"An' some of the shells."* Stevie chimed in.

She ran to the front door and opened it, peering out into the courtyard while at the same time, pulled on her boots. *"Stay here!"* She shouted urgently and left the house but before I knew it, Stevie had flung off his shoes, jumped into his boots and was outside. I hesitated - just for just a moment and then did the same. In the patchy moonlight, it was easier to hear than to see. Glass crunched beneath our footsteps reminding me that the window had fallen out and the other sound I recognised was the axe being wiggled out of the woodpile. Linda whispered to Stevie and with a passing cloud I saw the glint of the whittling knife in his hand. I felt faint, unable to speak as if my lips were stuck with glue and couldn't take a deep breath.

Linda was close enough for me to see her take the axe in both hands just as we heard the powerful blast of a shotgun. I jumped at least a foot into the air as it echoed around the courtyard, the sound appearing to bounce off every surface. Then another. With echoes fading, I was surprised to hear the clucking continue. Linda ran towards the chicken shed with Stevie close behind. I hesitated once again and then followed.

I wished I hadn't. I wished Stevie hadn't either. It was something he shouldn't have witnessed because when Linda lit the lantern the scene before us was indescribable. Everywhere, bloodied dead and dying chickens lay on the straw. Those still alive flapped around pathetically shedding even more feathers, while any untouched, cowered in terror. Death and suffering. Feathers, blood, and egg yolks mixed with straw. It was a nauseating sight.

"Somefing got in." Stevie said. "Why did it kill 'em an' leave 'em? Weren't it 'ungry?"

Eventually, I took my hand away from my mouth and took a deep breath. A metallic smell hit me, and I retched. Trying not to vomit, I didn't know what to say, or do and looked in Linda's direction in anticipation of her instructions. I hoped she would tell Stevie and I to go to bed. She hadn't moved, only to cast the lantern around the shed taking in the full horror and extent of the destruction.

"Alec." Linda said quietly. "Alec took the gun."

There was no sign of Alec, or whatever it was that had caused the carnage, but in the corner of the shed close to a loose board and an enormous hole in the planks of wood, was a pool of blood and bits of brown and white fur. Linda picked up a piece and whispered,

"Weasels. It was Weasels. A pack of Weasels. They bite and lick the blood. Then they move on to the next creature."

"Weasels?" I asked. "You mean like the ones in 'The Wind in the Willows'."

The look on Linda's face was enough to chastise my remark.

129

Once again, I looked stupid. This was real. Small animals had caused this mayhem; it was nothing like the book.

I didn't think I could help with the clearing-up, what with feeling sick and a little faint and thought I'd make us all a cup of tea. Linda ignored my suggestion though and told Stevie to fetch two pails from what she called '*The cold room with the green door*'. It was good of her not use the word 'slaughter-house' and Stevie dashed off to get them.

"*Right*", she said in an authoritative way, "*We need to put all the dead chickens to one side and the ones that have been bitten on the other*". Stevie returned with the pails and began to collect the dead chickens in one of them, while I watched. "*Are you just going to stand there? Or are you going to help?* Linda snapped. "*Well, I . . .*" Was my pathetic reply. "*I can sweep the floor a bit.*"

Linda shook her head and told me to get the broom. Totally deflated, I walked outside to get it knowing I would never have made a Land Army girl. Stevie once again came up trumps though and seemed to know what to do – even with this crisis; it was uncanny. By the time I came back with the broom, he had already filled one pail with dead birds and as I attempted to sweep away the bloodstained straw, watched him fill the other carefully checking to make sure that they were in fact dead. With both pails full, Linda suggested Stevie empty them out onto the 'cold room' floor and do the same again. However, the buckets were too heavy for him to carry and at last I felt useful by suggesting that I help him. I couldn't watch as he emptied out the contents in a pile onto the tiles though and kept feeling sick.

I followed him back to the shed with the empty pails, wondering how Linda would treat the chickens that were simply hurt and not dying. Can you nurse a chicken back to health? Perhaps I would be good at doing that with Stevie's help. Yes, I was quite sure I could manage this and marched into the shed to offer my services to do whatever was necessary to make them better. How naïve of me. I shouldn't have been horrified to see Linda using the axe to chop off their heads, but I was. It was all very upsetting, and I felt sick again.

At least half the chickens were dead. Linda said some of those remaining might die anyway due to shock, but we'd just have to wait and see. Once the horrible straw was removed, we sloshed buckets of water everywhere and at least I was useful at the pump. We couldn't replace the straw immediately; we'd need Alec to pull a few bales down from the haybarn to do that.

Alec. I'd forgotten all about him. He'd used the shotgun. Should he have?

Dawn replaced the moonlight. Linda went to change into her jodhpurs. There was no point in her going back to bed when the animals would soon have to be fed and the cows milked. Stevie said he wanted to help her but insisting that he try to get a little sleep, we used the foul toilet, washed at the pump, and went to our room where we changed into our clean pyjamas. I had intended to do some washing anyway and added our bloody things to the pile of dirty clothes on the floor.

It was quite chilly, probably due to the gaping hole in the window. I felt very guilty about this and wondered what Joe would say, although surely, I wasn't completely to blame. I had to make certain that the other side didn't fall out though and carefully positioned the blackout wood where it would have to stay until something more permanent could be done. This made a big difference to the chill in the air and darkened the room enough for Stevie to doze off as soon as he'd checked that 'Trucky' was still under his pillow. I slept on and off even though my mind was in a whirl and still felt sick.

By half past seven we were washed, dressed and at the back door with our potties. We both noticed the shotgun back in its place. I had mixed feelings knowing that Alec had used the gun, but he'd saved maybe half the chickens and knew exactly what he was doing. Instinct? A distant memory? We'd never know, but although I was happy that he'd probably killed some weasels in the pack, it was still rather worrying.

We swept up the broken glass outside and wrapped the pieces in newspaper. The wooden frame had rotted through, so it wasn't really my fault that it fell out. I put the kettle on, and Stevie went to find Linda. Pantry stocks were low apart from pickled vegetables, SPAM, corned beef, and very green cheese. What could we have for breakfast? Eggs wouldn't be suitable after the events of last night and there was no bread. What could I concoct?

After carefully considering the table layout, I sat down with my second cup of tea. Breakfast would be late today, which meant that our mid-day meal would be put out although with the distinct lack of food in the house that didn't matter. I hoped Linda felt able to take us into the village and would ask her when she came in.

I heard Linda and Stevie using the pump and quickly began to fry two tins of sliced SPAM and lots of potatoes. Right on cue, Alec and the dogs appeared. Both dogs had bloody muzzles, which looked dreadful. I assumed they had eaten chicken and it was abundantly clear that Alec had been up all night. His hands were red and black, and his beard matted with goodness-knows what. This morning, he smelled of something unpleasant too.

Linda told us that she had placed a couple of old tractor tyres against the loose board and the massive shotgun hole in the chicken shed, but repairs would need to be made soon. The window was more difficult. "*Sorry*", I said with a grimace. She shook her head in a forgiving sort of way and began to talk about the weasels. Alec didn't look up, but it was obvious that he knew what she was talking about. "*I hope some of those weasels are dead,*" she mused. "*I doubt they're running around with big holes in their heads though, eh Alec?*"

He didn't smile, although one side of his mouth turned up at the edges. He cleaned his plate and before I had time to tell him that Stevie and I were leaving the next day, he left the table with the dogs in tow. Maybe there would be time to do that during supper. I wasn't looking forward to being alone in the house later and wished Alec slept in his bedroom. However, I had mixed feelings about this since I was unsure about the rational side of his mind.

Linda would take us into the village, but first wanted to have a few hours' sleep. That suited me well because it would give me time to do our washing and get it on the line to dry. The most important jobs were done, and Stevie would do some of the other chores while I dealt with our laundry. We were both so busy, that the time flew by and it was suddenly half past one. As I said, there was no bread, so our midday meal was a strange mixture of corned beef and pickled vegetables. The apples I cooked were good though; well of course they were – covered in runny honey.

Linda came down looking more refreshed. I'd left a plate of food for her and she stood shovelling it into her mouth with one hand and wrestling with the money tin above the range with the other. Admitting defeat, she finished the food and used both hands to remove the lid, took out a few notes and threw them on the table. *"That should be enough,"* Linda said, *"I'll get Mildred and meet you outside."*

Assuming our usual positions in the trap, we drove to the village. Stevie and I were noticeably quiet and thoughtful on the journey and even the Home Guard were not at their post to give us some amusement. It was disappointing. As soon as we arrived at the memorial, Linda went straight into the pub to see her friend. Stevie found the bucket of water for Mildred and I joined the queue at the shop. It was ironical that we had all this down to a fine art just as we were leaving the farm.

The sweet jars were almost empty, but I asked for some anyway – even the broken bits at the bottom I said, knowing that they would be covered in a lot of sugar. There was a box of Mint Imperials on the shelf below. I was sure Gladys would like them. Dare I ask how much they are? I squeezed my little change purse to feel the contents and decided to buy them whatever the cost.

Gladys and Joe had left their Ration Books at home and as

they were expected back soon, I took advantage of their allocations by buying as much as we were allowed. The amount of money I had limited my purchases, but I felt I'd chosen wisely. I made sure the precious box of Mint Imperials sat hidden in the bottom of the basket and on top, piled two loaves of bread, a large a shank of beef, two tins of pressed meat, soup and even some bacon. Fortunately, with so many pickled vegetables in the pantry there was no need for them!

Heaving the basket into the back of the trap with Stevie, I took my seat. Linda left the pub without looking back and taking the reins, told Mildred to move on. Circling the memorial, I could see her companion sitting at a window and she watched as we drove by, but this time they didn't wave to each other. I supposed this was because they would meet again later. I was a little jealous that they had such a nice relationship and wished I too had such a good friend to spend time with; they were probably like sisters.

We didn't speak on the way back. Linda seemed far away, with a glazed look on her face, although she was obviously thinking about something pleasant because whenever I looked at her, I could see her lips were slightly upturned. Reaching the farm, I couldn't help noticing a distinct dent in one of the loaves. I held the abnormality in front of Stevie but instead of apologising for his need to nibble, he simply held up 'Trucky'.

"Oh, it was him, was it?" I said with a smile.

Linda and Stevie went off to do the afternoon chores, leaving me to put away the food; I hoped Gladys would be pleased with the choices I'd made. My other hope was that they would return from Birmingham safe, sound and soon, otherwise the beef wouldn't be used up. In the pantry, I discovered two rabbits, and a duck hanging where the pheasants had been and a small pot of honey courtesy of Kenny no doubt. I had to remember to tell Linda so she could pay him. Remembering to take our Ration Books from the pile in the basket, I was beginning to feel like a refugee.

Satisfied that we would leave the farm in good shape – *apart from the window of course*, I distributed the fresh food around the pantry shelves and left the mints on the stone shelf with a note thanking Gladys for her care. Stevie and I had learnt such a lot. Not only about living on a farm, but also about ourselves. I felt we'd moved on, although I was still worried about Stevie's emotions. Come to think of it, my own emotions had been rocked in a big way too. Bombs, death, and destruction in so many shapes and forms. Sadness, excitement, tears, and laughter; enough encounters for a lifetime, not a fortnight.

I took the basket back to the kitchen where Stevie was sitting at the table with his jigsaw. It was almost finished with only the blue sky causing a bit of a problem. It would be good to finish it before bedtime if we could - a sort of conclusion to our stay. I asked him what I should cook for supper, bearing in mind that Linda was going to the pub. He shrugged as he banged in a piece of jigsaw that obviously didn't fit. I could see he was upset and not only with the jigsaw. I sat beside him and said, "*We'll be alright, Stevie. Why not go and help Linda before supper?*" He smiled and put his hand on top of mine. It was such a tender moment, I wanted to cry but resisted the urge to hug him. As soon as he was out of sight though, I sobbed pathetically all over the potato peelings.

We were spoilt for choice as far as food was concerned, but I decided to stew some of the beef as a bit of a treat. I would have loved Linda to be with us on our last evening. She would cycle to the pub as soon as she'd finished with the animals and then we'd be alone until Alec and the dogs appeared for supper; at least we could say goodbye to them. I used up the last of the blackberries and apples, sweetening them with honey, which reminded me about paying Kenny, put them in a dish and did my best to make a pie crust top. Pastry-making was never my strong point, unlike Nan's suet crust.

Linda came down with her toothbrush and pyjamas saying that she was looking forward to having a bath at the pub. How wonderful. I was very envious. Stevie turned his nose up. She would be back at dawn, deal with the chores and then drive us in the trap to the station. We were to be ready by nine o'clock. The aroma from the range drifted through the air and Linda commented on the nice smell. "*Barbara's a good cook*, she said, "*She's good at a lot of things*", she added.

With a wrinkle in my nose, I repeated her words sarcastically under my breath. Stevie laughed and went outside to wave her off and then came back to lay the table with seven knives and forks. As I began to dish-up, Alec and his followers arrived. We ate in silence to begin with. The stew was tasty and once again, I wondered how.

When it came to cut the fruit pie, I said casually, "*Alec, Stevie and I are leaving the farm tomorrow, we're going to stay at a school for a while.*" There was no response. I really thought there would be some sort of reaction, but no. Not a thing.

"*Conkers.*" Stevie said. "*Pardon?*" I replied.

Shaking his head and looking at the ceiling, he replied. "*Can I get some? Wiv string?*"

"*We'll find some at our next place.*" I told him.

Obviously cross, he folded his arms in the way he did when he disagreed with one of my decisions and then the funniest thing happened. Alec folded his arms too. They both looked at me and shaking my head, I said again. "*There really isn't time.*"

I collected the plates and as soon as my back was turned, Alec and the dogs went on their way. I doubted we'd see them again and strangely enough felt quite sad. Thinking ahead, I cut the mould off the cheese in the pantry and made two cheese and pickle sandwiches to take with us the next day. Those and an apple each would keep us going on the journey to Swindon. I still had to pack all our things together somehow and knew that would be difficult, so quickly washed the dishes using the method taught by Gladys and went to our room, leaving Stevie to try and finish the jigsaw.

The carpet bag was so full, it wouldn't close. There hadn't been time to wash my dungarees, and reluctantly, I decided to leave them for Linda; they would be a bit short for her, but once they were washed, they'd be okay for wearing around the farm. We needed to look reasonably smart for our journey, so I chose my green dress with the Peter Pan collar and my brown cardigan. With brown shoes, I would look a bit like a tree, but it couldn't be helped. The dilemma was whether, or not to wear my one and only pair of nylons or go with the Lisle pair. Well, I was going to be a teacher again, so might as well look the part. Lisle it would be. Stevie would wear his short trousers, white shirt, long grey socks, and navy cardigan. Would this be the right time to give him his school cap?

Rubbing our shoes over produced a bit of a shine and dusting my gas mask box, I realised we hadn't thought about them since we arrived. Seeing Stevie's mask instantly took me back to that awful day. I shuddered and quickly placed it beside the carpet bag ready for the off. The envelope containing Stevie's paperwork and the lovely brooch thankfully slid safely down the side of the bag; that was terribly important and must stay safe. Looking around the room I was at first so shocked to see, I realised how lucky we had been. It was almost desolate, but I'd grown to love it. We had great hopes at the Reception Centre when we were told we would live on a farm, expecting a beautiful farmhouse with flowering window boxes, a bustling estate where handsome farmhands reared glossy-coated animals and made haystacks with gleaming pitchforks. It hadn't been like that exactly, but it didn't matter at all. When I went downstairs, I congratulated Stevie who had managed to finish the jigsaw. It was great fun messing it all up and pouring it back into the box. Then we lit a candle, turned down the wicks in the lamps, opened the shutters and went up to our room for the last time. I would never be frightened of stairs again.

"*Do we 'ave to go, Lelly?*" Stevie asked. "*Yes, we do, Stevie*", I said, "*But it doesn't mean we won't come back some day*". Before I blew out the candle, I removed the wood from the window and made sure I wound my watch. Without the blackout wood the breeze blowing through the hole was cold, but we had to rely on the sunrise to wake us up. Tomorrow was a big day.

CHAPTER NINE

A Gruelling Move

Stevie was awake before me. It was ten past six. A little earlier than I had wanted, but at least we wouldn't be late. I hoped Linda was back. Of course, she was. I wondered if Barbara had made a wonderful meal. Of course, I knew she had. Rather than go back upstairs after breakfast, we decided to say goodbye to our room and managed to take everything down with us including our potties, which we emptied and washed. Opening the shutters, brilliant sunshine flooded the kitchen with light revealing a mound of something dark and shiny on the otherwise empty table.

Stevie was there first. "*Cor!!*" He shouted. "*Cor!!*"

He couldn't believe what he was seeing, and neither could I. We both stared at the eight shiny conkers with knotted string attached. They were huge! Where had they come from? There was only one place. Alec! Alec had left them for Stevie. What a marvellous leaving present for him. Studying them one, by one, we didn't hear Linda come in. "*Good morning,*" she shouted twice. She looked very tired but was beaming.

The smell of SPAM fritters frying muffled my conversation with Linda, but right on cue, Alec and the dogs arrived. Stevie immediately stood up and went over to Alec holding out his hand. Alec just looked at it, but Stevie took his anyway pumping it up and down saying, "*Oh, thank you, Alec. Thank you.*", Alec sat at the table and seemed more interested in consuming the SPAM fritters, wolfing down three of them with several saucers of tea. He was still slurping as he stood up to go and I said hurriedly, "*Goodbye Alec. You're a lovely chap.*"

He went before there was time to say goodbye to the dogs, but there was no love lost there.

Stevie was desperate to inspect every inch of the conkers and held them up high, stroking the string and cooing over them. *"Time marches on"*, Linda said. *"Are you going to have one last walk round the farm?"* I nodded, digging deep in the carpet bag. It was now, or never to give Stevie his school cap. *"Oh, by the way"*, I said to him casually, *"Your cap turned up, you might as well wear it I suppose."* He took it from me slowly and placed it on his head. Memories flooded my mind. I hoped I'd done the right thing. Then he stood up and one by one, stuffed the conkers into his pockets. He looked very funny with bulging trousers.

I didn't know if it was a good idea to walk round the farm for the last time, but I thought if we didn't, we might regret it so that's what we did. As I stepped into the boots that had become my own, I wondered if I would ever wear Wellington's again. I'd been comfortable in my dungarees and hadn't been worried about combing my hair or concerned that I wasn't wearing lipstick. Being clean all the time seemed unnecessary although I longed for a bath knowing that things would have to change in that direction because a smelly lady teacher would be doomed.

We trod the same path, just as we had when we arrived, both still distressed by what had happened to us only a few days before. The farm we were now accustomed to wasn't what I expected, but it had opened our eyes to another world and in a few weeks had recharged our batteries for whatever was coming next.

Our first stop was with dear Roger, who was in his usual greeting position on the fence almost flattened by his weight. He was now so fat he looked as though he might burst. Under the circumstances, it was surely time for him to go and maybe that meant it was also a good time for Stevie to leave rather than witness the demise of a friend. I gave Roger a big pat, something I was no longer afraid to do, while Stevie wrapped both arms around his thick neck. We left him with his filthy string in his funny little house and had a pig been able to wave goodbye, I was sure that Roger would have.

The goat was happily chewing what looked like an old leather belt, at least we hoped it was old. I had no idea where it had come from, but she seemed to be enjoying it and the buckle was on the ground so it wouldn't be much use to anyone and at least she hadn't eaten that too. I told Stevie not to attempt to salvage the remains and deciding not to pat her we moved on. What was left of the chickens ran around in their usual panic-stricken way reminiscent of the night they were attacked; I could still hear those awful sounds and picture the grisly scene. The cows? Well, considering our milking skills, or rather the lack of them, I'm sure that like the dogs, Daisy Mae and Tess were glad to see the back of us.

Mildred was in the stable and we could say goodbye to her at the station, but I wanted to see the Shires one last time. They were enjoying a few days' rest in the top field while Joe was away and we trudged up the hill passing the stream, the conker tree, and the Blackberry bush, which was full of Blackbirds eating the remains of the fruit. Stevie ran ahead flying 'Trucky' through the air as if it were a plane and as I walked, I tried to breathe in as much of the countryside as I could. This time, the sky was filled with blue rather than aircraft. A colony of birds sat on a fence tweeting loudly, perhaps readying themselves for the long trip south and the mixture of shades in the hedgerows was something that even the best artist would find hard to recreate.

Magnificent as ever, Peggy and Polly looked up briefly before continuing to munch the grass. Stevie stroked the arch of Peggy's smooth neck speaking gently to her and I ruffled Polly's mane remembering how hard it had been to cling on to it for the ride. The girls barely noticed us, too occupied with eating to give us a second look, but it didn't matter because memories are wonderful things; they were the souvenirs we could take with us. It would have been lovely to stay there with them. To take in more of the view and the peace of that moment and smell the sweet, sharp earthy aroma of nature. But Stevie and I were heading into uncharted waters. We had to accept the next segment of our disjointed lives and move on.

Back in the courtyard Linda attached Mildred to the trap, and we loaded our luggage. I remembered our lunch at the last minute and went to collect the brown paper bag from the pantry while Linda waited in the trap. Reaching the kitchen door from the back hall, I stopped suddenly as I saw Stevie standing in front of the dresser. I was just about to ask what he was doing, when he delved into a pocketful of conkers and brought out a crayon. What was he up to? Taking a newspaper from the shelf, I watched as he tore off a piece and slowly wrote on it. Then he took something from his back pocket, carefully placing whatever it was beside the paper. He hesitated, just for a moment and then dashed outside without realising I'd been there. It was odd and I couldn't resist investigating his secret mission.

What I saw softened my eyes in the greatest of ways because on the scrap of paper Stevie had written '*for alk*' and beside it was his sixpence. If it hadn't been for Linda shouting for me to hurry up, I would probably have allowed myself to be upset; what with leaving the farm and now this, but anyone with a hint of feeling would have been touched by this gesture and for once I didn't think I was being pathetic. It took a good deep breath and some hard lip-biting to recover. Recover enough from this tender moment so I could go out into the sunshine and jump into the trap promising never to embarrass my Stevie by mentioning his generous act.

I didn't turn around to look at the farm, but Stevie was sitting with his back to us and would have had a good view of the house, the stable and a bit of the chicken shed as we drove past. He didn't cry; at least I don't think he did. What a dear sweet thing he was. The thought of him leaving me was unbearable. I truly hoped it would never happen and with each passing day, became more determined that somehow, or other I would find a way to keep him with me forever.

The station was in the opposite direction to the village and Mildred pulled us back the way we had come in the tractor all those days ago. We seemed to bob around in the trap for ages, until eventually we saw the sign for the station and took a sharp left just before the High Street. My heart sank to its lowest ebb. It was really time to say goodbye. Stevie helped Linda unload our things all too quickly until there was an awkward pause between the three of us and I felt a flood of emotion.

Through my tears, I managed to tell Linda about Kenny and rambled on about the dead things hanging in the pantry, told her to make sure she had a 'Mint Imperial', or two and that I had scraped the mould off the cheese, but completely forgot to say all the important things I'd rehearsed. Stevie's lovely eyelashes fluttered, but I was too distraught to notice if he was blinking back his own tears. I hugged Linda and then clung round Mildred's neck, hugged Linda again and started to go back to Mildred, until Stevie gently took my hand and pulled me away. Linda drove off without looking back. She was gone, seemingly without batting an eyelid and I'd behaved like a pitiful idiot again.

We were left on the gravel with our luggage and I knew I had to compose myself, but It was Stevie who fished-out the travel warrants from the carpet bag and went inside to the Booking Office. What would I do without him? He returned, saying we had to hurry because we would need to go over the bridge to the platform on the opposite side. The train to Liverpool Street was due any minute, at least that was what Stevie had been told by the *'man wiv the 'at'*. If we weren't on that, we might miss the connection from Paddington to Swindon.

If only I could be a stronger person, perhaps I'd be able to manage these situations in a more positive way. Mum was strong, Nan was strong, and Dad certainly was, so where did I get my inadequacies? I'd probably never know, but from that moment, I was determined to be more courageous. I would take control. Well, at least I would have a go. The journey was a bit complicated and we were both heading into unknown territory. Where would this courage come from? I'd have to dig deep.

Meantime, while I decided where to look for it, I was thankful that Stevie took charge again telling me to wipe my eyes and blow my nose. Then he stuffed the carpet bag under my right arm, threw the gas mask box over my other shoulder and threaded my handbag across my chest. This left him to deal with the remainder, which were difficult shapes and sizes. The apples and sandwiches, his own mask, the jigsaw, bulging pockets of conkers and of course, 'Trucky'. *"Right. Ready, Lelly?"* He said with great conviction by adjusting his school cap.

I nodded and wanted to cry again and had to remind myself that I was going to be courageous from now on. We tramped over the bridge and heard the train chuffing towards the station. That was good. See, a positive thing! We would be fine travelling from the lovely, safe countryside into the capital that for all we knew had been bombed to oblivion. The school would be lovely. It would have people who liked us. They would make us welcome and look after us. Stevie would have a wonderful education and I would excel as a teacher of toffs. Why then, was I full of doubt?

As the engine pulled into the station, my heart raced in time with the commotion surrounding it. Stevie couldn't remember travelling in a train and was terribly excited as we boarded. We were lucky to have a compartment to ourselves, although we pushed our luggage into the rack above us in case we were joined by others. Stevie bounced up and down on the springy seat in an exaggerated way as the train picked up speed and we chugged past brown fields some with haystacks, others being ploughed with a tractor and some with a Peggy or a Polly. People waved, we waved back. The sun shone kindly the way it does when autumn is close and although an obvious change in temperature caused the leaves to wilt on all the trees, the colours were quite spectacular.

The train slowed as we came into Newton Halt allowing us to see the man in the signal box leaning out of the window and the remnants of a rose garden, which must have been glorious earlier in the year. Jolting to a standstill, a huge whoosh of steam covered the windows on the platform side. It took a while to clear, but when it did, rather than the passengers we were expecting, we saw that the area was filled with boxes of pink Geraniums and white Fuchsias. It was so pretty. On the other side, our carriage was almost close enough to pick the fruit from a massive Blackberry bush, reminding me of the last time I picked berries beside the stream at the farm. A few doors clanged shut, the Station Master blew his whistle and we were off again. Were we really at war?

It wasn't long though before hedges and fields were replaced by big sheds and even bigger buildings and on the outskirts of the city with its shops and terraced houses visible signs of war were apparent. At one point, the train slowed almost to a crawl while men with ashen faces holding pickaxes stood back from the track. Air raid damage was very evident as we passed a smouldering home and saw deep craters where several others had been. It was horrible. Sparks flew into the air as Firemen directed their hoses into a big hole in a roof, while fellow workers rolled those not in use ready for the next time I supposed. I strained my neck to see if Dad might be standing amongst the rubble but could see no one wearing his distinctive helmet.

Stevie was content to look out of the window commenting every now and then about the carnage and when a tethered barrage balloon came into view, it had him jumping up and down in his seat. With the changing scenery though, his mood altered, and he became noticeably quiet and thoughtful. I squeezed his hand as we pulled into the next station and this time, a lot of people stood waiting on the platform. It looked as though we'd have some company for the remainder of the journey as four sailors joined us in the carriage. Each of them heaved their luggage onto the racks above us and sat down heavily on the seats. The atmosphere deteriorated suddenly with the smell of stale beer and tobacco, but they were all quite jolly and said hello. Stevie was captivated.

One of them reached into a pocket for his cigarette pack. Seeing this, another nudged him with an elbow and cocked his head towards Stevie and I and the sailor immediately put them back in his pocket. I was grateful because so far, the journey had been pleasant with the smell of fresh air and countryside and the new aroma was bad enough. They were all young and fit-looking. Their caps simply said 'HMS' and I knew we shouldn't ask anything about their ship, having been warned that careless talk costs lives and Stevie was too enthralled to ask any awkward questions. Three of them were quite daft, while the most handsome of them had Cary Grant's alluring eyes. He winked at me and I blushed. I don't know why.

Stevie asked the one with an anchor tattoo on his hand why it was there, and he said it was to remind him that he was a sailor and not a Blacksmith. It took a minute for this joke to sink in until Stevie beamed approval. Then the conkers came out and there was pandemonium as they all tried their hand at the game. It was very funny and so good to see Stevie laugh. Several red knuckles later and no 'hits' big enough to split a conker, they were put back in Stevie's pocket and 'Trucky' appeared from the safe place he was kept. Each of the sailors examined it enviously, with an *"Ooh"*, or an *"Aah"* every now and then. *"Lelly bought it for me."* Stevie told them proudly. *"Lelly?"* One asked. I blushed again as my childhood story was explained.

The young men had been such a diversion and seemed to soften the blow of leaving the farm, but now we were pulling into Liverpool Street Station. Stevie returned the sailor's cap he'd been wearing and saluted with the wrong hand and the sailor returned the salute and the school cap that *he'd* been

145

wearing. Pulling their belongings down from the racks, shouting their goodbyes and "*Good Luck*", they leapt from the carriage, with the last one being the Cary Grant lookalike who winked for a second time. Of course, I blushed again.

How we managed to get things together I don't know. With the uncertainty of what was to come next and all the other emotions churning in our minds, I think we were both more than a little scared of leaving the safety of the compartment. Composing myself to organise our exit, I told Stevie to put his cap on straight and as usual pull up the sock nestling round his ankle. The jigsaw was the biggest problem because it wouldn't fit into the carpet bag. I fumbled for the warrants while Stevie wrestled with the cumbersome box. Our gas masks were awkward enough and with apples and conkers bulging in Stevie's pockets and sandwiches in mine, we must have looked a comical pair as we fell out onto the platform.

I doubt anyone noticed us though. The combination of noises was as confusing as it was deafening. Clouds of dense, white smoke puffed from tall funnels giving the engines the appearance of huge restless animals. Passengers and Guards slammed doors shut in such a succession of bangs, it reminded me of the time my finger was caught in the door at home. It made me wince, adding to my foreboding. And as we came closer to the engine, hissing, warm steam threatened in the hope of making us jump from the heat. The distinctive tang of damp sulphur in the air echoed the coal fire at home and I wanted to rush there to toast marshmallows peacefully with Mum.

But of course, there was no peace and certainly no marshmallows. The mixture of emotions raced through my mind. Goodness knows what it was doing to Stevie, who had somehow attached himself to me by grabbing my thumb with one of his fingers. I assured him that we were alright. I just hoped I didn't look as scared as I felt. People were shouting to each other above the noise and their hurried footsteps made us walk more quickly too.

A voice over the loudspeaker gave some sort of information, but I couldn't understand it; I hoped it wasn't trying to tell us something important. A guard waved a flag on the opposite platform and blew his whistle with such gusto, the high-pitched warble made us both jump again. I looked down at Stevie and faintly smiled. My thumb had lost all feeling with the grip of his one finger and my head was reeling.

We joined the throng of people I couldn't have fitted a pin between and found ourselves swept along the platform with them. The queue at the end funnelled everyone through a tall gate between railings where the Ticket Collector studied each ticket before allowing people through. Eventually, we reached him. He examined the warrants carefully, gave them back to me and patted Stevie's head moving his cap to one side. Stevie frowned at him but could do nothing about adjusting the cap. At least he didn't kick the man in the shins.

The scene in the station itself was one of pure frenzy. My anxiety rocketed and my heart pounded to such an extent that I thought it would stop. I was also boiling hot with such a dry mouth that I didn't seem to be able to swallow. Porters rushed around pulling, or pushing trolleys laden with suitcases and bags shouting, "*Mind your backs. Mind your backs, please!*" A gaggle of tiny tots blocked our way at an evacuation assembly point. I wondered if some of them were being RE-evacuated, having returned during the Phoney War. Whatever the reason, they were a sad-looking lot. Wearing labels attached to their clothes as if they were items for sale, they clutched a teddy or a doll in one hand and a chaperone in the other. Most cried, or simply looked as bewildered as I felt. Tearful ladies waved hankies in the air, mothers held babies tightly in their arms and I couldn't help staring at a soldier kissing a young girl for such a long time I thought she would faint any second. Stevie tugged on my thumb interrupting my gaze, and speaking loudly above the noise I said,

"*We need to get to the Subway.*" Stevie looked at me blankly.

"The Underground. Can you see a sign for the Underground?" I added irritably.

He looked around, but I don't think he knew what he was looking for. How we would find the tube I wasn't sure because the amount of people to get through was enormous. Men and women in uniform were everywhere. All sorts of ranks, types and from far-flung places it seemed because English was not the only language we heard. I recognised French and then there was what sounded like German, but surely it was something else. Stevie turned his attention to a very grand-looking gentleman wearing a turban and shouted, *"WOW!"* When he saw what he thought was a cowboy, but I think he was an Australian soldier.

I had often taken the tube with Dad for trips to football matches at weekends. He was an ardent and loyal supporter of Arsenal player, Herbie Roberts until having broken his leg he was forced to retire in 1937, but until then, anywhere Herbie went, we went too. Stevie and I would have to use the tube to get to Paddington Station and he didn't question the route we were taking until I saw the SUBWAY sign and we reached the escalator.

There was an odd-looking queue of people forming to one side, a real mix of young and old waiting patiently, carrying Thermos flasks, pillows, blankets, torches, and all sorts of things. Their mood was good-humoured and the banter so sociable, it would appear they were going on some sort of outing. I was puzzled and asked a lady if she was waiting for a specific train.

"Train, love?" She asked. *"Nah! Wanna get a good spot for the night."*

A good spot for the night? Where, I wondered? Well, if we weren't 'queue-jumping', it would be okay to walk past them. Stevie let go of my thumb and I assumed he was following me, but it wasn't until I had one foot on the moving staircase that I realised he'd stopped walking. I stepped back quickly and asked what was wrong. It hadn't occurred to me that this was another new experience for him, so it was a surprise when he refused to go down. I told him we had to get the tube because catching a bus might take a long time. I pulled him once again, but he wouldn't budge. No amount of talking helped and it was obvious that he was too frightened to go down there. Whether it was fear of the unknown, or it reminded him of the school basement, I didn't know, but we were wasting time and people were pushing past us. It would have to be the bus, I told him.

We managed to get to the street outside where the chaos and confusion continued. Cars hooted, an ambulance with a bell clanging furiously picked its way through the traffic, people walked quickly with grim-looking faces. Which bus? Which direction? I didn't have a clue. Was it this side of the road, or the other? Stevie nodded towards a queue at a bus stop. Yes, I'll ask someone there if they know how we get to Paddington Station, but as I went towards them a bus appeared and they all got on it! The clippie hung out of the open platform, urging the people to move quickly and just as she rang the bell, I shouted *"Paddington Station?"*

"Other side of the road love", she shouted back as the bus moved off.

That was a start. We crossed the road and headed for the bus stop there. But what bus?

I was hungry and thirsty. Stevie must be feeling the same, although you would never know it. We had done so well to get this far and now I was failing. I bit my lip as tears welled up and was just about to apologise to Stevie and admit that I didn't know what to do, when a taxicab stopped beside us. A man wearing a bowler hat left the taxi and stood on the pavement while he paid the driver. The flag wasn't up to say that he was free, but in a moment of madness, I asked if he was ready for another fare.

By the time we were sitting in the back of the taxicab, I was feeling faint. I wasn't sure if it was due to hunger, thirst, or if it was because I was totally unhinged. Stevie was in complete awe, but all I could do, was wonder how I would pay for the journey. Well, we were there now and whatever the cost, I would have to pay-up so I might as well ignore the meter and enjoy the ride through the streets.

It was a long journey and the roads were crammed with traffic. We passed so many people all with a look of urgency on their faces hurrying on their way somewhere and I asked the driver how things had been with the air raids and if he was busy what with petrol rationing. Considering what he told us, he was quite jolly. He treated us like day-trippers, or tourists, pointing out various bombed buildings as though they were an everyday occurrence and gleefully said that yes, he was very busy because so many drivers had joined-up and lots of cars had been commandeered by the army. He told us how difficult it was to drive during the blackout and that white lines had been freshly painted on the kerbs and even in the middle of some pavements in a one-way system to stop pedestrians bumping into each other. Stevie laughed. I shook my head.

Clutching my handbag tightly as we neared the station, I pulled out my purse when we came to a halt. I still hadn't looked at the meter and was determined to maintain a dignified air as I had done when I paid the bill in the department store. As it turned out, the fare left very little from half a weeks' wages, but I was so relieved to have arrived safely this far into our campaign that I handed over the money almost gratefully and with further madness, added a tip! My advice telling the driver to look after himself followed by a corny joke about the white lines made my toes curl though and I had to accept the fact that trying to appear this confident with no income meant I was completely deranged.

Paddington Station appeared to be even busier than Liverpool Street. There were more electric trains than steam, but the noise was worse. It was almost two o'clock and we hadn't eaten anything since early that morning. I had relaxed a little in the taxicab but now felt that sense of urgency all over again. Stevie looked tired but hadn't complained at all and I didn't have the heart to tell him to pull up that errant sock. Eating and drinking must take priority and we should also find a toilet. I wasn't sure what to do about the rail warrants and whether I had to swap them for proper tickets this time. The Ticket Office had a long queue and I was torn between joining it and waiting until later.

I suddenly felt very contrary because I didn't want to be in this frightful place. Neither did I want to go to a strange school to work with a load of posh boys. This wasn't the happy Paddington I'd been to with Mum and Dad when we travelled to Reading for Uncle David's wedding. The curved roof of the station was familiar, and the sun sparkled prettily through the glass illuminating everything with white light, but the mood of the people was quite different.

Relieved to see a big red tin sign with 'LADIES WAITING ROOM' written in big black letters, I pulled Stevie towards it. We were lucky, only four ladies and a young girl with a baby were sitting inside and with the door closed, it was reasonably quiet. We sat down, spilling our bags and parcels on the floor and one of the ladies asked if we were going far. 'Careless Talk Costs Lives' went through my mind again, but before I could answer Stevie simply said, *"No."* She didn't ask us anything after that and none of the other ladies spoke, which gave us space to breathe and gather our thoughts.

We took it in turns to use the toilet and then ate the apples and sandwiches I'd made last night using the bread I'd bought only yesterday with the cheese I'd scraped and the pickle that Gladys had made. I was comforted by their origin as well as the nourishment and while eating, the last few weeks swam through my muddled mind. It was as if I'd been catapulted into another world. This war was turning all our lives upside down. What of Stevie? How was his mind coping with the enormous change of events in his life? He'd been through so much and ironically had come full circle because this was the area he'd been born.

The girl holding the baby left the waiting room and we were

joined by a Wren. I would have loved to ask all about her job, but of course that wasn't allowed. She was about my age and very pretty. The hair beneath her cap with the letters 'HMS' was turned over at the back in what Nan called 'sausage rolls' and apart from the smart uniform, she had the shiniest shoes and satchel. I was glad she was reading a newspaper. It allowed me to have a good look at her in an envious way and make a mental note to find out once and for all, exactly what Wren's did.

I was nervous and kept checking both my watch and that the warrants for our next journey were still in my handbag. If only there was time to see Dad; he was literally down the road, well almost. The train for Swindon was due to leave at ten past four, so there was plenty of time to have a cup of tea and maybe a bun, or a biscuit. Stevie liked the sound of a bun and making sure that he was aware of each parcel and bag and that he would stay put, I ventured into the station.

Noises and peculiar smells hit my senses once again and I thought twice about wandering around amongst the strange mixture of people, but we were both in need of a drink. Opposite the waiting room door was a newspaper stand with a placard saying, '*MORE ON GIBRALTAR RAID and BUCKPAL BOMBING*', both of which I knew nothing about. Buckingham Palace bombed? Was the King hurt? I thought I'd buy a paper later and meantime, asked the newsvendor to point me in the direction of the nearest café.

It wasn't too far, but I queued for quite a while to be served. Finally reaching the counter I asked for two currant buns and two cups of tea to take back with me. At first, the lady behind the counter was reluctant to allow the cups and saucers to be taken away, but when I explained that Stevie was only nine and sitting in the ladies waiting room, she relented provided I promised to bring them back. She did better than that because she put the buns in a paper bag, poured three cups of sweet, milky tea into a big enamel jug and gave me two cups to carry. Bless her.

I took the tea back to the waiting room where good as gold as ever, Stevie stood guard over our belongings and hadn't moved a muscle. The buns were delicious, and the tea washed them down a treat. I returned the jug and cups and felt much better about things; maybe I was just in need of a cuppa. Anxious to know about the King and Queen, I bought a newspaper and a 'Beano' comic for Stevie. He was delighted with my choice. I knew he would struggle with most of the words but at least the pictures would amuse him.

The newspaper was full of the war. King George and the Queen weren't hurt, but the palace was damaged, and the Queen said she was glad they had been bombed because now she felt she could look the East End in the face. She was such a wonderful woman and made a marvellous Queen. Nan used to cut out any pictures of her in the paper and they would hang around until the next batch was printed. Nan was a true Royalist.

Gibraltar had been attacked by Vichy France, whoever that was, the Supermarine factory building Spitfires was heavily bombed, which would put back production for some time and the ports of Southampton and Portsmouth had suffered badly at the docks and factories there, with more than one hundred civilians killed. The underground station platforms in London were being used as shelters, which solved my earlier puzzle and reminded me of Stevie's refusal to go down there and all in all, the stories were not only gloomy, but also very pessimistic.

Most of the news was about the destruction in the capital though, with one account from the Fire Service telling of blazing wood, flaming streams of rum from a warehouse, ships burning and barrels exploding high into the air. The crew of the Woolwich Ferry had ignored the sea of burning oil on the water and bravely continued to evacuate civilians. It was like a horror story and Dad was right in the thick of it. I longed to see him walk through the door right now and if he did, I would ask him to come away with us.

Time flew by. One minute it was half past two and the next,

it was ten past three. I panicked at first and stood up, dropping the newspaper on the floor. This startled Stevie, who looked up at me apprehensively and rather than admit that I had no idea where we needed to go next, simply said that I thought we'd better get a move on. With this, he stood to attention so I could have a look at him. I pulled his cap straight, buttoned-up his cardigan and told him to return the offending article round his ankle to his knee. I hoped he would be warm enough without a coat; maybe this was something the school could provide or at least lend him.

Being so engrossed in the newspaper, I hadn't noticed the change of ladies sitting amongst us. There were several new faces. The Wren had gone and been replaced by a rather grubby-looking lady wearing a scarf on her head, the type the factory workers and Land Army girls wore, and there were two very sleepy-looking children with an older woman. We began to organise our luggage and having eaten the sandwiches and apples found we each had a whole pocket empty, which was useful. The jigsaw was still the biggest problem though until the scarf lady suddenly spoke and produced a length of string.

"Eeryar luv," she said. *"This might 'elp ya."*

I took it from her and thanked her very much saying it was just what we needed and wrapped the awkward box together with Stevie's gas mask. It did the trick by allowing them to dangle safely from his shoulder, leaving an extra arm free.

"Need to be one a them octypusses", done you? The lady joked.

Nodding and thanking her once again, we left our foxhole for the madness of the station. Wandering around for a few minutes, people bashed into us blindly and one huge soldier made me drop my handbag; he didn't even apologise. I didn't know what to do and although I wasn't able to look at my watch, knew that time was of the essence. I was worried that we might be separated, and it was then that I was overwhelmed with that courage I'd been looking for.

Maybe it was the sweet tea, maybe it was the bun or even the sandwich, but I was suddenly determined to find the right

154

platform and get us to Swindon. The Queen had been bombed and if she could handle all this, so could I. I was in control. I told Stevie to hang on to my coat and not let go. I stuck out my elbows the way Nan had taught me when we visited a busy jumble sale, took a deep breath and without stopping, ploughed a way through the disorder towards a man in a station uniform. Stevie looked at me in a completely different way as I spoke.

"Tell me, my man," I said with authority, *"What is the location of the 4.10 to Swindon? Err, please."*

My confidence waned a little when he asked to see our tickets. I supposed this was in case we were spies, or Nazis on the run. It made me smile because I couldn't help remembering the dear men of the village Home Guard who were keeping everyone safe. I wasn't sure what having a ticket would prove either, but did as I was asked, which allowed him to give me the platform information and tell me that the warrants were as good as a ticket.

"It isn't in yet," the man said. *"It's the bombing you know. Been a lot of it. And what with every Tom, Dick and Harry sleeping on the underground platforms. Well, whatever next? I say"*

Thanking him very much with several nods of my head and my best smile, Stevie saluted with the wrong hand and showed him 'Trucky' with the other, while the man returned the salute and showed him his whistle. *"Come along now",* I said, turning in the direction of Platform Five, which was Platform Six on the other side, if you see what I mean. The area around the numbers 5 and 6 above the railings was empty and the gate was firmly shut, but we'd made it. I had managed to get us all this way. We were fed, watered and intact. I was so elated I could have milked a cow. Well, that was probably asking a bit too much, but perhaps I wasn't so useless after all.

Not wanting to be trampled upon by alighting passengers when the train did come in, we stood against the railings and waited. Then we waited some more, because by five o'clock, the train still hadn't arrived. Stevie had been studying his 'Beano' quietly, but my legs were aching, and I'd have loved another cup of tea. Trains were coming and going at every platform except ours', until at last, smoke in the distance headed towards Platform Five.

Passengers were opening doors and leaving some of the carriages running before the train had stopped, which I thought looked rather dangerous, although they managed to stay upright somehow. The train finally came to a halt in a great gush of smoke, steam and noise and a huge sigh, relieved to end its journey. Then all at once, the remainder of the people soon filled the platform. Soldiers, sailors, airmen and women, civilians, a great cross section of people involved in the crusade against the Nazis, although I was sure this was being repeated in Germany by mortals with the opposite idea.

It took a while for everyone to leave the train and squeeze through the iron gate having given up their ticket or perhaps had their warrant scrutinised, but once the porters had wheeled their barrows away, the platform was empty again. Some passengers disappeared almost in a puff of smoke amongst the confusion, some were reunited with a loved one in a flurry of excitement and emotion, while others looked towards heaven at the big clock hanging high above. I just wanted to sit down and be on our way.

Finally, when the man at the gate shouted, "*Bristol train, for Reading, Swindon and Bath,*" we gathered ourselves together. At last. We would take our time. Choose our carriage carefully, making sure we had window seats opposite each other. Perhaps have the company of more sailors, or even airmen. Thoroughly enjoy the last part of our journey. Swindon here we come!

How wrong I was. We couldn't move an inch! My orderly plan scuppered completely by the huge crush of people attempting to board the train. The frenzy continued for several minutes with no alternative but to wait until the crush became a trickle. The train was filling up fast and as soon as I saw a gap in the multitude, we made a run for it. Where was everyone going? They couldn't possibly all be heading for Swindon!

It was a corridor train and each carriage we passed appeared to be full to overflowing until I noticed a space outside the last carriage but one. Making sure that Stevie was safely on board first, I managed to pull the door shut behind me with the carpet bag pressed against my chest. *"Lot of people on this train, Lelly"*, Stevie said in a wry way.

The train was bursting at the seams. We were bewildered by it all. Standing like sardines in a can all the way to Swindon wasn't ideal, but then the journey shouldn't take that long if we could get under way soon. The important thing was to stay together, get there safely and make sure our parcels did too. The sliding portion of the window above me was open so that would give a bit of fresh air once we got going and I'd have to ignore the smelly man beside me. The real problem was that it was almost six o'clock and I had hoped we'd be on the bus to the school by now. Surely the train couldn't take any more passengers, so why weren't we moving?

It was then we heard a clanking and clunking sound and the train lurched a little. Someone said that an engine was now at the front, so we should be leaving in a minute or two. That was a relief to hear. That was until the air raid siren suddenly began to wail and there were groans, sighs, and lots of murmuring. Stevie looked up at me apprehensively and I managed to hold the top of his arm with two fingers and a thumb hoping that this would reassure him in some way. I supposed we'd have to get off the train and find a shelter, but just as I was steeling myself for the mass exodus, the train began to move, and we slowly left the station.

Being unable to see out of the window, meant I couldn't make a note of our progress although the last thing I wanted to see was bombs dropping all around us – *or on us!* The train picked up speed, rattling along the lines with the siren still wailing urgently in the distance. We seemed to be making a successful escape from the noise of explosions and my thoughts turned to what we may have left behind. I pictured the huge glass dome of the station crashing down just as the window at the farm had done. I still felt bad about that.

The carriage swayed and rocked gently while Stevie and I huddled together with our parcels locked firmly between us. With his head on one side, he rested it on top of the carpet bag gently moving his truck in front of him in a polishing motion. This was so unfair. Why should a dear little boy have to go through such an ordeal? I was glad I'd bought that truck. It had given so much pleasure and always brought him comfort in trying times like these. I felt so protective towards him and not for the first time, vowed to see that he was sent safely to a new home – even if that home was in Scotland.

There were planes above us. I heard them along with everyone else and panic erupted when there was a succession of massive explosions to one side of the track. The train seemed to roll with the rapid change in air pressure but carried on. Our speed increased and I imagined the men in the engine cab desperately shovelling coal into the firebox in a daring attempt to preserve us all. But then there were screams as the whistle blew in one disturbing, high-pitched blast. The carpet bag fell to the floor as I grabbed Stevie genuinely believing that this was the end for us. I wouldn't be taking him home after all.

Noises were mixed and confusing. I was terrified and Stevie began to cry. Screams from passengers were muffled by screaming of another kind as the engine driver applied the brakes so heavily, the shrill grinding sound of metal on metal went on and on until finally we screeched to a halt in complete darkness. Stevie called my name. Unable to answer, I simply held him close.

My eyes soon adjusted to the change in light and I could see that many people had fallen on top of each other. We were lucky, because the smelly man had reached across us both while hanging onto the handrail and we were all still upright. He was still holding on to us as a light shone through the window and I could see his face. *"We're safe. We're in a tunnel."*

He said softly. Even with this protection, explosions around us were loud enough to hear and big enough to feel the effects of and Stevie was still crying. All I could say was, "*Oh.*"

The light came from a lantern held high in the air by the Guard who was surrounded by dozens of people. I couldn't understand what was going on until the man explained. "*The tunnel isn't long enough to cover all the carriages, so, people in the ones left outside had to leave them.*" Once again, my reply was, "*Oh.*"

Some passengers left our carriage and stood on the track, which gave us room to sit on the floor and calm ourselves, but after more than an hour, we were still in the tunnel. We dozed a little until Stevie said he needed the toilet. I had no idea where it was, or even if the train had one, so suggested he relieve himself from the carriage door being careful not to sprinkle anyone. He wasn't keen to do this, but in the semi-darkness, he surely wouldn't be noticed. My situation was a little more awkward, but when he returned, I followed another young girl out onto the track and did what I needed in the most discreet way possible under the circumstances.

Bombs were still dropping. Two soldiers counted the space between them. "*Number eight will get us, Ben*", one said to the other. "*It's always number eight.*" He added. I told Stevie that this was all nonsense when he asked if we should count too. Ambulance and fire engine bells rang incessantly, and smoke wafted through the tunnel giving off such a pungent smell that some people donned their gas mask. We were hot, tired, hungry, and thirsty and didn't know where we were, but unlike me, Stevie hadn't moaned once. When would this misery end? Would we ever reach the school? There was no camaraderie or good humour and it was now almost one o'clock in the morning. We surely had missed the last bus to the school and the people there would think we weren't coming.

When we heard the faint sound of the 'all clear', the Guard came to tell us all that the track further up the line was being repaired, but the one behind us was blocked completely by the destruction of the last carriage, which meant that those passengers would have to squeeze in with the rest of us. *"At least we made it out of London,"* he said cheerfully. True, but thank goodness the people left that carriage. How we would fit them all in was another story.

Stevie and I must have been asleep when we moved off because the next thing we knew, the lights were on with the blinds down and we were pulling in to Reading Station. Two people were straddled across our legs, which was good of them considering they could have told us to stand up and make room. The smelly man was nowhere to be seen. I should have thanked him for hanging on to us, but at the time, my terror hadn't allowed me to think straight.

Several people left the train and suddenly, as if I had just seen a large chocolate cake, I noticed empty seats! My bottom had gone to sleep, and I had pins and needles in my arms, but despite this, I pointed them out to Stevie, who reached them quicker than me. It was heaven to sit on something soft and for a moment, I forgot that nothing had passed our lips for several hours. Our fellow passengers looked dreadful and I was sure we did too.

The journey seemed to go on and on until the train slowed once again. I desperately wanted the next stop to be Swindon. Fortunately, when we came to a halt, someone shouted, *"Swindon, Swindon"*, which was music to my ears. Carefully stepping out first, Stevie passed our luggage to me and I helped him onto the platform. *"Now what?"*

It was just after four o'clock in the morning when the train chugged away with three carriages missing. We were left standing forlornly amongst other weary passengers in the dark and weren't sure in which direction to move. An owl hooted mournfully. A dog barked. Apart from this, the air was still and slightly misty, with a half-moon high in the sky. We saw a light. Clearly, a man in pyjamas and a cap walked towards us holding a lantern, which he lifted high allowing us to see each other. The flag and whistle he carried in the other hand told us he was the Station Master and if that wasn't enough, the gold letters on the cap confirmed this. I hoped he didn't want to see our warrants as I had no idea where they were.

He led us to the Waiting Room, where behind the heavy curtain at the door a dwindling fire crackled and spat. Safely inside, the gentleman switched on the light. It was dazzling and woke us up a bit. Two people started to ask questions and another chimed-in, until with hands in the air, he said, "*Easy, easy. One at a time now.*" Stevie used the brief silence to say, "*Is there any tea, Mister?*" This made some of us laugh, while others nodded. Of course, we weren't surprised to be told that although the WVS ran a Tea Bar, it was never open at four o'clock in the morning.

However, this kind man went on to say that he would make a pot if we didn't mind taking it in turns, because he only had three cups and saucers and there were eight of us. We all agreed to this suggestion and when he'd made the tea, the first to get one was Stevie. Once we'd all been revived to a certain extent – even without the runny honey we were used to, it was decided that the six other people would have to wait there until the first bus arrived, but Stevie and I could ask the milkman if we could cadge a lift on his float. Witherleigh Hall was his last stop on the way back to the Dairy and he usually reached the school around half past six.

I wasn't sure at first. If we waited there for the bus, we could have a sleep and maybe more tea, but looking at the hard, wooden benches surrounding the room, decided that we'd speak to the milkman instead. While we waited, the others settled down as best they could with only the light from the few embers in the fireplace, and Stevie dozed with his head on my lap. I pulled off his cap and stroked his hair thinking about the last few weeks wondering what would become of us. We'd come a long way on an ever-changing road. We'd comforted and cared for each other. We'd been bombed but not bloodied and should be grateful for that.

My thoughts were interrupted by the Station Master who

appeared at the door silently waving his hand at me. I woke Stevie, who closed his eyes again saying, "*No. Sleep, please,*" although he did his best to stand to attention when I pulled him to his feet. I stuffed the cap on his head but didn't have the heart to mention the sock round his ankle. Dragging our luggage behind us, we left the Waiting Room with its sleeping passengers and in the darkness, I could just make out the milk float. I was surprised when the driver spoke though because it wasn't a milkman at all. It was as if we'd accidentally come across old friends when Land Army girl Bunty introduced herself and Samantha the horse.

Oh, how we talked, despite being dog-tired. Stevie was almost wide awake now extolling the virtues of fresh milk, the supervision of pigs and the perils of keeping chickens. I asked Bunty why the Station Master had led us to believe that she was a man and her answer was that many of the farmers found it hard to accept girls working on the land, although they were very happy with the end products. There had also been a bit of rivalry going on between them and local girls vying for the attention of soldiers on the many Ack-Ack Batteries in the area. "*Ack-Ack Batteries?*" I asked. There I went again, silly me, knows nothing. "*Anti-Aircraft guns and searchlights, you know.*" She said. I nodded and wished I HAD known.

The sun was making an entrance and everywhere sparkled. It reminded me of the countryside I'd become used to, especially when we passed a newly ploughed field with its recognisable smell. I was in seventh heaven again until we reached a gap in the road with a curved wall on either side and a big blue sign saying, 'WITHERLEIGH HALL' SCHOOL FOR BOYS. We had arrived at our next address.

It took a while for us to make our way down the long road, or I suppose what was the 'drive' for such a prestigious school. Stopping just in front of the tall oval front door inside a stone porch, Bunty off-loaded the remaining four churns expertly 'walking' them across the gravel path at the side of the building, while I stood surveying the scene. It was an imposing grey stone building with long leaded-light windows. "*Like a castle, Stevie*". I said. Stevie was not impressed. "*Done like it, Lelly. Less go.*" He said glumly. "*Go where, Stevie?*" I asked. He shrugged. Bunty came back to the float where Samantha was eating the flowers in a large tub. She pulled a face and then laughed, hauling our luggage down from the back of the cart. We were sorry to see her go but promised to remember the name of the dairy farm in case we could visit some time. This cheered-up Stevie no end as he waved them off, then turning to face the school in a less-cheerful voice, said, "*Might not stay.*" "*Okay.*" I replied.

We must have looked a sorry state so before ringing the doorbell, I straightened my clothes a little and licked my hair in place, then did the same with Stevie including the usual sock placement. We would have to do. Gingerly entering the cold porch, I pulled on the bell rope. Not a sound from within. I pulled again. Nothing. "*Okay, less go.*" Stevie said. "*Not in.*" Well, the bell was quite loud, and I thought it would be heard by someone, surely. It's not that early. They can't all be asleep. I was about to ring once more when footsteps crunched on the gravel at the side where Bunty had left the churns. An elderly man in a very frayed suit appeared. "*YES?*" He said loudly.

CHAPTER TEN

An Unwelcome Surprise

The man removed his cap and asked what we wanted. I told him we had been expected yesterday, that we had been delayed by an air raid on the railway line and that I was a new teacher and Stevie, a pupil, to which he scratched his head and pulled the bell in a more furious way than I.

A shuffling of feet and then by the sound of it, the door was being opened. It had several bolts on the other side and I wondered if they were to keep people in, or out. Eventually the last one slid across and the door slowly creaked open. I wasn't sure who, or what I was expecting but I was surprised to see another elderly person in the shape of a lady wearing a hairnet, dressing gown and slippers. "*YES?*" the lady said, stifling a yawn.

Not so friendly in this neck of the woods then. Stevie had backed-off and was standing on the drive ready to make a sharp exit as my own level of anxiety rose but before I could speak, the gentleman gave a potted version of my story. "*Teacher, boy, due yesterday.*" The lady at the door frowned and hesitated before saying, "*You'd better come in. Leave your things there*" I called to Stevie, who kicked a few of the gravel stones in defiance, before wandering in behind me. Leaving our precious luggage in the porch wouldn't do though and before the lady closed the door, I grabbed the carpet bag and Stevie slid the rest across the floor. We stood in a vast hall. There was a faint smell of Lavender mixed with something not as nice. The stone floor could have been marble. With dark blue and orange streaks running through the grey, it was silky smooth and almost monumental. I raised my eyebrows. Two

164

formidable-looking doors with brass knobs broke the expanse of dark wood panels cladding the walls and various hunting scenes hung from a dado rail. The wide staircase with a huge newel post led elsewhere. A second look at the doors told me that these were the domains of the Bursar and Headmaster, Mr. Fortescue and then I noticed a plaque above the front door. An arch of acorns and oak leaves bordered the words, '*Traditionem Excellentiam Indirecte*'. It was all rather fancy, and I had a horrible feeling we would look somewhat out of place at this posh school.

"*Sit there.*" The lady told us, pointing to a long bench leaning against the wall on the opposite side. We did. "*I'll speak to Matron,*" she added before shuffling out of the hall and into a corridor. I doubt she heard my thanks. "*Done like it. Smells funny*". Stevie told me, shaking his head. Neither did I, but I couldn't agree with him and admit defeat. So far, the journey had been awful, we were almost killed on a train and having finally arrived, we were hardly welcomed. Maybe Mrs. Johnson had failed to let them know we were coming. We would just have wait and see what happened next. We were good at that.

The only sound came from a Grandfather clock standing majestically opposite the bench. It swung its pendulum and ticked loudly with the hand displaying a time of ten past seven. Trying not to be mesmerised by the brass weight, I checked my watch. It agreed. I felt as though I was waiting to see the Dentist and was so apprehensive, I began to bite a fingernail. Stevie produced 'Trucky' and drove it slowly up and down the bench. I told him to 'shush', when he added engine noises, which he changed to a gentle '*brrm, brrm*'.

I had trouble keeping my eyes open until the clock chimed loudly at half-past-seven startling us both. It was then that the whole school came alive with bells ringing everywhere. Whoever they were meant to wake, they did the same for us and we stood to attention. Almost immediately, boys of all shapes and sizes emerged from the floors above. Wearing grey blazers with mauve piping and those acorns and oakleaves on

165

the breast pocket, matching stiped ties and gas mask boxes slung over a shoulder, they trooped down the staircase, spilling into the hall. Some ignored us, others gave a long look, but all had a sense of urgency, being drawn along the same corridor that lady had used.

When we smelt breakfast, it became obvious exactly what it was they were being drawn to. Stevie's eyelashes swept slowly up and down, and my own envy showed by several gulps and swallows. A young girl wearing a mob cap and white apron appeared. *"Cook says you're to have breakfast."* She said timidly. Leaving our luggage on the hall floor, we followed her at full tilt. Wild horses couldn't have kept us away from the aroma of toasted bread.

Chattering and the noise of crockery being scraped grew louder as we neared a door saying, 'REFECTORY', another panelled hall, although much larger. The young girl told us to join the queue of boys, take what we wanted and then find a seat. It was quite exciting, especially when we saw the trays of scrambled egg. Careful not to appear greedy, we took a plate from the pile and a moderate amount of egg, a knife and fork, two pieces of toast each and a mug of tea. It was sumptuous. I had eaten it with my eyes already by the time we found a space to sit.

Breakfast finished at eight-thirty and as swiftly as they had appeared, the boys were gone. Crockery, cutlery, big enamel milk jugs and napkins in rings piled up on one side of the hall systematically removed on oval trays by the young girl we'd seen earlier. Stevie and I waited at the empty table hoping we would be told what to do, or where to go but it was almost nine o'clock before a lady in a navy dress and frilly, white cap came in. *"Hello,"* she said, offering her hand. *"Matron. Matron Lewis, in charge of the boys here. Now, you need to speak to Mr. Fortescue."*

"Yes, I'm sure," I replied. *"Mr. Fortescue."*

"The Headmaster". Matron chirruped. *"I don't know what's going on here, but this is all very inconvenient."* What was

inconvenient, I didn't know, but we followed her back to the front hall and the appropriate door, which she tapped on gently with the knuckle of one finger. Seconds passed until we heard, "*Enter,*" and Matron opened the door for us to 'enter'. "*A young lady and small boy to see you, Mr. Fortescue.*" She said this almost sarcastically and leaving the room, added, "*They've had breakfast.*" Mr. Fortescue stood at his desk beckoning to a chair in front of it, so I sat down while Stevie hovered behind. The tall man wearing thick, horn-rimmed glasses took his seat and asked, "*Now, what can I do for you, Miss ... Err ...?*"

"*Carter,*" I replied, "*Lesley Carter and this is Steaphan, my charge – for the time being. You were expecting us yesterday, but our train was delayed.*"

"*Carter. Carter. Yes, we're expecting Leslie Carter, our new English Master - and a boy.*" He said looking in Stevie's direction. "*Well, we have a boy, but where is Mr. Carter?*" He asked.

"**MISTER** *Carter?*" I shouted.

I think the three of us realised the mistake all at the same time, but the only one to speak was Stevie, who said, "*Blimey.*"

Mr. Fortescue rifled through piles of papers on the desk until he found a letter, which he read with a sigh. Removing his glasses, he said, "*There's been a mistake, Miss Carter. We do not employ female teachers here. I'm sorry.*" The look of horror on my face obviously alarmed Mr. Fortescue to such an extent that he sat back in his chair prodding his chin with the glasses reconsidering his statement. "*Right, less go, Lelly*". Stevie said with conviction. "*No good ere.*" I was stuck to the chair. Where would we go? Stevie tugged at my arm. "*But, but*". Was all I could manage to say. Stevie had his hand on the doorknob by this time. "*Just a minute, m'boy,*" Mr. Fortescue mumbled. "*Let's see what we can do ... Matron would you come back in, please?*" She was just outside the door.

Deep discussion between the two followed. We were to stay. Under the circumstances, we were to stay. I would have the scullery maid's room, who had just married and now lived-out. It was next to the kitchen and had a bathroom and toilet adjacent. Apart from Stevie, I would help some of the evacuees – slow learners, with reading, writing and arithmetic and Stevie would be 'integrated' into the school – whatever that meant. He huffed and crossed his arms, but my relief was obvious.

The room was in the basement beside the enormous kitchen, just as Mr. Fortescue had said. It had a double bed and a small single, a chest of drawers and a wardrobe. There was electric light everywhere, a basin and bath with running water, a toilet that flushed with beautifully clean water and a scratchy roll of paper attached to the wall. Yippee! Then we were officially introduced to Mrs. Quick, the cook, who was the lady we first met and the newly wed scullery maid, Ethel. It was all quite surreal. Matron walked in. *"Well, this is an odd situation. Whatever next?"* She chuckled. *"I'll take the boy up to the dorm now. Get him settled. Oh, Cook will need you Ration Books, of course."* Stevie and I looked at each other in sheer panic. We'd been together for so long, how could we be separated now? *"Is that absolutely necessary, Matron?* I asked. *"Stevie hasn't been alone for some weeks and has had a bit of a rough time. Could he use the small bed in my room? Please?"*

"Well, he won't be alone." Matron scoffed. *"We have 260 boys here – 261 now. Steven is it? Follow me."*

Stevie didn't move, so I took his hand and pulled him up two flights of stairs to a long room with several single beds and lockers in a fashion not unlike the Reception Centre. There was an empty bed right at the end. Stevie was to have a bath and slip into a school uniform. Matron old him that he would soon 'integrate'. He would have new shoes, courtesy of the ex-pupil who had left them, a lovely pair of slippers and a dressing gown and I was meant to abandon him immediately, which would be 'for the best'. I was as distraught as Stevie when I left the dorm and a portion of my heart stayed behind with him.

I bathed and bathed. And then bathed some more. It was my first bath for weeks and the luxury of immersing myself in warm water and the perfume of the Camay was so good that I didn't leave the tub until the water was stone cold. Sitting on the side retrieving the soap, I felt so clean and warm, all I wanted to do was sleep. The knock on the door put a stop to that. It was Matron. I was to collect my gas mask and be taken on a tour of the school. Quickly dressing in my other change of clothes and remembering the infernal contraption, I went back upstairs to find Matron.

As we walked, she explained the blackout procedures and other emergency precautions including the location of the doors to the cellars where we would shelter in the event of an air raid. The caretaker, Mr. Thomas was responsible for fire-watching from the roof, ably assisted by several Prefects on a rota system. There were two gardeners, Mr. Sykes, and Jimmy, who had failed the army medical due to his flat feet. I had already met Ethel, the scullery maid and Mrs. Quick, the Cook, who had a bedroom and bathroom opposite mine. Mr. Hendrix, the local Barber came once a month to cut the boys' hair. The Launderess came in each day and her domain was in an outhouse where I would deal with my own laundry. The Sewing Room and Matron's bedroom were beside the Sanatorium, which was only for boys with a temperature above 99.9 degrees Fahrenheit. This was a strict rule and discouraged malingerers. It was a tight ship.

Master's bedrooms and sixth form studies were on the third floor. There was a weekly Tuck Shop in the small room off the Library beside the Refectory with a dwindling supply of sweets for sale. The Pupil's Common Room had a wireless activated by a designated teacher only and the Science Laboratory was kept locked. Assemblies were held in the chapel every morning at 8.45am sharp. Classrooms were all on the ground floor and I would be using a room called, 'Small Hall' to teach a special group of boys on Tuesday and Thursday mornings after assembly and each afternoon at 1.45pm. If I needed the toilet, I would have to go downstairs because there were only 'boys' and 'gents' facilities on that floor. The 'special' boys would join the others of their age for PT on Monday and Friday mornings and an Art class on Wednesday mornings. She rattled on-an-on. How I would remember all this, I didn't know. I should have taken notes.

Each dormitory had a bathroom with three tubs, six basins and four toilets. Women were not allowed in the Masters' Common Room, so all twelve of them would meet me in the Library before lunch, which was at one o'clock. Phew! My head was spinning, and I missed Stevie already. I found the way back to my room hoping that I might have sight of him 'en route'. No luck. I longed to see him, although we'd only been apart a few hours. Maybe I would be allowed to sit with him for lunch, although I hadn't seen any teachers at breakfast.

With my luggage unpacked, I realised how little I had, and felt tearful thinking about all the things left in our house. Rotten war. The room was nice though and running water with electricity was simply divine. It was odd to think we'd not had any on the farm. The farm. What a time we had there. How had Gladys and Joe managed in Birmingham? Were they back now with Linda, Roger, and the horses? Was Alec okay?

Before I knew it, it was twenty-to-one and I reckoned I should go to the Library to meet the teachers. I was a bit nervous and would have loved Stevie to be with me. The Library was full of books, funnily enough. Wide glass doors led outside, which I was yet to see, so I peered through the 'criss-cross' scrim to study the view. Trees, rolling hills and greenery seemed to go on and on and once again it was hard to believe we were at war. A few minutes later, the teachers trooped in. Each wore a black gown and mortar board and were of varying age, somewhere between forty and eighty! Well, there was a war on. I shook hands with them all and attempted some sort of cohesion, although most of them found it difficult to speak to me, apart from perhaps the youngest, Mr. Stone, who was very friendly.

Frank Stone had been teaching French and German at the

school for several years. He also spoke a reasonable amount of Dutch and Italian. German as a language was dropped in 1939 for obvious reasons. A weak-looking man about my height, Matron told me later that this was because he had contracted something called Trench Nephritis in the Great War. It was a disease of the kidneys apparently. Auntie Win's cousin had Gas Gangrene and lost some toes thanks to the mud in the trenches, but this sounded just as bad and the debilitating effects were obvious.

Ethel told me that the men took meals in their Common Room, which had a dumbwaiter connected to the kitchen and as I wasn't allowed there, it was safe for me to go to the Refectory. I didn't want to miss Stevie and stood at the door as the boys came in for lunch. My patience was rewarded when I did a double take on one boy who looked familiar. Matron had done wonders. Stevie had been transformed by the school uniform, which included the tie! Shiny black lace-up shoes made him appear a little taller and with long socks held tightly in place by garters, never again would the left one be seen at half-mast. My emotions were mixed about that. We greeted each other like long-lost friends, much to the amusement of some of the boys, but I didn't care. He even smelt different.

We lunched together and I told him that I would see him every mealtime, some mornings, and every afternoon, so he wasn't to worry and at other times, I was just downstairs. He still looked concerned though and I too, had my doubts about this arrangement working successfully. Well, we would have to try because there was nowhere else for us to go at the present time.

'Small Hall', a comfortable sitting room with armchairs and a fireplace, would be cosy on cold days should we be allowed to light a fire. The picture window looked out onto the side of the school, giving a different view of the grounds to the one from the Library and had a big table and upright chairs in front of it. It was a nice room and I would enjoy teaching there. My class of 'special' boys consisted of Stevie and four evacuees who all seemed disturbed in one way, or another. Two of them hardly spoke at all and it was obvious that something more distressing than simply being evacuated had occurred. Fortunately, it didn't take long for me to discover that their reading and writing abilities were similar when I asked them to write their name and age. Looking at Stevie's offering, 'Stevie Stewart, aged 9', reminded me that he would soon be ten. It was a pleasant afternoon and I think the boys were happy with it too. I was sure we'd all be fine.

Unfortunately, everything changed that night when I was woken by Matron standing in the middle of my room with Stevie in floods of tears. "*We can't have this,*" she said irately. "*You'll have to have him with you. It's the only way.*" Obviously, I had no idea what she meant until she explained that Stevie had woken twice in a confused state and in a panic that had erupted into incessant screaming. Terrifying some of the boys in his dorm, one of them had hit him with his slipper and a sixth form Prefect had to be called so half the school had been upset. I felt so sorry for Stevie. My apologies went on and on, but I had to admit that I was secretly pleased. Stevie stayed in the single bed from that night on and there was no more disruption. The boys in the dorm soon forgot about the incident, although Stevie found it hard to mix with any of those outside our little class.

I had been so intent on remembering Stevie's Birthday, I'd forgotten my own, which I realised with some surprise had been and gone while we were living at the farm. It didn't matter although suddenly being twenty-three now, I felt terribly old. The important thing for me was that Stevie enjoyed his tenth Birthday. I had already bought a card at the Post Office, with two little puppies on the front saying, 'Many Happy Returns of the Day' and later, asked Cook if on these occasions she usually made a cake. I was disappointed to hear that parents either sent them to their sons by post, or boys from more affluent families had them baked in town. She said that with so many boys in the school, she'd be making one every day, which wouldn't have been practical and not only that, with sugar so precious now it wouldn't be possible anyway.

In that case, I had to give him a nice present instead and decided to buy him something he'd really like. There was a small toy shop in town, and the next Saturday while Stevie was on the pitch, I went along to see what they had. On the upper shelf in the window there was a display of books, a few jigsaws, a couple of cars and a London bus. Finger puppets stood to attention in various shapes and sizes beneath this and seemed to be the cheapest option although hardly exciting. Then I spied something glinting in the far corner and went in to investigate further.

The toy gun in its holster and the cowboy hat I added at the last mad moment cost much more than the sum I had in mind, but I was really pleased with my purchases and knew Stevie would be too. Walking back to school, I noticed some small odd shaped bits of iron laying at the side of the road and after checking to see that no one was looking, scooped them up quickly into my handkerchief. They would be the cherry on the cake he wasn't having, because for some reason, it seemed that all small boys loved to collect bits of shrapnel. I had no idea where they had come from, or if this might be the real thing, but even if it turned out to be just bits of old iron, I would call it 'shrapnel'.

The bad start at Witherley Hall meant that Stevie had yet to make good friends, and this bothered me because his Birthday wouldn't be celebrated with any pals. The other four slow learners I taught were timid little things and barely spoke to me, let alone each other. The best I could do, was to ask Cook and Matron to join us at the Tea Room in town and with Stevie's Birthday falling on a Saturday, this was perfect. All I had to do was obtain permission from the Head of Lower School to take Stevie out for a couple of hours and this was my next mission.

Mr. Soames had been due to retire the year before, but with

so many teachers joining-up, he was staying on indefinitely. His beady black eyes and long nose were encased in a thin, waxy face framed by wispy grey hair. The cap and gown he wore every single day were both filthy, covered in a mixture of chalk and what could have been past dinners. He always carried a cane, which I didn't like at all although I was told it was more of a deterrent and rarely used. The biggest problem though, was that he was very set in his ways and flatly refused the permission I needed.

I was so disappointed and began to protest by saying that it was Stevie's first Birthday since his family had been killed and that he deserved a nice time. He was adamant that Stevie shouldn't be allowed a privilege under any circumstances and still refused. I went back to my room in a terrible mood. Cook heard me clunking around and knocked on the door to see what was wrong. When I told her, she smiled saying, "*Go back, ask him again and when he refuses say that Cook would be grateful.*"

Without knowing the reason for this guidance, I did exactly that. His face coloured and all he did was nod once, turning away quickly and wafting along the corridor leaving a peculiar odour behind. He wasn't one of my favourite members of staff for lots of reasons, but whatever influence Cook had over him had done the trick. I had my permission and that was all I cared about.

Saturday morning came and I woke Stevie by singing 'Happy Birthday'. Cook and Matron both had cards for him and between them had bought him a pair of gloves. He sat up in bed with 'Trucky' in one hand and I gave him a cup of tea in the other, while I piled the cards and presents on his lap. I had stuffed the iron in some cotton wool inside an empty wooden tea box with the word 'SHRAPNEL' written on it and balanced this on the end of his bed.

"*And we're going out for tea later*", I told him gleefully.

Expecting him to be overjoyed with this news, I was quite upset with his reaction. He wasn't crying exactly, but had tears streaming down his face. I took his tea, placed it on the windowsill and sat beside him.

"*Come on now,*" I whispered. "*Open your presents and after lunch we'll walk into town with cook and Matron and have a lovely tea.*"

Wiping his nose on his pyjama sleeve, he said, "*Thank you, Lelly, I'll open them later.*"

He washed and dressed and went off to the sports field without eating. Miserable and totally deflated, I heard Matron talking to Cook in the kitchen and went in to see them both sitting at the big table.

"*He's not very happy and hasn't even opened his presents.*" I said woefully.

Cook poured me a cup of tea and I sat with them. I refused to howl, but when they were both being so kind, it was hard to hold back the tears and howl, I did.

"*What did you expect, love?*" Cook asked. "*All the sad memories of his little life to disappear overnight?*"

Not knowing what I expected, I realised I'd been stupid to expect him to behave in any other way. A good cry did me good though and by lunchtime, I felt better and found it easier to handle Stevie's celebration.

I wanted to tell you that the Tea Party was a great success, but it wasn't. It wasn't a party at all and quite honestly, I don't want to talk about it, although Stevie opened his presents before bedtime and seemed to like them.

CHAPTER ELEVEN

Derring-Do

It had been almost a week since Stevie's Birthday and more than six weeks since that bomb dropped on us. I was supervising the lunch break in the quad, where Stevie was destroying other boys' conkers with the giants provided by Alec, when a Monitor arrived with a message that Mr. Fortescue wanted to see me in his study. Unable to leave until a Prefect took over my job, I began to think of all sorts of reasons for being summoned. My biggest worry was that there was news of Stevie's family and I went to see him with my heart in my mouth.

As I knocked on the study door, I heard Mr. Stone's voice and then Mr. Fortescue call, *"Enter."* Both men stood as I walked into the room, which was full of cigarette smoke. I coughed, more with nervousness than choking and Mr. Stone offered me his chair. I had been in the Headmaster's study only once before when I first arrived at the school and at the time, hadn't taken in the surroundings. The smell of cigarettes mixed with perhaps a whiff of formaldehyde was uppermost, but then there was also a musty smell. Stuffed animal heads adorned the walls and several smaller animals stared out from inside their glass domes. It was a most unpleasant room.

"Mr. Stone has some news that may require your assistance." Mr Fortescue told me. I sighed with relief and coughed again. *"Oh yes."* I replied.

"I'll allow Mr. Stone to give you the whole story and then you can make your decision." He added.

I felt rather exposed sitting on the chair and didn't know whether to cross my legs in a ladylike fashion, fold my arms, or what. In the end, I sat on my hands and kept my knees together but remained uncomfortable, wondering if I looked like a naughty schoolgirl. Then Frank began to unravel such a story, that if I was intrigued when he started, I was almost dumbstruck by the time he had finished. Apart from clenching my fists a few times, I sat perfectly still as I listened to his description of incredible past events, immense sorrow, and injustice. I stared at him in amazement as he unfolded his tale of derring-do.

When the Great War began in 1914, a young Jew, Reuben Van Bergen had been studying English in his hometown of Amsterdam when rather than go to war, the Dutch government decided to remain neutral. Reuben had other ideas though and with two fellow students, risked his life by sailing across the North Sea to England and enlisted with the British Army. Frank Stone had also enlisted and found himself fighting alongside Reuben in the trenches where their experiences together forged something special.

Throughout the horrors of trench warfare, they literally stuck together like glue amongst the mud and lice. Brothers in arms, they vowed to be friends forever and surviving the war, despite his bad health, Frank visited Reuben in Holland regularly. Frank had not married, choosing to dedicate his life to teaching, but by 1929 there was the addition of a wife, Aletta and three children for Reuben. 1935 saw the rise of the Nazi Party and the announcement in Germany of something called, the Nuremburg Laws, which Reuben viewed as such a big threat to his family, that he moved them to Luxembourg.

Frank had not heard from Reuben since the events of 1939. In May, the following year there was the disaster at Dunkirk and Germany had occupied Luxembourg with little resistance. His last two letters remained unanswered and all Reuben spoke of in the exchanges before then, was that he could see a need for another move perhaps to the south of France. His last words were that if nothing else, he hoped to evacuate the children Miriam 17, Noah 14 and Luuk who was eleven years old to a place of safety and that the only person he would trust to look after them was Frank.

Frank couldn't have known that disastrous events had already taken place though, because before any arrangements could be made, Luuk returned home from school one day to find that his family had been arrested by the German authorities. Sympathetic neighbours had quickly taken him in, risking their own lives by hiding him for weeks, until the whereabouts of one small boy ceased to be of further interest to the Secret Police.

During this time, a motley band of French people resisting the German occupation known as the '*refus absurd*' were also hiding stranded British soldiers left behind after the Dunkirk beaches had emptied. Not only were they urgently looking for ways of returning them to England to continue the fight, but the fact that Luuk's family, amongst others, had literally disappeared incensed them so much that Luuk was included in their rescue plans.

Any arrangements were intensely dangerous as not everyone could be trusted and consequently, French aid was thinly spread. Many soldiers had been rounded-up, had died of their wounds, or were too sick to travel. Luuk was suffering from malnutrition with the combination of sparse amounts of food and the obvious emotional impact of his ordeal. Moving him would be a further risk, but the alternatives were unthinkable.

With the help and support of a new department in England designed to communicate with these people, Frank at last received news that five weeks ago, Luuk had been smuggled out of Luxembourg into neutral Sweden where he would remain as a refugee as he had no papers. However, should Frank be willing to accept him, he would be hidden on board one of the Swedish timber ships sailing to America and dropped as close to our coast as possible. This was very risky because although neutral, the ship could be fired upon, or intercepted by German patrol boats along the way with dire, unlawful consequences should any fugitive be discovered. Lives were also at risk in the British boat meeting it.

Frank had replied through obscure channels that he would accept responsibility for Luuk and had taken advice from Mr. Fortescue, who was unsure about the legal side of things, but the priority was to get him here safely. '*Things would be sorted out*', he assured him. The latest message had been sent six days ago, which meant that the liaison with the ship was twelve hours away. The clandestine repatriation of Luuk and two Dunkirk escapees in a fishing boat would be paid for by the authorities here, although Frank would have to reach Hastings under his own steam.

It was a fantastic tale. I had never heard such a story in real life. '*The Spy in Black*', a film that Dad and I had seen at the cinema was exciting enough, but that was just a bit of a yarn. This was true and meant saving the life of a boy just like Stevie. We'd all heard horror stories of what was going on with Jewish people in the east, but this was rather close to home. Persecuted for being different, or following another religion was no reason to harm someone. What right did they have to do that? I was so inspired by this but then felt compelled to ask, "*Where do you think the family is now? Could they be looking for him?*"

Frank replied indignantly, "*I think they're dead. They've killed them all. All four of them,*"

An awkward silence was broken when I said, "*How can I help?*"

"*I knew you'd help*", he said. "*You're doing such a marvellous job with the others will you look after Luuk too?*"

Frank had misunderstood my answer, which was rhetorical rather than an offer to do something constructive. Sensing my apprehension, Mr. Fortescue chimed in, "*I'm sure Cook, and Matron will help out.*"

Doing a marvellous job? Was I? This little boy will be in a worse state of mind than Stevie was. Parents disappeared, brother and sister too. Smuggled away from the clutches of an

179

evil regime. Half-starved. The language barrier would be the biggest problem. Did I have a choice? How could I refuse to help with something so urgent?

Well, *"in for a penny ..."* as Nan would say.

"Of course," I whispered.

Shaking Frank's hand and wishing him good luck, I left the room wondering what on earth I'd done. Frank spoke Dutch to a certain extent, but how would I communicate with Luuk? I returned to the quad to find it empty and hurried to my little classroom to find my five slow learners, who were soon to become six. There was no point in telling Stevie about the boy who would be joining us until he was safely here because I had no idea when that would be, or if it would happen at all. I couldn't help looking at my watch for the rest of the day and into the evening, imagining all sorts of scenarios. It became so annoying when I had no specific time to go on but feeling honoured to be part of such a secret mission somehow thought I should worry. So that's what I did for most of the night.

Sure, as eggs-is-eggs, I slept badly and was glad it was a Saturday. The whole school would be outside for rugby and a paperchase and without a class to take, I could carry on worrying. Between changing our bed linen and dealing with the laundry, I spoke to Cook and Matron who were as unsure about this as I. *"Well, we don't know if he'll be normal, do we?"* was Mrs. Quick's fourpenny worth and Matron's contribution was equally negative, *"Should be with his own kind, really. I hope he doesn't have lice!"*

It was late afternoon when we heard that Mr. Fortescue had collected Frank and Luuk from the station and they were here at last. The boy hadn't travelled well and the whole experience had taken its toll on them both. Frank put him to bed in his room where he slept until Sunday evening and it was then I had a message inviting me up there, which was rather improper. I hadn't been to that part of the school before and felt like an intruder in an obviously male-dominated area but arrived after supper at the time arranged. Matron had agreed to a once only visit and expected the door to be left open to avoid wagging tongues.

Frank answered my gentle tap and I cautiously stepped inside. Luuk stood and bowed when he saw me, which I found very poignant. He wasn't the little boy I was expecting. Tall for his age, allowing Frank's pyjamas to fit him perfectly, he was emaciated. Hollow cheeks and a straight nose, in what was usually perhaps an attractive face, his skin sallow and ulcerated. I had never seen a child in such poor condition and was distressed by his appearance although I tried not show it by offering my hand. He wouldn't understand what I said but hoped my smile would break the ice. Patches of sore skin showed through his long, brown hair adding to his pitiful state. Luuk stared at me from sunken green eyes surrounded by dark circles and said softly, "*Uw Dienaar.*" I looked at Frank, who hesitated. "*Erm ... Your Servant.*" I smiled again and squeezed his hand.

Poor Frank had slept in his armchair the night before. He looked dreadful and I asked what the plan was as far as domestic arrangements were concerned. Apart from the three in the San., there was only one empty bed in the whole school – the one Stevie had used, but this was unsuitable. Luuk would surely feel alienated and alone amongst so many English boys. Without really thinking it through properly, I blindly suggested he sleep with Stevie in my double bed, while I use the single. It was the least I could do. The words tumbled out of my mouth leaving me reeling at my generous and impulsive offer, but then I reminded myself that there was a war on, and we all had to make sacrifices. Frank was overwhelmed by this and translated the idea to Luuk in words that were hard to believe made up a language, although Luuk immediately nodded his approval. Dutch was all double to me.

The next thing was to introduce 'my boys' to each other. I was making quite a collection. Before that though, a warm bath and a hot meal for Luuk was very necessary, so the three of us traipsed downstairs where I filled the tub with a little more than the few inches we were officially allowed; it wouldn't hurt just this once. Then, leaving Frank to sort out Luuk, I found Stevie with my other boys in the Common Room where I sat them down to tell the story of the Dutch boy's escape.

Suitably intrigued, Stevie and I said goodnight to the others and went to our room, where Luuk was already sound asleep in the double bed. Frank sat on the other and smiling at us both said quietly, *"Thank you for doing this. His family would be so grateful."* Stevie, never failing me, first put a hand on Frank's shoulder in his usual wise way, stood for a moment to look at Luuk lying there, then moved the eiderdown closer to his chin. I should have been used to his virtues by now, but Stevie continued to humble me with such noble qualities.

I woke early the next morning to find the double bed empty. Instantly worried like a mother hen, I went into the kitchen hoping Mrs. Quick was there. She wasn't, but Stevie and Luuk were. They sat beside each other at the long table with a glass of water each, while Stevie drew on a sheet of baking parchment. I hated to disturb them and listened at the door for a moment, where I heard Stevie say, *"Na, this is where we are na and this is where we ave grub."* He was drawing a plan of the school for Luuk. You see what I mean now, don't you?

Mr. Fortescue had contacted the Police to tell them about Luuk and Sergeant Prothero arrived after breakfast to take details. He thought that as the 'Bigwigs' had been involved in Luuk's escape, there would be no need to investigate under the Emergency Powers Act as long as he reported in weekly. Sometime later, Luuk would go before a Tribunal and all being well, they would issue Immigration papers, meantime he could stay at the school. It was a big relief to know that he could be with us and not interned. Clothes and shoes would be supplied from the bottomless pit Matron seemed to have. The doctor looked him over and fortunately, there was no lice to deal with, so a clean-up and good food would be all that was necessary.

In the days that passed, Luuk's health improved enormously. He became the subject of both curiosity and admiration, with the story of his daring escape from an occupied country, although he was unable to tell it himself and I'm sure Stevie enjoyed an embellishment, or two. Stevie was included in this acclaim and I could see that this, coupled with his strength of character and a different lifestyle was doing wonders for him. It was delightful to witness the boys' recovery, although none of us knew if their experiences would haunt them forever.

Frank though, was not doing so well. I wasn't the only one to think that his valiant plan to snatch Luuk from imminent danger had been a bit too much for him when he began to look terribly ill. We knew he'd seen the doctor and some of us were worried that he hadn't been given any sort of medicine to take. Frank appeared to be flagging fast and was simply accepting the fact. He was more than eager to help Luuk learn English and coached him at every opportunity, which made me wonder about the sense of urgency.

It was November 4th and plans were made for the next evening when it should have been a traditional Guy Fawkes Night. Of course, a man called Adolph Hitler had scuppered those plans and an alternative 'indoor' evening was arranged instead. It wouldn't be quite the same without a bonfire but would be better than nothing and we were all excited about it, although we teachers tried not to show our enthusiasm.

Mr Edwards had bought several boxes of indoor fireworks, which were not a patch on the real thing, but would be fun to light, the gardeners had collected hundreds of apples for bobbing and Mrs. Quick had been saving sugar and vinegar for weeks to make toffee apples. Mr Fortescue had asked the Bursar to provide some money to buy bran tub gifts and with great reluctance he did, and the older boys were charged with organising table games. The evening was good for everyone, although Luuk was rather bemused by the whole thing, especially the apple-bobbing.

Stevie and Luuk had gone to bed quite exhausted after the excitement of our odd Guy Fawkes night. It was a totally new experience for Luuk, and we saw him laugh for the first time, although I felt that the novelty had done wonders for them both. I was sure a bond already existed between them and it was comforting to hear them making sense of each other despite the language barrier.

Luuk often had a 'glazed' look though; the faraway one that Stevie sometimes had. It would have been amazing if they hadn't been affected by their dreadful experiences, but it was even more amazing that they had the strength of character to soldier on without complaint or hold a grudge against the injustice of it all. Such a terrible time for anyone - let alone youngsters. I so admired them both and felt they were survivors rather than victims. They would be fine. I would make sure of it.

CHAPTER TWELVE

Frank and The Fugitive

I had a letter! Matron popped her head round our door and waved it at me as if it were a flag. It was a wonderful sight, even more so when I recognised Dad's handwriting. I put it in my handbag until I had a moment alone but itching to know what he had to say, opened the envelope while the boys were still in bed. There was another envelope folded inside, with Nan's tell-tale letter 'L' at the start of my name and the swirl of her 'Y' at the end. Desperate to open them both, I was so excited, I left the boys to dress and read them three times sitting on the toilet with the door firmly bolted.

Nan had no idea where I was, so had sent the letter to Dad for him to forward. It was no surprise to hear that she was having a difficult time with Auntie Win, although cousin, Geoffrey had left for training camp and it was easier with just three people in the house. She talked about the weather, the seaside and the difficulty finding knitting wool. Reading between the lines, she sounded as miserable as sin.

If her letter didn't depress me, then Dad's news certainly did. One of his Firemen had been killed and four others seriously injured fighting air raid fires ravaging the city day after day. The devastation was unbelievable and casualties extremely high from every walk of life. Businesses struggled to continue, paperwork from offices fluttered around the rubble like confetti and many historical buildings were in ruins. Those shops still standing stoically kept their opening hours, some with a sign in the window saying, *'Bombed but not defeated'*.

That, he said was a potted version of the scene. It seemed

that the Luftwaffe was determined to finish us off and at the time of writing, there had been raids every night since early September. Our own street had been hit again and it was unlikely that we'd ever be able to return to our home, which upset Dad so much because he felt the house was our last link with Mum. It upset me too.

I cried each time I read the letters and my heart ached with loss all over again. Touching the one picture I had of Mum and Dad was some comfort and brought memories flooding back. I pictured the house and remembered the sweet perfume of Mum's favourite pink Roses either side of the front gate. The taste of her lipstick – the one she allowed me to use until I had my own. The sound of Dad's terrible singing in the bath and the peculiar-shaped carrots he grew. Thank heavens for memories and bolts on toilet doors.

Must pull myself together. Be strong. I dried my eyes and knew they must be red, so ran the cold tap in the basin, splashed some cold water on my face and took a few deep breaths. Placing the letters back in their envelopes and slipping them in my handbag, I patted the outside as if to tell it to look after these precious things. Realising how daft that was, I shook my head and said out loud, "*For goodness sake, Lesley!*"

The ruckus from the bedroom had stopped, which meant the boys had gone up to breakfast. The boys. Here I was a daft woman of twenty-three, whose best achievement to date was the ability to stoke a cooking range, responsible for children ten and eleven years of age. That thought reminded me - when would Luuk turn twelve? Something as small as this was so important to know. I was doing my best and with Matron's help at least the boys had some female influences, but they needed a family to love and nurture them. Was this a hopeless goal? The weeks were flying by with still no news from Mrs. Johnson and the longer Stevie and I were together, the harder it would be to say goodbye. It was a strange existence because on the surface we were both very settled although I kept reminding myself that our relationship could end tomorrow. I was also becoming quite attached to Luuk.

With the passing weeks, the now handsome Dutch boy had an Identity Card, a Ration Book and a gas mask and had picked up enough English to join in with my teaching of the Three R's – *well, to a certain extent*. His Dutch accent was very strong, which we all found amusing, although Luuk took it in good humour when we laughed at some of his words because a 'D' at the end of a word in Dutch is pronounced with a 'T'. The four evacuees had really come out of their shells, enough to make them naughty sometimes, but I saw this as progress, and we all seemed content. Stevie and Luuk enjoyed 'Treasure Island' so much that each evening, they relived the chapter we'd read, which meant I had the devil of a job getting them to bed between bouts of swashbuckling swordplay and giant leaps from bed-to-bed. I loved them both.

Frank thought that Luuk's Birthday had been and gone and that he was now twelve, but with no documents of any kind, the only way to be sure was to ask him. This might be awkward though and have an adverse effect, so I gave Stevie the task. Stupidly, I thought he would be diplomatic and spend time delicately asking pertinent questions using limited English and the special language they had between them, but no.

"*When's ya Birthday, Lukey?*" Stevie blurted out the moment Luuk came into our room. Luuk frowned with a peculiar look on his face, something between panic and curiosity.

"***BIRTH … DAY***" Stevie said loudly. Luuk looked blank and said nothing.

"*You know …*" Stevie continued, cradling his arms, and rocking them backwards and forwards, pointing to him.

The penny dropped. "*Aah*", Luuk chuckled. "*Augustus – Negun … Nine*".

So, he'd had his Birthday and was twelve.

"*Mine was in October … 'Oct … **Toe** … **Berrr**',* Stevie said in an illustrative way. "*I was ten and yours' is August, so you're*

187

... two years older than me". Stevie said cheerfully, *"But don't think you can push me around!"*

These words were lost on Luuk, who simply smiled and nodded before they marched off arm-in-arm into the kitchen.

Frank was now very unwell. He'd looked pale and fatigued and had spent the last three days in bed refusing to see the doctor. Matron had been so worried about him though and called him anyway. Frank had already been given the bad news and now we knew too. It seemed that the kidney disease he'd picked up in the trenches was getting worse and there was nothing to be done to save him. He was moved to the Sanatorium in town and the following Sunday afternoon I went to see him.

Standing at the door of the ward, I studied the occupant of each bed. Unable to see him, I thought I must have gone to the wrong place and turned to leave until I heard a weak voice call my name. Trying not to show my alarm when at last I recognised Frank's face, I smiled and went towards him. His appearance had changed dramatically, and it was obvious that this would be my one and only visit.

We embraced and in doing so, I felt every bone in his shrivelled trunk. He was more than pleased to see me, and I'd only just sat down when he said that he knew he was dying and asked if I would witness the signature to his will. Apart from being taken aback by his acceptance of an untimely death, I wasn't sure about signing a will. Dad had always told me to be careful about signing anything and I began to shake my head slowly with Dad's words ringing in my ears. Then he took my hand and said,

"Lesley, I have no family and the money I have should be going to Reuben, but with the likelihood of him being dead, I want Luuk to have it. He will be the sole beneficiary and the money will be held in a Trust for him by my Solicitor".

I had no idea how much money was involved, or even what a Trust was really. However, the circumstances were terribly sad and although I had never been asked to do anything

188

remotely legal before, agreed to do as he asked. Mr. Fortescue was prepared to act as liaison, so I thought it must be okay and a dated signature with my name and current address was all that was required. The ward Sister was glad to help and unlike my hesitant scrawl, she completed the task of second witness so confidently, I was quite sure she had performed this duty before.

With this done and the will safely in an envelope in Sister's office drawer, the pained look on Frank's face disappeared. He thanked me, saying how much he had enjoyed our friendship, but I gulped when he said he had even wondered whether we might have begun a romance. I nodded, smiling sweetly and fortunately at this moment he closed his eyes, so was unable to see the tears in mine.

It was a Friday morning two weeks later when Matron woke me with the news that Frank had died in the early hours. Mr. Fortescue would announce this during assembly and although we doubted Luuk would understand the English, he should be told straight away. That sinking feeling came over me. How many times can I be expected to break this type of news? Instantly, I removed my selfish head and replaced it with my compassionate one, because it would be Stevie, not me who would have to explain that the last known link to Luuk's family was gone. I woke Stevie gently and told him. Glancing at the sleeping Luuk, he said wisely, *"We 'ave to 'ave 'ot, sweet tea, done' we?"*

I nodded and went into the kitchen to do as I was told, returning with the tea just five minutes later to find Stevie cuddling Luuk who was crying. I never knew what had been said, but whatever it was, it was managed without the luxury of sweet words and must have been cruel.

We attended morning assembly together and when Mr. Fortescue made the announcement about Frank many of the younger boys turned to look at Luuk, who sat bravely between Stevie and me. When we were dismissed after prayers, a few of the boys spoke to Luuk and a couple shook his hand. It was very moving, and I believe he appreciated the gesture.

In the days that followed, school life continued in the ordinary way until a week later, we heard that Frank's funeral would take place the next Friday. Matron assumed I would want to go and asked if I had decided whether, or not to take the boys. This was an enormous decision to make and my immediate answer was that I thought it inappropriate given the recent events in their lives and said I'd 'sleep on it'.

However, sleep was almost impossible as I toyed with one scenario after another. Stevie had never been to a funeral, or witnessed a burial and for all I knew, neither had Luuk. The incident with Stevie and the rabbit was horrible. Would this trigger something else? What horrors had Luuk seen in Holland and in the months before leaving Luxembourg? I needed advice, but from who?

My restless night eventually saw Saturday, the day the younger boys have sporting activities in the morning and board games in the afternoon and for once in the week, Stevie and Luuk were up with the lark. Unwashed, they dressed in their borrowed white shorts and tops and quickly tied their plimsol laces before swallowing some bread and butter and a cup of tea from the kitchen and dashing off. I was at a loose end and decided to deal with my laundry and perhaps write to Dad and Nan. I was still battling with the decision about the funeral.

Laundry done and hung on the washing line, I wandered out in the peace of the quad. Everyone including Matron and Cook were watching the morning sports and apart from voices in the distance and the occasional screams of delight when someone had perhaps scored a goal or won a race, all I could hear was birdsong – maybe a Robin at this time of year.

It was a lovely school and I was happy to be there. Mr. Sykes kept the gardens beautifully. There was still a lot of colour with White Forsythia, dark pink Cyclamen and Purple Hazel and the herbs were still flourishing. I picked a little of the Sage and then the Rosemary breathing in their scent. It reminded me of the farm. What was Linda doing now? How did Joe and Gladys get on with their trip to Birmingham? Perhaps I'd write to Linda and maybe keep in touch, although she really wasn't the most feminine of women and I doubted we'd have anything in common outside the farm. It made me think again about her relationship with the barmaid who seemed rather dainty. Curious.

The sportsmen and their spectators were returning and suddenly the peace and quiet was shattered with noise and confusion. The ruckus on the first floor above us meant that the usual mayhem was in progress, with the juniors all trying to be first in one of the three tubs. None were cleaned between occupants, which meant that the last boy came out dirtier than when he went in. Half an hour later, the noise changed to what sounded like thundering hooves galloping down the stairs and the inevitable din erupted in the Refectory. Saturday lunch was always cold meat and cheese with chunks of bread and margarine and Cook had stewed all the leftover apples with a huge bag of sultanas she'd found at the back of the pantry. Of course, it would have been even better with butter from the Gladys churn and runny honey from the poacher.

With lunch over, the younger boys went to the Common Room to play board games or construct a jigsaw. Mr. Thistle was the Master in charge on this occasion, which was wonderful because he allowed the wireless to be turned on and would always find something to entertain us. Saturday being Tuck Shop Day it was extra special although the items for sale were hardly plentiful. The older boys were permitted to walk into town to the sweetshop so long as they were back at four o'clock and a long line of them left school banging the huge front door with each exit. The school was in a good mood, but I continued to grapple with the funeral thing.

In an atmosphere of blissful comfort interrupted only by the occasional blare of a trumpet from the wireless, or laughter from one of the boys, I sat in an armchair opposite the blazing fire, thinking. I knew that once a month the local vicar offered communion in the school chapel and tomorrow was one of those days. I had mentioned my lack of religious beliefs earlier, although lately my few encounters with the church had provided comfort, so I wondered if I dare take advantage yet again by talking to the vicar and asking for his advice. With no other brainwave this was what I would do.

It was a cold night, but the boys slept soundly until seven o'clock and I didn't toss and turn as much as I had the night before, although I was apprehensive about speaking to the vicar. I hoped he would advise me not to take them to the funeral and even if he thought I should, I didn't have to. After all, they were my responsibility and it would be my decision since I knew them better than anyone else. We went into breakfast. Luuk and Stevie chose some bread and dripping and a mug of cocoa, but all I could manage was a cup of tea. Communion was held at nine o'clock and I seemed to check my watch as every minute passed. I told Matron what I intended to do, excusing myself from the immediate job of clearing away the breakfast things and she gave me a little bit of confidence by agreeing that it was a good idea to "*get an opinion from a man.*" Linda would have winced if she'd heard her say that.

So yes, I snuck in at the back of the chapel about ten minutes before communion had finished and was surprised to see how many boys and teachers had attended. Some I didn't expect to see, such as sixth former, 'Petey' Sorenson who had a reputation for being a bit of a bully and Mr. Sears the History teacher who was always going on about 'killing the Hun'. I waited until everyone had left the chapel and watched as the vicar dismantled the altar.

Desperately trying to remember his name, he sensed my presence and turned around. "*Hello*", he said, "*Who have we here?*" Beginning with an apology for taking up his time, I quickly explained my quandary and the reasons for not wanting to '*open-up a can of worms*' for Stevie and Luuk. I blushed having said that because maybe it wasn't the right sort of thing to say to a vicar, but he didn't seem to mind and said,

"We prayed for Frank today and it will be me conducting his service next week. He was a popular teacher, so there could be a lot of boys feeling they should attend." He went on to say that logistically, if that was the case, it would be difficult to transport a large number to the church and it may even be necessary to obtain parental permission, which would be hard to do in the present climate with parents scattered everywhere. Then he came up with the perfect solution. *"Why not have a memorial service here before the funeral? That would solve all the problems."*

Not knowing that this was possible, my relief was evident. I could only hope he would excuse my enthusiasm when I clapped my hands together. He would speak to the Headmaster and make the necessary arrangements for an evening service, which anyone who wanted to, could attend. My troubles were solved, thank goodness, or maybe thank God! We shook hands, but I could have kissed him.

Supper was at six o'clock every day except Sundays when Cook prepared a 'roast' and because there were more pots and pans to wash, she liked to serve at half-past five. Lately, the 'roast' had consisted of potatoes, cabbage and swede or carrots, huge pies with indeterminable contents, or maybe braised sheep hearts. She always managed to conceal the rations with clever carving, a tasty herb stuffing, or thick gravy and being master of both disguise and quota, her personal knack of creating a meal the boys and staff would wolf down without question, meant we never went hungry.

It was chilly outside. Caretaker, Mr. Thomas had kept the fire going in the Common Room and I was grateful being the teacher on duty there. The Upper School boys with their privileges had taken advantage of this fact and disappeared in every direction, while Stevie, Luuk and the other young boys congregated in the Common Room once again, waiting for our 'roast' supper, whatever it may be.

As the Blackout Monitors closed the window shutters, I noticed the sky was clear apart from a few fluffy clouds. The nip in the air was most certainly a herald to winter and with the sun setting at just after five o'clock, the evenings were 'drawing in', although the government had decided that this year, England would not put the clocks back by one hour for reasons known only to them. The Common Room was last on the Monitor's list and I remember them 'shutting up shop' as they called it specifically that evening, because I had glanced at my watch thinking it was already quite dark. 'Children's Hour' on the wireless played in the background and was being ignored. Unlike the evening Princess Elizabeth had spoken on the programme when we all gathered round to hear her speak, no one was listening to the story being told. Stevie and Luuk were playing Snakes and Ladders in a competitive way asking for the overhead light to be turned on so they could finish their game and I had told them there wasn't time to do that.

It was a lazy winter's evening. Forever-hungry boys were coming in through the front door, making for the dining room in anticipation of roast 'something' and all seemed well within the school. After a few moans, Stevie folded the board and Luuk piled the tiddlywinks in the little pot and I told other boys to finish what they were doing to get ready to go into supper. It was about this time that we all heard the unmistakable sound of the town air raid sirens and everyone in the room instantly stopped what they were doing. Stevie and I looked at each other in recognition of the noise and Luuk put his hands over his ears, terror showing in his green eyes.

It was a shock at first, but the consensus amongst staff who soon began to appear and then disappear, was that it was a drill of some kind. We were miles away from anything remotely strategic apart from the railway and convinced ourselves that we were safe. There were no sounds of bombs landing in the 'crump' that had been described by those unlucky enough to witness the 'Blitz' and it had to be a false alarm. A bomb had dropped in the area during the summer holidays apparently, but that and one that landed in a field killing a cow was believed to have been a mistake made by the enemy.

Being the only adult in the room, I thought I'd better say, or do something, so casually told the boys to collect their gas mask and stand in a line at the door. The masks were piled on a settee and it was a good thing the room wasn't filling with gas because there were scuffles between them while they determined whose was whose. I took advantage of this by surreptitiously removing the lipstick and purse from mine scolding myself for using it as a handbag.

It was then that we heard a commotion outside and those of us in the Common Room crowded into the hall hoping to see what was up. The big oak door was wide open with the blackout curtain stuffed to one side and I quickly pulled it across. This did nothing to stifle the noise from outside where boys hollered and shouted, while others raced up and down the gravel drive. Suddenly, our fire bells began to clang furiously and then incredibly, the sound of guns firing from the Anti-Aircraft battery were heard.

I was rather shaky now and for some reason a picture of Stevie in his gas mask all those weeks ago flashed through my mind. Both he and Luuk looked frightened as the sirens continued to wail, and the boom of the guns increased in pace. Two of the youngest boys began to cry and I went to them, taking their hands to give some comfort but wasn't sure what to say when little Andrew Fuller asked if we were going to be bombed and die like 'Twinkle' and Aunty Susan. Luuk and Stevie moved closer to me. I really wanted to scoop them up and run away with them, but with other boys there I couldn't favour my two. Everyone was talking at once and just as panic began to set in, Mr. Fortescue came out of his study and we all fell silent. Disappearing behind the curtain, we could just about hear his voice above the sound of sirens, rumbles and bells as he instructed the boys outside to *"WALK"* around the side of the building and use the door there to assemble in the Refectory. It was a relief to have someone in authority.

The door closed with a bang and he stood in front of us, turning to Mr. Thomas first saying, *"I believe the school is alerted enough now to have the fire bells terminated, if you would be so kind, Mr. Thomas."* Touching his cap, Mr. Thomas trotted off. *"Now boys,"* he went on, *"Remain calm and all will be well. Place your gas mask over your face, form an orderly queue in pairs and walk quietly and sensibly to the cellars."*

I think I mentioned the cellar doors earlier; one in the hall and one in the kitchen. There were two flights from the hall, but only one flight from the kitchen because that was already one floor down in the basement if you get my drift. The cellars were deep down under the school, so we'd be completely safe – unless the building fell on top of us. The lights were turned on illuminating the steep, stone steps, giving an eery glow. Mr. Fortescue told us to tread carefully because at this time of year they were damp and slippery and anyone landing on the floor after a tumble would be seriously hurt.

The fire bells stopped. We began to form an orderly queue. Cook and Matron appeared looking rather dishevelled, making a beeline for two of the youngest boys and Stevie and Luuk held hands, leaving me to take charge of little Andrew. He was such a tiny little thing and so scared he held onto my hand with both of his. Behind the front door boys were taking their time to walk to the Refectory. Some yelled excitedly, *"Look, look. That searchlight has one!!"* *"Missed it. Missed it. I could do better than that!!* *"There. There. Look over there!"*

Eventually, the whole school had trooped carefully down the shallow stone steps and sat safely in the cellars while whatever was going on outside went on. I was amazed at the way the staff and boys had behaved. Mr. Fortescue must have been pleased that the drill was executed without incident, considering it had never been put into operation before. Everyone seemed to know what to do. The only part I played however, was to lift the bottom of my gas mask and say, *"Here"* when my name was called and every now and then, make sure my lipstick and purse were still tucked down the top of my corselet.

Cook pulled at the gas mask straps and wiped the inside with her apron, saying she hoped Enid, Mr. Sykes' wife was safely in their cottage and that Mr. Sykes was wearing his tin hat on the roof. Matron, who was taking her time putting on the ghastly contraption, said Mr. Thomas was mad for not going with them to the cellars. *"He always has to know what's going on,"* Cook said, *"He'll be rushing off to the village hall with his rifle by now,"* she added with a sigh. We all knew Cook had a soft spot for Mr. Thomas.

Wooden benches had been arranged in anticipation of a need to shelter in the cellars and the pecking order continued even now as we sat in our various classes. We were unable to see the senior boys and their Masters, who had come down last and were on the hall side, but we could hear them talking, while the smaller boys and we three ladies sat silently together listening to what sounded like the rumble of thunder above us. The cellars were cavernous. Lower school had congregated on the kitchen side and I was grateful for that because the toilet was just up the steps and around the corner. I hoped we wouldn't be there too long, because that would mean others using it and having witnessed some of the boys' habits knew that it would be in a right old state after a few of their visits.

The steel furnace and chimney were in an alcove on this side, so it was nice and warm and beside this, lay a pile of glistening black coal. It was delivered down a wide chute through the external hatches in the ground above and Mr. Thomas would argue with Mr. Sykes about the need to keep the area around it free from plants and shrubs. With things growing all over the hatches he said, the coalman would find it difficult to open them up and they had to be kept clear. They loved to argue, even about coal.

Seeing the pile of coal beneath the chute, I was reminded of Mrs. Atkinson next door at home when she was expecting Phillip, her second child, who I told you about earlier. She would chew on a lump of coal most days; a peculiar and quite revolting thing to do, although Nan said it was the same as her own craving for pickled onions when she was expecting. It turned out that Mrs. Atkinson had a deficiency of some kind and was compelled to do this. Her teeth were always grey, even after she stopped eating it. Funny how something can instantly jog your memory. Just thought I'd mention it.

We had water from the tap above a huge Butler sink and electric light and we even had music from Mr. Sanders and his Ukulele. However, when it was announced that the whole school would have to use Cook's toilet – and OUR toilet, because they were below ground level, I knew that sometime later, I would need to borrow Ethel's rubber gloves. The school seemed to have a Monitor, or Prefect for every occasion and two of the Prefects were given the temporary title of 'WC Warden' to ensure yet another orderly queue for this purpose. It seemed Mr. Fortescue had thought of everything, except the most important item as far as growing boys was concerned. Food!

About six o'clock the sirens stopped, and we were told to remove our masks. Then we heard a different sound. It was far away, but quite distinctive and at one time, I'm sure I felt the ground shake. Cook looked at Matron, mouthing the word, "*Bristol.*" I supposed she meant that now it was that city's turn to be bombed. I must have had my selfish head on again, because as awful as that was to think about, I hoped it would give Dad and his men a break.

Air Raid Warnings came and went over the next few hours and our gas masks were on and off like yo-yo's. Every now and then, we heard the guns fire at the hum of aircraft in the sky and then there came a new and much louder sound. It was a sort of high pitched, whining noise ending in a massive explosion, which made us all jump. Cook's muffled scream and several boys' gasps were apparent even through their masks and the ground did shake that time, because the pictures hanging on the walls for safe keeping were suddenly all askew. A cheer went up, which surprised me until I realised that the guns must have shot down an aircraft. Of course, that was a good thing, wasn't it?

By eight o'clock, we were all very hungry and during a quiet spell, Matron and Cook asked Mr. Fortescue for permission to go into the kitchen to grab as much food as they could. With help from the 'WC Wardens', they returned with bowls and spoons, trays of cold roast potatoes and a vat of rice pudding, which they dished up altogether from the sink drainers. Rice pudding at the bottom and a potato on top. It was a most peculiar supper and satisfied us all. Had she found the huge tin of jam she'd been saving for a rainy day though it would have been even better.

The sirens and all the noises that went with it continued until gone midnight, although the only proper explosion we heard was the big one. Most of the pupils slept on and off, either propped up against each other, or on the floor and while we were expected to stay awake, some of the staff dozed. The furnace had been stoked regularly, but it was cold enough to make our clothes damp and in turn, feel thoroughly miserable. The toilet was in dire need of a good clean and I longed for a warm bath and my squeaky old bed. This was just one evening in a shelter. How were others managing night after night after night?

It was almost one o'clock in the morning before the 'all clear' sounded and Mr. Fortescue decided that it was safe for us all to leave the cellars and go to bed. He thanked everyone for their cooperation and announced that the first lesson of the day would be cancelled. He hoped that Cook would be able to serve breakfast at nine o'clock and he would conduct assembly at ten o'clock. I think we all slept like logs although hardly woke refreshed.

Breakfast chatter consisted only of one subject. There was talk that a German aircraft had been shot down with no parachutes seen. This was confirmed by Mr. Sykes, who had been fire-watching on the roof and seen the plane come down in flames having been caught in two streams of light from the Battery. Enid Sykes had sheltered under the kitchen table in their cottage and said the noise of the crash had been terrifying. She was worried all night when her husband had cycled off to join the other members of the Home Guard, who had the grisly job of locating the bodies in the wreckage.

The aircraft was a Heinkel, which had five crew. It was found in a copse completely burnt out with two airmen laying severely burnt beside it and the remains of the other poor souls still inside. It would have been worse had they not already dropped their bombs, but Mr. Sykes said it was an inferno and must have been a horrible death, even if they were the enemy. It would take time to remove what was left of the three of them, but there were hopes for the other two who'd been taken to hospital under guard. An awful story, but it didn't seem to put anyone off their breakfast.

During assembly, we prayed for anyone who had been hurt, or worse in the Bristol air raid. There was no definite news of casualties yet, although 148 bombers had been counted, so it must have been bad. It would have been nice to have said a prayer for the German crew as well, but I suppose that would have been a bit odd even though they were human beings too. I thought how daft it all was. They kill some of us, we kill some of them and so it seems to go on.

Mr. Fortescue must have spoken to the vicar, because he announced that there would be a Memorial Service for Frank Stone on Thursday evening at 6.30pm for anyone who wished to attend, with the funeral being held at ten o'clock on Friday morning. Mr Fortescue would represent the teachers and I would attend with Cook and Matron. Six people in total, including the vicar and the verger. Not many to say goodbye to such a nice man. By Tuesday, we knew that there had been much devastation in Bristol. Dozens were missing, hundreds were injured, and more than two hundred people had been killed. It was very depressing.

The chapel was packed for Frank's Memorial and I hoped it

would make up for the lack of people at the funeral. The service was short and simple. Mr. Fortescue gave a potted version of his life, saying that he had been a hero of the Great War and Mr. Soames, the Geography Master talked about him as a colleague. Cook and Matron cried, but I managed to hold back my tears for Luuk's sake, hoping he would be able to understand enough to know that the tribute was fitting. I was sure he did though, because at one point he whispered, "*Doei, doei, Frank*", which I think was his way of saying goodbye. Stevie sat holding his arm with one hand and the other firmly on the pocket where 'Trucky' sat. Yes, we still used the truck for comfort in our hour of need.

Frank had made provision for his funeral. The hearse arrived at the top of the drive and we followed on in Mr. Fortescue's car. At the church, the vicar conducted a brief service with the verger playing the organ for one hymn. Cook and Matron cried again and this time, so did I. It reminded me too much of the day we buried Grandad and then Mum. Mr. Sykes had managed to find enough Forsythia and Purple Hazel in the gardens to make up a lovely wreath, which Mr. Fortescue laid before we walked away from the grave and afterwards, we had a glass of sherry in the school Library. I was glad when the sad day came to an end.

Leaving the quad with my laundry in a basket the following morning, it was hard to believe that another week had passed and there was still nothing in the post from Mrs. Johnson. I was beginning to wonder if Stevie would ever be settled properly. We'd both accepted life at Witherley Hall now and become accustomed to the security that routine brings. We were also playing a significant part in Luuk's life, but I longed to see Dad and Nan. It was in quiet moments like this that my mind wandered, and I was in danger of getting upset. Perhaps it was the funeral yesterday. I would snap out of it when the boys finished games.

I quite enjoyed taking advantage of the solitude that came with Saturday morning sporting events. It meant I was able to have my underwear discretely on and off the washing line before everyone returned, so knowing I was alone, I was startled to hear a noise near the greenhouse. Mr. Sykes was usually shouting his head off on the sports field, so it wasn't him, but it could be one of his cats, 'Fred', or maybe, 'Ginger'. Walking in that direction, sure enough, 'Fred' was sitting amongst several upturned flowerpots. He'd really made a mess with earth everywhere and I scolded him while turning them back over. He shot-off as I tried to scoop-up as much of the mess as I could, but then remembered that only yesterday, they were full of tomato plants and quite a lot of fruit. They'd done very well, considering it was almost December, but Mr. Sykes truly had a knack with plants.

Cook had her eye on the green tomatoes. It was unlikely they'd ripen now, and she'd be able to make chutney. Obviously, she'd nabbed them already. I carried on walking, deciding to use the other door down to the kitchen, rather than walk through the school and crunched down the gravel path at the side of the building. A few feet past the door, the big, wooden coal chute shutters were set in the ground surrounded by the shrubs that Mr. Sykes had insisted on planting. Some of the smaller plants had been trodden down and I could only hope that the perpetrator was the coalman making a delivery and not any of the boys. Didn't Mr. Thomas say this would happen?

It began to rain, which made me hurry through the door and down the stairs. Once through the warm and cosy kitchen, I reached our bedroom where I placed my clean clothes neatly in the bottom of the three-drawer chest. I couldn't resist peeking in the other two. The top drawer held most of Luuk's little world donated by the school and in the middle, lay Stevie's now abundant stock of clothes, which I lovingly stroked flat with both hands. There wasn't much of mine hanging in the wardrobe and even if I had money for new things, it would mean a trek into the small town with not much choice. With winter round the corner though, I needed a warm coat, a jumper or two and if we had snow, maybe even some boots. What I would do about this was the question.

The inevitable crashing and banging of saucepan lids interrupted my thoughts, as Cook and Ethel began lunch preparations. I helped take trays up to the Refectory when the food was ready, while the noise above signalled returning boys and associated mud. Before my second journey, I asked Cook if she'd found the tin of jam. *"No."* She said annoyed. *"Trouble is, I hide things away and then forget where I hid them!"* Ethel nodded knowingly and we all laughed. I asked if I could help make the chutney from the green tomatoes in the greenhouse and she told me she thought it was Mrs. Sykes' turn to make it. I missed cooking a meal and would love to have shown them the way Gladys dealt with pickling. Maybe I could help Enid instead. I told her about the mess 'Fred' had made and the plants being trodden down around the coal chute shutters and afterwards felt like a real Tell-tale-Tit.

That afternoon, an attempt at teaching the boys the game of 'Monopoly' failed miserably, so once again, it was 'Snakes and Ladders' and Luuk's favourite, 'Tiddlywinks'. I loved to hear them laugh. Then they dozed in front of the fire, while I read the newspaper, which was full of doom and gloom. The air raid on Coventry last week had been terrible and the cathedral was all but destroyed. In retaliation, the RAF bombed Hamburg, Berlin, and Bremen. Was that the right thing to do? I tried to do the crossword, but even that made me miserable and was glad when it was time for supper.

Cook was in the kitchen more than anywhere else and Ethel rarely had time off even though the sweet little scullery maid had recently married a boy from the Brewery. They were both so dedicated. How Mrs. Quick managed to feed us all was a never-ending mystery and although I helped in the kitchen whenever I could, made only a small dent in their work. This time, my help was gratefully accepted, unlike Gladys, preferring to do everything herself. The farm stories I told while we washed the dishes had them in fits of laughter one minute and tears the next and I vowed to write it all down one day. There was no need to elaborate, because the stories were funny, or sad enough. Stevie and Luuk had put themselves to bed. This was often the case on a Saturday after such a busy day and I tiptoed around without turning on the bedroom light. I was tired myself, although I hadn't done much all day. I must have gone to sleep as soon as my head hit the pillow, so had no idea what the time was when I woke up.

I thought one of the boys had stirred. I could hear them both breathing deeply though and turned over. And over. Then counted sheep. The 112th woolly jumper was almost over the fence when I heard something odd. Always plagued by mice, the kitchen had traps down and one had surely been activated because there was a sort of snapping sound. Yes, a mouse. Go back to sleep. Trouble was, I couldn't stop thinking about it. Had it been killed outright, or was it mortally wounded, eventually dying in agony?

A few minutes went by, which was enough time to convince myself that the poor little thing was writhing around caught in the trap. I wasn't keen to do so but would have to look. Slipping on my cardigan which I'd left at the end of my bed, I groped around beneath it to locate my slippers. Waking the boys now would be disastrous – I'd never get them back to sleep again but moving around in the dark was difficult. I felt my way into the kitchen. It was unusually cold there despite the range ticking over and I realised that the draught was coming from the cellar because the door was wide open.

A thin glow from beneath the pantry door meant that Ethel had forgotten to switch the light off again; she had trouble remembering the blackout rules for some reason and would be in trouble if Cook knew. It made it easier for me to find the small lamp on the enormous dresser though and I switched it on. The brilliant light made me squint as I opened the pantry door and cautiously stepping into the big room found the trap complete with nugget of fresh cheese - unlike the mouldy stuff

Gladys used. No mouse. Good. Switching off the light and closing the door, I looked for trap number two.

Now where was it? *Aah, yes,* under the table on the floor, where no feet could reach it. Bending down to investigate, something much larger than a mouse scuttled across the floor. It cast a dark shadow, the silhouette lengthening as it moved. *"Fred",* I whispered, *"How did you get in here? Naughty cat. After the mouse, were you?".* Cook would have a fit if she knew he'd been here. Better get him out before he does any more damage. He hissed and spat at me with ears flat to his head as I pounced, failing to grab him before he disappeared down the stone steps to the cellar. *"Oh, well. He'll have to stay there for a while. At least he's wearing a fur coat."*

A peculiar smell wafted through the air. Ethel would have loaded the range with coal before she left and at first, I thought it was that, although it wasn't the odour we had when the window vent shut accidentally. Unable to identify the whiff, I shrugged as I pulled the door towards me; the kitchen would be very cold by morning if I didn't.

But I didn't close it, because the shock of seeing what stood behind the door made me scream loudly and I stood back. I had never heard myself scream before and that startled me even more. It was the type of reaction to sheer terror that would have made anyone's hair stand on end when they'd seen a monster. I tried to run but was firmly rooted to the spot. Whatever it was, moved. I gasped and leaned backwards, turning my face away until I heard it gurgling through laboured breath rattling like crinkled paper and felt compelled to look back at the tall, ugly creature staggering towards me with arms outstretched just like the one Frankenstein had made. Its heavy footsteps slid across the tiled floor. I screamed again. Was I stuck in some terrible nightmare?

It stared at me from eyes sunken into a melted face distorted by black, charred skin and blistered lips. I tried in vain to scream again, my feet firmly stuck to the ground. Covering my face with an open hand, an overpowering stench reached me. I couldn't breathe. Through gaps in my fingers I saw it draw closer. Close enough for me to see that the monster was a man wearing a tattered, blood-stained tunic, where a silver badge in the shape of a flying bird hung from his chest and in its claws, it carried - a *swastika!* The melted face snarled grotesquely as the owner lifted a shaky hand holding a pistol – a real gun and it was pointing at me!

Out of the shadows came a commotion as Stevie ran from our bedroom. Something glinted in his hand and when I saw it was the toy gun, I shouted, "*No, Stevie! No!*" The toy and the pistol now pointed at each other. I knew I had to do something to save my Stevie, but just then, Luuk, screaming in Dutch, charged into the kitchen carrying a broom. He didn't stop his advance and with another almighty shriek, pushed the monster's chest with the bristle end, until he tumbled backwards down the stone steps into the cellar. As he did, the pistol discharged. The gun had been fired at Stevie!

Luuk let go of the broom, slammed the door shut and pushed the bolt across. Stevie was on the floor. I went to him, as someone switched on the light. Had he been shot? Was he dead? No! No, please God, no! Stevie opened his eyes and stood up. "*Wow!* He whispered. "*It's a German. We gotta German!*" He had simply fallen over the broom.

Mr. Thomas rushed into the kitchen. He must have run all the way from his cottage because he was panting and had a very red face. Wearing slippers and his tin hat, which looked comical with his pyjamas, he carried the all-important Home Guard rifle. "*Burglar?*" He gasped. "*Where is the blighter? Anyone hurt?*"

"We're not hurt." I told him. "*It's a German. He's in the cellar. And he has a pistol.*"

"*No, he hasn't.*" Stevie said gleefully, as he picked up the gun from the floor and placed it on the table. "*German? In the cellar?* Mr. Thomas said breathlessly as the kitchen filled with people. "*Then he can get out through the coal hole shutters or come up through the door in the hall.*" Mrs. Quick appeared in her dressing gown and hairnet and calmly put the kettle on to boil, while Mr. Thomas gave orders to several older boys for them to go outside as fast as they could and sit on the shutters. *"I'll lock the other door, then I'll use Mr. Fortescue's telephone to call the Police and the Home Guard ... With your permission, sir"*, he added when he saw the Headmaster standing amongst the boys. *"An ambulance, too,"* I said, *"he's badly hurt."*

The whole school was awake now and in such an excitable state, it was decided that although it wasn't yet six o'clock, the water boilers should be turned on in the Refectory and the Prefects make tea for those who weren't sitting on the shutters. I couldn't stop shaking and sat at the table while Mrs. Quick fussed around me. I think we were all relieved to hear bells ringing in the distance, heralding the arrival of Sergeant Prothero and Detective Saunders and not long after, three very puffed-out members of the Home Guard hurried into the kitchen.

"German is it? In the cellar, is he? Must have been in that Heinkel," one said, with another adding wisely, *"We wondered you know."* The soldiers crowded round the cellar door, rifles at the ready, as one of them gingerly unbolted the door. Sergeant Prothero switched on the cellar light and shouted down the steps, *"Come out with your hands up. And don't try any funny business."* There was no reply. *"Maybe he doesn't speak English, George"*, Detective Saunders whispered. The Sergeant mumbled something and turned to the soldiers, saying, *"Well, it's up to you, then. I'll take charge of his weapon."*

The soldiers looked at each other. A short discussion delayed their descent as they decided who would lead. One of them nodded and took a pace forward. *"Watch out, Joe"* One of them said, *"He might have a knife. Slippery creatures these Hun."* Joe cocked his rifle and the men bravely tramped down the steps together.

The pathetic creature was certainly an airman and unconscious with a deep gash in his head courtesy of the stone steps. Perhaps he'd been thrown out of the Heinkel as it crashed, but whatever happened he'd managed to stay alive with the help of Mrs. Quick's rations and some very green tomatoes. This was confirmed later when the big tin of jam Mrs. Quick sought so diligently was discovered unopened in bushes near the coal hole shutters – an easy way in and out of the kitchen.

Now Mr. Sykes arrived looking extremely puzzled. *"What's all this then? He asked. "Must be a dozen boys sitting on top of the coal hole shutters. Said it was a load of Germans."*

"Tea. Mr Sykes?" Cook asked casually.

Sitting at the table drinking a cup of steaming tea with a shaky hand, I looked up to heaven thanking God that Stevie hadn't been shot. It was then I noticed a big hole in one of the dresser shelves. Lodged in the hole was the bullet.

CHAPTER THIRTEEN
The Proposal

A stickler for routine, Mr. Fortescue held morning assembly at the usual time, saying that due to the bravery of two Witherley Hall boys, a dangerous German fugitive had been apprehended. The man had been removed by the Police and the Home Guard and taken to hospital, where his condition was serious, although he was expected to recover and become a prisoner of war. There were gasps from the boys hanging on his every word.

For days, Stevie and Luuk were hailed as heroes. Between meals, Cook allowed them to conduct a re-enactment of the incident and lead pupil 'Tours'. With great explanations including an inspection of the bullet hole - *although the bullet itself had been prised out by Sergeant Prothero*, Stevie's toy gun was carefully studied, the cellar steps examined in fine detail for signs of blood, the (approximate) position of the airman's landing point on the cellar floor identified and the broom proudly displayed.

Later that week, two people from the newspapers arrived and Mr. Fortescue was asked if he would allow photographs of Stevie and Luuk to accompany the story. There was much discussion and I was amazed when I was asked to give my permission as well. I thought it would be wonderful for them both and when the papers went to print, I bought three copies of each. The articles were quite dramatic, with photographs showing Stevie and Luuk pointing to the bullet hole and Sergeant Prothero presenting Luuk with the spent bullet. We all felt as if Luuk had managed to get a little of his own back somehow and that this incredible event must have helped him deal with the dark thoughts I knew he sometimes had.

Suddenly it was December. Thick fog at night interrupted the assault on Bristol and the different route the Luftwaffe took for the two air raids after that, meant that fortunately there were no more visits to the cellars. With help from the older boys, Jimmy and Mr. Sykes erected three Christmas trees taken from the copse behind the laundry. A small one in the front hall, with a Nativity scene beside it, one of medium size in the chapel and one, which must have been eighteen feet in height for the Refectory. Once decorated by the Prefects, they looked beautiful and coupled with the sound of carols softly sung, blazing log fires and some sunny, frosty days it was all very 'Christmassy'. The only fly in the ointment was the daily replacement of one of the Nativity figures in the stable by a person, or persons unknown. Mr. Fortescue threatened to 'take serious action' with the perpetrator, but by December 5th, the Wise Men and two of the shepherds had been replaced by Popeye, Mickey Mouse and three tin solders.

Revelry in school continued. For me though, fate played its part again at breakfast on Wednesday morning when I was summoned to the front door to receive a telegram. As I walked to the hall, I prayed it wasn't about Dad. The messenger boy asked my name and then handed me the envelope, which I held for a moment before opening slowly and read, 'STEAPHAN HAS RELATIVES. LETTER FOLLOWS. ANNABELLE JOHNSON'. "*Any reply*" The boy asked. "*No,*" I whispered.

I went straight to our room and sat on my bed. Cook and Ethel were in the kitchen and hearing the kettle whistle went to join them for a cup of tea. I certainly felt I needed one. Mrs. Quick told me I looked very pale as she handed me the cup and noticing the telegram said, "*Oh. Bad news, dear?*"

"*Sort of.*" I managed to say, pushing the envelope across the table. "*Oh, my goodness!*" She exclaimed, passing it to Ethel whose eyes almost came out on stalks. They both looked at me as I burst into tears. It was a good job I didn't have to teach the boys that morning because I couldn't have. Back in our room, I opened Stevie's drawer and went through his things one-by-one. The jigsaw was the last thing to take out. I had no idea why I was doing this, but for some reason I felt the need to torture myself. It was happening. Steaphan was finally going home. How I would explain this to him would have to wait until I received the letter from Annabelle, but whatever the details were, this meant goodbye.

The rotten morning continued into a rotten afternoon. I told my little class that I had a bit of a headache and they were to do some drawing. All this did, was make the afternoon even worse when two of the evacuees drew quite worrying scenes of bombs falling and planes crashing, another pictured an ugly witch on a broomstick and little Andrew Fuller drew a picture of the dead cat, 'Twinkle'. It couldn't get any worse, could it?

It did. Luuk's drawing was of a windmill, which at first I thought was rather nice until I realised the sails were actually 'swastikas' and Stevie drew another picture of Roger and his house, which was lovely apart from the outline of Linda standing beside it holding a pail of dead chickens. I told them to stop drawing and read them the last chapter of 'Treasure Island' instead.

I was surprised when the dreaded letter arrived the next morning, but decided that if it had to happen, it might as well happen soon. Annabelle told me everything the Police had discovered, which was almost unbelievable. Stevie's grandfather was a Laird, some sort of nobility and had an estate on the west coast of Scotland near a place called Clunes. Aisla had eloped with Alasdair, the Ghillie taking expensive jewellery with her and the family had accused them of theft, which was how the Police were involved. I didn't know what a Ghillie was and went to the library to look it up; it's someone who helps with hunting.

There was no theft, but the accusation hit Aisla hard and she vowed to sever all connections with her family. A marriage and two children later, the husband, Alasdair was killed and Aisla fell on hard times having to pawn the jewellery. The rest we knew, but the important thing for me was that Douglas and Elizabeth MacClintock were committed to having Stevie live with them. A telephone call would be arranged so they could discuss this with me and meantime, they sent their thanks for all I had done so far. So, was that it? Stevie would just go off to Scotland and live happily ever after? As easy as that? It seemed so. Well, I thought it was a rotten idea.

After lunch, which I couldn't eat, Mr. Fortescue sent for me. This time, I knew what it was about. He told me that as Stevie's grandfather lived in a remote area near Inverness a Trunk telephone call had been booked and would be received at five o'clock. I was to wait in his study in good time to accept it and he would make sure I was not disturbed. I had four hours to think about what I would say and went to the afternoon class feeling incredibly low. I clock-watched. Four o'clock came and when the boys left, I wanted to grab Stevie and hug him, but that would be wrong of me. I was being selfish but didn't know how I would get through this or even what would happen to me when he had joined his family. Goodness knows how we'd even get him there. That would be interesting. Inverness. Literally the other end of the country.

I washed my face and combed my hair, even though Mr. MacClintock wouldn't be able to see me I thought I'd better spruce myself up a bit. There was plenty of time before the call, so I went to the Library and pulled out an Atlas. Scotland looked very lonesome. There was a page showing something called the topography - the hills, rivers, lochs, and things like that. There was a lot of them, and I turned several pages to find information on Inverness. Of course, this is where the Loch Ness Monster lives, but since the 'Night of the German', I had a real aversion to those and slapped the book shut.

Mr. Fortescue opened the door when I knocked. I think he realised I was dreading what was to come and said that it was in Stevie's best interests. He'd never called him by that name before and I was surprised. The telephone rang and he answered. A minute, or so later, he said, "*Yes, good evening Sir. Miss Carter is here.*" I took a deep breath as he handed me the receiver and left the room.

His accent was sometimes hard to understand, but we talked for twenty minutes. The call must have cost a fortune. I did feel a bit better about everything afterwards though. At least I think I did. Some of the questions were hard to answer but I did my best. I thought it important to tell him that Aisla had called her son '*Stevie*' rather than Steaphan and that at least, would help him adjust and that despite his ordeal, he was brave enough to confront a German with a gun. He was rather impressed with this piece of information, saying he would look forward to seeing the newspaper cuttings. He told me that his wife, Elizabeth had been terribly affected by Aisla's disappearance and knowing she was dead had not only inflamed her distress but the fact that she'd had a daughter and used her name had fuelled the fire even more. That hadn't dawned on me until now. They wanted Stevie and so did I, but they had a claim to him. His rightful place was with them. Of course, I knew that. When I replaced the receiver, I sat still for a moment and went over the conversation. Yes, I HAD agreed to take him to Scotland in less than two weeks' time. I was to stay for Christmas and for as long as liked after that. An arrangement would be made with the Bank in Swindon who would give me enough money for the journey, and I was to buy Stevie anything he needed and that included me too. There would be a letter in the post to Stevie, which would give me enough time to explain all this and the family couldn't thank me enough. That was it in a nutshell. I had twelve days to sort everything out.

There was a knock on the door and Mr. Fortescue returned wearing an optimistic smile. I reiterated the conversation whirling in my mind in as much detail as I could, saying that in the final moments, Mr. MacClintock had made a daring proposal. This suggestive piece of information alarmed Mr.

Fortescue and before I could explain myself, he said with disgust, "*My dear girl ...*" Realising my failure to report the plan of action properly, I quickly interrupted him with the assurance that nothing improper had been discussed and the conversation lightened. Mr. Fortescue listened intently while I revealed the finer points, but it was clear that I had doubts about the whole thing. This altered his whole demeanour; it was as if he'd turned into Dad. He said I wasn't to worry. The Bank Manager was a friend, so that side of things would be easily taken care of. He would sort out the journey with the Swindon Station Master and although it would be a journey of Herculaneum proportion, I wasn't to worry. Frankly, I think he was inspired by the mechanics of the mission.

That night was spent deciding the best way to tell Stevie he had relatives. Somehow, I would explain that strangers had appeared out of the blue expecting him to make a long journey to live with them in an unfamiliar place. A cold, barren place where they spoke in a strange way, men in skirts played a wailing wind instrument by squeezing a bag and they ate meat cooked in an animal's stomach. On the plus side, I would tell him that there were hills and lots of grass to run around in and he would have everything he ever dreamed of; he would be happy there because that was where his mother and father had lived. Would it be enough to convince him that this was a good thing? We had been together for just four months, but in that time, we'd clearly learnt to trust and care for each other. Stevie, a little boy I had grown to love with all my heart, surely loved me too. Suddenly feeling the pain of loss all over again, I sobbed silently into my pillow until it was wet through with tears.

The next morning, I received a lovely long letter from Nan, which I read while my assortment of boys battled with their arithmetic. The main news was that Nan had bought a bungalow! It was all very 'spur of the moment' apparently because it was put up for sale almost overnight and Nan had snapped it up for a ridiculous price. It was still in Whitstable, but further down the coast away from Auntie Win, who now had a man-friend, much to my cousins' disgust. It even had an inside bathroom with a toilet and a small garden front and back. It wasn't hard to imagine, and I longed to be there with her. My emotions were so mixed-up though because I wanted to be with Stevie too.

Nan had heard from Dad. London was having a bit of a respite since Adolph had switched to bombing other cities. Southampton had been devastated with hundreds of casualties and more than one hundred dead. The interlude was giving Londoners time for a clear-up before the next wave, however, bodies were still being discovered amongst rubble and food supplies were low, which was even worse with Christmas coming,

Mr. Fortescue sent for me yet again. Now what? I was anxious to read Nan's letter for a third time and write back, enclosing one for Dad as she obviously knew where he was staying, but left the boys with Luuk in charge. So long as I managed to make the evening post, she would receive it with my latest revelation and if more arrangements were made meantime, I'd be able to add those too, so I hurried off to Mr. F's study.

There were indeed more arrangements. The Bank Manager and Mr. MacClintock had spoken at length and once money from Scotland had been transferred, I was to collect the vast sum I would need a wallet for. Mr. Reynolds, the Station Master had formulated a plan for the journey, investigating suitable hotels in both Liverpool and Glasgow for overnight stays and Matron was assembling as much as she could fit into a spare suitcase for Stevie.

We were to travel on the 18th. All being well, we would arrive at Inverness station on the 20th, where we would be collected by car and driven to Harley Muir, the MacClintock's home. If I said I was scared, it would have been an understatement. The thought of travelling with Stevie for that length of time and staying in a hotel for two nights was terrifying; the journey from the farm to the school had been bad enough and on top of that, all these plans and preparations had yet to be revealed to him. It would be almost as bad as telling him that his mother and sister had been killed and I was the one to do it.

The noise erupting from 'small hall' as I turned the corner, meant that Luuk had not been able to keep order. I clapped my hands as I went in and told them we would mark their arithmetic and after that, they could have a short break outside. Stevie and one of the evacuees had done quite well, with eight of the ten sums added correctly, while Luuk had them all right; he was a bright child and a few years older than the others, of course. They stood to leave, and I asked Stevie to wait a minute. When the others were out of earshot, I sat in one of the armchairs and patted the one beside it, which he bounced into. *"I have some wonderful news, Stevie,"* I said as triumphantly as I could.

Driving 'Trucky' up and down the arm of the chair, he listened intently and several minutes later, sat staring at me with the sideways look he conveyed when he thought I was having him on. The fire crackled and spat as he took a deep breath and said casually, *"Nah, "I'll stay with you Lelly. Done wanna go to no Scotland place. Can't leave Lukey can I?"* As he stood up to leave and join the others without a hint of a second thought, I broke out in a cold sweat, the realisation of what he'd said changing everything. Oh, my God! Luuk. What about Luuk? *"Come back, Stevie,"* I shouted as he skipped off. His head appeared slowly round the door and I asked him to sit down again. Huffing irritably, he sat down with arms folded and I tried to explain. There was no alternative. He had to go. There was no one else. They were family.

Staring deeply into the fire, the flames reflecting in the tears welling in his blue eyes, he said *"Done you love me anymore then, Lelly?"* The answer was obvious. Pulling him onto my lap as I'd done in the church, we hugged and cried together in front of the fire. He asked if I would stay in the 'Scots place' with him. *"For a while"*, I said. *"For as long as I can."* I promised. Suggesting we keep the news from Luuk for the moment, I said I would talk to Mr. Fortescue about him, but what he would say was anyone's guess. Stevie went outside. I returned to the Headmaster's study and without thinking, walked straight in without knocking - something I'd never have done before, but I was in desperate need of a solution. He was as surprised as me and didn't appear to be annoyed at all. In fact, while I babbled at him, he nodded and smiled then patted my hand as a signal to stop my flurry of words.

He told me that this had already crossed his mind because unlike the other boys with family, Luuk was a refugee and had to be placed somewhere. The perfect answer would be for the boys to stay together and this was what he would propose. I wasn't to get my hopes up, but he felt optimistic. I offered to pay for the telephone call, which prompted Mr. Fortescue to mention a completely different subject. *"That reminds me, Lesley,"* he said *"You're owed quite a lot of salary. Some from your post in London, which has come through and the remainder from deductions here."*

Anything would have been useful considering I had to buy a new coat. The offer from Mr. MacClintock was kind, but I couldn't accept it. I was completely bowled over though when I opened the brown envelope to find the money and a slip detailing the payment of twenty-six pounds and eleven shillings. Rich beyond my wildest dreams, I seemed to ping-pong from one emotion to another at such a great rate that I thought I may be in danger of falling victim to some sort of nervous disorder.

It wasn't until Friday the 13th – *'unlucky for some'*, that we heard with great relief and excitement that the MacClintock's would happily accept responsibility for Luuk in the short term at least. They fully appreciated the situation and felt that having Luuk with them would help Stevie to settle. Whether he would be allowed to stay indefinitely would be up to the authorities, but Sergeant Prothero was to deal with the legal implications and the three of us would travel together, paid for by the MacClintock's.

As difficult as it was to know if he understood every single detail, I doubt Luuk would have cared where he was going, so long as it was with Stevie and vice versa. He accepted the news gratefully, although he seemed a little unsure exactly where Scotland was. I made a mental note to have a geography lesson during free time the next day. He was deeply moved when he realised just how generous Frank had been when he was told that under the terms of Frank's will, Luuk not only inherited his money, but also his belongings. It was bittersweet. It magnified the relationship the men had enjoyed on the one hand and compounded the assumption that his father and the others in his family were dead.

There was much to prepare and little time to do it. Frank's clothes almost fitted Luuk, which was better than everything being too small and would last a fair while. Stevie's were all second, or third hand but Matron managed to supply a pair of reasonably new plimsolls and sandals, a duffle coat, his first long trousers, woollies and shirts galore, and even wellington boots all in the next size up, so he was ready. He looked lovely in the heavy navy-blue coat and school scarf and paraded around in them for us as if he were a fashion model. I was in a bit of a pickle though. My mackintosh would keep out the rain, but not the cold and the Swindon shops were unlikely to have all the things I needed.

As well as practical planning, I had to remember the other boys in my slow-learners class. They were sweet little things and I would miss them terribly. I was unlikely to return to the school after the trip to Scotland and doubted I'd ever see them again. Fortunately, we had news that a newly qualified teacher would take my place, in the shape of Mr. Saunders, who had been deemed unfit for active service. It would have been nice if he'd been a young lady to give the boys a little feminine influence, but at least they were saved from joining a class that was way ahead.

It seemed to me that everything was falling into place for Luuk. Stevie was simply happy to be with his Lukey and my only regret was knowing that I was to be parted from the boys, although I was so busy with everything, I hardly had time to think beyond the journey to Scotland. Luuk had such a lot to take with him, that Mr. Thomas dug-out an empty trunk from the attic and Stevie now had so many belongings he needed two suitcases.

On the Saturday, I took the train into Bristol. It was a place I'd never been before but acting on advice from Ethel who assured me that I'd be able to buy everything on my clothes list in one fell swoop, decided to go. She told me to aim for Wine Street, which was full of shops in an area around the pretty medieval district of Castle Park. Of course, she had no idea that while trying to get there, a Policeman would tell me that it was all gone. Four churches, St. Peter's Hospital and a 17th century timber framed Dutch house all in ruins, together with shops, pubs, restaurants, and 'Jones' the department store. Everything there had been destroyed on November 24th.

I was directed to a shoe shop away from the carnage and bought some fur lined boots and a pair of flat shoes. The chemist had everything I needed in the personal way, including a bottle of 'Aspro' and in a milliner's, I treated myself to a very fancy Cossack-looking pillbox hat. No one was selling stockings. The winter coat I hoped for was not to be, but I was delighted to find a pair of dungarees similar in style to the ones I'd left with Linda. Ethel was horrified when I told her about the destruction in the city.

On Sunday afternoon, I gave Luuk and Stevie a geography lesson making it all as exciting as I could. We tracked the distance on the map, which looked even more daunting now and looked at the topography page I'd seen earlier and read about Inverness, a big town with a cathedral on the River Ness. Neither of the boys were taken in by the photograph of the 'thing' that's supposed to live there, but we had great fun discussing it.

Soon after assembly on Monday, I saw the boys off to their PE class and went into Swindon, where I posted a letter to Nan at Auntie Win's address and included a letter in the envelope for Dad, giving them the all-important news and an address of sorts hoping a letter would find me there. Mr. Fortescue was quite sure that 'Harley Muir', Clunes, Scottish Highlands, was safe enough to use. It sounded very grand. Then I had to see the Bank Manager and talk to the Station Master too.

The Bank had a strange odour. Maybe it was the smell of all that money. I wouldn't know. Mr. Soames told me that he had been instructed to raise a large sum for me. Large sum? The notes he counted out and placed in a canvas pouch seemed to go on and on and by the time I left, I was concerned about carrying so much in my handbag. I smiled when I remembered the similar worry with the small amount from the Post Office all those weeks ago.

At the Railway Station, I asked to see the Station Master, Jack Harrison. This huge, jolly gentleman welcomed me into his office, and we sat together at his desk concealed by reams of timetables covered in cigarette ash and an overflowing 'IN' tray. The thing that caught my eye the most though was a set of dentures sitting on top of a box marked, 'LOST PROPERTY' and I couldn't help picturing someone somewhere walking around without teeth. Jack rifled through the debris, finally producing the itinerary he'd drawn up for us. "*First things, first*", he said. Did we have much luggage to take? I told him we had lots! Then we would need to pack a small bag with overnight things as well. He sat beside me and pointing to each stage of the journey explained what I was to do. It was all '*perfectly simple*'.

We could have travelled into London and caught the train to Edinburgh although it would be long and arduous and the next leg just as awkward, so it would be better to make the journey in stages with overnight stays. There was a train to Bristol at 8.20am the next morning and I was to purchase 1st Class tickets to Liverpool via Bristol. 1st Class! The luggage would be loaded into the Baggage Car by the Porter, who should be paid for his time. Upon reaching Bristol, I must find a Porter telling him that we are for the Liverpool train. He will know where to go. If the train isn't in, we should go to the Ladies Waiting Room until it is, and I mustn't forget to pay the Porter. Porters seemed to figure greatly in Jack's mind and already wavering under the enormity of it all, I discovered there was much more to come.

In Liverpool, we must wait for our luggage to be unloaded and have it taken to the Left Luggage Office, then take a taxi from the rank to the Adelphi Hotel, where a room had been reserved for the night. At breakfast the next morning, I should ask to have sandwiches made for later. I was so glad this was all written down. The words between the instructions paled into insignificance as I picked out the most pertinent details. At the station, I will buy 1st Class tickets for the 9.15am Glasgow train and see the luggage loaded. I knew the drill with the Porters by now. We would use the Left Luggage Office again and as the Grand Central Hotel was attached to the station it was within walking distance. Ask for sandwiches for the next day. Purchase tickets for the 9.50am Inverness train the following morning. Have luggage loaded. Yes, yes, I understood everything so far, although my stomach had Pterodactyls flying in it.

The actual time of arrival was difficult to determine, dependant on the weather and the Luftwaffe. That alone was totally unpredictable and heavy snowfall that far north could make a huge difference. However, the MacClintock's would receive a telegram with the details and be there to meet us. All would be well, he assured me. Tucking the itinerary safely into my handbag, I wished I had his optimism, but gave him my thanks and we shook hands. I felt as though I was going on some sort of secret mission having been given an impossible assignment in enemy territory although I tried hard to give the impression that I was in complete control. In fact, I stood outside his office for a moment with my eyes closed hoping to be transported back to the farm.

I had to finish my shopping. I didn't want to miss lunch with the boys and tried hard to concentrate on what I needed, although my mind kept wandering back to trains, hotels and not forgetting to pay a Porter. Shops in Swindon were limited, although I bought two sweaters, a woolly scarf, and some underwear. I was disappointed about the coat, especially with money burning a hole in my purse. I'd have to make good use of the scarf and wear the jumpers together. If the boys were warm and dry, we'd survive the trip.

CHAPTER FOURTEEN

Completing the Journey

———

Then it was Tuesday, the day before our epic trek across the country. My apprehension was turning into sheer terror, especially when we were finally all packed and ready to go with the luggage in the front hall. After breakfast, a large envelope arrived addressed to *Master S. Stewart.* Stevie had never received post before and when I handed it to him, he said, "*For me?*" I thought he might rip it open immediately, but instead, he carefully examined the stamps and reading the date stamp whispered, "*In-ver-ness.*"

He waited until we were together as a class before opening it and using a ruler to slice it open, tipped the contents onto the table to find a letter and several photographs. Stevie stared at the first one for a long time. It showed a huge house, with turrets standing alone amongst tall hills, dotted with sheep; it was almost as big as the school. On the back was written, 'Harley Muir', 1938. It was Stevie's new home. Passing the photograph round the table, the boys, 'ooh'd' and 'aah'd'. Another showed the head of a big, shaggy cow with long horns and on the reverse was written the name, 'Fergus'. Another showed a herd of Deer and a wonderful picture of three dogs, who sat together in front of a vast fireplace bigger than any I'd seen before. Their names and breed were on the back. 'Sky', was a scruffy-looking Scottish Terrier as black as Newgate's Knocker, 'Sheena' a sleek Collie and 'Jessie' a massive grey Wolfhound. My imagination ran riot again as I remembered 'The Hound of the Baskervilles'; I should stop reading these scary books.

The last photograph was the most interesting. It was a

close-up of Stevie's grandparents, Elizabeth and Douglas MacClintock taken in the summer of 1937. Elizabeth looked just like an older Coral, I mean, Aisla, with the same colouring and turned-up nose. Douglas and Stevie seemed not to have much of a likeness, although I wondered if the eye colour might be the same; it was unclear with the photo being in black and white. None of this mattered, of course. They simply looked a nice elderly couple. The letter was from Elizabeth, which I helped Stevie read.

Dear Stevie,

By now, you will know that you have a family in Scotland because your mother was our beloved daughter.

Your father's parents both died suddenly last year, but they leave you an auntie, an uncle and four wee cousins whose names are Finlay, Mungo, Maisie, and Kyla.

Your grandfather and I would love to meet you and especially hope that you will want to come and live with us. Our home is in a beautiful glen surrounded by lots of animals including sheep, deer, and our Longhorn cattle.

Miss Cooper has told us all about you and has kindly agreed to bring you here on the train before Christmas as soon as this can be arranged. Meantime, I enclose some photographs for you to see, wish you a safe journey and send you all my love.

Granny

Stevie went through everything several times and we read the letter again until finally he asked, "*So, my mummy lived there with them people?*" I nodded and held his hand. "*They're your* **mummy's** *mummy and daddy.*" I said slowly. "*Your Grandparents, Stevie.*" I wasn't surprised that he was having trouble taking it all in, these revelations were mind-boggling to me too. We sat at the table together focusing on Stevie, until little Andrew Fuller, the boy so affected by the loss of 'Twinkle' and Aunty Susan began to cry.

Whether it was the sound of the choir practising "In the Bleak Mid-Winter", the orange setting sun, or the pink streaks in the sky, I didn't know, but suddenly we were all incredibly sad. Luuk had bitten his bottom lip so hard, it was blue, and the three other evacuees begged to come with us. *"Me … Too … Please,"* Andrew managed to say between sobs. The thought of taking six boys to Scotland using a child evacuation plan like 'Operation Pied Piper' amused me one minute and then the realisation that this was impossible bought me back down to earth with a bang. Yet another emotional wrench was about to occur. How much can a soul take? The evacuees were so tearful, all we could do was huddle together until the pink streaks had disappeared and we were roused a little by the choirs' rendition of 'Ding Dong, Merrily on High'.

After a restless night and several attempts at counting sheep, morning came with all three of us awake just after six o'clock. Cook had offered to make us breakfast in the kitchen and Matron joined us at ten past seven where they presented me with a pair of gloves. Bless their hearts, I would miss them too. The boys were excited, although it didn't spoil their appetite. I forced down some toast and two cups of tea but couldn't stop thinking that I'd forgotten something. We'd said our goodbyes the night before, everything was packed, so it was probably self-doubt.

Then before we knew it, we had to go. Armed with an old square-shaped whisky bottle filled with water, sandwiches, and Garibaldi biscuits, which Stevie had convinced Luuk were filled with flies, we three ladies locked in a tearful embrace. I felt as though I'd known them for years. Our first meeting had been frosty and neither Stevie, nor I had wanted to stay, but now it was a different story. I promised to let them know we had arrived safely and write often, wear my gloves and assured Matron that her advice to *'keep my throat warm'* was very sensible. The boys tried hard to accept their sloppy kisses but avoided a second round and Mr. Thomas patted them both on the back before he loaded our luggage into the Head's car. It was good of Mr. Fortescue to take the time to drive us to the station and see us off.

I felt rather swanky asking for our 1ˢᵗ Class tickets and was becoming accustomed to peeling-off pound notes from a wad of cash. Once we'd handed over our luggage to the Porter and I'd dispensed the half-crown from my pocket, we stood together on the far end of the platform chatting about everything except the journey until the train announced its arrival with a blast on the whistle. Luuk, once again held his hands over his ears as he had when the air raid siren sounded, while Stevie jumped up and down as if on springs; two totally different reactions. Did Luuk just have sensitive ears, or was there a more sinister reason?

An empty compartment came to a standstill almost beside us and Mr. Fortescue opened the door saying, "*Your carriage awaits.*" This was it. I took a deep breath. A six-hundred-mile journey ahead of us and me in charge. What was I doing? As if to guarantee our departure, he waited until we were on the train and closed the door behind us and I lowered the window to lean out and say goodbye. Assuring the boys that he would know if they hadn't behaved themselves, he took my hand and said softly, "*Well done, Lesley. We were lucky to have you.*" This declaration settled my nerves a little and I knew we'd be alright.

We reached Bristol unscathed, although the station was terribly congested and confusing. Big signs saying, 'IS YOUR JOURNEY REALLY NECESSARY?' were all over the place. I supposed ours' was. The Porter was helpful and touched his cap when I gave him a half-crown; I hoped it was enough. The next leg was arduous, and the train stopped constantly for no discernible reason. The carriage was packed, and I was so grateful to be in 1ˢᵗ Class with well-dressed ladies and a few un-smelly gentlemen. We made sure we saved each other's seats when we used the toilet, munched the biscuits with 'flies' and ate our sandwiches, but we'd have to wait until the engine was changed in Birmingham before we could have a cup of tea.

It was the middle of the afternoon by the time we reached Birmingham, the halfway mark and all I could think about was Gladys and Joe and the family that died there. The train was meant to be in the station for at least twenty minutes, so I gave the boys some money to have a drink at the tea bar on the platform and stretch their legs and when they returned, I would do the same. However, the moment they bounced back into their seats, the whistle blew, and we were off. I was so glad I hadn't left the train! However, this left me with a dilemma because I was so thirsty. Slurping from the bottle of water wasn't very ladylike and I could even be mistaken for an alcoholic, which would be dreadful. Instead, I visited the toilet with my handbag and guzzled from the bottle in private.

By half past five, we had passed Crewe. Almost there. No, there was an air raid somewhere and we stopped again. The boys had been so good up to now but were bored and I had a real job to stop them lifting the blackout blinds to see what was going on. It was difficult to decipher the noises outside, which sounded far off. Oh, good, we were moving again. Boys sleeping. Dozed myself.

At last, Liverpool, where phase two went into action! Let's hope the hotel can feed us. Once we had fought our way off the train, we saw our luggage being loaded onto a trolley and I quickly told the Porter what the plan was. Another half-crown later, we were in a queue at the taxi rank. Mr. Fortescue had been right to exchange a few of my notes for the big, shiny coins.

The Adelphi Hotel wasn't far from the station, but it was necessary to drive in a big circle due to the amount of bomb craters in the roads. We were unable to see much in the blackout, although it seemed as bad as everywhere else that had suffered from dear old Hitler. I was getting quite used to travelling in a taxi and giving helpful people half-crowns and felt quite the Lady. None of us had ever stayed in a big hotel, or any hotel for that matter and when we arrived, a man in a top hat and tails opened the door for us. Should I have given him a half-crown as well?

I wasn't sure what to do next, until the top hat man asked me if we were resident. Resident. Were we? Yes, of course we were, we had a reservation. Pull yourself together, Lesley. I nodded and he led me to a big desk where a gentleman asked for my name and details. I wondered if we had to show our Identity Cards and give them our Ration Books, but he didn't mention them. All he did, was to ask if we would 'take' dinner and at what time we 'required' breakfast.

Our room was huge and heated by radiators. Bliss. There were two single beds and a double, a very ornate wardrobe, a massive marble fireplace and a basin. With a toilet right next door, I felt horribly spoilt, especially when I realised the curtains were velvet. Opening the overnight suitcase, I pulled out the spongebag and we washed our hands and face, hung up our coats, or in my case, my mackintosh and combed our hair. We looked reasonably presentable. Now for the dining room.

Everyone was chatty, especially when some overheard Stevie tell the waiter that we were on an adventure. The three of us swallowed a glass of orange juice and I looked at the menu, which was in French in big letters, with English underneath. I showed the boys. Stevie mouthed the words he could read, then exclaimed loudly, "*Ear. Was this poisons?*" I laughed, but Luuk gently told him that it was '*Poisson*' – fish. Stevie and I looked at him in amazement. Why didn't I know he spoke French?

I decided to talk to him about this later. We were all very hungry and it was after eight o'clock. I gave the waiter our order. Minestrone Soup for three with Dinner Rolls. Stevie and I would have the Plat de Jour, which was Lamb Cutlets and 'associated' Vegetables, the Tripe a La Mode reminded me of Nan's culinary habits and was something I couldn't begin to fancy and Luuk asked for the Cod. Perhaps fish was something he'd been used to having – he was full of surprises.

Having munched our way through two courses, the waiter asked if we would like to see the dessert menu and we said we certainly would! Plum Pudding and Custard for me and for the boys? Oh, what a treat. Raspberry Jelly and Ice Cream. They were ecstatic. It was good to watch them enjoying themselves. I declined the offer of Cheese and Biscuits and having never tasted ordinary wine, also refused a glass of Dessert Wine, whatever that was.

We hadn't done much but were exhausted. Bath and bed came next. I wasn't sure where the bathroom was and back in our room, I told the boys to brush their teeth while I investigated but before I left, Luuk pointed to a door beside the wardrobe that I hadn't noticed; if I had, I must have assumed it was a cupboard. I turned the knob, opening the door with trepidation and stepped into a wonderful bathroom with shiny green and white tiles.

I couldn't believe it, our own beautiful bathroom with a toilet. I ran a bath for the boys and once they were in bed, did the same for me. While I lathered my Camay and scrubbed every nook and cranny, I rehearsed for the next day. We had done well so far, and I went to bed feeling an optimism I hadn't felt for a long time. That night, I didn't need the sheep.

Breakfast was more than adequate, after which I requested lunch sandwiches and for the bill to be made up; I was really getting good at this now. Trying not to look horrified at the total on the bottom of the itemised bill, I handed over the money. At least there wasn't quite as much in my bag now. Remembering to fill the whisky bottle with fresh water, we left the Adelphi.

Luuk carried the overnight case. Stevie carried our sandwiches wrapped in baking parchment and the two conkers he had left were safely in one pocket, while 'Trucky' travelled in the other. We each had our gas masks, although we still didn't have a box for Stevie's. This left me with my handbag, which was so much easier than having to manage as we did before. That was a real struggle. Thank goodness the jigsaw was in Luuk's trunk. The top hat man opened the door again, asking where we had to go and as he did, he stood in the middle of the road and whistled to a taxi parked outside another big building. The boys jumped in while I performed the now familiar 'presentation of the coin' and off we went.

In daylight, we could see that Liverpool had suffered greatly. The city was on the banks of the River Mersey, so perhaps it was some sort of strategic target, or maybe it was hit just because it was a busy port. Whatever the reason, it was sad to see the destruction. I was getting used to the scenes in railway stations now and wasn't as nervous as I'd been, so it was easy to find a Porter and have our luggage loaded onto yet another train and yes, I knew I would have to collect more coins soon!

Liverpool to Glasgow. We would soon be in Scottish territory and closer to our destination. I was getting excited too. There was time for a drink, and we stood at the tea bar with a glass of milk each. Next door was a newsagents' stand where I bought The Beano and The Dandy comics for the boys and the Girl's Own, which would help pass the time on the train. Purposely giving the vendor a pound note, I asked him if he would let me have a couple of half-crowns in the change. "*A shilling, or no more than two Bob is enough,*" his accent was almost melodic. "*Don't want to give them fancy ideas!*" I hadn't mentioned the Porters but somehow, he knew why I'd asked.

Well, the 1st Class tickets I bought for train number three were worth every penny, because it was jam-packed. I was a bit flummoxed when I'd been told we had to change trains though. The boys sat with their comics, giggling every now and then with Stevie dangling a conker from each ear, while I read all about '*Worrals of the WAAFS*' in the 'Girl's Own'. By one o'clock, we were hungry enough to eat our sandwiches. The hotel had been very generous and included three pieces of Swiss Roll, which was yummy. Not long after that, we reached Carlisle where not only did we have to change trains, we also had to get to another station.

I did think about what the newsagent had said, but still gave the Porter who dealt with our luggage a half-crown. This time, we had to get everything in a taxi, which was more than a bit of a squeeze. The driver was helpful though and said that Carlisle hadn't been affected by any bombing yet, although no one living there was complacent. He gratefully accepted a tip.

Train number four and I think Porter number five, or was it six? Mind you, we couldn't have managed without them. Carlisle to Glasgow. This journey was affected badly by all sorts of things. Air raid warnings, cows on the line and that was apart from the fact that we stopped at each station we came to. The boys drank from the bottle when they went to the toilet and I refilled it a couple of times, although the water tasted rather strange. Once again, we were tuckered-out when we arrived in Scotland.

Glasgow Station – maybe a bit like Paddington. It was here we saw our first kilt and heard our first bagpipes, both of which, caused the boys great amusement. The Grand Central Hotel for our second overnight stay was attached to the station and within walking distance, so following the inevitable trooping to see our things safely installed at the Left Luggage Office and customary donation towards the Porters' Fund, we found ourselves in the enormous hotel.

I had never seen anything like it and obviously, neither had the boys. The staircase in the middle of the entrance hall was wonderful with a beautiful chandelier hanging from the ceiling, which seemed to go on and on. Our room was even bigger than the Adelphi and the bathroom very plush. I really felt as though I shouldn't be there and worried that a meagre half-crown tip would be frowned-upon.

We repeated the same format as the evening before, although the Dining Room was called a Restaurant and we felt the need to whisper; driving 'Trucky' around THIS table was most definitely taboo. Dinner was marvellous. We started with Brown Windsor Soup, then had something called, 'Chicken a La King' with Rice, followed by Peach Melba. We had never eaten so well in all our lives.

It was difficult to leave the bathroom, where even soap had been provided. The crisp, linen on the beds had a luxurious

231

feel, the pictures on the walls were works of art and we had been treated like Royalty. It was at that moment that I decided I would need to marry a millionaire. The next morning after a breakfast of Haddock and Poached Egg, Stevie took it upon himself to ask the waiter for our lunch sandwiches but was bewildered by the reply. He frowned and examined a conker while he thought. "*Nah!* He began, looking at the waiter haughtily, "*Fink we'll 'ave cheese and pickle. Not cumba, or the smokin' fing, tar.*" The waiter suppressed a smile and said, "*Of course, Sir.*" Stevie was probably right, his choice was far better than cucumber, or even smoked salmon.

We saw nothing of Glasgow City. Once on the train for the final leg of the journey though, the view from the window was one of pure beauty. The route would take us to the other side of Scotland, travelling through Perth and on to somewhere called the Cairngorms, a mountainous area apparently, or so the Scottish lady sitting beside me said. The boys were certainly enjoying the sights, what with snow-capped hills, shaggy cows, woolly sheep, great flying birds, and glittering water tumbling across rocks into fast-flowing streams. Stevie's delight at seeing a cow "*like 'Fergus'*", meant he'd taken stock of the photos from his grandmother.

The strangest part of my life was coming to an end. I would stay in Scotland only a short while because as soon as I knew the boys were safe and sound, I would leave. Luuk's fate was in the hands of the authorities, but at least the MacClintock's had some influence over his future. How I would return to anything remotely normal would probably depend on the war. There would be a school somewhere that needed me, maybe near Nan's new bungalow so I could live with her, or perhaps take a job in another boarding school. But then there was Dad. Was that it? Was that all I would have? I wasn't exactly inspired by this prospect, especially after reading about '*Worrals of the WAAFS*' and wondered if I should make enquiries about becoming a Wren.

The boys looked so well compared to the time Stevie and I

were in hospital and that first meeting with Luuk. What if they'd been girls? Could I have done a better job? I would still have devoted every waking moment to them, watched over them, helped them through difficult times and dried the same tears, so maybe not. They weren't my flesh and blood but being fixed firmly in my heart, I couldn't imagine feeling more love for them if they'd been my own. Handing them over to the MacClintock's I would make sure that love was transferred to allow the healing to continue. I would have to take the chance that they would forget me, even though I knew I would never forget them.

Lunchtime. The 'sandwiches' were minute. Filled with cheese and something resembling pickle with the crusts cut off - *I hoped they'd been used elsewhere*, they were gone in a couple of swallows and this time, no Swiss Roll. Noticing our disappointment, the lady I mentioned delved into the bottom of her bag, producing two very sticky boiled sweets and gave one each to the boys. They seemed content and I didn't need to tell them to say, 'Thank You'. Chugging along the winding track to Inverness, the lady eagerly pointed out things of interest; even the elderly gentleman in the carriage listened to her running commentary. A big lake, called Loch Insh, rolling hills decorated in red, brown and green hues, a herd of running Deer led by a huge stag with antlers to match and some of the time, we drifted past a river, but apart from the occasional shepherd, we saw no people. Scotland looked desolate in its own beautiful way.

We travelled through a valley, which the lady said was a 'glen' by way of the magical Cairngorms and with Ben Macdui in the distance, a mountain more than a thousand feet high. Snow was more in evidence here and the temperature in the carriage dropped enough for us all to put on our coats, although my mackintosh did little to help warm me up. So many Deer. Such lovely things. They ran like the wind when the train approached. Cows were almost as plentiful. I was corrected however and told they were 'Highland Cattle'. Well, whatever they were, they seemed oblivious to our presence and weren't frightened by the train at all.

The nice lady told us that the next stop would be the last one before Inverness. I thought we should tidy ourselves up a bit to meet the MacClintock's and sent the boys off to the toilet, while I combed my hair and swept a hint of lipstick across my lips. The engine was slowing steadily, and my tummy started doing somersaults. Stevie and Luuk were suddenly quiet and we tried not to look at each other; goodness knows' why. We came to a halt and rather than hurry, we took our time to get ourselves together. I wondered if the MacClintock's were feeling just as apprehensive.

Thanking the lady for her knowledgeable narration and saying goodbye to her and the gentleman, we stepped out onto the platform, where the icy wind hit us like a ton of bricks. I told the boys to button their coats, pull their caps down a bit and wished they'd been wearing long trousers. It was no longer necessary to tell Stevie to pull up the errant sock. That was a distant memory now and one I missed for some stupid reason. The saucy Cossack hat would keep my head warm and the gloves were very welcome. My feet nestled cosily in new boots, but the rest of me would freeze.

It wasn't difficult to find one last Porter, which was a good job because it was also my last half-crown. Once he'd loaded a trolley with our possessions, we followed him through the station to the road outside, where at first it seemed there was no one to meet us. Stevie pulled 'Trucky' from his pocket, which was something he still did when he felt anxious and Luuk stood to attention in wide-eyed anticipation. The Porter waited for a moment and then said, "*Phwell, here they be. The Laird in his red fire enjun.*"

I wanted to ask him what he meant. Who be where? It was a mystery with no one in sight. Then, hurtling round a bend in the road came a line of traffic. Well a van and a Land Rover led by a very noisy, open top, bright red sports car, which screeched to halt in front of us. The driver was an elderly man wearing a Sherlock Holmes type of hat. He even had a pipe sticking out of his mouth surrounded by a bushy ginger beard. I recognised this gentleman instantly as Douglas MacClintock.

Confusion reigned in one fell swoop as the Wolfhound we'd seen in one of the photographs leapt out of the Land Rover. Truly, the biggest dog in the world, standing with his head almost on Stevie's chest, he was joined by men in kilts who surrounded us shouting, "*Braw. Braw*" and "*Helloo. Helloo*". The lady wearing a beautiful fur coat and matching hat I supposed was Mrs. MacClintock – *it was difficult to see her face under the hat*. Coming towards us with a beaming smile, she held the Scottie dog and Collie in the same photo with one hand on their leash and threw the other arm around Stevie's shoulders. We were literally scooped-up, flung round and kissed in a whirlwind of welcome and joyful expression. Nan would have said it was like a 'three-ring circus'.

"*Hoo are ye, hen?*" A tall man, the image of Stevie asked. It might as well have been Chinese. Shaking my hand until I thought my arm would fall off, he continued, "*Jack. Jack Stewart. And this must be wee Stevie*". He said, looking at him with a grin just like Stevie's. "*Aah, but yas, yas, he hees the Stewart ays.*" If he was talking about big, baby blue eyes, he certainly did. With unruly hair in the same colour and texture and imperfect teeth, this had to be Stevie's uncle.

Mrs. MacClintock jabbered away in a heavy accent as she led me and the dogs to the Land Rover while her husband squeezed both boys in the front passenger seat of the red car. It would be a rather chilly ride for them, although their excitement would keep them warm. Jack and two other men, who hadn't introduced themselves loaded the luggage into the van and once the huge dog had leapt back in, the boys and I rode away in a flurry of relief that the natives were friendly.

'Harley Muir' was a twenty-minute drive from the station. We drove west, towards the sun sinking in a spectacular way behind great white peaks and waterfalls frozen in time and with the constantly changing light throwing a blue tinge on the dusting of snow, the scenery was both captivating and eerie. It was a wonderful sight. Hoping I had nodded and said all the right things in answer to Mrs. MacClintock's questions, it was perfectly plain to me that I would struggle with the accent. There was one very poignant moment when she told me to call her Elizabeth and I thought of little Beth and her mother who had grown up here.

I could still see the red car carrying the Laird and its precious cargo. It was getting colder and I worried that the boys would have sore throats or something worse by morning. Fortunately, as I was about to raise my fears the red car made a wide turn onto another road until eventually, the Land Rover crunched down a sparsely gravelled track behind it. We had arrived, although there hadn't been a house name, or sign along the way.

The sunset silhouetted the white house sitting proudly against the purple sky. Much of it was in the shadows but what I could see was magnificent. A tall building with a small turret hanging on the side of a big turret, all it needed was Rapunzel leaning out of the top window. A steep roof with an almost silvery glow to it was interrupted at intervals by windows sitting above a sort of balcony big enough to walk along. That was all I saw before we were hurried inside; there was still the blackout to consider.

It would have been difficult to ignore the centre of attraction in the hall, a Christmas tree stretching to the top of the ceiling upstairs. A big carpet almost covered the wooden floor and the log fire blazing in a grate was unusual; I'd never seen a fireplace in a hall before. Elizabeth let the dogs off the lead, and they padded over to it hugging the warmth of the fire. They were soon joined by the one as big as a pony and it was then I realised this was where the photograph of them had been taken.

But I didn't tell you about the tree. The beautiful blue-green Pine tree had such an aroma, it took me back to the time I'd walked in the grass barefoot at the farm. It was that sweet, earthy smell, the one I found so calming and peaceful. Someone obviously possessed an artistic bent looking at the way it had been decorated with coloured glass baubles in the shape of teardrops and tinsel catching the light trailing from every branch.

A portrait hung above the fireplace. Two children, a young girl about Stevie's age astride a rocking horse and an older boy standing with an arm around her had been painted in oils. The girl showed a remarkable likeness to little Beth. Should I tell her grandmother, or would that be cruel? Someone took our coats. I don't know who it was because I was too busy looking at everything. Then we were ushered into a room with another blazing fire, where the boys and I sat down with Elizabeth, Douglas, and Jack. It was all a bit strange. Douglas wore curious brightly coloured Plaid trousers and Jack looked quite unnatural sitting on the settee in a kilt or '*quilt*' as Stevie had called it. His thick knee-high socks were the colour of porridge with red Tartan zig-zag bits dangling on either side and with legs wide apart in a most ungainly way, I looked away quickly in case I should catch sight of anything I shouldn't.

The fire crackled and a clock on the mantlepiece chimed the half hour, but neither of the boys spoke and I felt quite awkward. The ice was broken however, when an elderly lady came in pushing a trolley with two teapots, an assortment of crockery and a large sponge cake with what looked like jam inside! "*Thank you, Aggie*", Elizabeth whispered. "*I'll pour.*" It wasn't until we each held a plate with a slice of sponge that Jack said, "*Well, ye three wall need a bitty tame to settle in.*" Both boys frowned. "*Erv course, yeel be needing ye supper, a bath and ye bed in thet arder.*" Clearly, it was going to take a while for us to get the hang of the local lingo. I smiled. The boys stuffed cake in their mouths.

I had a room to myself with a bathroom next door. The boys would stay together for as long as they wished. Their bathroom was a few doors down. We unpacked, had a bit of wash and brush-up, and then joined Elizabeth and Douglas for dinner served by Aggie, who had been with the family since Douglas was a child. I dreaded to think how old she was. The Beef served with a potato dish called 'Clapshot' was delicious and the Cream Crowdie was more than amazing, considering we'd been used to frugal offerings at the school. Douglas offered me a "*drammawhiska*", which confounded me until I saw the bottle and graciously declined.

We made small talk for a while until Jack said he'd better get home to his wife and their two children and we'd see everyone on Christmas Day. Elizabeth told us there would be fifteen for lunch, cooked by Mrs. Murray, who had prepared dinner. Jack and Flora would bring Finlay and Mungo and his sister, Morag - Stevie's aunt would come with Ivor and their two, Maisie and Kyla. Callum, the Estate Manager, one of the two men who met us would also be there and of course, Aggie. The boys not only looked bewildered, I was sure they weren't able to take all this in, so I suggested we went to bed.

Elizabeth and I saw the boys settled in their room. The fire in the grate would last until they were in bed and after making sure the guard was in place, we kissed them both Goodnight. Thank goodness they had each other and 'Trucky' was there if necessary. Sitting on the bed in my room, Elizabeth chatted while I poked the fire in my own grate. They were quite used to children. The house had twelve bedrooms and for the first nine months of the war, they'd taken charge of ten evacuees from Edinburgh until they trickled back home when the threat of bombing passed. Now things looked different again and eight of them were to return. That sounded good to me.

I slept like a log until the boys woke me with a start. Breakfast was as plentiful as the previous nights' dinner giving us the energy to go outside and explore. Elizabeth helped the boys into their coats and wellingtons but seeing my mackintosh she shook her head and told us to wait a moment. Waiting for much more than a moment, the boys were getting impatient, but the wait was worth it for me when Elizabeth returned with a gorgeous Beaver Lamb coat. "*For you*", she said quietly, "*I know it will fit, she was about your size.*" I resisted at first, knowing how hard it must have been to make this gesture, but said I felt honoured to be given something of Aisla's. Elizabeth simply nodded her approval when I slipped it on.

It was a cold and frosty morning, despite the sunshine and I was so grateful to be wearing a heavy coat. The boys and I agreed to walk round the house together first to get our bearings and as it turned out, it was the most intoxicating walk for all three of us. Cattle wandered in their own shaggy coats, a small group of Deer were busy with heads down in the distance and squirrels in a tree squeaked at us before scurrying away. The strange thing was, they all seemed to be the same colour, a sort of orangey brown.

The peaceful scenery was 'wild' and barren in a most captivating and beautiful way. Stopping to survey the slopes and ridges above us and watch the trickling stream below, we shielded our eyes to spot the lichens and moss we'd seen in the book at Witherley Hall. It was a wonderful moment, not only because of the magical scenery, but because I valued every waking moment with my darling boys.

Turning back towards the house that would one day be his, Stevie said, "*Are we really gonna live here, Lelly? Will it be alright?*" I nodded. "*You wanna stay, done you?*" He added. Quickly moving away from the subject by pointing to a massive Holly Tree, the distraction did the trick and gave me the time I needed to disguise the tears in my eyes.

That afternoon it began to snow heavily. Douglas drove us in the Land Rover to register Luuk at the Police Station and then did the same with our Ration Cards at the shops in town. He took his time to return us to 'Harley Muir', driving along Loch Ness, a wonderful body of water. There was no sign of 'Nessie' unfortunately. "*Maybe next time*", Douglas told us. Reaching the house late that afternoon illuminated by glistening white snow, it looked just like a fairy castle. The war was far away, and all was well with my boys. I was content and proud that I'd been able to make the journey and tried to put leaving them out of my mind.

I was keen to give Elizabeth all the documents I had, including Aisla's lovely brooch before supper that evening, so asked Aggie if she would let her know that I would wait in what they called the Drawing Room. I waited anxiously, because I felt that this was the moment to physically hand my Stevie over to her and it meant a lot to me. It was hard.

When the time came, there was only word I could use to describe Elizabeth's manner. Being a true Lady, she was 'gracious'. Sifting through the papers, nodding every now and then and reading the article about Alasdair twice, her face beamed when she saw the newspaper cutting and photograph of Stevie and Luuk capturing the German. Then the brooch slid out of the envelope. Staring at it laying there in a moment of recognition, Elizabeth clasped her hands tightly around it with eyes closed as if in prayer. It was very moving and somehow, I felt we were holding some sort of ritual for Aisla and Beth; Elizabeth was letting them go. Thanking me, I knew my goal was complete. I had successfully returned the rightful heir to the estate. I had done the job fate had set me. It was meant to be. Kismet. Why then was I not elated and satisfied? Why did I feel so left out and unable to let Stevie go?

Elizabeth handed me the brooch. As I took it from her the stones sparkled and flashed in the light of the fire, the Lilac thistle reflecting my favourite colour. It was quite beautiful. *"It's yours' dear,"* Elizabeth said. *"You have it, Lesley, you deserve it".* My head shook from side-to-side for at least a minute. I told her I couldn't possibly accept something so valuable. I already had the coat. She went on. *"While we're about it, you're to have a dress, or two and some sweaters - something nice for Christmas day."* There would be no argument.

That evening we heard that Liverpool was in the line of fire. We had been there only two days earlier and were lucky to have missed the raid because the railway lines had been bombed and we wouldn't have made it to Inverness. Hundreds of people had died, some in shelters. This piece of news bought memories flooding back to me in a whirlwind of confused images and later in bed, I found it hard to close my eyes.

Christmas Eve. The house was filled with wonderful aromas. Nutmeg, Cloves and Cinnamon mixed with that crisp cold scent of snow that rushed in every time the kitchen door opened. Freshly cut Holly and Ivy with bright red berries now adorned the top of every portrait, candles nestled amongst branches of Pine and cones in a swathe across each mantelpiece and a wreath had been fixed to the front door with a big tartan bow. Parcels appeared mysteriously beneath the tree in the hall and a large gold star had been attached to the very top. The boys were in awe and in high spirits and so was I. The dogs bounced around excitedly surely without really knowing what was going on and when the boys armed themselves with shovels to make a snowman, I knew that Christmas was here.

Just before bedtime, Elizabeth gleefully produced a pair of long roughly knitted socks and told the boys to hang them either side of the fireplace in the Drawing Room, assuring them that the fire would be out by the time Santa came down the chimney. Stevie did this immediately, but Luuk stood with the sock in his hand and a confused look. He was even more confused when Aggie came in carrying a small tray with a tot of whisky and a carrot. *"I do not know why."* He said in his own endearing way.

It took a minute for the penny to drop and when it did, I didn't know what to say. We'd forgotten that Luuk was a Jew and knew nothing about celebrating Christmas. Stevie seemed unaware of this crisis and lay on the floor driving 'Trucky' around the rug, while Elizabeth and I sat Luuk down to tackle the subject. With limited English, it was difficult. He knew there were Christians and Catholics and understood their ways were different. He'd seen decorated trees before but had never questioned the reason behind them.

Luuk managed to explain that Hanukkah, a celebration of

light devoted to a temple, occurred about this time each year. A lamp with seven candles was lit in a window and people ate what sounded to us, something like doughnuts. At least this is what we understood. While we talked, it suddenly dawned on me that Jewish people didn't eat Pork and from now on at least, that would have to be considered. Elizabeth knew of a small Synagogue in town and would speak to the Rabbi there after Christmas. Meantime, there wasn't much more we could do.

Luuk put his long sock on the table and went up to bed with Stevie in tow. As usual, I kissed them both goodnight and as I sat beside Luuk, he said, "*I beg your pardon, Lelly.*" I asked him what he was apologising for. "*Ik ben Joods*". He replied. With no idea what this meant, I told him to go to sleep otherwise Santa wouldn't come.

Elizabeth had left some clothes in my bedroom as she promised. Two dresses that I could never have afforded, three cardigans and two jumpers. I felt like Princess Elizabeth and tried everything on there and then in a sort of frenzy. One of the dresses was a little tight, but I could probably let out the darts and it was so nice, I wouldn't mind breathing less. I slept fitfully though, being worried about Luuk and how we would manage his beliefs. Stevie worried me too. He'd settled into life at 'Harley Muir' so quickly. Should I warn Elizabeth about the incidents at the farm?

Christmas morning. It was still dark and snowing heavily when I heard the boys running to the bathroom. I walked to mine. Although spoilt for choice, I decided to wear the dress that fitted best with the softest cardigan in the world. I wondered whether Elizabeth was expecting me to wear the brooch, which would have looked lovely on the cardigan, but because I was in two minds decided against it. Chasing downstairs shouting, "*Happy Christmas*", Stevie dashed into the Drawing Room, with Luuk following. Sure enough, the carrot and whisky had gone. "*See? Told you.*" Stevie directed to Luuk in a patronizing manner while at the same time pulling the bulging sock off the mantelpiece. Digging inside he produced a set of toy soldiers, a yo-yo, a balsa wood aeroplane kit, several walnuts and in the toe, a small orange, which must have been dropped from heaven. Luuk was in a state of awe.

"*Come on, Lukey.*" Stevie told him, nodding to the table where Luuk had left his empty sock. Now it was overflowing with the same things. With each presentation he whispered to no one in particular, "*Dank U. Oh, Dank U.*" After breakfast in the kitchen, Douglas told me that everyone would be going to church and they really wanted Stevie, to join them. Of course, Luuk and I were welcome too, but this was difficult because none of us knew if Luuk was permitted to enter a Christian building, although I did say that he'd often been in the school chapel.

I wanted to go, not only because it was Christmas Day but because Stevie's other relatives would be there too. Elizabeth came up with a brilliant idea. The church had a big porch with seating either side. Luuk and I would sit there and listen to the service and almost be amongst the others; they were coming for lunch at the house anyway. So, we snuggled up on the stone plinth with a big rug from the Land Rover and listened to carols being sung, prayers being said and heard the vicar's short sermon. It worked perfectly.

Stevie's aunts and uncles brought strange traditional gifts with them to the house. A piece of coal, a pot of salt, bread, and whisky and before we sat down to eat, a small branch of a Rowan Tree was burnt in the hall fireplace to loud applause and Ivor making a racket with his bagpipes. I was pleased that on this occasion, Luuk didn't cover his ears. The men all wore kilts complete with sporran, but the thing that impressed Stevie and Luuk the most was the dagger tucked inside one sock.

Everyone was very jolly, and the boys were instant friends with the cousins. It was a miracle they understood each other with such different accents, but play doesn't seem to need words. The never-ending table in the dining room set for fifteen of us had been decked with glowing candles smelling of sweet honey. Crackers made from red tissue paper sat on each chair and Holly and Ivy entwined in antlers hung amongst the iron light fitting swinging above us. It was an unforgettable fairy tale scene.

Although Christmas, it was a normal working day in Scotland. Douglas had not replaced Alasdair now that war had put a stop to all country pursuits and a Ghillie was hardly necessary. Nevertheless, Jack and his brother-in-law Ivor worked on the estate. They hadn't been called-up because their job was deemed a reserved occupation due to livestock production being such an important industry. As soon as we finished our delicious 'Cock-a-leekie' soup, wonderful Roast Beef and Clootie Pudding served with clotted cream, the men went to do whatever it was they did with cattle, leaving their wives and children with us and it was then that Douglas collected the parcels from under the tree.

The boys were given a Meccano set each and immediately went to work on them. Maisie and Kyla delighted us all with the tea party they gave for their dolls using their gift of a tea set and the Aunties and I received pretty lace edged handkerchiefs embroidered with a thistle. I hated the fact that I was unable to return the favour, but as Elizabeth said, I had '*done my bit*' and shouldn't feel awkward. With a Roast Beef sandwich for supper, the Hogmanay party to come on New Years' Eve and the tempting suggestion of trying Haggis on Burn's Night in January, I felt very content that all would be well for my boys. They were in safe hands.

The days slipped by and there was even more action in the kitchen. Big preparations were being made for the last night of the year, which was the one most celebrated in Scotland often lasting three days! I helped where I could and entertained with my farm stories, while the boys enjoyed each day making snowmen and generally enjoying themselves. The Meccano sets had been a big success, with Stevie making a garage for 'Trucky' and Luuk showing his prowess by building a car with a crane attached. When it was too cold to be outside, they 'flew' their aeroplanes around the house, marched the soldiers up and down the stairs and practised spinning their yo-yo's. Every minute was used in a good way and I was proud of them both.

It was soon the day before the party, and everyone was busy preparing. Ivor was going from room to room with his bagpipes practising the pieces he would be playing to '*get the acoustics right*' and it was these squeaks and wails we listened to, rather than the wireless. So, it wasn't until after lunch that we heard the news that London had suffered enormous damage and hundreds of casualties in an air raid the night before. I began to worry about Dad, wishing I wasn't six-hundred miles away from him at the other end of the country and wondering how long I could stay in Scotland when in that short moment, my life was turned upside down yet again.

I heard the telephone ring in the study and Douglas left the table, returning almost immediately to tell me that there was a Trunk Call coming through from Mr. Fortescue. It was a relief to know it was him, obviously wishing us a Happy New Year and to hear how the boys were doing. How kind and thoughtful of him. The boys would be able to speak as well, and we all crowded round the telephone waiting for it to ring again.

Douglas told me to wait until the long 'ring' had stopped before picking up the receiver and this was what I did. It was lovely to hear a familiar voice and I began the conversation in quite a jovial way by saying how nice it was to hear from him and asking if he had a good Christmas; you know, all the things you say at this time of year. I went on to ask about Mrs. Quick, Matron and Ethel, but he stopped me halfway through a sentence by saying, "*Lesley, he's alright, but your father has been hurt.*" His words puzzled me initially, but then I felt a bit faint. Douglas pulled a chair towards me when he saw that this was not a social call and stood beside me with a hand on my shoulder.

"*What?*" I whispered. He told me that Nan had telephoned the school because she had no other way of contacting me. My heart was racing now. Elizabeth took the boys out of the room, leaving me with Douglas while I tried to absorb what I was being told. The air raid on London the night before was the worst one yet and Dad had suffered third degree burns when a building collapsed on top of him. He was being transferred to a hospital in Sussex specialising in this sort of injury and it was vital that I made my way there as soon as possible. Sussex? How do I get to Sussex in a hurry? Douglas took the receiver from me. I can't remember what was said after that. Aggie bought in a tray of tea, but Douglas told me to swig the contents of the glass he was holding instead. It tasted horrible but made me focus.

A news bulletin gave the grim details of the previous night. The air raid was concentrated on the area around St. Paul's Cathedral and fires were so intense, that night was as bright as day. The watermain had been hit and Firemen had tried to draw water from the Thames, but this coupled with strong winds hampered attempts at dousing the raging inferno. It was so terrible it was being called the 'Second Fire of London'.

The rest of the day was spent planning my route. I don't know how I would have managed without help from Douglas because I was panic stricken. Elizabeth made light work of packing my clothes in my carpet bag and a leather suitcase with the initials F. MacC which must have belonged to her son. I vowed to return it one day. I had spent eleven wonderful days in Scotland. I was leaving prematurely, but with good reason and the boys understood that when I explained what had happened. "*You come back?*" Luuk asked. "*Course she will. Just a cuppladays away, eh Lelly?*" Stevie said cheerfully. "*See 'er ole Dad*". I told them I would get back when I could and that they were to be good boys. I would hear about it if they misbehaved and then there'd be trouble!

Douglas was to drive me to the station early on the 31st.

Believing that my time away would be short, it was easy for the boys to say goodbye and wave me off, although Elizabeth almost had to prise me off them, which they thought was funny. My throat was closing-up with a huge lump in it, I couldn't swallow and halfway to the station, I was in such distress that Douglas stopped the car until I was able to compose myself. The snow on the roads made the journey longer than anticipated and I just made it onto the train before the whistle blew. If I could have stopped it leaving, I think I would have, but the engine soon increased its speed and tore me away from the children I loved.

If the journey to Scotland with the boys had been a pleasant experience, the four days it took me to reach Dad in hospital were the dead opposite. Eight trains, four buses, three hotel stays, air raids, confusion and boredom all took their toll on me and when I finally reached East Grinstead in Sussex, I was lonely, longed to be with the boys and felt quite ill.

The desk in the front hall of the hospital was presided over by a formidable-looking older nurse and despite being on the point of collapse, I politely asked where I might find Dad. Checking a list in front of her, she told me I couldn't see him because he was allowed only one visitor a day for fifteen minutes and that person was still with him. I wanted to howl. Who was with him? It should be me. I was his daughter. "*Come back at two o'clock tomorrow*", she told me curtly. Totally deflated and devastated with disappointment, I turned to walk away with my hankie at my nose when I heard a voice I recognised.

"*Lesley. Lesley. Oh, Lesley.*"

Engulfed in emotion, my heart pounded as I ran into Nan's open arms and we howled together. We'd not seen each other for months and the comfort I took from her embrace was overwhelming. Tired and both upset, we questioned each other frantically between kisses. "*How did you get here?*" we asked in unison. "*You've lost weight*", I told Nan. "*You've put ON weight. What a lovely coat!*" Nan replied. Our laughter was the nervous type, since we were so taken aback by the unexpected meeting.

Still holding hands, we walked outside and sat on a bench in the cold, misty air. Dad was out of danger now, but Nan had left Whitstable to be with him when it was unclear how bad his injuries were. She had been staying at a local pub. Dad was lucky because the men with him at the time the building collapsed were killed. He was trapped in the rubble, with blazing wood laying across the right side of his body, which was burnt so badly, he would need skin grafts. This was bad enough, but I knew something worse was coming when she took my other hand and said, "*Look at me, Lesley*". With tears in her eyes she went on. "*His right leg below the knee could not be saved and they amputated yesterday*".

Once the shock of this news had subsided and I stopped crying, we talked and talked until the sun began to set, and it became even chillier. The pub was a bus ride away and although closed to customers, the Landlord kindly gave us a tray of tea in the Snug. There were no rooms free, since they were inundated by visitors to the hospital, but I was welcome to use a camp bed in Nan's room. I told him I would sleep on the floor of the cellar if necessary.

A few days later, I wrote to Mrs. Johnson.

The Swan Public House, High Street, E. Grinstead, Sussex.
January 6th, 1941.
Dear Annabelle,

I trust that you will receive this letter and can only hope that you and your husband are safe and well after the massive raid last week. I know there were hundreds of casualties and more than a dozen firemen – perhaps as many as sixteen killed. My dad, being in the thick of it all, was trapped by falling masonry. He survived, although suffered extensive burns and was transferred to East Grinstead Hospital where he is having skin grafts and had part of one leg amputated. His days as an active Fireman are over and when he recovers, he will go to live with my Grandmother in Whitstable.

Stevie is settling down with his new-found family in Scotland and I am so grateful to you for persevering with the hunt for them. They are lovely people and I know they will all be happy together. You didn't know that Stevie took a companion with him – a Jewish refugee of similar age, who the MacClintock's hope to adopt when it is certain that he has no living relatives.

It was quite a miracle that something as good as this could come out of such a tragedy not only for Stevie's sake, but also to save the family bloodline, which after losing both son and daughter, is particularly important to them. Stevie's future is assured, and I feel this is what his mother would have wanted.

I finally reached the hospital to see Dad on January 4th and will stay at this address with Nan until he improves. I will be looking for work as soon as possible, but while Dad is still in hospital, I am loath to leave him.

As I said, I pray that you are well and wish you a much happier New Year.
With my love,
Lesley

Those few days in Scotland had spoilt me rotten and I missed the boys in an unimaginable way. The camp bed was terribly uncomfortable, I was constantly hungry and any weight I'd gained soon fell off. Nan and I existed on a sandwich in a little Teashop each morning, took it in turns to visit Dad at two o'clock and had an evening meal of sorts in a cafe. This routine went on for weeks with Dad having painful saltwater baths and one operation after the other, until one day, he was not as sedated as he had been and opened his eyes to look at me. That was a real turning point and from that moment, he was soon well enough to be transferred to the cottage hospital in Whitstable.

We were so grateful to everyone at East Grinstead and admired them greatly for their expertise. The doctors who'd saved Dad's life, the pioneering work being done with horribly burnt people and I truly admired the nurses who'd given him such care and attention. Nan and I were also amazed at the way fellow patients dealt with their injuries. Apart from Dad, most of the others had been RAF pilots during the summer they called, 'The Battle of Britain'. It was easy to pick out the ones who'd left their goggles and helmet on when the plane was hit and caught fire, because they looked like a cross between a Panda and a Raccoon. Dad's face was intact, theirs' were not.

It was now the second week in February. Dad had been taken off in an ambulance, but of course our journey took us back into the chaos of London to catch a train to Whitstable. The whole day was taken up with travelling and we were exhausted by the time we reached Nan's new bungalow. Dad was safely in hospital by that time, which was either a twenty-minute walk, or a bus ride away. We were able to see him each evening and in the afternoon at weekends and by the end of March, he was well enough to be discharged with crutches and the promise of a 'new' leg as soon as he was completely healed.

I hadn't seen Stevie, or Luuk for three months. I'd written every week though and they'd both replied, although it seemed that neither of the boys had noticed the weeks go by without me. Elizabeth had sent a photograph of the two of them with the dogs, which showed them looking healthy and content and kept me up to date with their progress. All seemed to be going well and I was a little jealous. One half of me wanted them to settle down and live their new lives happily, while the other part of me felt redundant. I constantly reminded myself that thousands of mothers were separated from their children and these weren't even mine. It was still hard though. I missed them so much and longed for the time I could visit.

The problem now, was that I didn't have any money coming

in. With Dad using the second bedroom, I slept on Nan's settee in the living room and that was okay for the moment, but I couldn't stay there forever. I was torn between working locally and renting a room or going back to Scotland. Stories from the boys at school were mixed. Luuk was in a different class to Stevie. This had been a problem to begin with, until Stevie decided he was comfortable with the company of two of his cousins and Luuk the same with the older two in the Stewart family. I was upset to hear that Stevie was not allowed to take his beloved 'Trucky' to school with him and this also caused uproar. If only I'd been there to explain.

Elizabeth told me that the new 'Harley Muir' evacuees consisted of five girls and three boys and were a real handful. Uncle Jack hadn't helped by making several wooden swords for the children and wearing an assortment of paper hats, Stevie led a daily 'charge' around the house carrying an ancient family shield. I could picture it. Just like Stevie. A born leader. Elizabeth had to admit that although the gang terrified Aggie, the remaining staff thought it hilarious and after all, it would be Stevie's house one day. The village school had thirty-two extra children in total and with the imminent arrival of a dozen, or so more, the existing teachers would need help - *if* I decided that Scotland was my choice. I think she would have liked that.

Being torn between seeing Stevie and Luuk every day – *the selfish choice* and joining the Wrens, which was admirable, my feelings were that there was something missing in both. I knew I should move on. In which direction was the problem. The few weeks that followed saw a lot of soul-searching, where I considered every aspect of my life concluding that what I needed was a challenge.

One morning after another uncomfortable night of tossing and turning on Nan's settee having counted enough sheep to feed several armies and poring over photographs from Scotland, I came to a decision. I would take the admirable route and do my bit for the country.

Next time, I'll tell you more about Stevie's war and the road he trod towards becoming the Laird at 'Harley Muir', not forgetting the little Dutch boy who grew more than just in height. So, can you picture me in a Navy jacket and a hat bearing the initials HMS? Well stop right there because my new uniform has Lilac and white stripes with long, billowing sleeves and white cuffs. I'll tell you all about that one day, too.

ightning Source UK Ltd.
on Keynes UK
V011829181220
UK00001B/67

Lightning Source UK Ltd.
Milton Keynes UK
UKHW011829181220
375492UK00001B/67